In the Ghost Detective Universe:

R.W. WALLACE

Author of *Beyond the Grave*

FAMILY HISTORY

A Ghost Detective Short Story

Family History
by R.W. Wallace

Cover by R.W. Wallace
Cover Illustration 10926765 © germanjames | 123rf.com
Cover Illustration 263199440 © Nouman | Adobe Stock
Cover Illustration 192365728 © Natallia Haidutskaya | Dreamstime

This story was first published in *Pulphouse Fiction Magazine*, Issue #14

www.rwwallace.com

ISBN paperback: [978-2-493670-09-0]
ISBN ebook: [978-2-493670-10-6]

First edition

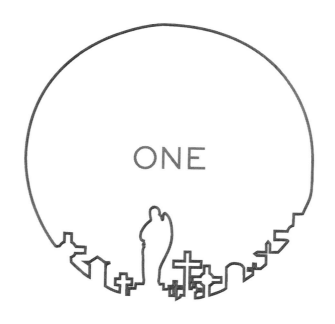

ONE

OUR CEMETERY IS a small one. I haven't actually counted, but there can't be more than three hundred tombs total and at least ninety-five percent of those never became ghosts.

The ones who did have all found their peace and moved on—present company and Clothilde excluded.

The people of our little town don't fall dead like flies or anything, but little by little we're running out of space. Some years ago, the municipality gave us a neighboring lot, but even that's already half-full.

The new section is not as fun to walk around in as the older parts because nobody can afford—or are willing to part with large sums of money for—the huge stone constructions with statues and seatings and columns that were in favor a century ago. Today everybody goes with the classic tombstone, a short inscription, and possibly a plaque with a picture of the deceased. And let's not forget the plastic flowers.

The new tombs in the north section are arranged in neat rows with straight, clean paths, whereas the oldest section to the west has winding paths, overgrown passages, and some graves that have completely disappeared beneath overenthusiastic weeds.

There's no such thing as an eternal resting place, of course—not in a graveyard like this, anyway. It's possible to buy your lot "*à perpétuité*," for all eternity. Except in the French graveyards, eternity means one hundred years.

Lately, the church or municipality or whoever it is who's responsible for the graveyards have been digging up the old graves where the hundred years are up and there are no descendants to pay to keep the lot, in order to free up space.

In a couple of cases, the descendants were found and decided to keep paying. They even came in and cleaned up the tombstones, making sure there was room for more family members. It certainly makes the place look more pleasant.

In most cases, though, the tombstones are removed, whatever remains still intact are removed, and the lot cleared for new arrivals.

In all honesty, it's a bit disturbing to watch this happen, especially for a pair of ghosts who still haven't moved on and can't help but wonder what will happen to them if they still haven't done so when their time is up.

Watching someone exhume a body isn't particularly fascinating. But it's the only entertainment we have. Whenever a new ghost arrives, we make sure to be ready when they exit their caskets, to explain the ins and outs of being a ghost in this cemetery. Most importantly, we help them figure out what it is they need to move on, what unfinished business we can help them wrap up.

When there are no other ghosts, we watch the excavations.

"Do we know who was in this one?" Clothilde asks me.

We're sitting on the neighboring tombstone—the Lambert family, whose first family member arrived in 1859 and most recent only two years ago; one of those places which always has fresh flowers year round—having watched the excavator remove the tombstone, now giving place to the manual labor of three young men.

I shake my head. "I never managed to read the name. Seems like it's only one person, though, and I'm pretty sure he or she died in nineteen seventeen."

"Municipality certainly isn't losing any time," Clothilde comments dryly.

I don't exactly know why we're sitting here watching, but it just feels right. Paying our last respects to the deceased, maybe. Hoping someone will do it for us when our time comes.

Because, let's face the truth. If we don't get any visitors now, we certainly won't have anyone to pay to keep our space in seventy years.

The men doing the excavation aren't the usual gravediggers. It seems like the municipality isn't working on the same contract as the people responsible for putting people *into* the earth.

3

I don't like these guys as much as the usual team. I don't expect them to stay perfectly serious for hours on end, but the jokes I'm hearing are anything but respectful. These guys are doing the job because it's the only job they could find, and they're not pretending to like it.

"Seriously," one of them says as he throws a shovelful of dirt haphazardly onto the path next to the grave, "I don't see why we have to to this manually at all. Can't they just use the excavator to get everything out? Who cares if they accidentally get part of the idiots from the tomb next door? It's not like anybody'll know."

We'd know.

But we can't tell anybody. My frown mirrors Clothilde's.

The second guy, a weaselly-looking guy with a shaved head and dark, close-set eyes, grunts in agreement. "The dead don't care. If I keel over tomorrow, just throw me in a ditch somewhere."

I open my mouth to say something to Clothilde, but I'm interrupted by a shovel hitting wood. The casket.

"Got 'im," Weasel-face says. "Let's see what state he's in."

During past excavations, they've unearthed caskets and bodies in various states of decomposition. Sometimes the casket is intact and the skeleton laid out prettily inside—possibly with pretty decent clothing. Sometimes the casket has disintegrated completely, and only parts of the skeleton can be removed, the rest having been eaten up by the earth, ending up who knows where.

When they get a whole skeleton, they have to take in to some sort of pauper's grave. For obvious reasons, they can't just thrown them in the trash.

The three workers remove the earth, bringing to light a casket that still has the shape and look of a casket, but looks like it could disintegrate any second.

"There's no way that's coming out in one piece," one of the men says.

"I'm not touching any more dead bodies," the second says, his hands raised as if giving up. "We're not paid enough for his shit."

"Maybe we won't have to." Weasel-face steps up right next to the casket, raises his shovel above his head, and brings it down full force on the center of the flimsy wood.

The entire lid cracks under the pressure, and goes from being a large, even surface to a million splinters in two seconds flat.

Weasel-face nods in satisfaction. "I'm thinking this is one of the graves where we didn't find anything."

His colleague lights up with a wicked grin. "Oh, I see. Let me help." He takes his own shovel and hits the side of the casket, with much the same result as earlier.

"I really don't like these guys," I say as I turn to Clothilde. "How come there's no—"

"Robert." Clothilde's voice is shaking and her eyes are wide and non-blinking. You'd think she's seen a ghost, pun intended.

She points to the grave and my gaze follows, puzzled what has her so shook up.

I let out a strangled cry.

There's someone in the casket.

A young man, maybe in his twenties—it's difficult to tell with all the splinters and dirt superposed with his form—is lying in the casket, his arms crossed and an annoyed frown marring his smooth forehead.

A shovel runs right through his abdomen and he winces.

"Well, this is certainly uncomfortable."

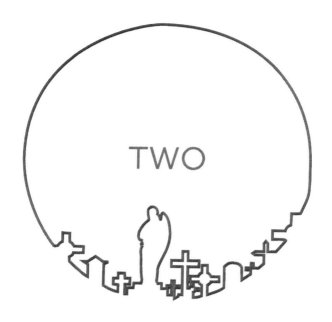

TWO

THERE'S A GHOST in a hundred-year-old grave.

"How long have you been down there?" I ask, dumbfounded.

The three workers are discovering that their method is working and all start hacking at the casket and its contents with more energy than I've ever seen from them. Two out of three hits go right through the ghost and I can see him flinching every time they hit the bones.

I can see he's going to answer my question, but I cut him off. "Please come out of there, that can't be comfortable." I extend a hand—as if he needs it or can indeed grab it—urging him to move.

Reluctantly—I can see the defeated sigh and note how he studies the three men before deciding that they have no intention of stopping anytime soon—he sits up, then quickly jumps to his feet and steps out of the casket.

"Come up here, why don't you?" Clothilde pats the slab of smooth granite next to her. "Let the idiots do their vandalism in peace."

With another sigh, the man complies, though he takes a while to figure out how to get out of the grave. It's a whole new world to get used to when you become a ghost, where you have to decide which part of the physical realm you want to respect, and which one you'll ignore.

Clothilde, for example, has a great love for the *tops* of tombstones—great seats—but has no need for the sides. She always sits the same way; her butt on the top and her feet swinging straight through the granite as if it weren't there.

The man figures it out fairly quickly, all things considered, and is soon sitting—back straight as a ramrod, hair brushed to a perfect early-twentieth-century haircut, straight parting and all, and his suit and bow tie immaculately ironed—next to Clothilde.

"I guess we should start with introductions," I say lamely. "I'm Robert."

"Clothilde." She offers her hand for him to shake, and after a very short hesitation he takes it.

"Bernard Lebrun," he says, his voice cultured.

I have no idea what to say to the man, so I just launch into my usual spiel for when we have new arrivals. "We're the only ghosts currently in residence in this cemetery. If you need any help with moving on, we'd love to help."

He studies me for a second. "Moving on?"

"Yes. Uh…you know. Moving on to wherever ghosts go when they've handled their unfinished business."

"For obvious reasons," Clothilde interjects with a smile, "we don't know where that place is, since we haven't gone there ourselves yet."

"Yet you are more than willing to help me move to this place."

I frown. "I'm one hundred percent sure it's a better place than here. So of course we want to help."

Monsieur Lebrun's presence deeply disturbs me for some reason. How could he just be lying there in his casket without us knowing about it? Has he seriously been there since he died? For over a hundred years? The idea is baffling.

And actually…the most important question might be: Why didn't he come out?

A ghost is kept in place by his or her casket as long as they haven't accepted that they're dead. If the acceptance isn't there, the casket stays a prison. Personally, I spent four days screaming and banging at the walls of my casket before I came to terms with my fate and was let out. Some were quicker, some slower.

But a hundred years?

And what will it mean if he *hasn't* accepted that he's dead? Could he be some sort of danger to us or others? If nothing else, if he's been stuck in a casket for that long, his mind should have broken long ago.

"Why are you so keen on assisting me, if you have not yet obtained this 'moving on' for yourselves? I never had much faith in so-called philanthropists."

All right, his mind seems to be in working order.

Clothilde flashes a huge smile. "We're complicated, is all," she says. "We're kind of limited in our field of action here, so we're waiting patiently for our opening."

I still don't know the details around Clothilde's death, I just know it made quite few waves when she died, and that as a result, nobody ever comes to visit her grave. My friend is as close-mouthed as they get, on top of being stuck for all eternity with the aggressiveness and resistance to authority of a teenager, so I don't push for information.

Some day, she'll tell me.

Monsieur Lebrun glances around the cemetery, taking it in for the first time. "I presume the field of action is the cemetery?"

"You presume correctly!" Clothilde winks at me, her smile still in place.

I can't hold my questions in anymore. "When did you die?"

Monsieur Lebrun's sharp gaze meets mine and holds it for several moments. I'm not sure what he's looking for, but he must have found it, because he answers. "November nineteen seventeen." He takes in my clothing, Clothilde's clothing, the three men continuing their gleeful destruction of his last resting place. "What year is it now?"

"Twenty nineteen," I tell him, watching closely for a reaction. "The reason they're unearthing your grave is that the *perpétuité* is up."

His eyebrows make a minuscule jump. If I hadn't been paying close attention, I might have missed it. This man is very, very good at keeping his feelings to himself.

Clothilde shifts sideways on her seat so she's facing our new arrival. She doesn't even try to hide her curiosity. "You must have had *some* inkling of time passing. You've really been down there all this time?"

Monsieur Lebrun brushes a nonexistent piece of lint off his pants. "Where else would I have been?"

"I don't know." Clothilde raises her hands and shoulders in a way that is very close to, but not quite, mocking. "I'm just curious as to why you wouldn't have come out sooner, is all." She waves a hand between the two of us. "We've both been here for thirty years, and we've never had *any* idea that there was someone in this grave."

"I was perfectly comfortable where I was," Monsieur Lebrun says, his back becoming just a little bit straighter. "I don't see what the point of coming out would be."

Clothilde gapes at him. "So you were happy to just stay down there for all eternity?"

"I was comfortable, as I said. And nobody bothered me. I don't see why I would seek out a place filled with people screaming all the time."

"Ah," I say. "So you heard the screams of the new arrivals, huh?" I cock my head at him. "You never thought to go check?"

He meets my eyes, and I'm not entirely sure if it's indifference I see, or if it's some sort of very strict view of what's proper or not. The man's unreadable. "It was not my place."

"Who cares about 'your place'?" Clothilde says with an eye roll. "You're dead."

"All the more reason to behave in a proper manner."

An awkward silence descends, only interrupted by shovels hitting wood and bones. I can tell when they're hitting poor Bernard Lebrun's skeleton both by the difference in sound and the tiny shudders wracking his body at each hit.

Clothilde chews her lip as she surveys the ongoing massacre. "So what's the proper etiquette for when someone's whacking your casket and dead corpse to pieces?"

Monsieur Lebrun's eyes move to look down into his own grave and I realize he's avoided looking at it ever since he came out.

He gulps. "I don't know."

THREE

"THERE MUST BE *some* sort of unfinished business for you to resolve." Clothilde sits on the edge of the hole that still holds Monsieur Lebrun's remains but looks like a newly dug—and empty—grave. Her ankle-length jeans and worn Converse swing back and forth, into the air, through the dirt, back out in the air.

Monsieur Lebrun leans against the Lamberts' tomb next door, apparently the most relaxed position he's capable of adopting. Not needing to breathe doesn't stop him from sniffing. "I would never leave any business unfinished, Mademoiselle. Once one starts an action, one follows through."

I know Clothilde well enough to know she's laughing on the inside, but luckily she keeps it internal. "And what if one dies while in the midst of an action?"

"That was not the case." Lebrun adjusts his bow tie. "Everything was in order in the shop. It was the first of the month and I'd done the finances and checked the stock. The shop was clean and ready for the month to come."

"You died in nineteen seventeen, right?" I ask.

Lebrun nods. "First of November nineteen seventeen."

"How come you weren't on the front lines? I'm surprised an able-bodied man in his early twenties was still managing his shop in the peaceful part of the country."

Lebrun meets my eyes and it's the first time I see emotion in his eyes. There's some anger, some annoyance...and shame. I'd recognize that look anywhere.

God knows I saw it often enough in the mirror when I was still alive.

"I may not have moved around much since I arrived in this cemetery," Lebrun said in a low but firm voice, "but I've become very well acquainted with how a ghost's 'body' works. It behaves and looks like I expect it to. Mademoiselle here expects the ground to stop her body from falling into the ground, but she does not expect it to resist when she wants to swing her legs." He puts a hand on his right leg. "I now expect my legs to work, so they do. But while I was alive, this was not the case. I suffered an accident from horseback when I was seventeen and had to make do with a bum leg that just barely accepted to hold my weight with the help of a cane. I was not able to participate in the Great War."

And that was his greatest shame. I didn't need for him to elaborate to know that. While I was alive, I'd participated in the November eleventh arrangements in this village several times, and the list of dead was impressively long for such a small place. I'd often wondered if there were even any men left to create the next generation—which would get the honor of dying in the next World War.

At least one man was left behind—but if he'd died before the end of the war, he wouldn't even have been able to help reboost the population.

"How did you die, anyway?" Clothilde's thoughts must have gone in much the same direction as mine.

Lebrun's lips thin as his gaze goes from Clothilde to the open grave to me. "I do not know," he finally says.

"You don't know?" Clothilde meets my eyes. "That's new."

Lebrun's forehead creases slightly into a frown. He's either becoming more expressive or I've just gotten used to him and know how to read him. Right now he's annoyed and defensive.

"I went to sleep on the night of November first and never woke up."

"So…" Clothilde glances between the two of us. "A stroke, perhaps? Heart attack. Choked on a spider in his sleep?"

I hold back my laugh. Barely.

"Do any of those options sound probable to you?" I ask our new friend.

He shifts a little but is still stiff like stick against the Lamberts' tombstone. "I certainly did not choke on a spider. One never knows for a stroke or a heart attack, but I was in fairly good shape, bum leg notwithstanding, and only twenty-three."

"Maybe that's your unfinished business," Clothilde offers. "To figure out how you died."

I shake my head. "Too weak. I've never met a ghost who just needed to know *how* he died. Catching their killer, sure. Tying up loose ends with friends or family, certainly. But the how is a lot less important than the why."

Clothilde shifts her gaze to Lebrun. "Do you know *why* you died?"

Lebrun just stares back woodenly.

"You're certain there was nobody you needed to say goodbye to?" I ask. "Or tell them you loved them—or anything in that vein?"

Lebrun shakes his head curtly, though I think I might have seen his left eye twitch at the mention of love. Or I might have imagined it. There are statues in this graveyard with more facial expressions than this guy.

I clap my hands briskly. "Then I propose we work on the assumption that you were murdered and that your unfinished business is to at least identify who the killer was."

Clothilde's eyebrows shoot up. "We're going to catch a murderer from nineteen seventeen? Unless it's another undiscovered ghost in this very graveyard, I have no idea how we'd go about that."

I nod. "I'm sure the presumed murderer is dead. But ghosts are all here for a reason. If Monsieur Lebrun's business was impossible to wrap up, I'm sure he would have moved on. There's no point in holding him here for all eternity."

A softness creeps into Clothilde's eyes. "You really believe that?" Her voice is softer than usual and her eyes are searching mine for truth.

"Of course," I tell her. "Our time will come, Clothilde. The world just isn't ready for us yet." I wink at her and get the hoped-for smile in return.

Clothilde's carefree demeanor pops back into place. "So where do we start?"

Lebrun clears his throat, in that way that people like him have, where you clearly understand that they're annoyed at you. "I did not give you authorization to search for anything. You will not be looking into my life and my business. I would have been perfectly happy to stay in my grave forever, and it was in no way my choice to be here in your company."

"Aw, we like hanging out with you, too," Clothilde says.

"You came out of your grave now for a reason," I tell him firmly. "Something will happen that will lead us to your murderer—or whatever else your unfinished business is. Believe me, you do not want to stay in this cemetery forever. Clothilde will make you want to die all over again within a month."

"Hey!"

"We will help you in this, and you will find peace." I might not be able to find it for myself yet, but I've made it my mission to help others get there. In fact, I'm absolutely certain it's part of my own path to redemption.

Lebrun shakes his head, but doesn't say anything, so I take it as approval.

"So what's the plan, boss?" Clothilde asks with a wink.

"The plan?" I look around the cemetery, but everything is at it has always been—dead and barren.

I shrug and lean back on the path behind me, imagining being able to feel the heat of the sunlight on my skin. "We wait."

FOUR

ALL IN ALL, we don't have to wait long.

Five days later, the Lamberts come on their monthly visit to refresh the flowers on their tomb. It seems to be some sort of regular Sunday outing for the family, where at least two family members will come on foot, stroll through the cemetery, and spend some time at their lot.

I find it admirable that they're all so dedicated to maintaining the last resting place of their dead ancestors, but also find it a little bit weird. No other family is this regular and they aren't even particularly religious.

Sometimes it's just two adults; sometimes it's entire families, with kids of all ages, from newborn to sullen teenager. None of them ever complain. Then again, seeing how they'll bring a picnic when the weather permits, maybe it isn't all that surprising. If you're not bothered by the fact that it's a graveyard, it's just a calm spot and a nice opportunity to catch up with the family gossip.

At least once a month, we hear the story of how this tradition started—how Mamie's mother came here every week without fail, to give thanks to her husband for coming home long enough to give her her family. If it weren't for that short month, none of them would have even existed.

Today, it's a small procession, but it encompasses no less than four generations of Lamberts, all women. The youngest is no older than a year and is the reason it takes the group forever to cross the cemetery. She wants to walk by herself, but isn't particularly stable on her feet and gets distracted by the real flowers, the fake flowers, the shiny lettering on the gravestones, and the pebbles on the road. When her mother gets impatient and picks her up, the poor baby starts screaming her heart out and is quickly put back down.

The mother is a beautiful young woman in her mid-twenties. She has long, golden hair, dark brown eyes, and a slightly upturned nose. Her own mother walks next to her, with the same brown eyes and the same nose, but with darker and shorter hair. I'd say she's approaching sixty.

The group's eldest member is Geraldine Lambert, known by everyone as Mamie Lambert, and she's eighty if she is a day. She's been a regular here since way before my arrival thirty years ago. She loves walking, so no matter what the weather's like, she'll show up on foot. Possibly with a raincoat and boots, with her pants splattered in water and mud, but she'll be there.

The first time I saw her, she could already qualify as an elderly woman, but she carries herself with such grace, it feels wrong to comment on the deepening lines of her face or the sagging skin at her neck. Her class and inner calm shine through everything, and there's no doubt the young men must have been standing in line to court her in her youth. Her hair is now all white, but I know it used to be blond like her granddaughter's, and her eyes are still a soft, calming brown. And she has the Lambert nose, of course.

The reason why this is still a Lambert grave, and not a Vanderwalle one, is one of the family's favorite stories during these outings. Mamie married young, before she even turned eighteen. She had the time to pop out one daughter and get pregnant with a second one before becoming a widow. Considering two years of marriage wasn't reason enough to go through life with a name she could hardly spell herself, let alone anyone else, she changed it back to Lambert and renamed her children while she was at it.

Mamie Lambert's daughter, Sylvie Lambert—she was a Bertrand for fifteen years, but took her maiden name back after the divorce—carries a bag, which I'm sure contains fresh flowers. Her sister sometimes try to put up fake flowers, claiming it'll save them all money, but Sylvie will have none of it. She'll remove anything plastic whenever she comes, and replace it with the real stuff. Today, we're getting some purple flower that I don't know the name of.

While Sylvie takes care of the flowers, the three others approach the freshly dug hole in the lot next to theirs.

"What happened here?" Mamie asks.

"Probably nobody wanted to pay once the *perpétuité* was up," Sylvie says as she arranges the flower's leaves just so. "Remember they contacted us almost a year ago and we had to pay to keep our place?"

Mamie's wrinkles deepens as her face folds into a frown. "That. Wanting to kick us out of our cemetery."

"They didn't want to kick us out, Mamie," Sylvie says soothingly as she brushes her hands on her pants. "The time that Grand-Mamie paid for was up, is all. Now we're good for another hundred years of Lamberts."

Mamie grunts but lets the subject go.

Us three ghosts are standing on the other side of the open grave, observing the family. Clothilde and I usually come and hang out with the Lamberts when they visit because they're so lively and gay, unlike most of out visitors. For Lebrun, this is his first visit ever and I'm not quite sure how he feels about it.

While the three women study Lebrun's final resting place— or what's left of it—Lebrun goes over to study *their* tomb.

He runs a finger over the large "Lambert" engraved in the arch on top. A shiver runs through him as he realizes his fingers aren't giving him any additional information and he puts his hand behind his back instead.

His eyes moves over to the names of the family members interred here. There are over a dozen, but his gaze seems to lock onto the first one and stop there.

I know the names by heart, not only because I've lived here for thirty years and have gotten *very* bored at times, but also because the Lamberts always tell numerous anecdotes during their picnics, keeping the story of their family alive.

That first name: Pierre-Antoine Lambert. Born the first of September 1895, dead the third of March 1918.

"He died during the war?" Lebrun asks me when I step up next to him.

"Technically, yes," I reply. "But he was back from the front by then. Came back injured, and just had enough time to get his wife pregnant before succumbing to a bacteria he probably picked up during his convalescence."

"He came back?" Lebrun's eyes stare directly into mine for the first time. "When?"

I exhale, trying to remember the details. I've heard that story at least a hundred times, though. "His wife received the news just before All Hallow's Eve, and he arrived for Christmas. 'Best Christmas gift a wife could hope for.' Mamie Lambert was born in July 1918—a little early, but in great health nonetheless.

Lebrun stares at the women looking into his own grave, his eyes unfocused.

I'm about to ask him if he knew the original Lambert, but I'm interrupted by a scream.

I catch a glimpse of something pink pitching into Lebrun's grave.

The young mother jumps into the hole.

Sylvie screams, her arms out, trying to hold back her daughter a few seconds too late.

Mamie Lambert leans forward to look into the freshly dug grave. "You should keep better watch on your offspring, Audrey. She could fall into a grave or something."

FIVE

CLOTHILDE IS LOOKING up at me from the bottom of the grave when I join the commotion. "She's fine," she says, and I can tell from the lack of mischievous glint in her eye that she'd been genuinely scared for the little girl. "She's mostly just scared."

The little girl is screaming her heart out in her mother's arms, large tears streaming down her chubby cheeks. The mother seems to be taking as much comfort in her daughter's arms as she's giving. Her eyes are squeezed shut and she's sitting in the fresh dirt in total disregard of her pastel pink jeans, rocking her daughter and touching her everywhere, searching for wounds.

"I think she's all right," she says, her voice cracking.

"Thank God," Sylvie sighs. "Why weren't you watching her?"

"I was watching her!" Audrey screams. "But you can't watch a kid every second of every day. She wanted to pick a flower from the next grave over and tipped over backward into this nightmare."

I jump down into the grave to join Clothilde behind the mother and child. Lebrun has stayed by the Lambert grave and although I can't be one hundred percent certain, I think his eyes are glued to the name of the original Lambert, the one who died just a month or two after him.

Mamie Lambert takes charge of the situation. With a hand on her daughter's shoulder, she addresses her granddaughter. "Accidents happen with toddlers all the time, there's no way to avoid it. We all do our best, as I know you do, Audrey."

Sylvie visibly takes a deep breath, her eyes closed. "I'm sorry, honey. I shouldn't have yelled at you like that."

"Now." Mamie Lambert looks around the empty graveyard. "How do we get you out of there?"

Getting the little girl out would have been easy—if she'd accept letting go of her mother. While Audrey can reach the top of the grave with her hands, she can't pull herself out, especially with her girl clinging to her like a monkey. There's no real hand-hold or stepping stones and the one time she tries to kick a step into the dirt, part of the wall falls down.

"We're going to have to call for help," Audrey says to the two women watching her from the foot of the grave. "I can't risk bringing the walls down on the both of us."

Audrey sits back down in the dirt with her back against a

wall. Clothilde and I sit down next to her. She might not know we're there, but people can sometimes subconsciously realize we're there or even integrate some things we say to them.

The little girl has stopped crying and is currently pulling on her mother's hair, shoving it into the dirt. The fact that Audrey doesn't even seem to mind shows how wiped out she is.

Sylvia is on the phone with someone, explaining the situation, when the little girl lets out a happy gurgle. She holds something in her chubby little hand and holds it up in front of her mother's face.

"What have you got there, honey?" Audrey says. "Is it a rock?" She takes the object from her daughter in order to hold it farther away from her eyes.

"Uh," Clothilde whispers. "I think that's a bone."

I lean in to study it. "Oh, yeah. That's a human bone. Maybe something from the hand? Or the foot?" I glance up at Lebrun, who's flexing the fingers of his right hand. Guess that answers it.

Audrey sits frozen, staring at the bone. The little girl, unhappy to have lost her new toy, grabs for the bone.

"No!" Audrey throws the bone away, so hard it flies right out of the grave and lands at her grandmother's feet. The baby starts screaming.

Mamie Lambert bends down—slowly, to make sure she'll be able to get back up—and picks up the bone. "What have we here? A bone?" She looks into the grave, at the Lambert tomb right next to it.

"I do believe we're leaking."

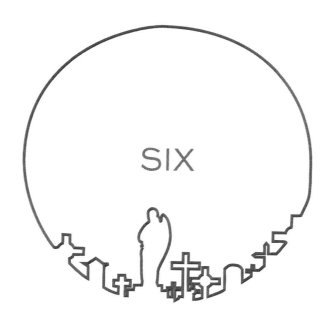

SIX

In the end, a group of firemen come to get the two youngest Lamberts out of the grave and the whole family takes off, taking the bone with them. I keep a close watch on Lebrun as they leave, wondering what would happen when one of his bones leaves the cemetery, but apart from a twitch in his right hand when they pass the gate, he shows no reaction.

We go back to waiting, Clothilde and I making our usual rounds in the cemetery and hanging out on her grave as is our habit, while Lebrun stays close to his own grave. He alternately stares down into the hole that hold his earthly remains and studies the Lambert grave, reading all the names and dates as if they hold the answer to some mystery.

On Wednesday, some middle-aged man comes to look at Lebrun's lot, apparently with the aim to buy it for his recently deceased wife.

On Thursday, one of the usual gravediggers drops by to inspect the empty grave, scraping at the wall closest to the Lambert tomb, shaking his head all the while. Then he opens several of the compartments of the Lambert grave and takes out pieces of God knows what to put them in little containers.

Two weeks later, the Lamberts are back. The same three women as the last time, but they've left the baby behind. Guess they don't want a repeat of their last visit.

Audrey carries a small package that we soon discover contains the bone from Lebrun's hand, and Sylvie carries a thick envelope. It all feels a lot more official than the usual family outings.

Clothilde takes a seat on the top of the Lambert tomb and for once I decide to join her, getting a perfect view of the assembly. Lebrun stands next to the Lambert women, his eyes on that first engraved name again.

"Well," Sylvie says to the package in her hand, "this is it. We're going to find out who you are and put you back where you belong."

"This family is weird," Clothilde says. "Anyone else would have just thrown the bone away or shoved in into any part of their tomb. Who cares which Lambert it belongs to?"

"To be fair, it doesn't belong to a Lambert."

Clothilde huffs a laugh. "Good point. What's in the envelope, do you think?"

I shrug. "Seems to be some proof of whose bone it is."

Giggles. "I wonder how far they'll throw the thing when they discover it's nobody from their family."

Lebrun has moved to stand next to Mamie Lambert. He's bending down to look into her wrinkled face, studying her from less than ten centimeters away. He studies her eyes, then goes so far as to reach out to let his ghostly finger pass through her nose, making the old lady sniff.

They're standing so close, facing each other, I suddenly have an epiphany. I haven't studied Lebrun's face too closely since he got here. His old-school clothes and hair draws my eye every time. But now that he's in profile, with Mamie's profile mirroring his.

"They have the same nose," I whisper.

Papers rustle and my attention is drawn to Sylvie when she exclaims, "What the hell does this mean?"

Audrey grabs the papers. "It's highly probable it's my great-grandfather…even more likely it's your grandfather…basically certain it's Mamie's dad. But…nothing in common with Pierre-Antoine Lambert."

"But…" Sylvie's mouth hangs open as she scans the pages for something that would make sense. "What does it mean? Didn't they bury the right body? Is grandfather's body buried somewhere else?"

Mamie Lambert doesn't seem to quite be following the conversation between her daughter and granddaughter. She's looking left and right, lifting her hand as if searching for something she cannot see.

Her hand passes through Lebrun's ghost several times, but the man doesn't move. He's staring at her face, mostly at her nose.

The same upturned nose as his.

The Lambert nose. Which appears to actually be the Lebrun nose.

"Uh," I start. I hesitate before deciding that I'm allowed to pry. "Lebrun, you wouldn't happen to have known Lambert's wife? Laetitia, wasn't it?"

Lebrun takes a step away from Mamie Lambert and dips his head just a fraction—I think it's his version of hanging his head. His eyes jump to the grave again, where Pierre-Antoine and Laetitia appear together at the top of the list.

"He'd been away for three years," he says in a defeated voice. "We'd been friends since we could walk and I'd always loved her. She married my friend instead, but once she got lonely during his absence…"

"Difficult to resist the woman you love, isn't it?"

Lebrun raises his hand to cover his eyes. I can see his lips trembling. "I know I shouldn't have done it. I deserve my punishment for what I did."

"Oh, is that why you stayed down there all this time?" Clothilde asks. "You thought you were doing penance?"

Lebrun doesn't answer but his expression is answer enough.

Sylvie and Audrey are still arguing, each with a wad of papers that she's shaking under the other woman's nose.

Mamie Lambert seems to snap out of her reverie. "It means Pierre-Antoine wasn't my real father, that's all. It was whoever this bone belongs to."

All eyes go to the little package with the bone.

"Who *does* it belong to?" Sylvie says to nobody in particular.

"It's from the grave next door!" Clothilde shouts at them.

Lebrun's eyebrows shoot up toward his hairline. He seems genuinely shocked by Clothilde's behavior.

I hope he won't have to stay long, because I don't think these two would be compatible over a longer period of time.

"Sometimes it helps talking to them," I explain. "They can't exactly hear us, but sometimes they do anyway."

As if on cue, Mamie points to the newly emptied grave. "Who was in that one, already?"

Sylvie emits a sigh, as if somebody poked her with a needle and all the air was leaking out. "I guess we'll have to find out."

૭૩

SOMEBODY MUST HAVE made the idiot gravediggers admit what they'd done because only days later a team of police experts came and dug up the bottom of Lebrun's grave. Without great surprise, they found what they were looking for. They put the bones in a casket and left the cemetery.

Once they passed the gate, Lebrun went with them, sitting on his new casket like some wound-up cowboy riding into the sunset.

SEVEN

He comes back a week later.

He has a brand new white and shining urn and the entire Lambert family attends his second funeral, this time in the Lambert family tomb.

"I still don't understand what happened," Sylvie says to Mamie Lambert as the urn is placed in its final resting place—let's hope for real, this time. "Your mother always forced on all of us how much she loved her husband. It's the reason we all come here every single week. And now we discover she wasn't even faithful?"

"That's probably why," Mamie replied calmly. "Guilt." She looks away for a moment—straight at Lebrun, who is once again

32

standing right in front of her. In front of his daughter.

"I'm sure she loved Papa just as much as she said," Mamie finally says. "But she made a mistake while he was away and expressing her love for him and making his grave into a family shrine when he died was her way of repenting."

"I feel sorry for her," Audrey says, her voice low so that the rest of the family won't overhear. "Even if she did love Pierre-Antoine more, she must also have cared for this Lebrun guy. She lost both of them within a couple of months."

All heads nod in agreement and they finish the interment in silence.

೦ಽ

"She's right, you know," Clothilde says to Lebrun once the Lambert family is gone. "The two of you died almost at the same time."

"There was a war in progress," Lebrun replies curtly. "Millions of people died that year."

"But you weren't at the war. And you died anyway. For an unknown reason."

Lebrun doesn't have an answer to that as he stands in front of his new grave, staring at the name of his one love. Is he going to stand there for the next hundred years?

"Apparently being buried with your actual family members isn't enough to let you move on," I say to Lebrun. "I'm honestly thinking you were murdered and you need the culprit to pay."

Lebrun stays silent, staring at the gilded letters.

"You know who the culprit is, don't you?" Clothilde asks as

she walks up to Lebrun so he'll at least see her in his peripheral vision. "She killed you when she learned her husband was coming home?"

Accepting that the love of his life didn't love him back. That she killed him to protect her own reputation. That would be a hard pill to swallow.

Could that be all he needed?

"Does it sound at all possible?" I ask him softly.

His face is as impassive as always, but I can see the moment the acceptance eases up some of the tightness of his features.

"Hey, at least you fathered a daughter," Clothilde chimes in, surprisingly compassionate. "Who had kids of her own, and so on all the way down to that baby who fell into your grave. They might have given thanks to the wrong guy for a century, but now they know you were at their origin, I'm sure they'll remember you in their own way during their family outings. That's not so bad."

Clothilde and I share a look. None of us ever have any visitors.

"I guess it could have been worse," Lebrun whispers. He grazes the name of Pierre-Antoine Lambert with his hand—and disappears.

AUTHOR'S NOTE

THANK YOU FOR reading *Family History*! The inspiration for this story came when we visited a small cemetery in the countryside and several of the tombs had... eviction notices, for lack of a better word. If nobody pays the bills, the grave will be dug up and the slot given to somebody else. So, naturally, I took that idea and ran with it!

Family History is the sixth Ghost Detective short story I've written. You can find links to all the others (ten at the time of writing this note), and to the series of novels set in the same world with the same characters, in the next pages.

If you want to make sure never to miss a new release, remember you can sign up for my newsletter on rwwallace.com.

R. W. Wallace
www.rwwallace.com

Also by R.W. Wallace

Mystery

Ghost Detective Novels
Beyond the Grave
Unveiling the Past
Beneath the Surface

Ghost Detective Shorts
Just Desserts
Lost Friends
Family Bonds
Common Ground
Till Death
Family History
Heritage
Eternal Bond
New Beginnings
Severed Ties

The Tolosa Mystery Series
The Red Brick Haze
The Red Brick Cellars
The Red Brick Basilica

Short Story Collections
Deep Dark Secrets
A Thief in the Night

Time Travel Secrets (short stories)
Moneyline Secrets
Family Secrets

Romance

Find all R.W. Wallace's books:

rwwallace.com/allbooks

ABOUT THE AUTHOR

R.W. WALLACE WRITES in most genres, though she tends to end up in mystery more often than not. Dead bodies keep popping up all over the place whenever she sits down in front of her keyboard.

The stories mostly take place in Norway or France; the country she was born in and the one that has been her home for two decades. Don't ask her why she writes in English—she won't have a sensible answer for you.

Her Ghost Detective short story series appears in *Pulphouse Magazine*, starting in issue #9.

You can find all her books, long and short, all genres, on rwwallace.com.

Printed in Great Britain
by Amazon

14701275R00025

PROTECTOR

THE FULL-BLOOD SERIES: BOOK ONE

SERENA NOVA

This is my place to escape. I hope it will be yours too.

And mom, I know you are going to read this.
Please skip chapter 26, thank you!
And for my amazing, crazy and loving team that helped me
through this all. Thank you for being part of this weirdness, for
not laughing too hard or get to angry for me spamming you with
spoilers.
O and don't forget the boyfriend, thanks honey!

1

"I'm one of the last Full-Blooded Witches alive," I whispered to Astra, my hands fidgeting in my lap. I'd never told this to anyone. My grandmother told me to keep it a secret. Astra looked at me, her eyes wide, saying nothing. Her mouth opened and closed. I rubbed my hands on my pants, trying to stay calm, instead I wanted to jump up and walk a hole in the ground. Okay, so maybe I have a *slight* nervous fidgeting habit. "You need to say something," I tried to whisper to her, but my voice pitched higher.

"Why are you a Null then?" Astra whispered back.

The sound of footsteps silenced my reply, we hunched down behind the bookcase we were hiding behind, holding our breath. Astra put out her Witch light and covered us in a shroud of darkness again. Our hiding spot was a secret. I bit my lip and focused on the sounds around me, attempting to hear if the person was coming closer or walking away. Our school had a night curfew, and the teachers were strict with following that rule.

They patrolled the school at night, keeping everyone in line, and making sure we kept to the rules. We never followed that rule. Luckily, we'd also never been caught. Still, it was always nerve-wracking when we heard them walking right past us. The soft blue glow of a Witch's light casted shadows across the walls, only to never reach our hiding spot behind the enormous bookcases, which filled the library we were hiding in.

The library had been built first, this massive building was now encased by the rest of the school. When the sun hit the few windows it had, the golden light filtered into the library, showing the dust that danced around. Inside, the library was packed with bookcases. Staircases swirled up towards the second floor to the galleries above, which were filled with even more books. The center of the building was left open, allowing you to see the interior rafters. In front of the windows, were seats with cushions, with side tables next to them, for students to place books on. On the ground floor, were rows of tables, accompanied by desk lamps and comfortable chairs. In the front, stood the librarian's desk, where the librarian could aid students in signing out their books and also answer their questions.

The librarian was an old lady, her grey hair was always in a neatly-placed tight bun on her head. She loved floral prints and never wore plain-coloured clothes. She looked like a nice old lady, with her wrinkled face, however she turned out to be the nightmare of the school. She was always so strict with the rules; kept on saying we needed to whisper when we were in the library, and lift up the chairs, not scrape them on the floor. She made us place the books back where we found them, *exactly* where we found them. She never cracked jokes, or got one, so we made fun of her by asking the most strange or personal questions we could think of.

Astra and I once asked when she had her last period. We were dead serious, or that was what she thought. Her face turned red, and she tried to give us an answer. Nothing really came out, and before she could get mad, we walked away, giggling. To be honest, it wasn't nice to torment the old lady. Only, she made it hard to be nice towards her; her rules needed to be followed no matter what, and her punishments for not lifting up chairs were always strict. One time, we had to clean all the beams of the roof. Another punishment was to clean the lower shelves of the bookcases. She always gave us these strange punishments.

One time, she made me reorganize the whole library, alone. I kind of deserved that one. I hadn't slept well for almost a week, and I was cranky as a pig who hadn't eaten for weeks. So yeah, I ate in the library, pulled the chairs out, started yelling at someone, and almost burned down the building. To be honest, I didn't mind it; it helped me relax, and she let me read all the books I wanted. I got to know the old lady during that week. And once you'd broken through her tough exterior, she was a real nice lady; the absent grandmother everyone wanted. She reminded me of my own grandmother. Sweet but strict. I kept working in the library after that, helping her out, and reading as many books as I wanted.

I found this alcove one day while I was rearranging the books on the shelves. It had been hidden well, and I had almost missed it. I dropped a book next to the bookcase; after picking it up and hitting my head on one of the shelves, I found out that the bookcase was placed in front of an opening, an alcove. There was nothing inside, just a small bare area. I placed some pillows in the space to make it more comfortable, and you could find me there when I wanted to escape the world or talk with Astra–in our own secret hideout.

We used this corner to gossip about the teachers–for Astra, it meant talking about which teacher was the hottest. For me, it was talking about the hard training Instructor Lavina put me through. Instructor Lavina was the combat teacher and solely trained the Protectors. Astra, as a Witch, got totally different classes than me. The Protectors were trained to keep the Witches and Elementals safe, and the Witches. . . . Well, they learned to be a Witch.

And now we were discussing my heritage.

This would be the last time in our secret hiding spot; we were almost done here; graduating. The Witches would go through a selection process, while the Nulls, would show off their skills as Protectors.

That's what I would be doing. I would be showing off my amazing fight skills. After that, I'd disappear, like my grandmother had told me to do. It was something I'd promised my grandmother a long time ago, however I wasn't sure I wanted that anymore. The only thing I knew, was that I had to tell my best friend what I was. She needed to know . . . or maybe I just wanted to tell someone the truth, *someone I trusted.* I wasn't not sure . . . I couldn't handle the heavy weight of it on my heart–not telling my best friend, it felt like a burden that had been strapped to my chest.

We were both frozen as we waited for the footsteps to leave. The light dimmed, and the person walked further away.

"Why didn't you tell me this sooner?" Astra asked when we were sure that the teacher was gone.

"I wanted to, I didn't know how or when. I promised my grandmother." I shrugged at her, only she couldn't see me; we were still in the dark. Without a word, I made a light ball form in my hand. My light wasn't as blue as the other Witches, it was more of a pure white. Astra stared at my hand, as I gave the light ball a small bounce to lift it a little above my palm, I let it hover in the air.

Astra followed the ball of light with her eyes, her mouth opened again. "I-I didn't really believe you, when you said you were a Witch. Now seeing, the light . . .," she said, trailing off. Her eyes were still wide. She shook her head as if clearing her thoughts. "Why didn't you tell me this sooner?" she whispered again.

"I wanted to. Only, my grandmother kept me from saying anything. The day she placed me here at the school, she made me promise never to tell anybody what I am. It'll mean my death." And she didn't say it nicely, she shook me roughly whilst she made it really clear what she meant by death. I sat fidgeting with my hands in my lap, thinking about that memory. I looked up at Astra. Her eyes were downcast, and for a second, I thought she would start yelling at me, until she looked up and tears shone in her eyes.

"It's okay," she whispered softly and grabbed my hands. I knew it was the right decision to tell her. From the moment I walked into this school, she became my best friend. She believed I was a Null but never cared about it, or gave me shit for it. Astra was always there for me, *always*. "What can you do?" Astra asked me.

I expected that question. Pressing my lips together, I blew out a breath and said, "Everything." I kept my eyes focused on her, waiting to see her reaction to it.

"You-you . . . 'everything?'" She did *not* whisper that at me. I placed my hand over her mouth and made a shushing motion.

Pulling my hand from her face, I said, "Sorry, I'm kind of nervous." I gave her a crooked smile and wiped my sweaty palms on my pants. Astra just smiled back at me, she didn't care about it.

"You really meant it when you said you are a Full-Blood?" Astra asked me, this time she whispered.

"Yeah, I'm sorry I never told you before." I kept looking at my hands in my lap.

Astra grabbed my hands again, squeezing softly. "It's okay, Isa. I would have liked it if you told me earlier. But I get it."

We stayed silent for a few minutes. Letting that all sink in before Astra started speaking again. "Are you . . .?" She paused, and I waited for her to finish her question. I had an idea of what she wanted to know. And I knew that I would lie about that, for her safety. "Are you family of the last Queen?" Astra's eyes were focused on me. I kept my face as neutral as I could, not showing that my heartbeat had picked up.

"No," I answered. Knowing I needed to say more, Astra could be too smart for her own good. "I'm not sure who my parents were. Gran raised me. She told me that they went into hiding when the Gate opened and stayed in hiding after that." That was partially the truth.

I could see her thinking about that, hoping that she would accept that half-lie for the truth. Knowing that I'm the last Full-Blood already made it dangerous for her. Telling her that I'm the last Savill Royal alive? No need to add more danger to all this.

"What are you going to do now? When we graduate? You have to go through it as a protector, right?" she asked me. I let out a breath that she had accepted the lie. Still, my stomach cramped with it, and the lie added a new heaviness to my heart that I hadn't had before. Feeling gratitude towards Astra for believing me, for having her as my best friend, and relieved for her question, I gave her a small smile.

I could see her thinking of something else when her eyes widened. "Are you going to test for the Selection?" she asked me, her voice pitching a little higher.

"No. As, I don't want to be that. I want to go home, to my house in the forest and live a quiet life," I lied again. The short reprieve of the heaviness shattered fast when I replaced it with more lies. *I haven't thought this all through*, I thought while giving myself a mental eye roll.

Astra snorted. Yeah . . . me . . . a quiet life. We always got into trouble at the school. Maybe it would be different when I was living in my own home, without other people around me, boring and alone.

"I would never be part of the Selection, Astra. It is your place, not mine," I promised. Placing my hand on top of hers.

"Why did you tell me this?" Astra asked. "Why now?"

I looked into her eyes, finding curiosity and nothing more. I started to speak. "Because you are my family. You are the person I trust with everything I have. And I didn't want to leave here and never have told you who I am. It's lonely." My throat tightened up, swallowing away the tears that pooled in my eyes. "I needed you to know." I finished, one tear falling down my face to splatter on our hands. She wiped away the fallen tear then looked me in the eye and nodded. She got what I was saying and dropped it all. Not asking more about it or wondering why, and I was relieved with that, I couldn't handle more lies. We talked about the last days of school and what Astra would be doing after we graduated. Her parents and family were really strong Witches and Elementals, she had a great future in front of her. If she made it through the test, it would mean she would get a good chance of a high place in society.

And when she won the Selection, she would also be in the running to become a Queen for one of the Kings. The Selections were held every year when the Witches graduated from school. Nobody knew what they needed to do in the selection process, it was always kept a secret. One thing we knew for sure, was that the strongest were chosen to go to the castle, who would then add to the new government of this world. That's how it had worked for years. They get further tests in the castle, and after that, they can choose to go for a position inside the government or choose to be married off to someone from the highly established houses.

When the Kings were ready for marriage, they used the Selection to find their future Queens. That meant that this Selection would be more important than other years, because they were searching for their Queens. Not once had they found their perfect match, in over three years. They still kept looking for the right Queens. This was great news for a Witch like Astra, it meant she still had a chance at becoming a Queen, with her being powerful and all.

For Astra to become Queen would be the best way out of her miserable family. They may be the strongest but they were also terrible and harsh on her. For her, being the strongest Witch in the school meant that she had a really good chance to win the Selection. I believed that Astra would be an amazing Queen, and it would shut up her parents about it. Which would be a nice bonus.

And for me, I would go through the Protector test and graduate, and then I would go away. Only there were a few things wrong with that plan. First, I wouldn't see Astra anymore, second, I would have trained my whole life to become a Protector to end up sitting on my ass, and third, I didn't know if I could ignore some things from my past. Like my parents, who were still alive. At least I thought they were, though I'm not sure where they were now.

They had left me with my grandmother, and she died five years ago. She left me alone in this world, she left the house in the woods as my heritage. Which was great, but that's it. I wanted the family she told me about when I was younger; she told me about her daughter, my mother. That she was a Full-Blood Witch, too, and that my dad was a Full-Blood Elemental. She always said I looked like my mom. Gran also told me that I have the stubbornness of my dad. She didn't know my dad for long, because he left shortly after I was conceived.

In almost all ways, I looked like my mom when she was younger, the same black hair and brown eyes according to my grandmother. She said my mom was too stubborn and too caring for her own good. She also told me I was the spitting image of her mother, my Great-Grandmother, whom I had never met. The biggest thing that would be different between my mom and me was that my body was trained as a Protector, all muscles with female curves. I had hips and boobs, not too big but nice to grab. I was 5'8," a little taller than most girls, that was fine by me. I loved working in the sun, giving me a nice tan, I burned easily, which I got from my dad. *So, thank you for that, dad.*

"What do you think the Selection will be like?" Astra asked me, interrupting my train of thought.

"I don't know," I answered her.

"It is a test, right? So, we have to show how strong we

8

are. The strongest are sent to the castle," Astra said, her hands fidgeting in her lap, showing me she was nervous about the whole selection process.

"You know, As, you are the strongest one here. So, stop doubting yourself." My voice pitched higher with the emotions behind it. I breathed out and continued, "It will be fine, and you'll probably have to show your powers, do some spells and tricks, you will be great!"

She nodded at me. Still, I could see there was some doubt in her eyes. Her stupid parents placed so much pressure on her. They wanted her to be even better, they wished she was a Witch, which she wasn't. They had hoped by mixing their genetics, they would make a Full-Blood. Except they weren't enough, and now Astra had to live with that, they blamed her for it.

"Come on, let's go back to bed, and we will see what will happen over the next few weeks." We got up, and I put out my light as Astra made a small one, so we could see where we were going. Listening for the sounds of the teachers who walked in the hallways, we waited until we could move out of the library. We had done this so many times, we knew when and where the teachers would be. Still, we needed to listen for them, to be sure and not to get caught. We made it to our room without being seen, and we both slid into our beds. Astra put out her light, and I heard her sigh. "It will be alright Astra, I'm here for you, and I will always be there for you," I said to her. We didn't have to whisper anymore, still, I kept my voice low.

"I know, Isa, but you will be leaving after the graduation. And then I have to go through it all alone." I turned over and looked at her, our beds were across from each other, with two small bedside tables next to each of them. Mine, full of books and Astra's filled with magazines and makeup. Astra looked at me, her blonde hair falling over her shoulders. She had always been a pretty girl, and she had grown into an even prettier woman. All the right curves that would make her a model if she wanted to be.

She was a little shorter then I was, which she was happy about. It meant she could wear heels and be the same height.

"It will be fine Astra," I said again to her. I sighed and wished her goodnight, not knowing what to say anymore. I couldn't go with her, I'm no Witch. And to be honest, I loved being trained as a Protector. It gave me a real goal, more so than learning spells and doing things without getting up. *Still, it is pretty amazing if you can fill your bath from the living room.* Only, leaving Astra alone would be the hardest thing I would ever do. Feeling tears pooling in the corners of my eyes, I blinked them away as I looked over at her. She had turned around, I listened to her breathing, which evened out, letting me know that she was sleeping. This would be a long, long night for me. I sighed and moved on to my back. "Gran, why do I have to keep this all a secret? Why couldn't I stay at your home in the woods and be happy?" I whispered to the ceiling. Knowing I would never get an answer from her, I turned, laying on my side.

My thoughts went back to the evening my Gran told me that I would go to Sevilay, the all-female school for Witches and Protectors. I was eight then, a normal age for girls to be placed in such a school. It was one of the best things I had ever heard, that I would be a Witch for real. Until she dropped the big news. "Now you must listen to me, Isadora," she started, "It is really important that you never use your magic again. When you are at that school, you will be a Null." Her cracking old voice sounded strong that night, filling the small room we were in. Holding her hand up before I could even open my mouth to say something, she went on. "You will be a Null, Isa girl. You are the last Full-Blood Witch there is. And that means that you are special." That made me smile, I liked being special. But that smile disappeared with what Gran told me next.

"People will be looking for you, those people will not be nice to you. They will try and kill you, Isa girl. And it won't be a nice death, those people are bad, Isadora. Remember that." My grandmother wasn't the sugar-coating type of woman. I got used to it in the eight years I lived with her. Only, hearing that you would be killed, die horribly when you tell someone who you are is a little harsh. And Gran knew that as she took me into her arms and hugged me. "Isa girl, you need to remember this and repeat this, okay?" As she squeezed me tighter to her, I agreed to it. "Okay, good girl. Now you can't tell anybody who you are. Never tell them that you are a Full-Blood Witch, never tell them that you are a Savill Royal, never show it. And I mean it, never show it in front of people from the palace. Okay, Isa girl?" My grandmother pinned me down with her grey eyes. I nodded and was pulled in for more hugs, she placed her chin on top of my head and sighed. "You need to be careful, Isadora, you need to train hard and become the best Protector there is. You have to be strong for what is to come."

I looked up at her and told her, "I'm already strong, Gran." I meant my magic. I could do a lot, for an eight-year-old.

"I know, Isa girl. You need to be strong in body and not only in your magic. You have to train. And they won't allow any Witches to become a Protector. You have to be a Null for that, and more importantly, act like one, too. . . . No more magic for you okay, Isadora?" My Gran touched the tip of my nose while she looked at me, and I nodded again.

"I promise, Gran."

She never explained why I needed to be strong or why I needed to hide after all this. I never asked her about it, I was eight and wanted to be a Unicorn Princess.

The next day, she dropped me off at the school, breaking my dream of becoming a Unicorn Princess. She looked down at me, I saw tears in her eyes. "Remember what I told you, Isadora. Promise me, Isa girl," she said again. She had been repeating that throughout the whole drive towards the school.

"Yes, Gran, I promise," I answered her.

"You will be great, Isa girl." And then she hugged me; tears blurred my eyes, and I wiped them away. I didn't understand it all, but I knew that I needed to keep my promise to her. She had never asked anything of me before, except this. My grandmother never did or said something without a good reason, so I needed to be strong for her. And I knew she was a Full-Blood, too, with a powerful foresight. She made me listen to her, demanded that I would remember this. She didn't use any magic on me, didn't magically bind me to keep it a secret. I'm really good at keeping secrets, most of the time. Gran turned around and walked away, leaving me alone.

Before I even turned around, I heard a voice behind me. "Are you alone, too?" That was the first time I met Astra; she smiled at me and I at her. "Come," she said and took my hand. We both walked into the school where a teacher was waiting for us and the other children. That was my first day at this school.

And twelve years later, we would soon be done. Thank everything for that. I loved being in school, and the teachers were amazing, but being back at my old home and using magic again would be great, too. I had kept the biggest part of my promise towards Gran, I had become the best protector there was. And the part about not telling anybody? I didn't think she would mind. I had kept it for so long, and Astra is family. You trust family, right? And with that thought, I finally fell asleep.

2

"Come on, Astra, let's get some breakfast." I heard her grunting under the covers. "Come on, girl. We have history in an hour."

"We still have an hour," she answered, her voice muffled through the covers.

"Yeah? So, come on. Food is waiting." Turning around, I walked towards my desk to get my books and knives. No Protector left a room without her knives. Before I could tell Astra to get out of bed again, a bell sounded, and we both listened to the announcement.

"Last years, be in the dining hall in twenty minutes for an important announcement." The voice of our headmistress died off.

I looked at Astra, her head now out from under the covers. She looked at me and jumped out of bed. She sprinted towards the bathroom, and I heard the shower turn on. It made me chuckle. In record time, she was showered, had makeup on, and was dressed in her outfit for the day. I had never seen her that quickly out of bed. Laughing, I swung my backpack over my shoulder and walked after Astra out of the door.

The halls were full with Witches and Protectors. They were talking about what the announcement would be.

Most of them thought it was about the graduation or the Selection. I walked next to Astra. Before we reached the double doors that lead to the dining hall, I heard my name. I looked around, finding DeeDee, Madalena, and Banu walking towards us. They were three of the Protectors who were in my class. We hung out with them, and luckily, they liked Astra, too. Not all Witches and Protectors got along. Astra had Witch friends, but they didn't like Protectors. It meant that most of the time, it was just her and me.

It wasn't always like that; Witches hating the people who protected them. We fought together with them, and now, they hated us. Most Witches at the school were major bitches, they thought that being a Null meant that you were nothing. They thought themselves better than anything else in this world. They were a mean bunch, not knowing what was good for them, and hating the people who they needed to keep them safe. It wasn't smart to make enemies out of the Protectors. Still, if a protector didn't do their job, they were executed. *Harsh I know, laws and stuff.*

Astra and I were the only Witch and Protector who shared one room and were friends. They'd tried to make Astra ditch me by using spells. Still, she stayed by my side, friends for ever.

"What do you think this is about?" Banu asked me when they reached us.

"I have no idea. We will hear it in a moment," I answered her when we started walking again. We reached the double doors that led us into the dining hall. The teachers stood on the raised podium at the other end of the room. Our headmistress, Miss D'Moray, was standing in the middle, talking with Mister Ragdan, our history teacher. I looked around, all the other students were looking towards the podium, waiting for Miss D'Moray to start talking. When my eyes landed on Thalia, I found her looking at us, though when she saw me looking, she turned around, her head held high. She was one of the other powerful Witches around school, and she thought that she was the best at everything. Her two friends, if you could call them that–Sada and Elodi–looked at us and started laughing when they turned around. I rolled my eyes and looked at the teachers in front of us, not knowing what their problem was. Miss D'Moray walked to the front of the podium and cleared her throat. All the conversations stopped, and we focused on her.

"Good morning, ladies. I'm glad that you are all here. We have some important news about the Selection that will take place this year. We received a message from the Kings that this year's Selection would be different." The Witches around me had started to whisper. I looked towards Astra who had stayed silent, her eyes focused on Miss D'Moray.

"We will be holding a competition."

With that, all the Witches fell silent. "How do you mean competition, Headmistress?" one of the girls in the back asked.

"Isn't that normal?" another Witch asked. More questions were shouted. The Headmistress motioned for silence, raising her hands up. The tension in the room grew thicker. You could almost slice it with a knife.

"No, we normally have a test. Please hold all of your questions till I have explained. I believe that the majority of them will be covered by what I have to say."

"Yes, Ma'am," we all answered.

"The normal Selection test consists of a power test. We use a powerful spell to measure your magic level. It is painless, simple, and always accurate. When we know your power level, you girls are placed in categories, and the Selection members choose the Witches they think are strong enough to enter the government or other important positions. You are then sent to the castle for more testing and to meet the Kings."

A Witch next to me raised her hand. "Yes?" Miss D'Moray answered to the girl.

"What is different this year?" I looked back towards the headmistress, waiting for her response.

"This year, as I said, we will have a competition. We will test not only your magic levels, we will also test how you react to a certain situation." The headmistress looked at us all, making eye contact with every Witch here before she turned around to give Mister Ragdan room to speak.

"Okay, girls, we know that you didn't train for a competition. We told the Selection council that as well. They told us it was an order from the Kings, and they couldn't do anything about it. They gave us instruction about what we could tell you and what not. We will explain it all in your first classes." He folded his hands behind his back. "Go have breakfast and save the questions for later, please." His eyes landed on me, my hand was raised up into the air. I let it slowly fall back down. He nodded and turned around. The teachers walked off the podium, and we all went to get some breakfast.

"What was that all about?" Astra asked me when we stood in line for some food.

"No idea. Do you have an idea what this competition would be?" I asked her. She shook her head, her blonde hair moving around her face. "Do you girls have an idea?" Turning around, I looked at the other three Protectors. All three of them shook their heads no. The line started to move, and we reached my favourite breakfast stand. Pancakes. They made the best pancakes here, best thing about this whole school. The kitchen!

We grabbed some food and walked towards our usual table, next to one of the high windows. The dining hall was big, with a full wall of giant arched windows. There was a large double door that led into an outdoor eating area. We sat at a table facing the windows and the beautiful gardens outside. The room looked really cold; stark white tables, blue chairs, and grey walls. Only the food made it one of the best areas in the school. The smells were amazing. I took a big bite of my pancakes, already forgetting what Mister Ragdan had said.

"What do you think they will tell us?" Astra asked. We all had history together, meaning that we would find out together. I felt nervous, my stomach protesting the food for a second, until I smelled my pancakes again.

"Why did you just sniff your food?" Banu asked me, with her eyebrows shooting up towards her hair.

"I thought about what they just told me and needed some comfort," I answered with a broad smile on my face.

This made them all laugh, while I just shrugged and started eating again, enjoying my pancakes. We ate in silence, and there wasn't much noise in the dining hall. Normally, it was really busy, everyone talking and laughing. They were all eating and thinking about what the competition would mean for them. They talked about the Witches and not the Protectors; it made me wonder if things would change for us, too. We would find that out soon enough.

"Come, let's go." Banu got up after we finished our plates. We followed her towards the hallway that led us to the classrooms. The hallway had no natural light, but lamps hung from the ceiling–they gave the hall a doomed feeling, with the grey stone of the building on each side. Heavy brown wooden doors led towards the classrooms. We entered the door to our right; a small golden plaque on the door showed us it was the History classroom.

We walked into a room filled with chairs and tables all placed in a half circle, facing the desk of Mister Ragdan. He was already there, seated behind his desk. A board behind him was filled with the tasks we would be doing. A few bookcases lined the walls, and some geographic posters hung above them. They showed the old divided kingdom; how it was thousands of years ago, and how it became when a Queen took over the world, progressing to how it was now with the four Kings on the throne. I took my seat in the second row with Astra and Banu next to me and

DeeDee and Lena behind us. We waited for the others to walk into the room, too. The first bell had sounded when we took our seats, so we didn't have to wait long for the rest.

Mister Ragdan stood up and walked around his desk to lean against it at the front. He folded his arms over each other. Mister Ragdan was one of my favourite teachers, he had short brown hair with grey streaks in it and kind brown eyes. He was an old Protector who was injured in a fight. His right leg was badly damaged; it made him lose his function as a Protector, making him ideal for the function as History teacher. He looked us over, waiting for us to be quiet, before he started speaking.

"Good morning, ladies. Thank you for being silent this quickly." He gave us a smile before he continued. It made me chuckle a little. We were never quiet that quickly, only today.

"You all know now that this year's graduation test will be different. I think all your minds went on a walk, and you tried to come up with an idea that will replace this year's test. I can tell you, you all will be wrong." He unfolded his arms and placed them on the sides of his desk.

"The Witches are going to fight Ilunias." And with that the whole room exploded into sound. People talking across each other. I looked over at Astra; her eyes were wide and her face pale. I grabbed her hand and squeezed. Ilunias are dark-world creatures, terrible creatures.

"Quiet!" Mister Ragdan said, his voice silencing us all. "They decided to test you all differently this year, like we said in the dining hall. They want to see more of you than your power and strength. They want to know how you handle situations, how you react to things. And fighting Ilunias will give them that." I arched my eyebrow with his last statement.

"Mister Ragdan," I started, he looked at me and nodded, so I went on, "Why do they need to do it that way? You can make other tests that will show those skills." I heard others agree with me.

"That is true, Isadora. Only this was decided by the Kings and the Selection masters. We can't say no to this, otherwise nobody will end up in the Selection." And with that, the whole room went silent; so silent you could hear a pin drop.

"Witches get three weeks to train for this, there is information in the library, and you all get six hours of fight training each day during those three weeks. You are fighting Ilunias–a scary bunch of dark-world monsters. Research as much as you can and train as hard as you can. And for the Protectors . . ." My head snapped around, I had been looking at Astra, checking how she reacted to all of this. Once Mister Ragdan had named us, he received my full attention. "You girls will be the security detail for this fight. The Selection wants to see what you can do. You are only security, remember that. This will also add to the test that you ladies will take the week after the Selection fight."

"Wait, what?" I asked out loud.

Mister Ragdan looked at me and sighed. "The test for the Protectors has changed, too. You have to fight the Ilunias, too, a week later than the Witches." My breath hitched in my throat. We never had to fight creatures. Only the teachers, also the Witches' teachers. This was something new. I felt Astra squeezing my hand, and I squeezed back.

"Why?" Banu asked him, I heard others question it, too.

"That is what they want," Mister Ragdan answered.

"Are there problems in the world?" I asked our teacher, and hoped he would answer honestly. He looked back at me then, I could almost hear him deciding how much he should tell us.

"There are always problems in this world, Isadora." He gave me a weak smile, hoping to redirect me from my train of thought.

"What is going on then? Why change so much now?" I

asked, meaning the Selection test changes.

"Look, ladies. I know you all have questions about this. We are ordered to do it this way. Kings rules, I can't go against them. I don't know what is going on. Except that the Gate isn't sealed fully. You know that, too. This means that creatures keep coming through it." He looked at us all and pushed off his desk to walk from one side to the other.

"Look," he waved his hands in front of him, "I don't know what is going on. Normally, they would have found Queens by now; they would have been married, and the spells to close the Gates further would have been placed." Mister Ragdan rambled in front of us, his brow wrinkled. He rubbed his chin before he continued speaking.

"The thing I know is that you all have to fight strong creatures from the Dark-world. There are worse creatures you could find there, believe me." He sighed, and sat down on his desk again. "You all know the story of how the Gate came here. How the last Queen tried to protect us and was killed for it." He looked up at us all and paused. We were silent, we knew this story. They teach it in the first years of school. He continued telling us anyway.

"The Gate one day appeared in this world, letting dark-world creatures in to wreak havoc. A war raged between the dark-world creatures and the last Queen's army of Witches, Elementals, and Protectors. She failed," he said.

"She failed, and four of the ten High Houses murdered her for that. They thought they could do it better, leaving the four High Houses to seal the Gate, but that didn't work entirely. They made a bond between four powerful Elementals, the strongest of the houses, making them the Kings, the ones who used their magic to close the Gate." He looked us all over after his short reminder of what had happened. He continued with our history, kept on rambling.

"That didn't work, either, it closed partway, making it so that the creatures still came through, though not as many as at first. Still, enough to kill us, which meant being a Protector now meant fighting at the Gate, and tracking the creatures that came through the Gate. If you chose that path, you became a Hunter." He looked at some of the Protectors who wanted to be a Hunter and kept on talking, "You all know what happened next." Some of us nodded, and he went further with his story. I sighed, we had heard this story from the first year of school.

"The High Houses pulled all the fighting Witches and Elementals back, they needed to keep the magic lines safe. Left the fighting to the Protectors, found them less important, replaceable. And with no Full-Bloods left, they needed the strongest for themselves. And now, the strongest Protectors are recruited to become a personal Protector to a Witch or Elemental." He ended his short history ramble, it wasn't even a real lesson. We knew this story by heart.

What mister Ragdan said wasn't something I would choose to be in my life. If I'd had a choice, I wanted to be a Hunter and fight at the Gate. But I had promised Gran that I would stay away from the Gate, too. I'd already broken one promise. I wasn't breaking this one, too.

"You girls need to study hard, train hard, and help each other out," Mister Ragdan said, interrupting my thoughts. I looked up at him as he sat in his chair.

"You have three weeks, girls. Three weeks, use them well. Schedules are on my desk, they are all adjusted to the upcoming competition." He waved his hand to the stack of papers in front of him. And with that, we were dismissed. Chairs scraped over the floor, and people murmured to each other. I let go of Astra's hand as I got up and walked towards Mister Ragdan's desk. I grabbed a Witch schedule and one for myself. A question popped up in my mind. A dangerous one, one I needed to ask.

"Mister Ragdan." I waited for him to look at me, before I continued. "Why aren't there any Full-Bloods anymore? Weren't they strong enough to close the Gate?" I kept my voice low, not wanting the others to hear me.

He sighed. "Isa, the last Queen was a Full-Blood, and not even she was strong enough to close the Gate. I don't think they would have killed her if she was." He leaned towards me before he said the next thing, "And all the Full-Bloods went into hiding or were killed in the war. They were the strongest in magic, making them the first targets the creatures hunted. We never heard from them again. People who looked for those who went into hiding came back empty-handed. And to be honest, if there was still a Full-Blood who could help us, they would have said something." He looked at me, his brown eyes searching something in mine.

"I don't know, I wished they were still alive, so they could close the Gates," I quickly said.

"Oh no, Isa. Don't get me wrong, we don't know if they ever could close the Gates. The Kings possess a lot of magic, and they can't even manage that. The last Queen, the strongest Full-Blood alive couldn't even do it." He leaned back into his chair. "I know you are worried about Astra and this test. But they need the strongest, the Kings need to bond with their Queens. They will help close the Gate more. They will never let anything happen to the Witches in the test, Isadora. Don't worry."

I looked at the piece of paper in my hands. "Yeah, you are right," I said to him and walked out of the room. Astra was waiting for me in the hallway.

"What was that all about?" she asked me when I handed her the Witch schedule.

"Nothing, just a few more questions." We walked towards the dining hall; it wasn't time for the next lesson, so we sat down at our normal table. Banu and the others sat down next to us. I looked at the schedule, there wasn't much changed. Only that we would have six hours of fight training a day and two hours of study in the library, every day for three weeks. One good thing about this all was we didn't have the boring classes such as politics or etiquette. I never liked them; was never good in them. I used them to catch some extra sleep.

"What are you guys going to do, when you've graduated?" DeeDee asked us.

"I want to work at the Gates," Banu answered her. I gave her a small smile. She'd talked about that the last few years. She was an amazing protector and a tough lady. We both looked at DeeDee, wanting to hear her answer.

"I hope to get selected to protect a Witch or do something other than Hunting at the Gates." DeeDee was the most girly girl from the group except for Astra. Her parents were Protectors, too, so she had to follow in their footsteps.

"I want to protect a Witch, too," Madalena answered. "And you?" She looked at me. With that question, Astra also looked at me, arching a brow.

"I don't know, I'll see what happens," I answered as vaguely as possible.

"Nothing big planned?" Banu looked directly at me, a smirk on her face. "You are the best among us, so you'll probably get to protect the Kings themselves," she said, and the smirk on her face widened towards a full smile, making me blush. I turned my face away from them. They cracked a laugh, making me laugh, too. We talked about school and what we did when we were younger, bringing up some memories; like when we hid the blackboard chalks, or ate ice cream late at night—which we'd stolen from the kitchen. We'd done so many things together. I looked at those four ladies, these would be our last few weeks together. After this, we all would go our own ways.

I felt myself tearing up and swallowed past the lump that had formed in my throat. "Come, let's go and train already. I think they won't mind if we start early." I got up from my chair, and the others followed me. This would be the hardest three weeks of our schooling, training for the most important thing in our lives; graduation and surviving the test.

3

The three weeks flew by. We all had trained hard, and Astra had really shown improvement. We spent many hours in the library, looking up everything we could find about the Ilunias. I asked the Librarian if she knew of any books about the Ilunias. She had given me two, and we finished both of them in record time.

We were forever at the library, looking over those two books and some others we had found. We sat at one of the tables, knowing that the test would be soon. I read in silence until I heard a grunt from Astra in front of me.

"Why isn't there any part about their weaknesses?" Astra complained, her hands were in her hair while she hung her head over the book in front of her.

"Probably because nobody really fought them and explained what it was like, or nobody survived fighting them. So, nobody could tell us afterwards," I told her.

"Or the teachers have taken that part of the information out," a voice said from behind us. I turned around to find Thalia and her two puppets.

"Why would they do that?" Astra asked her. I fully turned around in my chair to look Thalia over. She still looked like an annoying bitch of a witch, only a little more tired. All the Witches had trained hard and for once, were really studying. The Witches got basic fighting the first few years in this school. When they knew the basics, they began learning magic and spells. For the competition, they needed to train more and be prepared for the fight. All of them went to the training without complaining, much. Astra took more training than she had scheduled. She trained with me and the other girls late in the evening. It was a good thing, because the information we found on the Ilunias wasn't good, and she would need all the extra benefits she could get.

"Because we need to show them that we are the best," she answered Astra. Discontent lined her voice, and I swear if that girl could roll her eyes she would have done so. Instead, I rolled my eyes for her. Like that answer explained everything.

"Yeah, that is it. So, go along and do something else we're studying here." I waved my hand at them, motioning for them go away.

Thalia snapped at my hand movement. "You aren't going to win," she said to us, then turned around and walked away.

"Why would she say that to you?" I asked Astra. I knew that she and Thalia used to hang out sometimes. They weren't friends, not like Astra and me. But still, all the Witches were nice to each other.

"I don't think she was talking to me," Astra answered, a little concerned towards me.

"Why would she say that to me? I'm no Witch, and I'm not even taking your test. I'll leave that up to you." I gave her a half-hearted smile. I tried to cover the fact that my heart was beating out of my chest, from the idea that someone may know more about me than they let on. I suppressed the movement of looking around, to scan the area for threats.

"Who gives a shit, Isa? Her hobby is being mean to you. You know that, and this is one of those moments. Let's focus on finding something on these monsters."

"Creatures," I corrected her.

"Huh, what?" was the smart answer I got back.

"They aren't monsters, they are still living things. They may be scary and want to kill us, but still, a cat kills a mouse because it needs to eat. And a lion kills a threat to her cubs, and we don't call them monsters. It is nature." I looked at the book in front of me. There was a short list of what the Ilunias could do, and one thing about their weakness.

The list said that they could use all the elements of magic, they had the power to turn into shadow, and they could blind their opponent. The two things known about their weakness was that they were overly confident and there were always three of them. Sisters, the book said.

"Come, let's go to bed. We can't find anything here, and we have to do the test tomorrow." Astra got up and closed her book. She placed it on the counter, so the librarian could put it back. We didn't know where she'd gotten them, except that those two books contained the most information about the Ilunias.

I closed mine and walked over to the desk, placing my book on top of hers. "I'll see you in a moment. Going to look for something to read." Astra mumbled a yes back at me, and I walked towards the back of the library. The smell of old books, dust, and old leather filled my nose, it made me think of my youth. I raked my fingertips over the book covers and the wooden planks they were standing on. I needed a moment for myself, to breathe and relax. Tomorrow may not be a big day for me, but it would be for Astra. It was her graduation test, her way to get a better life away from her parents.

I stood still at the end of the rows, surrounded by the high bookcases, and listening to the silence. Taking a big breath, I blew it out slowly. Reaching out my hand, I closed my eyes as I felt the woodgrain under my fingertips. My thoughts moved towards the test, and how they would have caught the Ilunias—that they even managed to find them, bring them here and use them for a test was remarkable. If it had been me, I would have been pissed off like the hottest fire in Hell. It made me grimace; the idea of them angry. My anger rose towards the Selection council and the Kings for choosing something this dangerous to be used in a test for Witches. I touched the back of my neck, my mind wandering back towards Astra and whether or not she would be prepared enough to handle it.

I shook my head at that thought. She was the strongest witch I knew; the smartest, too. She could handle it. The next question was, could I handle living without her, never seeing her again? This was one of our last days at the school. Astra would pass the selection. She would be chosen, and then she would leave. I would pass my test, and I would be going home.

Home, that word rang through my head. A place where I would be safe, in the woods, surrounded by the sounds of the trees, the birds and the other animals that lived there together. But I would still be all alone. A small pain in my chest made me gasp for breath. Lonely, that is what I would be, even lonelier than I already was. Alone with the smells of the earth, the creaking wooden planks of my house, and the memories of my Grandmother who'd lived there.

I opened my eyes, blinked a few times, removed the tears that had pooled in them, and stuffed those feelings as far away as I could. I didn't want to think about it anymore. The library was still silent, my other home. A place that had been my home for twelve years, a place that would be my home forever, maybe even more than my home in the woods. It hurt to leave this all behind, to leave Astra behind and go into hiding. I wiped the fallen tears off of my face, took a deep breath, then turned around and headed back to my room. Feeling tired and sad, I needed sleep to remove those two things out of my body and mind.

I needed to focus. When I reached our room, Astra was

already in bed, asleep. I silently put on my sports bra I used as a pyjama top and my sweatpants, and went under the covers.

———

Somebody shook me, then pulled off my covers, leaving me exposed in the cold air. I searched blindly for my covers, to get back to the comfortable warm shell I had created. I almost succeeded, until she started to talk.

"Come on, Isa. Wake up and get out of bed. We need to have breakfast and then the Selection starts." I opened my eyes and looked at the clock next to me. It was six in the morning, and breakfast didn't start until seven. I groaned and turned around, finally managing to get my covers back. "Isa. Come on, get ready," Astra almost yelled at me as she pulled at my covers again. I held them so tightly, I hoped they wouldn't rip.

"As, we still have an hour to get ready, please go back to bed or do something else. Stop bothering me." I pulled the covers over my head.

I hadn't really slept the night before, nightmares had plagued me constantly. The usual stuff, not really making sense, and most of the time they were too strange to decipher. Last night was no different, I didn't even start trying to figure it out. Spider-dogs that wanted to eat me weren't real. I needed to sleep more.

"Let me sleep for an half hour more, As. Okay?" I groaned out through the blanket.

"Yeah, fine." I heard her walking towards her bed, it groaned a little when she laid down. A deep sigh made me look at her, my lack of sleep forgotten.

"What is it, As? You can't be worried about today. You will be fine, you are the strongest Witch here."

"No, it isn't that. I'm just wondering how this all goes. And, Isa, you are the strongest here," she pointed out to me.

It made me groan, knowing what she said was true. "Don't start pointing that out, okay?" I mumbled at her.

It made her smile, the thing I had wanted to achieve. "Still, forget me, you are the strongest that will take the test. You will be fine. And you will meet the Kings." I waggled my eyebrows at her. "Have a happily ever after." I gave her wink, which made her laugh.

"That is it, Isa. I'm going to have an *amazing* life." She looked at me. "Without you," she added in a whisper. That got me out of my bed, as I reached for her. I layed down next to her and pulled her into my arms.

"It will be fine. You will be amazing, and I will always be there for you." I pulled her tighter against me, squashing her.

"Okay, okay, let me go. I can't breathe." Astra chuckled, and I let her go a little. Still holding her, we stayed silent for a short while. This was the last day we would be together, and we both had a hard time dealing with it.

"Come on, As. I'm going to get dressed. I can't go in my pyjamas to the Selection, right?" I said, smiling at her. I was rewarded with a smile back. We let go of each other, and I got up. I changed into black cargo pants, a sports bra with green leaves on it, and a black long-sleeve shirt; standard protector's outfit. I pulled on my boots, placed my knives in their holsters and my two swords on my back. The handles stuck out over my shoulders for easy access. They were made specifically for me; we all have our own weapons. They were always made specially for the Protectors. None of those weapons were the same. The weapons were a personal thing, nobody but that protector could touch those weapons. It wasn't really a rule, and maybe the other girls didn't have such a personal relationship with their weapons. For me, it was a no touch policy for everyone, or they would lose a limb.

After pulling up my long hair into a ponytail, I walked out behind Astra. We walked into an already filled dining hall. Normally, we would have been the first there, but not then. Not on the day of the Selection. No everyone seemed too pumped up to have slept in late.

We walked towards the food line, looking over all the Witches and Protectors, I saw a lot of yawning people with bags under their eyes. Chuckling at the sight of one of the Witches sleeping on the table, we reached the food line. I reached out for the pancakes and hot chocolate. Then, I grabbed a few donuts and some bacon and eggs.

"Are you going to eat that all?" Astra asked me as we walked towards our table. I waved towards DeeDee, Banu, and Madalena who were already seated.

"Yeah, of course, why not?" I answered back, as I took my seat.

"Morning, ladies. You all look rested," I joked, knowing I probably looked as bad as they did. Getting a mumbled response from them, I started eating.

"I can't eat when I'm nervous," Astra told me. I knew this already, so I wasn't sure if she had been talking to herself or me. I looked her over and bumped my fist against her shoulder. "Come on, As. You know that you can do this. Stop being nervous and enjoy the fact that you will graduate today!" I smiled at her then. "You can do this, girl." I gave her two thumbs up and got back to my food.

The other three smiled at us, cheering up a little, too. "How did you guys sleep?" I asked them, knowing fully well that they hadn't slept at all. Their eyes had bags under them that would hit the floor if they didn't look out.

"We didn't," Banu answered, she was always sort of the leader of the three.

"Why not?" I looked at them. "We don't have to take a test today." I had asked Banu, instead DeeDee answered me.

"No, we don't, indeed. We still have to stand guard, and we have to fight those things later this week. We are the ones who need to react when something goes wrong." Her normally cheerful voice sounded strained. I gave her a small smile, knowing full well what she meant.

"I don't think the Selection council or the teachers would let anything happen to the Witches. We don't have to worry about that," I told her, before stuffing my mouth full with the bacon and eggs. They were worried, I could see that in their eyes and the not so empty plates in front of them. That meant it was time for one of my amazing pep talks.

"Ladies, you will be fine today. And for our own test. We. Will. Be. Great." I punctuated every word, holding my fork in my hand pointing at each of them. My face was dead serious, which made them laugh. The tension disappeared at that moment, I could see them relax. They started eating, which made me relax even more, knowing that they were feeling better.

Our Headmistress walked into the dining hall then, making the whole room hold their breath. "Witches, you can go to the Arena. Mister Ragdan will be there to guide you towards the Gates. And good luck, ladies." She motioned for the Witches to get up and leave the room.

The headmistress waited for the Witches to leave before she started speaking again, making me squeeze Astra's hand quickly before she walked away from us.

"Protectors, you will go with Instructor Lavina, she will show you where to go and what we expect from you. I wish you all good luck." The headmistress then walked away after the Witches, leaving Instructor Lavina alone with us in the dining hall.

"Okay, Protectors, listen up." Her voice reached us all, and we fell silent again. "Today is the Selection for the Witches. This means that they will graduate today. They are going to do their best to show the Selection what they are worth. They need to show how good they are. This is important to them." She looked at us all. "And for you girls, I know this isn't your test, yet. Remember that what you do today can help you in your own test. We need to keep the Witches safe and protect them. When we reach the arena, you will be placed along the ring on the sand. You're not to interfere. Do not help! Doing so could lead to problems for any Witch. They have to do this on their own." Instructor Lavina stopped talking, letting what she said sink in. "If something goes wrong, and we need your help, you will get that order from me."

I looked over to Banu, she shook her head, also, not fully understanding what Instructor Lavina meant. She looked back to our teacher while Instructor Lavina continued.

"When you get the order to act, and only when you get the order from me, you will secure the Witches and contain the Ilunias. There is a do not kill on the Ilunias, they are to be contained only. Am. I. clear?"

"Yes, Ma'am," we answered her.

"What do you think will happen?" Madalena whispered from my right.

I shrugged my shoulders and shook my head. "I don't know. Let's just follow orders and hope that they can pull it off."

"Miss Lavina." I raised my hand up, to get her attention before she walked away.

"Yes, Isadora?"

"Isn't it unfair that we will see these Ilunias today and get to see how they fight, while the Witches see them for the first time?"

Instead of answering right away, Miss Lavina rotated her head and rubbed her neck as if trying to get rid of some tension. I could almost hear her swallow. Knowing that she agreed with what I said made me nervous. "Yes, it is unfair. Only, this is decided by the Selection and the Kings. We can't go against them." She started walking towards the double doors that led outside and towards the arena. I followed her with more questions.

"Why are we allowed to see them first? Why not use graduated Protectors to protect the Witches, why us?" I asked her again. Something was bugging me about that whole thing. She motioned for me to walk next to her.

"This will be explained soon, so it can't harm you girls to know it now. You get to see the Ilunias because you all have to fight them one on one." And that stopped me in my tracks, making me freeze where I stood.

"What do you mean, you guys are going to let us fight them one on one? Not in teams?" You could hear the shock in my voice and in the gasps of the girls next to me. Miss Lavina kept on walking.

"Are you nervous now?" I heard Madalena behind me.

"Yeah," I answered on a breath. I was nervous, I never expected that they would have made us fight one on one. "I never expected that the Kings would be this heartless, letting us fight creatures that are known for their killing rate." Madalena nodded at what I said.

"Don't hesitate, Isadora, ladies. Come on, the Witches are waiting for us. We need to take our positions!" Instructor Lavina yelled at us from outside. We started walking towards her, towards the arena.

We walked outside, into the sunlight that came over the surrounding walls of the school. Towards the big building that stood in the back of the school yard.

The big brown building had four doors that all pointed towards a different direction, giving the round building four different entrances. All four doors had two statues next to each of them, reaching to the top of the arena. Those eight statues all represented a different Witch or Elemental, the best of our history; the ones who were heroes to us. Now, they were forgotten and only honoured in stone at the school.

The arena didn't have a roof, magic protected it from the weather, kept the spells and magic inside, too. There weren't any windows, instead the doors and the open roof to let in light. It was made like this to keep everyone inside, it was a prison before it became an arena. You could feel the cold history of the building, the death that was brought here. It made me shiver every single time I entered those doors. We walked past ·Anriama a powerful Full-Blood who'd fought in the war and the Elemental Narlym. I bowed my head in respect to them, thanking those warriors like every other time I walked into the arena; thanking them for their sacrifices. You would never see a Protector standing at the gates of an arena–made of stone to be honoured. Only Witches and Elementals were important enough to be honoured. It made me bristle at the unfairness.

The cold and the darkness greeted me when I walked inside. The walls were lined with torches, lighting the paths inside the Arena. I touched the walls while we walked towards the gates that led to the middle of the Arena. The frosty air greeted me like an old friend, the magic kissed my fingertips, almost like a long-lost lover. It made me relax, letting go of the doubt and focusing on my duties; protect the Witches from harm and follow orders, not my strongest point that last one.

For a second, my focus wavered, and I could feel them. The dark-world creatures, they were in the building, contained in the magic that rested in the stone. Their blackness was a dark shadow over the natural magic in this world. I pulled my fingers away from the wall, losing contact with the building. I focused on where Instructor Lavina was.

She stood before a big iron gate. Behind her through the bars of the gate, was the arena. The sand reflected the sunlight, making it shimmer, making it too bright to look at from the dark hall of the arena.

"Listen up Protectors." Miss Lavina waited until she had our full attention before she continued, "I want two rows, one goes left and the other right. Spaced evenly. Make sure that every angle is covered. These creatures are horrible, strong, and want everything to die."

"Yes, Ma'am," We all answered her, moving into two rows.

"Banu, Isadora." She looked over at me and then Banu who stood a little behind me. "You two will be next to the holding gates. You will release the Ilunias when I give the signal." We both nodded at her.

"Go," she said when the gate raised up. Her voice rang out in the stone hall. When I walked out into the arena, the sunlight hit my face, making me squeeze my eyes shut. I gave them a second to adjust to the bright light after standing in the hall. We had been there many times, but still it was impressive; the stone building, with seats that reached all the way to the top. A box for the teachers directly facing us.

And in that case, for the Selection council, too. I looked up to see six people in robes who stood next to our teachers and the Headmistress. Some of them were in conversation, talking to each other and ignoring us as we walked into the arena. I walked over towards the holding gates with Banu, we took our sides. My gaze went back to the box, to the Selection council. I didn't recognize any of them. Instead, I checked out their robes.

The most powerful Witches and Elementals wore those robes to show which different kinds of magic they had. A bald male talked with Mister Ragdan; the man wore a grey robe for air with red for fire and brown for earth, making him an Elemental in control of three of the five elements. Having three elements made him strong. Another Selection council member talked with one of their own and our Headmistress. They both wore robes of dark blue and brown, showing they were powerful healers. A lot of Witches who had water and earth control were strong in healing.

You still wouldn't want to make them mad, earth is a powerful destructive magic, too. It could be used for healing, but water is always the main magic in healing. Two other women were talking with each other, they stood a little to the side of the rest. One wore red and the other wore grey. The women looked like each other, and I assumed they were twins. It was not unheard of to have twins with opposite types of magic. With just one colour, they had to be strong to get into the Selection. The most powerful Witches and Elementals were allowed into the Selection council. Most of the time those people were Council members or rulers of the High Houses, they loved their pure blood lines, their power.

I almost missed the last one, he stood more towards the back of the box. His dark-blue robes hid him from view. I squinted my eyes to get a better look at him. Not getting a clear view of him, I gave up and started to look at the other Protectors in the arena. Only, I saw him move from the corner of my eye. When I looked back, he looked directly at me. I could see his colours better, dark-blue of water and red of fire. A strange combination in any Witch or Elemental.

Normally, water and fire didn't mix, they are opposites of each other. Where fire and air complemented each other, water and fire worked against each other. Killing life with fire and giving life with water. I shrugged off his scrutiny of me and looked back towards the arena, filled with the protectors. The gates in front of me then opened up, letting the Witches in. Astra walked in front of the rest, they walked up towards the box to my left, standing still as they waited for the Selection to begin.

"Looks like we are beginning," Banu said to me, she was also focused on the Witches.

"Witches, take up your positions and remember, fight well," the Headmistress said. I saw the Witches spread out in front of the box. Instructor Lavina walked up towards Banu and me.

"Banu, Isadora, if you girls both take the handle at your sides and pull them down when I reach three, then the gates will open and let the Ilunias out. Let go of the handle, and the doors will close. They have to be closed when the creatures are out," she said while she looked at me in particular. Not wanting to roll my eyes, I nodded and looked towards the handle she had indicated.

"One," Miss Lavina started.

"Two."

I could feel the eyes of the Witches roaming over the gates; the fear and the excitement that filled the air. Nobody here had ever seen an Ilunia. Nobody knew what to expect.

"Three." Banu and I pulled down the handles. The gates opened with a screeching sound, like nails that raked a chalkboard, and the hairs at the back of my neck stood up. The gates lifted higher and higher until only the tips showed themselves. The darkness made it difficult to decipher anything in it. Before I could react, something flew by me, screaming. It made my eardrums rattle. Banu even placed her hands over her ears, others did the same. I gripped the handle harder, not letting it drop. Some Witches screamed, adding more noise to it all. I felt two more creatures pass by. "Let go of the handle!" Miss Lavina yelled, trying to be heard over the screaming. I let go of the handle, which dropped the gate down. The earth vibrated beneath our feet from the impact.

I looked up from the gate to the Witches in front of me. To watch them and the Ilunias fight.

4

I found only chaos, utter and total chaos. There must have been around forty-five Witches in the arena, and most of them were running around like headless chickens. I looked around, hoping to find Astra. When I saw her, she was fighting with two of the Ilunias. The creatures seemed to have known who was the strongest around them. She spotted me and even from that distance, I saw her blue eyes light up. Her power swirled around her. Astra mastered three powers, that made her stronger than most Witches. If you had mastered four powers it would be extremely rare, and the current Kings had four. And being like me, well that was extremely rare with a cherry on top.

Most Witches have two powers. And most of them are only extremely strong in one. Not Astra, she fought hard to gain control over all three of her powers, she wanted to show her parents that she wasn't a failure.

I watched her using water and earth, she created a mud pool to trap the first Ilunia. She used fire to create a cage to trap the second one. She got two down, and I wanted to cheer her on, but I kept my mouth shut, so I wouldn't distract her too much.

The mud-trapped Ilunia got free, she used air to fly out of there, and it didn't surprise me that she did that. They could use every element there was. Still, it left my mouth hanging open, seeing it happen right in front of me. And I wasn't the only one; other witches who were still fighting looked, too. Momentarily forgetting to watch the other Ilunia, they were attacked.

It made me wince in pain when I saw a few of them fall down, hitting the sand hard. I heard screams and groaning coming from them. The moment they hit the ground, a protective shield erupted around them. It kept them safe from other attacks. I released the breath I had been holding. The anger that had started to build, stopped. It became clear then that the Selection hadn't wanted the Witches to get hurt much, and that was a good thing. They still could have chosen a different kind of test. That anger was still there, combined with the fear for Astra.

Astra was still fighting with two of the Ilunias, while the third one played with the other Witches, like a cat that played with her catch. A few more of them fell down. I looked around to the other Protectors, we were trained to protect them, it was drilled into us from the moment we had started at school. A few had their hands hovering above their weapons.

"Do not interfere!" Instructor Lavina screamed at us.

Most of the Protectors pulled their hands away from their weapons, while I gave her a scowling look.

Astra kept on fighting, and used her fire to block incoming attacks. She made sure she kept on the move, the most important thing she had been taught. Move, keep your body moving. Make sure you never stood still, never became a target. One of the Ilunias jumped into the air, though I'm not sure if it was the same one. Those long slender creatures, women. With their long black hair, falling towards the floor, faces white as snow, with eyes as black as the night. They wore sleeveless dresses, torn at the bottom, from being dragged over the floor, flowing around their bodies. You could see their bones sticking out, slender fingers and tiny wrists, connecting to bony shoulders, and necks that were so thin, they would break if you looked at them too long. Long legs peeked through the slits in their dresses, as they walked barefoot on the sand of the arena. They sauntered around their prey, and Astra had become that too quickly.

I looked over towards Banu to see a horrified expression on her face before I looked back towards the fighting. Most of the Witches were down, they had started with forty-five, and only nine were left standing by that point. In minutes, the Ilunias had cleared the field of most of the Witches. I watched Thalia who was still standing, though I wasn't sure if I should have been happy about that, or totally surprised at it. I hadn't expected her to last that long. The Ilunias were finishing them off without breaking a sweat. Still we couldn't interfere, we needed to stay still and keep our mouths shut. This was their test, not ours.

We just watched; watched how the Ilunias used their fire to keep the Witches separated, and made sure they couldn't work together. Not that they would have done that, egos and all that. The Ilunias used their air to lift them up and let the Witches fall down again, hard enough to break bones. They threw earth disks at them, and used water to try and drown them. The Witches couldn't die in the test, the Selection council made sure of that. Before the Ilunias could do any real harm, the Witches would be covered by those shields, and pulled out of the fight.

My eyes flew over the fight, moving from Witch to Witch, and I watched Astra fight the hardest she had ever done. It made me proud. I then diverted my gaze towards the box, where the Selection council and teachers had been watching the fight. I watched their mouths form words, their hands glowed when they placed a shield over one of the Witches. I found disappointment in their gazes, and the irritation had risen, knowing they hadn't found what they were looking for. The Witches hadn't been good enough. My anger had flared up at them, the Kings, and that whole messed-up idea of the test.

Those Witches fought with everything they had, fought with everything they had learned, instead they were dismissed as worthless. I felt the sting of my nails dig into my palms, and directed my glare towards them. And if they could hear me, they would have heard the growl that escaped me. Rage surged through me, made my blood boil. The Kings were the ones who had agreed to it, those high-up shit-heads. They had decided that they needed the strongest, and that this test would be the only way to find them.

"Son of a donkey's ass," I mumbled to myself. "Why are you doing this?" I kept mumbling, questions as they ran around in my head. They came and went until one stayed with me, on repeat.

They needed to find the strongest Witches, the strongest. My eyes widened with the realisation that hit me. They were there to flush something out, to find something that they believed still existed. To find me? I shook my head, they weren't looking for me, they were looking for someone *like* me.

I looked down at the sand, my shoes covered in the small grains. My fists were still clenched from all the thoughts and emotions that ran through my head. They weren't looking for me, they didn't know that I was alive. Nobody knew . . . except for Astra, and she would never say anything. She was family; not by blood but by choice. That was something stronger than blood, when you chose to walk that path with that person.

I looked back towards the box, the teachers, and the Selection council, and I forgot the fight. I watched the Selection council more closely, and looked at the teachers. They had raised me. If they had known, they would have been the ones to tell the Kings. A chill went down my spine; it made me shiver, the idea alone. That they had betrayed me. Tears threatened to fill my eyes, and before one could fall down into the sand, I heard my name.

"ISA!" I looked up to see Astra flying. High up near the wards that covered the arena.

"Don't interfere!" Instructor Lavina screamed to me, she stood a few Protectors to my right. I glanced at her. She then yelled the order to me. "Don't you fucking interfere!" I gave her a small nod, which was the only movement I could make while my body was locked with the fear and shock I was experiencing. I looked back to Astra, who had started falling down. I quickly looked to the box, and hoped one of the teachers would break her fall. I saw Miss D'Moray's hands move, I felt the magic that took shape around Astra.

I breathed out again, when Astra's fall slowed down, when I could see the shield shimmer around her. She had been the last of the Witches, the last one standing. And then it was done, the test was over. And I knew for sure that they hadn't found what they were looking for. The anger still shimmered under my skin, a silent creature that lay waiting to explode.

The Ilunias stood before the box with the Selection members, who were ignoring them as they talked to each other. Obviously, they had forgotten that the Ilunias weren't back in their cells yet.

I looked over towards Lavina, waited for orders when a shrill ice-filled voice sounded through the arena, and my head whipped around to find the source.

"You think capturing us would do you any good?" We could hear the promise of death, spoken with each word. I swear I saw the room vibrate with the power behind that voice. The whole arena was now focused on them.

"You think that those things," the middle Ilunia pointed towards the Witches under the box, "can stop us?"

Some of the Witches had scrambled together behind the big shield that the teachers had pulled up around the box. It had been pulled down towards the sand floor and covered the Witches when they were pulled behind it. This was easier for the teachers to maintain then a single shield on every Witch. The girls pushed themselves against the wall of the arena, closer to each other, and tried to escape the wrath of the Ilunias. Others just looked at them, and a few of them even laughed, feeling safe behind that shield.

Astra just stood there, in front of the others at the edge of the shield. A murderous look was in her eyes, her mouth was in a straight line, and her hands glowed with power. She was ready for another fight, if it came to that.

Before anyone could react, the Ilunias let out a high-pitched scream. People fell to the ground, covering their ears. Protectors were down on their knees. More Witches scrambled further back towards the wall; away from the Ilunias, away from the threat in front of them.

My magic reacted on instinct, it covered my ears from the worst part of the scream. Still I looked through squinted eyes towards Astra, who had her hands to her ears, still standing.

The air vibrated, the sand grains started to shake, and the shields exploded. The one that kept the Witches safe, and protected the box with the teachers and Selection. Luckily the ancient shield around the arena held steady. The magic that exploded from the shield rained down on us; it made my skin tingle where it touched. The ground shook with the force of power that had been released. Some of the people in the box fell down. Others grabbed the railing in front of them, steadying themselves.

The Ilunias were now smiling, something you would never have hung above your bed. The scary level of those smiles would give me nightmares for months. Their hands glowed with their magic; wind whispered around them, their long hair dancing. All three of them looked towards one single Witch. Astra.

My heart jumped into my throat–the beat increasing– and my hands had started to tremble. I could see the Ilunias starting to aim, pointing their fingers towards Astra, who stood in front of all of the Witches, her arms glowing with her magic, her ears were bleeding like so many of us. My feet were already moving towards her, my body had made the decision to keep Astra safe, and my mind was right behind it.

I screamed when the Ilunias released their combined magic. It bolted towards Astra.

Everything slowed. Astra turned her face towards me, her blue eyes wide. My heartbeat drummed in my ears, so hard it drowned out my footfalls. I pushed my body to move harder, pushed magic under my feet, I used the air, so I would fly towards her. Just before the surge of power reached Astra, I grabbed her, my back turned towards the Ilunias.

I saw the shock on her face turn into fear as her eyes widened. Her hands came up to catch me if I fell. Because a normal Witch would have fallen down, would have been killed from a blast like that. And a protector, the Nulls, would have been decimated, gone, turned into dust, nothing to bury. But Witches had a higher tolerance for magical attacks, our bodies could handle more. I wouldn't say that we were made of magic. Still, with the magic inside our bodies, we were more resistant than Nulls.

I watched Astra's mouth form my name, the blast of the magic too loud for me to hear her voice. I felt it crawling over my skin, it made the hairs on my neck stand upright. Their darkness, their slick and oil-like magic had sucked the air out of my lungs. Tears streamed down my face, making Astra a blur in front of me.

With effort, I sucked it all inside of me. I pulled the magic into myself and turned it into my own. A ragged breath escaped my throat. It had been a long time since I had used magic; took magic, and I had forgotten how hard it could be. Cursing my Gran for making me keep it a secret, I straightened my back, rolled my shoulders and looked into Astra's wide eyes. I wiped away the tears in my eyes and gave her a half smile before I turned to the Ilunias.

"Now, let's finish you three," I mumbled to myself, my anger close to the surface.

The ring of steel rang through the arena when I pulled my swords out of their sheaths on my back. They glinted in the sunlight. The leather hilts fit perfectly in my hands, the weight balanced over the swords and the edges sharpened enough to cut heads from bodies. That was something I planned on doing three times; nobody touched Astra without paying for it.

With a smirk on my face and death in my eyes, I walked towards the Ilunias. Their mouths were open and their black eyes wide, their hands still hung in the air from blasting their magic. Fingers twisted before they lowered their arms. I stopped in front of them, both swords loose in my hands, next to my body. Their tips almost touched the ground. The Ilunias stood there, their brains slow to react to what they saw.

"Boo," I said. All three of them scrambled, moving apart from each other.

"The game is on," I said as I rushed towards the left one. I used air to speed up, reaching her in seconds. I swung my sword towards her head, but she dropped down, disappearing into the earth, dust rising up where she stood.

"That trick doesn't work with me," I told the empty space in front of me. I stomped down with my feet and pushed her upwards. A cry escaped her mouth before I cut off her head. She gurgled for a second before the head dropped on the ground with a thud.

The whole arena was silent, no sound inside the walls. Until two screams filled the arena. "Sister!" one wailed, with a high-pitched ice-filled voice.

"What have you done?" the other screamed at me.

"I killed her." Before I finished my words, I felt magic being gathered. I wasn't keeping my magic inside myself anymore; my senses were heightened, and my surroundings were clearer. I gave myself a second to shake off the doubt that had rushed through me with exposing myself to the Selection council, the teachers, and the others in the arena. I shook the feeling of being whole again off of myself, before I focused on the magic I felt behind me. I moved, using air to go faster, moving out of the way from the magical blast the other two Ilunias had thrown at me.

I turned around, threw air towards the right one and fire towards the left one. They both pulled up shields, blocking my attempt to finish the fight fast. Fire balls were thrown at me, so I used air to infuse my swords with the magic to slice them in half. I cut through them like a knife through butter. The heat still blasted in my face, and had made my lips dry up.

Running towards the left Ilunia, I made stepping stones out of earth. Running higher, I reached above her head before I jumped. I had planned on cutting her head off, instead I was thrown out of the way by a blast of air. I hit the ground hard, feeling the sand scratch over my arms and face. My knees burned with the impact, and I felt blood dripping down one of my legs. Ignoring it all, I got up and braced myself for the next attack. My swords were next to my body, I shifted my weight to my heels, balancing on them, ready to move when they did.

"Who are you?" I heard one of them ask.

"Your worst nightmare," I answered, and with that, they flew towards me, screaming. I braced myself and jumped high into the air, flying over them. With a thud, I landed behind them, turning around, swirling with my blades. I cut one of them across her back. Black blood flowed down her back as she fell down to the sand. The other Ilunia, her sister, stood in front of her. Protecting her.

Air attacked me from the sides, making me stagger before the earth dropped from underneath me. I pulled on my own magic, getting the earth to close up under my feet before I fell down into the hole, shielding myself with an air wall from the strongest attacks from her. I kept pushing my magic out, pushing my air shield until I knew I could blast her with my own air.

She fell backwards, over her sister who was still on her knees. I rushed towards them, only to be met with darkness. Total darkness. I couldn't even see my own hands in front of my face. For a moment I felt panic clawing at me. I shoved it back down, and I listened to my surroundings.

I heard a whisper around me–not knowing where it came from–say, "Give us the darkness to defeat our enemies." I turned around, slowly circling on the spot I was standing on. The air was cold, almost freezing, and the silent darkness pressed against me.

Then all hell broke loose. I heard people screaming. "Isa, where are you?" The voice of Astra reached me above all the screaming. "What happened?" I heard the panic in her voice.

"I have no idea, stay where you are. I'm handling it," I yelled back at her.

"No, you are not." I recognized the voice of Thalia.

"Oh, shut up, apple pie. I'm doing more than you did," I told her. I was still turning around, trying to find the Ilunias. I hoped that the screaming didn't mean they'd gone after the other Witches or the Protectors. My stomach turned around at that thought, my mouth went even dryer, not knowing what had happened around me. Whether the girls were all right or not. Astra sounded okay, that was good. I focused back on myself and my surroundings.

"Stand still, Isa, it doesn't work, turning around in the dark. There is nothing you can see," I said, giving myself a pep talk to keep my own nerves calm. Standing still in the dark, I could hear the movements behind me.

"Little girl, little prey, you are so dead." I felt their breath touch my ear, their whispered words sending chills down my spine. I turned around, swinging with my swords, cutting through air. A laugh sounded from my other side, I moved that way, cutting with my swords, and hitting nothing but air again.

"You are nothing, little prey!" one of them screamed.

"You will never be anything," the other whispered. Again, I moved, faster than I had ever moved before, hitting air.

I bared my teeth, knowing they wouldn't see it. A growl escaped my throat, my hands clutched my swords. I felt my muscles cramping from the tight grip I kept. Something hit my back, making me lose my breath, and I stumbled forward. Another blow to my ribcage, which made me blow out the last of my breath. I lost my balance after the blow to my face; my cheek throbbed with the impact. I felt the ground before I noticed I had been falling, the darkness made me lose my orientation. The impact rattled through me, and I almost lost my swords, before I clutched them in a death grip. I sucked in a breath of air, dust and sand filling my mouth. Coughing, I laid on the ground.

The laughter of the Ilunias filled my head, the darkness pressed in on me. It wanted to chew me up, eat me alive and spit me out as a shell of nothing but emptiness. The sand pressed into my skin, and the leather of my swords was warm in my hands. I took another breath filled with sand and darkness.

'When you are down, you get up, Isa girl. You get up, take a steady breath and look at it differently,' I could hear Gran saying, as if she was right there, next to me. I pushed off of the sand, getting up as I took a breath. The darkness still pressed against me. I took another breath and let the words of Gran sink into me. Look at it differently, look differently. An idea formed in my head, and I closed my eyes. I relaxed my stance, balancing on my feet, my swords, again, loose in my hands.

And then I embraced the darkness, the magic in it and made it my own. I listened to my surroundings. It wasn't that suffocating anymore since the darkness had stopped working against me. I pushed my magic around, slowly searching for the ones responsible for this. The last two Ilunias in the arena, and the two who would die.

I felt the first one, right behind me. I stood still, waiting for my target to move closer. I didn't move a muscle when I felt her moving towards me, letting her think I was still unaware of where they were.

"You are so–"

Before she could finish her words, I turned around, slicing my swords through her throat, cutting her skin and bone and removing her head from her body. "Dead." I finished her sentence before the head hit the ground. Warm liquid dripped down my face. Wiping the blood away from my eyes, I focused on the other, she had kept quiet that time. No screaming over her fallen sister.

I kept my eyes closed, my magic around me, and I waited again, listening for the last one. I heard a rustling to my right, but continued standing still. A rustling at my front; she was playing with me, trying to make me move around, and hoping I would make a mistake.

"You think you can beat me? You think that I'm weak without my sisters." The voice came from in front of me, filled with hate and pain. Pain for her lost sisters or pain for knowing that she would be losing this battle, too, I did not know.

I could feel magic moving in the air, dark magic. Even darker than the darkness around us, a magic that wasn't of this world and shouldn't have been there. I braced myself for the power that she was collecting in front of me. Reaching down towards my own power, I pulled it up and pushed it around me, collecting it and building it into the things I wanted.

I pushed out the shield behind me the moment the Ilunia let go of her dark magic, knowing she would not only target me, but the people behind me. I could feel the magic cross over my skin, like an oil that sticks to you and would never really wash off. I pushed my own magic into it, forming a copy of myself as I turned into a shadow. I moved to the right, the Ilunia now focused on my illusion, and crept closer.

"You can't win this, little prey!" she yelled at the illusion. When I stepped behind her, I placed my swords on her throat. She froze and the darkness, the concentration she had, fell away with the shock of being at the end of her life.

My illusion fell away with the darkness, too, and I dropped my shield as fast as I could to keep some of the magic I had, a secret. My swords were still against her throat, a small trickle of black blood trailed down her neck, where she'd pushed too hard, testing my skills.

"Don't kill her!" I heard someone yell from the box. I looked up at the person. It was the bald man from the Selection.

"You think you can tell me what to do?" I said to him. Before he could answer I pulled my swords through her neck, separating her head from her body. It slumped down to the ground, her head rolled towards the box I faced, coming to a stop in front of a few Witches. For a second it was still, then they screamed.

5

"Silence!" Miss D'Morays voice boomed around the arena. The screaming Witches froze, mouths open. They were screaming without a sound. I still stood behind the dropped body of the Ilunia, my swords dripped with black blood. Feeling the blood that slowly glided down my face, I knew I must have looked like a nightmare. Which was good, they needed to be scared, I needed as much of a cover I could get.

"Who are you?" someone asked from the box. I looked up at them. All of the council were at the railing, anger and disbelief rolling off of them. I could feel their magic in the air around me. I pulled mine back inside myself, to that hidden place within me. The one I'd learned from my Gran, the place where I had held my magic all those years. Nobody could feel anything from me now. I was as much of a Null as if I was born one.

Two of their faces morphed into something ugly, concentrating. I could feel their magic going over me, and I let it. I didn't show I noticed it, but I felt it. One of them lashed out, using their magic as a whip over my back. I gritted my teeth and stood still, putting more effort in keeping my magic away. Now that I had used it, it took me more effort to keep it down. Still, I pushed it down.

Before it could happen again, Astra moved, breaking their attention off of me.

"Are you alright?" she asked me when she stood in front of me. I nodded, not wanting to say too much. She moved to my right and stood next to me. A silent support.

"Who are you? And answer this time," a woman asked. I looked at her, her hair was in a high bun on top of her head. She was one of the healers in the group. She held her chin high and looked down her nose at me.

"Isadora," I answered. No point in not saying my name with all the teachers around them. My eyes roamed over all the people in the box. I ended on the bald man wearing the most colours. Knowing he would be the leader, I kept my eyes on him.

"Why did you kill them?" another woman asked me, one of the twins.

"To save you all," I answered.

"We asked you not to kill the last one, you didn't obey our orders," the bun lady said, more anger radiating from her.

I cocked my head to the side. I looked her over again, her face had started to turn red. Still I didn't answer. Why would I? I wasn't there to explain that if I kept the last Ilunia alive, she would bring more problems or they would have tortured her. Death was the better option.

"You are a Protector, you obey our orders!" she screamed at me.

"No. She is not," Miss D'Moray answered before I could say the same. "She still needs to graduate, you don't have any authority over her. Yet." Miss D'Moray turned towards the bald man, saying something that I couldn't hear.

"You aren't a Protector. Right?" the bald man asked me, when he turned back from talking with Miss D'Moray. I kept my mouth shut at that, letting them guess.

"You need to answer the question!" the bun lady yelled again, turning even redder. It made my lips twitch in a smile. Before I could answer, I heard people moving over the sands. As they moved towards me, I remembered that I wasn't the only one there.

"You got this," Banu said from behind me. I heard a few more saying the same, and some of them told me they had my back. It gave me a warm and fuzzy feeling that these girls would have my back. It helped that they hadn't really liked the Witches. Still, they chose to stand behind me, a Witch.

I looked at the teachers and the Selection, I knew I needed to give them something, to get them off my back.

"Yes, I'm a Protector."

"You aren't," Thalia said, her finger pointing at me. For a second, I was tempted to just chop it off her hand. She always wanted to have all the attention. I shifted my gaze back towards the box. Instead for that turtwaddle of a Thalia to started talking again; testing my patience. I still had black smelly blood on me, and a shower would be the best solution to that problem.

"You are a Witch. We all saw it, you used magic." Her finger was still in the air. I gripped my swords harder, heard the leather creak under my hands. "No Null could ever resist that much magic and live," Thalia said.

"She isn't worth it," Astra said when she placed a hand on my shoulder, willing me to relax.

"The Witch is right. You are a Witch. The question is, why are you dressed as a Protector, a Null?" the bald man asked as he held his hand up towards the bun lady, silencing her. She folded her arms in front of her chest, which made her look like a mad child.

"Why not?" I answered back, my voice ringing clear in the silence of the arena.

The bald man slowly studied me, he turned his head a little. As if seeing me from another angle would change who stood before him.

"You need to answer the questions we asked. We are here in the name of the Kings!" the bun lady spat out, her face was still red. The anger now seemed to vibrate from her, almost heating up the area around her, if that could happen with her ice-cold heart.

"Ladies, let's not start this here," the bald man spoke up again. He looked at his colleague, urging her back towards a seat. I couldn't hear what they were saying, I could see the wild hand gestures which showed me he was mad. When the bun lady sat down, he turned back towards me.

"Listen up, young lady. Miss D'Moray may be right, we don't have any say about you right now. However, remember that we get a lot of say in your life when you graduate. And looking at the fight you just delivered, you would pass that test with your eyes closed."

That had me chuckling, I had indeed won with my eyes closed. Yeah, I had been blinded by the darkness the Ilunia made, still the same thing.

"It is wise for you to answer the questions we asked you," he continued, not noticing my chuckle. Since the fight had ended, my emotions had calmed down, and my adrenaline surge had stopped. It made me feel exhausted. That was the first time I had used that much magic in years, it made me ache. I now wanted to get into a hot shower, to make sure my muscles wouldn't cramp over.

"No," I responded. Most of the people around me gasped for air. I could see a smile on Ragdan's face, it was there and gone in a flash.

Before the bald man could speak, I continued, "Listen up, you guys made a bunch of Witches fight against Ilunias. How you managed not to get them killed is a miracle. I'm not sure why you guys kept going with this test. I don't think any Witches from the other school passed the test?" I looked at them all. They didn't answer. "No, I thought so." I wanted to place my hands on my hips. Only I still held my swords. Not wanting to get the sheaths dirty I kept them in my hands, next to my body. The black blood had already dried on them, which meant that it would be harder to clean them.

"No, I will not answer your questions. I will not listen

to anymore of what you have to say. I saved your sorry asses. I made sure none of you were killed, and I showed the Ilunias some kind of mercy."

"'MERCY?'" the bun lady yelled. I just rolled my eyes at her. Why couldn't she shut up?

"Yes, mercy. Because you would have experimented on them, used them as you see fit. Like you used these Witches. And don't start with the, 'it is for the good of the world and the Kings' and all that slapstick shit. You are just a selfish bunch of people who don't understand the world."

"And you do?" the man who had stood in the shadows asked, when he stepped forward. I heard Astra sucking in a breath. Out of the corner of my eye, I saw her stiffen when she noticed him. Not wanting to show I had seen that in front of the man that made Astra react like that, I answered.

"No. I don't know shit about the world. But I know more about the people who live in it." My family's past was on my mind. "If you all would excuse me, I need to clean my swords. And you should clean up this mess." I used the tip of my sword to indicate the dead bodies of the Ilunias on the floor.

With that said, I turned around. The Protectors that had been behind me opened up, letting me pass through them towards the entrance we'd come through. The doors were open, and I walked into the darkened halls of the Arena. The cool air rushed into my lungs when I took a deep breath. I wiped my swords clean at the sides of my pants, they were already dirty, before I placed my swords back in their sheaths. I moved my shoulder to relax my muscles. I could hear footsteps behind me, I let my magic go a little, feeling who it was.

A power greeted me back, friendly and something I had always felt around me. Even without my magic roaming free. I could feel her water, fire, and earth magic dancing around her. It always reminded me of a waterfall in the spring; the power from it and the soft feel of the spring weather.

"You feel different," Astra said, when she caught up to me. I had slowed down for her.

"I know, you can feel my magic now." I gave her a small smile, focused back on the walk towards the school. All the magical creatures had their own feel of magic, almost like a scent.

Before we could talk more, I felt someone coming before I had even heard them.

"Isadora," a male voice had called out to me. It was only a matter of time before one of them would have followed me. They would never have listened to me. A sigh escaped me before I turned around. Astra stood next to me with her hands clenched at her sides and her back stiff. She didn't like this man. It made me step a little in front of her, to protect her.

I focused my attention on the man in front of us. Luckily for him, he was a few feet away.

"My name is Icas Nox," he said, and I heard Astra swallow. This made me switch my balance, widening my stance, so I could get into action when needed.

"I'm not here to fight you," he said, his hands palm open towards me.

"Yeah sure," I answered.

"Look, what you said—you are right. You did the right thing by killing those monsters. They would have done a lot of harm if they had the chance."

He waited for an answer. I waited for him to keep on talking.

"Okay, listen. The whole goal of this test is to find the strongest Witch." His eyes flicked for a second towards Astra. I positioned myself even more in front of her. His eyes moved back towards me, a brief smile on his face and a flicker of satisfaction in his eyes.

"And we found her." With that he smiled, through it never reached his eyes. I didn't move a muscle, just looked at him. Waited for the end game of his whole performance. His eyes flickered back to annoyance, and I could see his hands flexing and feel his magic gathering. He was losing his temper.

"You need to come with us to the Kings."

This made me laugh, really loudly. I stopped abruptly and said, "No." Then, I turned around, pulling Astra with me.

"We can order you," he said then.

"Oh, hell canaries no," I said back, and kept walking towards the doors that would lead us outside.

"Listen." I could feel his magic closer now. It made me stop; I didn't want Astra to get caught in the crossfire because he was strong. I looked over my shoulder at him. He stood there, his hands still open towards me, his nice gesture completely failing. It made me roll my eyes, I would roll them out of my head if I kept doing it.

"You are more than qualified to become a Protector," he said with a sneer on his face. "That means you will graduate, you will fall under the order of the Council. And with me in that council, I will bring you to the castle, to the Kings." He waited for a reaction from me.

I gave him nothing. I was the Full-Blood here, he was nothing, and that meant he couldn't do anything to force me.

"And if you try something." His eyes moved towards Astra again, a hungry gleam in them. "I will make sure you come, there is always some motivation to be found."

That had me reacting.

"You want to blackmail me? A Protector who just killed three Ilunias, and I'm not even graduated," I said as I turned around, making sure I would be facing him. My voice dropped low, nobody threatened Astra. Me, I was fine with that, Astra was the wrong direction. I had to give him credit, he didn't flinch.

"No, not blackmailing. Just finding the right motivation

. . . to make you see my side of things." A smile crept onto his face. I had to suppress a shiver.

"There is only one decision for you. And that is to come with us to the Castle. And you choose to make it a hard decision or an easy one." And with that, he turned around.

If I had balls, he would have had me by them.

I turned around, too. Astra had moved next to me, her face a little pale. Before we reached the door, we were caught up with three other ladies. Three I was really happy to see.

"What are you going to do now?" Banu asked. I didn't hear anything in her voice, no hatred or disgust. Except her honesty and her friendship.

"I'm not sure." I wasn't, not after the talk with that Nox guy. Astra grabbed my hand in hers and squeezed. "You can't let him blackmail you. You have to go and hide, like you said you would do." Her blue eyes were filled with tears, hopelessness written on her face. It made me stop.

"And leave you here, with him and what he planned to do?"

"What are you talking about?" DeeDee asked. I ignored her, they would find out soon enough.

"You have to, Isa, if they get you. . . ." She didn't finish her sentence.

"What–?" DeeDee started again, always the nosy one. I held up my hand to silence her for a moment.

"Come to my room. I need to shower and clean my weapons. I will explain a few things to you girls." I looked back towards Astra her hand still in mine. "And we will talk about that whole blackmailing shit, also." I pulled her with me, out of the Arena and into the sun.

6

We entered the dining hall. The room was filled with the rest of the students. The whole hall went silent when we entered. I knew I must have looked a mess, covered in blood with a Witch next to me and three other Protectors at my back. I'm sure they had felt the blast of magic the Ilunia used to shatter the shield, and their curious looks confirmed my thoughts. Nobody said anything when we walked past them. But when we walked through the door leading to the hall, the whispers started.

We walked through the hall that led us towards our room. A walk we had made daily for years. And this would be one of the last times that we would walk it together. I squeezed Astra's hand, she squeezed back. I'm sure she thought the same thing.

Astra opened the door for us, and we walked in. The room felt cold, this place where we had grown up and lived for years. My mind took a darker turn, sadness surrounded me and for a moment I wanted to lay under the covers and cry the ugliest cry you could think of.

"I'm going to take a shower," was all I said instead. I heard murmurs from the others, even though I'd already blocked them out. Before I reached the bathroom door, I pulled off my swords and placed them against the doorframe. I would clean them later. I entered the bathroom, the scent of the shampoo Astra had used that morning still lingered. Lavender, a smell I didn't like, normally. Now, it reminded me of what I would have lost if I hadn't reacted earlier. My breath hitched inside my body, my throat closed, and I felt the warm liquid of my tears running down my face. I hiccupped, catching the breath I had desperately needed. My lungs filled with air and the smell of lavender; I was lost.

That ugly cry had arrived. I turned on the shower fast, not wanting them to hear me. While the room filled with steam, I got undressed, pulling off the clothing covered in blood, which had already crusted over. I pulled the elastic from my hair, it fell down and brushed my naked back, it still hurted a little after the impact of that much magic, luckily it was already getting better. Still a shiver ran over me, not from the cold but the relief to be out of those clothes, to let them be a memory and nothing more. I stepped under the shower, the hot water warming my body, as it turned black around my feet from the blood of the Ilunias. That was when the anger reached me. I screamed.

The door burst open, and Astra and the girls filled the room. Astra looked at me, and the others looked around, searching for the non-existing threat. When they couldn't find anything, they turned their eyes to me. I felt them burning into me.

"It is okay," Astra said. She always had known what was going on with me. "I'm safe. We are safe, and you did good." She stood in front of the glass doors, I saw her shape in front of it. Her blonde hair was reflected by the bright light of the bathroom. They had it turned on, I hadn't even noticed that I hadn't.

I heard footsteps, they left the bathroom. Except Astra, she and her blonde halo stayed right where they were. I released the sob I had been holding. "Shh, it is okay, Isa.

You can cry." Astra's voice was low and soft, soothing. So, I cried, more and more.

I released the fear, the pain, and the anger I had felt. I kept the hate for the Selection council. The hate that they would use creatures like that, would place the Witches in danger without so much as blinking at it. I would need it for the next time I would see them.

After a while, Astra's soft voice filled the room. She had been talking the whole time, only it had taken a while to reach my ears. It was what had calmed me down. I stayed there for a few more minutes, listening to her, letting the warm water run down my body and calm the rest of my emotions. I needed my brain awake and alert.

I turned off the faucet and walked out of the shower. Astra handed me a towel and left the bathroom. One of them had left me clean clothing on the chair we had in the bathroom. I pulled it on and walked out. Determination ran through me, we needed a plan.

When I entered the room again, the others were all sitting on the beds. Banu was holding my swords. "I cleaned them." She offered them up to me.

"Thank you." I took them and placed them against the closet.

"Isa," Banu started. I looked at her to see a question in her eyes. I nodded.

"Why didn't you tell us that you were a Witch?" There was pain in her voice. Madalena and DeeDee both looked at their feet or hands, not looking at me. Shame filled me. They had always been there for me, and I hadn't trusted them.

"I-I couldn't," I said and pulled the chair from under my desk and sat down. "I wanted to. I promised my Grandmother to never tell anybody."

"You told Astra," DeeDee said.

"Yes, I did, three weeks ago. Believe me when I say that I trust you. I would never harm you guys or put you in any danger. Not even you, Astra."

"What do you mean?" DeeDee asked.

"Look, I planned on graduating, moving back to my Gran's house, and disappearing. That was my goal in life, still kind of is. Only, things got a little more complicated," I said to them, not wanting to stay on the topic of who I was any longer. They knew enough of me being a Witch, they didn't need to know that I was the last Full-Blood, let alone the last Savill Royal.

"I never planned on really telling anyone. Only, I got lonely. And Astra had been my best friend from day one. If I told you guys, I would break my promise to my Gran even more. I didn't want to put anyone in danger by knowing who I was." I had said too much already. I could see it in their faces as they worked on what I told them.

"Look, we need to do something about this mess," I quickly said. I hoped to distract them enough from my confession. And luckily for me, Banu had answered, giving me the break I needed.

"What is going on?" Her I'll-always-have-a-cool-head was working again. Her face was blank, no emotion, all business.

"This guy."

"Icas Nox," Astra said before I could say more. I nodded to her and let her continue.

"He is a council member and an uncle to one of the Kings. He is also powerful, and my parents arranged for me to marry him." That last part left on a breath.

"Wait, what?" DeeDee turned around, to face Astra who had sat next to her.

"What DeeDee said." I wasn't the only one who had kept a secret it seemed.

"My parents planned on me marrying him when I graduated."

"Aren't the council members like, older than old?" Madalena asked, her soft voice filling the room, a disgusted look on her face.

"Yes and no, most of them. I don't know," Astra

answered. "Icas Nox is the youngest of them. thirty-nine I think now. Look, my parents promised me to him when I was a newborn. They arranged it all, there was one good thing about it all and that was that he wanted me trained as a Witch. Wanted me to be perfect and not untrained. So, they sent me to this school as soon as I was old enough. Meaning that I wouldn't have to marry him before I graduated." She sighed.

"And that is why you wanted to become the best, so you would make it into the Selection." Astra nodded at what I said.

"And that is why you were so happy to hear that the Kings still hadn't found any Queens. If you marry one of them, you wouldn't have to marry him." My best friend-someone I would always protect-looked at me with her blue eyes.

A plan started to form in my head. I needed to protect her. That was the goal.

"I know that smile. What did you think of?" Astra asked.

"I think I found a way for you to still be a part of the Selection. A way to keep you out of the hands of that Council guy."

"And how is that?"

"I'm going to the castle."

It was silent for a second. My smile was still on my face. Because that was the perfect plan.

"No. No. No." Astra held her hand up, waving a finger at me.

"Yes." I grinned.

"No, listen up. If you go there, they will find out what you are."

"How do you mean what she is? She is a Witch, right? That is a good thing, right?" Banu interrupted us.

"She is a Full-Blood," Astra answered for me. My head whipped from Banu to her. Who pulled up her shoulders in a shrug.

"Wait, what?" DeeDee and Madalena asked together.

"Yeah. I am. Still no big deal. Only you guys know that." I turned back towards Astra. "And that is enough." I lowered my voice, and hoped she caught the fact that I hadn't appreciated what she had done.

"Not a big deal? You are the most powerful Witch here. Alive, even," Banu said, her voice filled with awe, her eyes wide.

"Yeah, still not a big deal. I'm a Protector first. I'm still the same person as I was before you guys knew this. And please keep it a secret." I shook my head at the two of them with their mouths hanging open, and Banu's eyebrows almost shot up from her face.

"Okay, Isa, what is your plan?" We turned our attention towards Astra.

"They want me to go to the Castle. And there is merely one way I would go and that is for her," I pointed towards Astra, "to be a part of the Selection."

"This will make her safe from that Nox guy. And it will allow me to keep an eye on her and make sure the Kings will like her, and she gets picked."

"And then, when that happens? What will you do?" Banu asked me.

I turned my head towards Banu, looked into her eyes. "Then, I will disappear. Leave Astra to her happily ever after. And I will do what I promised Gran." I crossed my arms over my chest, looked them all in the eye and waited for their response.

"And how are you making sure that we both get into the Castle?" Astra asked, when my eyes landed on her.

"Good question, Astra. It's simple, I will demand it." I gave her the biggest smile ever, maybe more an evil grin. Doesn't matter which one, it made them chuckle.

"You will demand it?" Lena laughed out.

"Yeah, I'm the most powerful person here. You said it yourself. So, yeah, I will demand it." I shrugged with that.

"And what if they don't agree?" she asked then, no laughter in her soft voice.

"Then I will take Astra, and we leave. Go to my Gran's home and see from there." I grabbed Astra by her hand and squeezed. "I will always protect you, As, remember that okay?" She nodded.

"Okay, then it is time to pack a bag for a quick escape and pack the rest of your stuff." I released her hand and looked over to DeeDee. "Can you tell the Headmistress that I want to talk to all of the Selection in twenty minutes?" She nodded, got up and walked out the door.

"What can we do?" Banu asked.

I looked around the room and said, "Help me pack?"

We worked in silence, packing our stuff into suitcases for Astra and duffle bags for me. We made two small backpacks where we would keep important things and a clean set of clothing, money, and in my case, my weapons.

A knock sounded on the door, I looked up at Astra who walked towards it and opened it.

DeeDee stood there, her face a little flushed. "They are ready for you," she said. I nodded.

"Okay." I turned towards Banu and Madalena. "I want you two to take these two bags and keep them with you. We don't want them to think we are planning on leaving somewhere else than with them." I turned back towards DeeDee. "Can you come with us and watch our backs?"

She nodded. I looked at Astra. "And I want you with me in that room. Only, don't speak unless you think it will help us. Otherwise, let me do the talking, okay?" I pulled up my brow with that question. She needed to know that it was serious. That I needed to handle it.

She nodded. And with that, we all moved out of our room. Banu and Lena took the two backpacks. "Can we do something else, after we drop off the bags?" Lena asked.

I shook my head. "No, stay in your room. Keep the bags safe, they have all of our important information in them. And my weapons." This made her chuckle.

"Okay. Keep us updated," Lena said towards DeeDee and me. She and Banu nodded at us when we reached the hall that would lead to the Headmistress's office.

"Good luck," Banu said and turned around, Lena followed.

We reached the door to the Headmistress's office. Voices could be heard through them. The wood didn't mute anything they had been saying.

"She wouldn't do," some female voice said.

"We need her," another said.

"You saw what she did to those Ilunias," yet another said.

Astra elbowed me softly in the side. "They are talking about you. Maybe you should tell them how rude that is when you aren't around." A smile was on her face, and her blue eyes twinkled with mischief.

"Yeah, maybe I should. Remember, let me do the talking." She nodded, and I pushed the doors open.

"It isn't nice to talk about someone who isn't there," I said, my voice calm. The whole room turned around to look at me. The Headmistress sat in her chair. She gave me a nod. I lowered my head a little in greeting.

"We can say what we want, about who we want," the bun lady said. She really needed to shut up, she had started to irritate me, and that was never a good thing.

"What is she doing here?" the bald man said, as he looked at Astra.

"She is here because I asked her to be," I answered back.

"You asked us to talk with you. We thought only you," Icas Nox said, his eyes moved over my body, giving me chills. I was all cleaned up; I *so* hoped at that moment that I didn't look like my ancestors.

"I didn't ask you here to talk to me. I asked you to meet me here, so I could explain a few things."

"That is not how this will go." The bun lady stood up from her chair and moved toward me. I let a sliver of my magic go, pushed it towards her and formed it into a solid wall of air. She walked right into it. "Oomph." She stumbled back, clutching her nose. I dropped my wall, and filled the room with my magic, letting them know that I was powerful and angry.

"Listen up. I will only come with you to the Castle if Astra," I pointed to her next to me, "comes with me. She will be part of the Selection. She is the strongest Witch in this school. You all saw that." I raised my hand to stop the bald man from speaking. "I will not be part of this Selection stuff." That made the room explode. "Oi!" I yelled out, filling the room with even more magic. The Twins had paled visibly, and the bald man stepped back a little. "I wasn't finished." When I had all of their attention again, I carried on. "I will not be part of this Selection thing. I'm no Witch, I'm a Protector."

"Are there more things?" Icas Nox asked. He leaned against the desk of the Headmistress.

"Oh, yes," I said, smiling.

"I won't let you all control my life, if you try or think about it once, just remember how it felt in this room. And believe me when I tell you that this isn't even scratching the surface of what I can do." I let my magic roam around again, filled the room even more. It would have felt like they were drowning, pressed down by that much magic. I kept it off of us and the Headmistress. But the others; I could see sweat forming on brows, and the other two selection members dropped down in their chairs, white as paper. Icas Nox, the bald man, and bun lady were the last ones standing, with difficulty.

I pulled all the magic back into myself, they sucked in a breath together.

"I hope, for your sakes, you all agree with my terms?" I asked them.

The bald man answered. "Yes. Astra will come with you, and she will be part of the Selection." I cleared my throat when he didn't continue. He swallowed. "And you will not be a part of the Selection. "

"One more thing, when do we leave?" I asked the bald man.

"Tonight," he answered, his voice shaking.

"Good." I nodded toward the Headmistress, she gave me a smile, and I turned around on my heels. Astra followed me close. I pulled open the door, letting Astra walk through it first. Before I walked through it, I looked over my shoulder to them and said, "Remember, I'm nobody's bitch, and if you like your own lives, stay away from mine." With that I walked away and towards a life that became a whole lot more complicated, and yet still made me feel more alive than I had felt in years.

7

"Are you sure they will allow me to get into the Selection?" Astra asked me. We were back in our room, waiting to leave. Banu, DeeDee, and Madalena were in their own rooms. Banu had given us our backpacks when she heard we got back.

"Yes, they will. Don't worry. You heard what they said. And you know what I can do," I said to her, while lighting my fingertips on fire. I could play with my magic again since I had stopped hiding it. The feeling of not suppressing my magic was amazing, liberating. It felt like taking a breath for the first time, being able to fully be me.

"We will leave for the Castle tonight. And meet the Kings," Astra said, her voice hopeful and awestruck. I moved my attention from my fingers towards her. She looked at the wall, deep in thought. She had never met the Kings, she had seen them on posters and on the TV, still she was smitten. I rolled my eyes at her. "I saw that," she said, a smile crossing over her face. "I hate waiting." she added.

I looked over at the clock on the wall; two more hours, and it would be six. "I think they plan on leaving soon. It is getting darker."

Before we could say anything else, a knock sounded on

the door. We both perked up from our beds, our eyes met, and Astra got up. She opened the door to a younger child standing in front of it.

"You two need to go to the big hall. You are leaving," she said and turned around.

Astra looked at me with both eyebrows up in her hair. "That was short." She laughed, nervously.

"Come one, let's go. Let's get this over with."

We both grabbed our bags and walked out of our room and into the hallway. Doors were being opened, and some of the Witches stood peeking at us. Some of them nodded, smiled, or just looked at us. I heard a whispered, "Thank you." I looked over towards Astra, and she had a smile on her lips.

"That was unexpected," I said to her when we walked into the main hall. The big double doors were opened, showing the darkening sky. There were four huge black cars in front of the stairs. Next to them stood the drivers, all in black suits. They left the sunglasses off, not fully going for the *Men in Black* look. We stopped next to the bald man.

"The drivers will place your bags in the car, and we will bring you both to the castle. You will be introduced to the Kings when you get there," the bald man spoke to us. A line of sweat showed on his brow. Why would he be nervous? It was just a car drive.

"When we arrive at the Castle and you meet the Kings remember, bow when you are introduced to them. They are 'Your Highness' to you and always, remember, always be respectful." He looked at me when he said that. I gave him my best smile, the one I knew would give him night-mares. I hoped it did.

"Why are you looking at me? I'm the most honest person alive," I half-joked, and I heard a snort coming from Astra. I could see him swallow. What or who had him by the balls that made him react like this? I didn't think that my show of magic in the Headmistress' office would impact him so much.

"Don't worry, I will keep her in line," Astra said, while she placed a hand on my arm and nudged me towards the cars.

"Hmph," the bun lady said when we reached them. I couldn't see where the others were, probably already in the cars. "Keeping her in line, that is a job in itself," she said when the driver opened the door for us. I moved inside the car. Before I sat down fully, I looked over my shoulder past Astra and stuck out my tongue. It didn't help me with anything, still it was fun to see Bun Lady's face turn red, again. I had no idea why she hated me. Maybe if she didn't have a stick up her ass, she would be nice and maybe beautiful. She looked young, maybe twenty-five, that stick made her look more like forty.

Before Astra could get into the car with me, the driver shut the door. I heard him say. "You go into the other car." I wanted to open the door, to protest, instead I was stopped by the Bun lady getting in the front seat. "She has her own car to go with," was all she said. Before I could even open the doors, they were locked.

"Listen up," I started, my anger filled the car with magic. "Let me out, or let Astra in."

"Don't worry, you will see her back at the Castle," Bun lady said. Before I could respond the doors were opened and Icas Nox got into the car next to me. I was relieved to see him here, but I wasn't happy, either; it only meant he wasn't with Astra. He had this vibe coming off of him. Not sure what it was, just that it put my neck hairs straight up. He gave me a smile that still didn't reach his eyes. Almost as if he went through the motions, and that was it.

The driver started the car, a low rumbling sound and a soft vibration went through the car. We had modern technology, TVs, cars, computers, and stuff, we just didn't use it much. We are magical beings, why would we use a car if we could fly?

Still, they were being used, for day to day stuff. Magic costed power for most Witches. And it was inconvenient to have to nap throughout the day to recharge.

We reached the big gates, the iron one that kept people out and in. The ones that opened once a year for the Selection and the new students. We drove through it, leaving the place I had called home for twelve years, behind. I released the breath I was holding.

"Did you expect to be struck by lightning, when you passed through those gates?" Bun Lady asked, her sneer sounded through her voice.

"What did I do to you?" I murmured.

"Violet, don't," Nox said.

This had me looking at the back of her head. A giggle escaped me when I said, "Your name is Violet, after the colour?" I choked out, couldn't hold the full laugh I felt coming up. Violet turned around so fast, her bun almost seemed to move out of place, almost. Hair, violet. Before I could keep my mouth shut, I laughed some more. "You should turn your hair purple. If you can't I can help with that." I held up my fingers, twirling one around.

Violet pointed a finger at me and spat out, "You can't talk to me like that, I'm part of the Selection. I'm in the council, the Heir to one of the high houses. If you insult me again–" her eyes darkened with her threat.

"If I do, what will you do, Bun?" I asked her. My mood turned around. She wanted to feel important, needed to let me know who she was. I didn't care.

"You-You. Watch your back." Violet turned around.

"Violet," Nox said, "shut up."

I turned my gaze toward the man sitting next to me.

I had seen him in the arena and in the hallway a little closer. Sitting with him in the car gave me the chance to look him over. Really look at him. Blond hair, cut in a modern hairstyle, short at the sides and long on top. I was being stared at by light-blue, almost white eyes. A smile was on his lips and solely there. He was handsome, but not so handsome you would jump into a bed with him.

Astra told me that her parents wanted her to marry him. That he was a bad person. A chill crept over my back, he looked nice, almost as if nothing was wrong with him.

"Are you done?" he asked. My eyes widened a little. I hadn't noticed that I had pushed my magic towards him, sensing him. I focused on my magic, what I felt from him. His fire magic and his water magic, nothing more. Nothing that would explain the chill he gave me; the neck hairs that rose up every time he laughed.

I pulled back my magic and answered, "Yeah." I turned my head to look outside. I could see the trees, the evening darkening the forest faster, letting the shadows grow and play.

"Why did you become a Protector?" he asked me. I didn't turn my head when I answered. I could hear the leather seat in front of me creak and knew that Bun Lady turned in her seat to listen.

"Why not?" I said. I couldn't tell them it was because of Gran, because I was a Royal. My mission was to keep it as vague as possible.

"Do you like it?" Nox's next question. That was a question I could answer. "Yes, it is great to know how to fight with your hands, to hit someone in the face and feel their nose break," I said, smiling into the window. I remembered the first time when I'd broke someone's nose. Thalia's nose.

The crunch it had made, the blood that rushed out of it. The way her head moved back, she stumbled, didn't fall. I would never forget that day, she deserved it. Thalia had used her magic on one of the Protectors in my class, we were young, thirteen years old. That girl didn't know how to defend against magic yet. Alexa had been in the hospital for weeks. It took her a long time to get back on her feet, and she still has the ice burns on her arms that Thalia made. I punched Thalia the moment I saw her doing it. It was worth cleaning the dining hall for a week.

Violet puffed out a breath. "You are a Witch, why would you become a Protector? Your status makes people do those kinds of things for you." Violet's voice pitched higher when she spoke, her anger still lining her words. I looked at the back of her seat, rolling my eyes at her.

"No, because when they all are dead, you will be, too, and me, I will be fighting my own battles, staying alive with what I learned. So, yes, I'm grateful and happy to be a Protector. Better than being a stuck-up Witch."

"Where did you come from?" Nox asked me, he ignored Violet who bristled in her seat.

"A home," I answered him, back to looking out of the window.

"Where?" he asked again.

"Somewhere." I answered, and before he could ask more, I said, "Why are you asking me that?"

"I want to know you, Isadora." My name was drawn out, almost as if he was testing it on his tongue.

"Who are you?" was his next question.

"Nobody," I answered.

That made him laugh. Before he could ask me something else, I turned in my seat and looked at him. "Who are you?" I said.

He laughed again, knowing that I was deflecting him.

"I'm Icas Nox. Council member and the Heir to the house of Nox," he said.

This made me look at him again, he was from one of the houses that had started the uprising. Who'd planned most of the whole thing. I breathed out, slowly.

"My nephew is King." A sly smile crossed over his face, and his eyes turned even colder. Before I fully registered it, it was gone. It left me wondering if I saw it correctly. The council of the high houses are called Heirs, they weren't the Heirs to the Kings. They fought over that, made sure that the strongest of them got on the throne. It was always Kings, never Queens that got the throne. They were there for the baby making.

"Fun for you," I answered him. We had learned about the council in school, how the Kings ruled the world. How they used the council to assist them. All the boring stuff. I never got why we needed to know that. We Protectors were good for one thing, that was as bait, sacrificed to do the dirty work, to fight the creatures they couldn't stop. They taught us how good the Kings were, how they fought for us, and kept this world safe. They didn't.

If you were lucky, you had money to keep you safe, living a life of luxury, freedom, and maybe even peace. If you couldn't and you were a Null, you become a Protector, you sacrificed your life to keep your family, and the world, safe. There was one good thing about this all was it paid well.

If you had magic, it was easy. Even if you were a weaker Witch or Elemental. Magic was seen as a status, it gave you power and a place in the world; without it, you were nothing, replaceable.

I was done with the questions from him. I was done with him and the whole trip.

"Wake me up when we arrive," I said and closed my eyes.

———

"Miss," someone said. I bolted upright. I hadn't noticed that the car had stopped driving. My mind felt foggy, and there was a lingering feeling in there. I looked around, finding a man, next to the opened car door.

"Yeah?" My mind was still sluggish and slow.

"Welcome to the Castle," the man said, and I looked behind him. We were in front of a stone staircase, which led up to steel doors. They were open, showing an entrance lit by a chandelier. I unbuckled my seatbelt and got out of the car. My eyes moved over my surroundings, finding a fountain and the castle walls and a big iron gate. No other cars.

"Where are the others?" I asked the man, who still stood next to me.

"Which others?" he answered. "Will you follow me inside, miss?" he asked before I could fully react.

I looked around again. Maybe I had missed them, my mind was still foggy. I searched for Astra's car. She should have been there, she had been in front of us when I had fallen asleep. I saw the Protectors by the walls and the man at the entrance. Nobody else.

"Where is Astra?" I asked him. I saw Violet walking towards the entrance.

"Remember this the next time you demand something," She laughed and turned around.

The man by the door looked at her and back at me. "The Kings will be seeing you in the throne room."

"Good." I stormed up the stairs. Astra was missing. They were the people I needed to talk to. I stormed past another man and walked into the high hall. The chandelier hung in the middle of the room, and there were two stair-cases—one on either side of the hall. Two doors led towards two other rooms. One was filled with chandeliers and windows that lined the wall, but was otherwise empty to the end. The other had two big chandeliers hanging from the ceiling, a golden light coming from them. At the end of that room stood four chairs, the throne room.

I moved towards the open door and into the hall. Windows lined the wall at my left side and paintings hung on my right. A marble floor let the sound of my feet vibrate through the room. The room itself was stunning in the dark, except not at that moment. Normally, I would have sucked in a breath, stood still, and enjoyed a beautiful thing like that. Just not then, not when Astra was missing. I had one mission. Getting her back.

I reached the raised platform, the four empty chairs in front of me mocked me. Nobody was there. My anger rose.

"You have to wait," Bun Lady's voice sounded behind me. I turned around on my heels, the anger radiating from me–all pointed towards her. She flew towards the wall, I kept her there. My wind magic blew my hair to the sides, and the chandeliers swayed in the wind.

"If I were you, I would let her go," a male voice said behind me. His low tone caressed me, and a shudder ran through me. He sounded amazing.

I kept my shock away and my anger in place. "Why should I?" I ground out, still I let her drop to the ground when I turned around to meet the person who had spoken to me.

I was met with four pairs of eyes, all locked on me. Four males stood in front of me, my breath hitched, and I stood there enjoying the beauty.

8

"Thank you," one of them said, as he smiled at me. A smile that warmed me from my toes to my head. I wanted to smile back at him, almost forgetting my anger. Then I remembered why I was there. That Astra was gone. I heard Violet muttering against the wall. None of the Kings, they must be the Kings, had walked towards her to help, to check if she was fine. She was, except her ego, that one got some bruises.

"Who are you?" the first one to my left spoke. I looked at him, checking him out. His obsidian hair was braided in two rows, bright silver-grey eyes assessed me. He had a strong chiseled jaw, and lips every woman would have wanted to kiss. His arms were folded in front of his chest, his t-shirt straining under his muscled arms. Arms I would love to have felt around me.

I shook my head, getting those thoughts out of there before I answered, "Isadora."

Violet finally found her feet and walked towards the Kings, she stood close to them. Almost touching them, and my anger surged forward; my breath hitched with the burst of emotion. I was not a jealous person, until then.

"We found her in the Selection. She is a Witch." Violet's finger pointed in my direction, her scowl deepened.

She really wasn't attractive looking like that, and it made my strange jealousy lessen as I rolled my eyes at her and looked back to the Kings.

The one who had smiled at me, the third one in the row, was still smiling, almost if it was glued to his face. It made me feel awkward, and I scuffled on my feet a little. I couldn't resist my own smile, giving him a small one in return, which lit up his handsome face, and for the second time that day, my breath hitched.

Again, I shook my head, I needed to remember Astra, not drown in those beautiful males that had stood in front of me.

I swallowed, folded my hands behind my back, and adjusted my stance to the rest position of the Protectors. All four Kings raised their eyebrows at my movement, and they seemed to ask me a question.

I answered the unspoken question.

"I'm a Protector."

The King that stood the most to my right spoke up, "You are a Witch and a Protector?" I looked him over, the soft light of the chandeliers had given his copper hair a golden sheen. His hair fell loose around his head, giving it the perfect 'just out of bed' look. His green eyes, radiant and soft looked at me. His eyes lowered over me, the same way I had done to him. He had on black jeans, and a grey shirt, showcasing his pecs. Yes pecs, the real deal, those were what every woman dreamed of. I needed to start thinking normally. But those pecs, yeah, I wanted to trace my tongue over his body. And I hadn't even seen him naked. Down hormones. I closed my eyes and focused back on my anger, on Astra. Not his body. Naked. Shit.

"No, I'm a Protector." I kept my voice calm when I spoke. I looked him straight in the eyes, his beautiful forest-green eyes.

"You used air," the first one said.

"Witches can't be Protectors," the green-eyed one said after that. I wished I had paid attention in the class, where they explained who was who. I had slept great in that class, to be honest.

I think those two were the oldest of the four. They had an air around them that told me not to mess with them, with any of them.

"I am. Whether you like it or not, isn't my problem." Violet sucked in air, I looked at her and smiled. I really didn't like her anymore, and she had moved even closer towards the Kings.

A laugh startled me out of my hate stare towards Violet. The dark-russet-haired one was laughing. His hair reached his shoulders, hanging loose and inviting me to comb my hands through it. Dark eyes watched me, the laugh had ignited a sparkle in them that I hadn't seen there before. Still, wariness took away that light. He mimicked my stance, showing his powerful body when he moved. What did they feed those men?

"Listen up. I need to find Astra Bronac," I said, getting straight to business.

"You don't speak to the Kings like that!" Violet screeched at me. I shrugged and ignored her. I had important business to attend to.

I looked at all of them, and lingered on the smiling one. His honey-blond hair was cut short, though not too short that you couldn't run your hands through it. His hair looked like silk, softer than my own. Striking blue eyes shone with mischief. They were looking at me, or rather straight into me, into the depths of myself. Places I wouldn't even visit, he found them.

He was the shortest one of the four, leaner, though still with powerful shoulders and arms, leading towards abs that showed through his shirt. Didn't they have a tailor who knew how to make clothing that fit, because otherwise they had bought a few sizes too small for themselves. You could almost hear the stitches scream when they had moved around. I snorted, an un-lady like sound. I hadn't cared in the past, I wouldn't start now.

"Violet." Violet looked up at the first king. "You can leave." He dismissed Violet. She glared at me, and started to protest.

"We said leave," the redhead told her. She bowed and turned around, mumbling.

I waved at her and smiled. "Next time, bring some cookies," I said after her. A chuckle sounded from one of them. I didn't know which one. When Violet walked through the doors, they closed, and I placed my hands on my hips. Time for business.

"I need to know where you guys took Astra," I demanded.

"Who do you mean?" the smiling one asked.

"The other woman, the one that would be entering your Selection. My best friend, Astra Bronac," I told them, like that would explain everything.

"We will look into that," the redhead said. I needed to recall what they were called. We had learned it, but I'd never memorized it.

"What are your names?" I asked them. The blond one smiled, again. I'm sure it was glued to his face.

"You don't know who we are?" the first king asked, one eyebrow pulled up.

"Yeah, yeah. I know you are the Kings, never remembered your names, though. I need names," I told them. I kept myself from snapping my fingers, by keeping my hands behind my back.

The King with the dark-black eyes, eyes that reflected the night, took two steps towards me. I braced myself, balancing on the heels of my feet. His whole body screamed danger, powerful.

When he started speaking, his voice was soft, low, and strong. Power and authority sounded through his voice. He was the one who saw to the military parts of the kingdom, the commander of the Protectors. I knew for sure, because he gave me the feeling I should have surrendered. Nobody had ever given me that feeling.

"My name is Flynn Nox." The others looked at him, confusion crossed over their faces. Gone before I could ask them why. Flynn turned and pointed towards the first king.

"His name is Averey Thorne. The one on the end, the redhead; his name is Cian Reeve, and the last one, the cheerful one is Rayan Leighlin."

Averey had taken a step closer, too. "And we are the Kings, the rulers of this world. We would appreciate it if you started explaining a few things to us." He pointed behind me. I looked over my shoulder to find a door behind the four thrones.

I got the hint and turned around, walking towards the door. I heard their footsteps behind me. Knowing they were following me, I put a sway in my hips. And then, I rolled my eyes at myself. *Why did you do that?*

When I reached the door, Rayan slipped before me and opened it. I smiled at him and watched as his eyes roamed over my body; the heat started slowly building up in my body. I shivered and willed it all down. No time for this.

I still wore my Protector's outfit, black cargo pants, and black t-shirt. For a second, I thought about my bags, where they had gone? I forgot in the moment I entered the room, a light switched on, and the room lit up with a yellow glow. It showed two sofas, a fireplace, four desks lined in front of the wall and a lot, a lot of paperwork. Maps lined the walls, and a few bookcases filled the room. There were two swords hanging on the wall above the fireplace, their steel reflecting the light. The room was filled and felt homey.

They moved past me, sitting down on the sofas. I stayed standing, arms folded behind my back again, not letting myself relax.

"I need to find Astra. And I think Icas Nox has taken her," I told them when they were seated. All their heads snapped up to me.

"You mean my uncle?" Flynn asked. I nodded.

"Why?" Averey asked.

"Because Astra's parents arranged a marriage between them when she was younger. And with her in the Selection, she can't marry him."

"Why would he take her?" he asked again, his hand under his chin rubbing a day-old scuff I hadn't noticed.

"You haven't seen him looking at her. He wants her, knowing that she is the most powerful Witch from our school." I looked at them one by one.

"Violet said you are a Witch, too. Why are you here then if she is the most powerful?" Cian's warm voice reached me, I looked at him. His green eyes were filled with curiosity.

"Long story, not enough time." I answered, it was the truth.

"Listen up, I'm going to get her back. You guys can stay here. I can handle it," I told them and turned around.

"Wait," one of them said. I stopped in front of the door, my hand on the doorknob.

"Do you know where you are going?" the voice asked. It must be Rayan's. I hadn't heard him speak.

"I'll figure it out." I opened the door.

"Are you coming back?" Cian asked.

"Yes. I promised Astra I would get her here." And with that, I left.

I entered the throne room; the door was still open. I heard fabric move, knowing one, or all, of them were standing.

"We need to help her," one said, but I didn't hear what the answer was. I was too busy walking towards the first servant I could find.

Flynn

We sat down on the sofas in our office. She stayed standing, her arms behind her back, the way a Protector stood when he relaxed. I didn't know why I had introduced us, I never spoke to new people. It was always much better to keep silent and observe. Except the first moment I saw her, standing there in our throne room, my heart skipped a beat. I saw the most beautiful women ever. And the best part, I saw the outline of weapons on her body. My heartbeat had started again, with more speed to it. It wanted to be with her as fast as I could.

I heard my uncle's name. "You mean my uncle?" I asked her, and she nodded at me. Her hair falling alongside her body with the movement. Her black hair, that reached over her shoulders, and fell in a wave down her back. Her brown eyes moved between us, serious and hard. She kept talking to us, her sensual mouth forming words I couldn't hear.

My mind had pulled away from the thoughts I had been having, when she got all bossy and left. For a second, I just stared at the empty spot where she had been. I got up.

"We need to help her," I said to the others when the door closed.

"Are you sure?" Rayan started. "She was pretty set on handling it alone."

"We need to," Averey said, he was still looking at the door, almost as if he could have willed her to turn around and ask us for help, which she would never have done. My judgement of her was that she was a powerful woman and knew what she wanted. She wouldn't be pushed into something easily and wouldn't follow orders without questioning them.

She was the sort of woman who I had always wanted to meet. And she had left to confront my uncle. The others argued, only to stop when I moved towards the door.

"I'm going after her," I told them. There were a few reasons I had wanted to go after her, the first was the fact that I had wanted her. I had never wanted something so badly as her. From the moment I saw her, I knew it; she was my Natural Bonded. She was my other half, and she had walked away. And second, you never knew what my uncle would be doing in that house of his. I left through the door, and heard the others getting up, too.

My heartbeat had picked up again when I stepped into the car, that time for two reasons; seeing her and hoping she was safe. My protective instincts had gone into overdrive, and I couldn't believe I had let her walk out of the castle. That I had lost every sense of what happened when I saw her. My body had reacted so quickly, it had destroyed all that was in my head then, leaving her in it. I was lost from the moment I saw her, and I needed her back.

Isadora

"I need a car and the directions to Council member Icas Nox's house," I said to the first servant I found. He pointed me towards some people. I moved towards them. I found a driver who would take me to Icas Nox's house. His house would be the first place he would have taken her. He was that kind of person who didn't think he would get caught. He forgot Astra was my sister, and I would do everything for her. Even get her back, present her to the Kings, and make sure she would have a happy ending.

It was a short drive, twenty minutes. We followed a road that led through another forest, away from the city that was located on the other side of the forest that surrounded the Castle.

We reached a high wall and an iron gate that was closed. The driver stopped in front of it, and I looked through the window towards the big drive that ended at a house covered by the trees. Only the lights along the road showed me the end.

"Thanks." I got out of the car.

"Do you need help?" the man, a Protector, asked. I smiled at him.

"No," I first said, then added. "if I'm not back in an hour or so, call someone," I closed the door.

I looked up at the stone wall, it looked easy to climb

over, the rough stones sticking out. I hadn't found my bag
before I had left the castle, so I only had my knife in my
boot. I felt naked, wanting to have more weapons with me,
but I shook the feeling away and looked up at the wall.

I walked backwards and ran towards it. Jumping up, I
reached for the top, scraping my fingers a little. Holding
on, I got myself up. The Protector in the car started it and
moved towards an alcove in the woods. He had turned off
his lights and shut off the engine. He saluted me, and I
dropped over the edge of the wall, landing softly on my
feet. I started moving through the trees towards the house
at the end.

A big villa greeted me, some windows covered in red
drapes lit by a light behind them. Other rooms were dark. I
pushed my magic out, sensing nobody was around me as I
moved closer.

The house was big, white with wooden ornaments. It
would have been beautiful if not for the man who lived
there, or the family who owned it. I pushed my magic
around again, searching for a trace of Astra. I pushed over
the house, it was covered in magic, which made it harder
to find anything. I pushed deeper, into the house.

When my magic reached the back, I felt something;
Astra's fire. The happy warmth she always threw out. I had
known she would be there. Needing to get her back, I
moved silently towards the house, keeping out of sight,
and keeping the darkness around me.

That was a good trick I had picked up from the fight
with the Ilunias. I moved around the house, towards the
back door where I had felt her. The door was open, and
with a soft push I moved inside.

9

I entered a dark room, the moonlight filtered into the room through the windows. I closed the door soundlessly behind me. I listened to the sounds around me, trying to figure out where I was and where the people would be. A house that big would have some help walking around.

I kept standing against the door, listening. Only my own breathing could be heard. I focused on the room. A kitchen or something like that, a big table stood in the middle. A fireplace was to the right of the room and countertops lined the wall opposite from where I was standing. There was no stove, so it wasn't a kitchen. There were cabinets, so maybe a second kitchen. It didn't matter, I needed to find Astra, and she was not there.

I sent out my magic, feeling inside the house. It was easier now that I was in the house. I couldn't find her, so I started to move towards the door. The floor beneath my feet cracked, and I froze. "Shit. Shit," I muttered. I looked down seeing the old worn wooden floor beneath my boots. This would be harder. I moved my weight a little, no creaking sound followed. Moving one foot and then the other, I used some air to make myself lighter. Not too much, I didn't want anyone to notice my magic.

I moved through the room, reaching the door that led to a hallway. Small and dark, no lights on. I let myself adjust to the darkness, not wanting to use my Witch light, I waited, listening. After a few seconds I could see more of the hallway. There were three other doors, one at the left end and one on the right end, and another a little to the left. I moved towards the first to my left and tried to open it. Locked.

I looked over my right shoulder and then left, not sure which way I wanted to go. Before I could decide, I heard people talking behind the right door.

"What are we going to do with her?" a male voice asked.

"We leave her in the room for a few days." I recognized that voice. Icas Nox.

My anger rose, and my hands clenched at my side. I had known he would have her.

"Aren't you scared that they will come for her. The other girl is at the Castle. She would have told the Kings about her. They seemed pretty close."

The other male must have been someone from the Selection. Nobody else would have known that Astra and I were close. Before my thoughts focused on who it could be, I heard the doorknob turn. Decision made, I sprinted towards the left door. Luckily for me, the hallway wasn't that long. I reached the door, pulled it open softly, and closed it just as the other opened. I froze, listening to the two males in the hallway.

"Who are you?" a soft voice asked from behind me. I remained rooted to the spot. *Shit, the freak.* I didn't look around at first. I was too focused on what the two men would say. Eventually, I turned around slowly, finding a little girl behind me. When I looked at her, I was reminded of a certain King. I was being stared at by two dark eyes, dark-russet hair cascaded in curls down her back. Her face was more rounded and softer than that of Flynn, still you couldn't miss that they were family.

"Eh, hi." I gave a small wave of my hand, still listening to the hallway.

"I have that covered. The Kings will be occupied with that Protector girl. She is a handful, and she's their problem now."

"Why didn't you take her? She is strong," I heard the other male saying. I fully turned back to the door, the girl totally forgotten; until I found her standing next to me, her ear against the door and a smile on her face. I smiled back at her and held a finger in front of my lips. She nodded, and we both listened to the men behind the door.

"She isn't that strong, and she's too stubborn. She would be annoying. That Bronac girl is already promised to me by her parents. It would be easier to keep her here and marry her. Nobody would object."

"That is not true, you said she would be part of the Selection. We all agreed to that term."

"Yes, we did, however the Kings didn't know that. And with only Violet and me in the Castle, they will never know. The other members don't care." Icas Nox laughed at that.

"What are you going to do if she shows up here?" the male asked. Their voices grew louder. I looked at the girl, my eyes big and then looked around, trying to find a place to hide.

My eyes landed on different things: another door, a curtain, a staircase. I was in a hall, and judging by the big doors at the right, the main hall. Shit, I needed to move; their footsteps were coming closer. Someone pulled at my shirt, I looked down seeing the girl. She pointed towards the stairs and started running towards them. Her feet were silent on the stone floor, her hair flying behind her. I moved, following her.

We reached the stairs, she opened a door underneath it and got in. I got in, too, and closed the door. Again, just in time. We heard them walking into the hallway, then for them to move to the other side, leaving us alone. "I would kill her if she became a problem," was the last thing I heard before their voices moved too far away to understand.

I looked around where we were hiding, a closet. The little girl stood next to me, and when I was focused on her I could see she was wearing her pyjamas, pink ones with bears on them. The fluffy sweet kind.

Lowering to the ground, so I was eye level with her, I started to speak. "Hi, sorry to come into your house," I told her, not sure how to start. I just broke into the house where she lived.

"Are you looking for the girl?" she asked me, her voice soft and small.

"Yes." I had hoped that Icas Nox had taken As and not any more girls.

"She is upstairs. Uncle Nox said that she needs to stay there, and that nobody can visit her." She twisted her hands together. "I wanted to say hello to her, it has been a long time since there was a new girl in the house." Her eyes were cast downwards.

"What do you mean a new girl?" Worry entered my voice.

"Uncle Nox has a group of women, they are his wives." That shocked me.

"Where are they now?"

"Not here," the girl answered.

"What is he planning on doing with the new girl?" I asked her. I needed to know what would happen if I couldn't free Astra.

"I-I can't say," the girl said, her voice even lower. I took hold of her hands, they were still fidgeting. She looked up at me, her dark eyes twinkling, now with tears and not with the laughter I had first seen. That had my heart stopping for a moment.

"Listen. You need to tell me. That new girl, she is my sister, my best friend, and the one person in this world I can't live without. If your uncle plans to do something bad to her, I

need to know. I need to know how to get her free." I squeezed
her small hands, trying to let her know how important it was.
She didn't respond, instead she looked at my hands over hers.

"What is your name?" I asked, trying to use another way
to get through to her. She was scared; something even a
blind person could see.

"Mara," she answered.

"That is a pretty name, Mara. Do you want to help me?"
I asked her. She nodded, and I could see curiosity flowing
into her eyes. "I want to find the girl, the one we talked
about, and save her." She nodded again. "Do you want to
help me, be a Protector?" She nodded, her curls bouncing
with the movement. "Okay, good. Will you tell me something first?" I kept my voice soft, my hands still over hers.
She nodded. "What does your uncle do to his wives? And,
Mara, you can tell me. I will keep you safe. I promise," I
told her. I poured all my emotions into that promise, I
made sure that she would understand that I was serious
about protecting her. That was my job, that's what I had
always wanted to do. Help and protect people who needed
it, like that little scared girl. I would take her with me when
I found Astra. And then I would ask, no beg, the Kings to
keep her at the Castle. She was Flynn's family for God's
sake.

Mara hesitated, her mouth opened and closed. After a
few more seconds of silence she nodded, more to herself
than to me, and started speaking. "He used them, married a
really strong Witch and then used them." Her voice was
just a whisper.

"How do you mean used them?" It had been normal for
Witches and Elementals to have a harem in the old days. It
wasn't so normal anymore. And a man like Nox didn't fit
the profile of the 'ever-loving' husband to one woman
never mind to more.

"He takes their magic." Her eyes filled with more tears,
and I had to do my best not to squeeze her hands to mush.

I breathed in through my nose and let go through my mouth.

"How do you know that?" I asked her. A child her age should have never witnessed things like that. Magic is connected to a person. Without it, a Witch or an Elemental would die, slowly and painfully.

"I'm good at hiding, he didn't know I was there. I walked into the basement. I wanted to know what they were talking about. The servants, they talked about the screaming and the blood." She looked at me, horror in her eyes. She was a brave girl, a little strange maybe, but undoubtedly brave. To be honest, I would have been curious about it all, too. Ghost stories were my favorite growing up.

"I saw what he did to Naommi–his last wife." She shuddered, and I stopped her.

"You don't have to tell me. It's okay. We need to save Astra, the new girl."

She nodded, her face hard, the tears left unshed in her eyes.

"Can you bring me to her, so we can get her out, and you, too?" I implored her.

She nodded again and moved towards the door, I stood up and waited for her to open it. She peeked through the crack and then pushed it further. I followed her as we moved towards the stairs we had been hiding under. Silently, we walked to the second floor. I couldn't hear anyone else.

"Where are the servants?" I whispered to her, not wanting to be overheard.

"He sent them away. It will be a few days before they come back." We reached the top, and Mara moved to the left while I tailed her. I was equally relieved to know we wouldn't find anybody else up here and worried that Nox had sent all his staff away and left a little girl alone.

We reached another hall with three doors on the left side of us and a row of windows to our right. We moved fast, past the first two doors. As we reached the last one, Mara pointed at it without getting any closer.

I moved towards the knob and pulled at it. It didn't budge. I let my magic go and felt for the door. It was protected, probably warded, too. If I shattered it, the creator would know. I stepped back, Mara next to me, and we both looked at the door, almost as if our will alone would have opened it. Then I looked towards the wall. I let my magic move over the wall next to the door.

"Yeah!" I said while I fist pumped the air. This made Mara chuckle. I gave myself another fist pump in my head and moved towards the stone. They hadn't thought to protect the stone next to it. I placed my hands against the cold wall and let my magic flow, wishing for it to move. I pushed some air with it, to make it silent. The stones moved away, giving me a small space, I could move through.

"Who's there?" I heard Astra's voice, and I was relieved to have found her.

"It's me, As. I'm here." I moved into the room and got tackled by a flying Astra.

"Oh, I'm so happy to see you here," she whispered. I grabbed her hand and pulled her towards the crack I had made. "We need to go." She moved with me, her hand in mine. We pushed through the crack, entering the hallway. I looked to the left and right, no Mara. Worry flooded through me, she knew this house. Hopefully, she would be fine. I would have to come back for her.

I turned around to close the gap I had made, slowly letting my magic go. Nox didn't need to know that Astra was gone.

I pulled Astra back to the stairs. We waited at the landing near the door, listening for someone. I heard nothing, so we moved silently down them. We reached the bottom, and I contemplated whether to go through the front door, make a break for it and run as fast as we could or go back the same way I had come. I looked around, hoping to find Mara, she would have known where to go. Only she wasn't there. I moved towards the door that would lead towards the spot I had come in.

"Look what I found," a voice behind us said. I knew who it was. I would recognize that cold voice anywhere. We both slowly turned around, I glared at Icas Nox. He stood in the doorway, at the other side of the hall. We had almost reached the door that would lead back to the small corridor.

I was suddenly relieved that Mara hadn't been there, I didn't want to get her into trouble.

"Where do you girls think you are going?" Icas asked, while he moved closer. Astra and I took a step back, almost at the door.

"For a walk," I answered cheekily, while we kept moving, Astra angled behind me, her hand in mine, trembling.

Icas's face turned dark. "Nobody comes into my house without an invitation. Nobody takes what is mine."

"I'm not yours," Astra spat out. I was happy that she still had some spine even while she was cowering behind me. It all must have been one hell of a roller-coaster for her. It made me proud of her that she still could stand up for herself.

"Oh, yes, girl. Your parents promised you to me. I have it all on paper." He waved a hand in the air. He now stood still in the centre of the hall, blocking the main entrance. The door was at our backs, and if we moved fast enough, we could get through it. I wasn't sure it would work, he would be after us in seconds. I needed to think of something else.

The driver popped into my head. I needed to stall, and I hoped that the hour I had said to him would be over soon. And that he would come to my rescue. I hated needing to be rescued, but I needed it then. Wishing with all my heart that someone would barge into the door, knock it off its hinges and save us.

My thoughts hadn't even finished when the doorbell rang. We all looked at the door, confusion on Icas's face. I didn't dare to be relieved, didn't dare to let that feeling go through me.

Nobody moved. Someone rang the doorbell again, followed by a loud pounding on the door that startled Astra. I felt her huddle more behind me. That was the moment for us to move. Before we could turn, the door blew open.

And I didn't *expect* them.

10

"Your Highnesses." Icas Nox bowed low to the four males standing at his door. I stared at them. Astra dropped my hand and moved to stand next to me.

"Your Highnesses." She bowed, too. I still stood there, with my mouth hanging open.

All four of them looked at me, and suddenly, I remembered to close my mouth.

"What are you guys doing here?" I asked them, still not connecting the dots.

"Saving you, it seems," Rayan said, a grin on his face. I looked them all over, but he was the only one smiling. Cian looked pissed, while Averey and Flynn didn't show a single emotion. That scared me more than Icas Nox did right now. He was still bowing towards the Kings.

"I don't need saving," I answered. I heard Astra's humpf at that. "Yeah, cliché. I get it, As. But it is true. We didn't need any prince on the white horse shit. I was handling it," I whispered to Astra. Not low enough, apparently, since I heard Rayan laugh. I was getting annoyed that the Kings themselves had come. Yeah, that was something that irritated me. If it was the Protector from the car, I wouldn't have minded, instead it was them. I bristled, my fingers twisted.

Before I could say anything more, Averey stepped into the hall.

"Why is this girl here?" I moved in front of Astra; a reflex. Averey frowned at me. He lowered the finger he had been pointing towards Astra and looked back towards Icas.

Icas looked up, his face in a scowl for a second before relaxing. Astra looked back at me, she had seen it, too. I shrugged and waited for what he would say. I hoped Averey had seen it, too.

"I wanted to give her some time to visit her family before she would be introduced into the Selection process. It can be demanding of someone's time." His face was smooth, nothing looked out of place with that lie.

"You're lying!" I said while I stepped forward, my fists clenched. "Mara told me."

Someone to my right sucked in a sharp breath. I whirled around to see Flynn's eyes were big, his posture stiff. Cian and Rayan's eyes were wide, too, except there was no pain in their faces, not like Flynn's had.

My body reacted to his pain, and I took a step towards him, and he took a step back.

"Who is Mara?" I heard Astra asking behind me.

I turned towards her. "This little girl that lives here, she helped me find you. I promised I would protect her and take her with us."

Astra narrowed her eyes at me. "What little girl?" she asked, the question clearly sounding through.

"The one that helped me find you. Dark-brown hair, dark eyes. About twelve years old, I think. She wore pink pyjamas with these cute bears on them."

Astra shook her head, frowning at me as she answered, "I haven't seen a girl, Isa."

"I know, she disappeared when we got out of the room he kept you in." I pointed towards Icas behind me. The room was utterly silent, listening to our conversation. "I think she hid somewhere, she was scared. She led me to you. She-she helped me," I told her again. I had started doubting it all.

"There is no little girl in this house. Hasn't been one here for years," Icas said. I whirled around to face him.

"I know what I saw, who I spoke to," I said, my temper taking over. The whole thing had become confusing in seconds.

"Isadora, it is only Icas in this house and his staff. And believe me, there aren't any children here," Averey said, his voice low, almost as if he needed to keep a trapped animal calm.

That was the moment I realised I had taken a fighting stance, ready to protect what was dear to me. Ready to fight that monster in that house. The one who killed his wives and let a child run around alone.

"We need to go," Flynn said from the door. I tried to relax my stance as Astra moved closer to me.

"Yes, we need," she said, while she placed a hand on my shoulder.

Flynn turned around, his movements harsh and quick. I looked at Rayan, an eyebrow pulled up in question. He shook his head, and my gaze moved towards Cian. But he had already turned around to follow Flynn.

"We will talk about this another day, Icas," Averey almost growled out. He, too, turned around and walked after the others. Astra pushed me a little, and we walked past Icas. I glared at him, and his eyes turned cold as a grin spread over his mouth, chilling me to the bone. Rayan waited for us to pass him before he then walked after us.

We walked into the night, the sky filled with stars and a slither of the moon visible. We walked towards the two cars that were waiting in the driveway. One of them with the Protector who had driven me there.

I gave him angry look. He chuckled in response. "You said, after an hour I needed to get back-up." He pointed towards the Kings, who had moved into both of the cars. "They were already on their way so that was easy."

Astra and I moved to the last car, the same car as Flynn and Rayan sat in. Flynn sat in the front, and the Protector got in next to him, the Protector started the car right away. We drove behind the other car, back towards the Castle. Following the same route I first had taken. The darkness hid the forest, and the lamp lights of the car showed there was life in the forest. Eyes lit up in the dark shades, almost if ghosts were staring back at us, hovering in the air.

The silence in the car was deafening. Even Astra was silent. I got that, she'd had a long night. I squeezed her hand, happy to have her back safe.

My mind wandered back towards the little girl, Mara. I couldn't hold my tongue anymore.

"Who is Mara?" I directed my question to Flynn; they were the spitting images of each other, after all.

He froze, and for a second, I thought he would stay like that. But he moved to look out of the window, without answering.

The answer came from next to me, from Rayan.

"Mara was Flynn's little sister."

The *was* vibrated through me. Still I asked. "What do you mean, 'was?'" I hadn't wanted to believe what he had been implying. Not after I had felt her, held her hands in mine. Saw the twinkle in her eyes, the spark of courage that shone through her fear. I would never forget the fear that I saw.

"She died," I heard Flynn answer.

"I'm sorry," I told him, while reaching out my hand to touch his shoulder over the back of his seat. I hesitated and let it hover in the air for a moment, merely to drop it down. I was not sure why I wanted to touch him, comfort him like that. I meant it, I was sorry. I hadn't known that she was dead. And it hadn't explained how I had talked with her or even saw her.

"They were young, she was twelve when she died–" Rayan said, He was cut off by Flynn's "Don't." And with that, the car had turned silent again. We drove for a few minutes before I couldn't hold my question any longer. Again.

"How old were you?" I asked Flynn.

The silence remained, and I didn't think he would answer me. The silence became deafening just before we reached the driveway of the Castle. We passed through the gates, stopping in front of the steel doors. A déjà vu feeling invaded me, and I grabbed hold of Astra's hand.

"I'm here," she said, almost as if she had read my mind. I let go of her hand, so she could get out of the car. Rayan had gotten out, too, leaving me alone with Flynn.

"I was fourteen," he said before he got out of the car. She had been twelve years old. I had talked to a girl that had been dead for years. A chill crept over my back, slowly up my spine.

I had talked to a ghost, it was the only explanation I had. A spirit.

My thoughts were interrupted by Astra. "Are you coming, Isa?" she yelled from the top of the stairs. The Kings weren't with her, just the Protector who had drove me.

"Yeah." I moved out of the car, my mind still on Mara and the promise I had made to her. To keep her safe, to protect her. I would find a way to keep that promise. She should be happy somewhere and not trapped in that house. My mind was made up. I placed the problem away, it was something I needed to figure out later. When I was alone and able to use my magic without any witnesses, I could try and summon her, see if I could do something from there.

Astra linked her arm with mine when I reached her, practically dragging me into the Castle.

"Can you believe we are finally here?" she asked, almost sounding cheerful, but I heard the exhaustion lingering in her voice.

"Yeah, great," I mumbled in answer.

"Ladies, if you would follow me. I will take you to your rooms," the Protector said. I didn't know his name. That needed to change, and I needed to thank him for helping out.

"That would be great . . ."

"Lars," he said.

"Thank you, Lars, for tonight also," I told him.

He directed us toward a big staircase in the middle of the room. How I had missed that one the first time I had walked in here, I didn't know. We went upstairs, and he led us towards the right.

"Your rooms are at the end of this hallway, they are near the Kings' quarters," Lars told us while we walked through a big hallway lined with doors to our right and windows to our left. I could feel the protection magic vibrating off of the glass, letting me know it was well-protected. The curtains were all open, letting the moon-light through. We could see the other side of the Castle and in the middle, a garden. The garden was covered in shadows from a few trees that reached the roof of the three-story high castle.

I stopped walking when I spotted him. I knew it was Flynn, his bulk standing out from everything else around him. I couldn't see his eyes, still I knew for sure he had been looking at me.

"Are you coming, miss?" Lars asked when he noticed I stood still.

I turned my head his way and nodded. When I looked back into the garden, Flynn was gone.

We reached the last two doors at the end of the hallway.

"Miss Bronac, your room is this one." He pointed to the door at his right.

"Miss . . ." He left it open for my name.

I answered with "Isadora."

"That one is your room." He pointed to the door at his left, the one closest to the double doors. I looked up and noticed there were figures on it, carved out of the wood; aged by the years, worn by the use.

Before I could study the doors better, they swung open, revealing Rayan standing there.

"Ah, exactly the people I was looking for. Lars, you can go. Thank you." Rayan looked towards the Protector and then back to me.

"We want to talk to you both tomorrow. We would like it if you both could come for lunch."

He looked at me, instead Astra answered, "Of course, Your Highness."

"Try to get some sleep, okay?" he said while he folded his arms in front of his chest and leaned against the door-frame. He looked sexy like that, his blond hair glistening in the lights of the moon and the lights of the hallway. I shook my head at that thought, willing it out of there. It was so not the time to think of those things. I yawned and looked back at him.

"Okay," I said, while I tried to stifle another yawn. Rayan's eyebrows flew up, and his mouth opened for a second only to close fast. He had expected me to go against him, however I was so freaking tired, I hadn't noticed it. Still, I had fought Ilunias, Astra had been kidnapped, and I had gotten her back all in one day. And after all that, I was back in the freaking Castle. With four good-looking Kings. If that was the first day, I shouldn't want to know what the next ones held.

"Um, your Highness," Astra said.

"Yes," Rayan answered, his gaze still on me.

"My suitcases were in the car that took me to Icas's house. I have nothing here; do you know if I could get them back?" she asked him. I had totally forgotten about my bags, too.

"Oh, shit, where are mine?" I looked around me, as if they would have been summoned to me by my question. A chuckle had me looking up.

Cian walked up towards Rayan. "What is she doing?" He pointed my way.

"Looking for her bags, I think." Rayan gave me his signature smile; the one he seemed to have on his face all the freaking time, the one that gave a girl weak knees and drool in the corner of her mouth. Cian chuckled again, a low and deep chuckle that did funny things to me.

"I need to get some sleep," I mumbled to myself.

"Yeah, you do," Cian answered. "And as for your bags, they are in your room." He pointed to the door Lars had showed me.

"Good. As, you can borrow something from me if you want. For tonight." I told her, when I pushed open the door. I had totally ignored the two Kings that stood in the doorway. It was late, really late, and my mind couldn't handle anything more at that time. I kept seeing them naked. It was a shame I was tired, it would have been a fun and nice moment with myself.

Astra followed me into my room, where my bags were placed on the sofa that stood in the middle, in front of it a small coffee table; two chairs were on either side of it. A fireplace dominated the room, and big windows looked out towards the wall that surrounded the castle. There was also a small table with two chairs to eat at. Another door led towards the bedroom, I caught a glimpse of a bed in that room.

I pulled out some stuff, placed my weapons lovingly on the coffee table, and grabbed a pair of pyjamas for Astra, more of t-shirt and sweatpants. I slept in sports bras and sweatpants, it was all I could have given her.

She grumbled a thanks and took them. Before she could move towards her own room, Rayan entered. "I'll see you girls at breakfast tomorrow morning. I'll pick you up here around eight, so I can show you the Castle."

"Thank you, Your Highness, but that won't be necessary. I think we can find the kitchens on our own. We wouldn't want to keep you from your work," Astra said, politely.

"Oh, no problem at all. I want to. It will be fun." He winked at her and then moved out of the door.

"Good night," Cian said, and he waved at us before he walked away, too.

Astra and I looked at each other. I shrugged, not knowing what to do about that. A yawn took over again.

"Let's get some sleep, Isa," Astra said, while she walked towards the door. Her eyes were downcast and her movements hesitant.

"Are you okay?" I asked her. She stopped and turned around. Her face was all I needed to see before I rushed towards her and pulled her in for a hug.

"It is okay, As, you're here now, you are safe. I'll protect you, I will!" I whispered into her ear.

"I know," she mumbled into my shoulder.

"I was so scared, they bound my magic. I couldn't do anything. Not until we left the house again." Relief surged through me. Because if she had still been bound, that would have been a problem. Something I could have fixed, but it would have been a little painful for her.

"I think they spelled the car and the house, As. I was spelled, too. I slept like the dead in that car."

"You always sleep like the dead," Astra joked. I did not, you learned to sleep lightly in the school, part of the Protector training. Always keep an eye out for danger.

"Are you good to sleep alone?" I asked her while I pushed her away a little, holding her by her shoulders, so I could look at her again. The doubt flickered into her eyes. "Come, you can sleep in my room tonight." Seeing her relax and watching the relief filter over her face, I knew it had been the right thing to say. I wouldn't want to have slept alone after something like that, either.

So, we walked into the bedroom, I turned on the lights, the curtains were already closed. A four-poster bed greeted us. We both changed into our pyjamas and slipped under the covers.

The soft sheets moved over my exposed stomach, and the pillows felt like a cloud. I knew I would be asleep in minutes. Luckily for me, I heard Astra's words just before she, too, fell asleep.

"Thank you, Isa. Thanks, Sis." And with that I was out.

11

A knock sounded on the door, rousing me from my slumber. I stirred and turned onto my side, my eyes still closed. The knock sounded again. I wanted to yell at the bastard who stood there to go away. Until I remembered, Astra. I opened my eyes, finding her on her side. She faced towards me, still asleep, her breathing soft. I got out of the bed and walked to the bedroom door, luckily that one had still been open. Moving into the next room, I walked over towards that door and yanked it open.

"What?"

"Hello to you, too," Rayan said, his ever-present smile on his face.

"Please stop smiling." My head wasn't working yet, I was talking to one of the Kings, and nobody spoke like that to the Kings.

His smile faltered for a second, then he kicked it into high gear.

"Why? Aren't you happy to see me, Babe? I am," he answered.

"You are happy to see yourself?" My mind wasn't there yet. I didn't blame her.

He laughed.

"Ssh, Astra is still asleep." I shushed him and pushed

him back into the hallway. "What do you want? I would love to get some more sleep," I said to him, my arms crossed in front of my chest. It pushed my breasts up. His eyes flickered over them and then lowered to my stomach and pants. I kept myself breathing normally, willing away the blush that wanted to creep onto my face, and wiped the annoying look off my face.

I was used to walking around like that, I had trained in clothing like that at school. In front of people. They may have been only women and the occasional male teacher, but that was it. Not a handsome King who seemed to enjoy what he was seeing. I enjoyed the feeling it gave me, for two seconds. Maybe more.

"Are you done, Babe?" I mocked him while I arched an eyebrow and kept my arms crossed in front of me, he then winked at me. "What did you want, Rayan?" I asked him again.

"I came to get you, and Astra, for the tour of the castle." He motioned around him.

And that was when my head started working. "Oh, pink pigs. Yeah, give us twenty minutes, and we will meet you here?" I asked him. He had said last night that he would take us for a tour through the castle.

I turned around towards the door, the knob in hand when I remembered something. "What time is it?"

"Almost eleven."

"Oh."

He chuckled and said, "We let you girls sleep, thought you both needed it. We will do a quick tour of the castle and then have lunch with the others." He moved towards the door, the one I was holding. "I think I'll wait in your room." He placed his hand over mine. His warmth immediately seeped into my hand, radiating off of his body into mine as his magic wrapped around me. He smelled like a refreshing summer rain.

"Water," I mumbled when I managed to push the door open.

"What did you say?" he asked me when we both moved into the room. We bumped once into each other as we moved through the door at the same time, giving me chills on my back; the good kind, the kind I wanted so much more of.

"Oh, your magic. Water, it is your preferred magic," I told him. The Kings were strong in all four of the elements, but still they had a favourite. You couldn't be strong in all of them equally. Except when you were a Full-Blood like me. We were balanced because of the Spirit we had. It took a lot of willpower and training to reach a master status with all four of the elements. You constantly had to balance yourself. If you didn't, you became darkened.

"You can tell?" he asked, when he stepped away from me, towards one of the sofas. I missed his heat immediately, and my body took a step his way. I pulled myself to a stop and moved towards the bedroom door. It was still open. Astra still slept. That girl must have been exhausted. I placed a finger in front of my mouth and pointed towards to door, showing Astra and made sure he would be quiet.

He nodded, and I moved to the bedroom. Time to wake up Astra.

I moved to her side of the bed. "As, wake up, Babe." I touched her shoulder lightly.

She mumbled.

"Come on, As. We have company."

"Send them away," she said, her voice croaking since she'd just woke up.

"I don't think Rayan would like that."

And with that, she sat upright in bed, her hair a bird's nest on top of her head.

"King Rayan." She had tried to whisper it. I laughed and pointed towards the door.

She looked and saw him sitting there. He waved. She squealed, pulled the covers towards her and looked at me. If looks could kill, I would have been dead.

"Why did you let him in here, let him see me like this?" she hissed.

I shrugged. "He walked in. And you were still sleeping."

"I knocked," he said loudly from the living room.

"Not helping," Astra and I both answered back.

He chuckled, which made us laugh, too. I walked to the door and pushed it closed.

"Come on, let's get dressed and ready for a late breakfast." Astra nodded as I walked to the other door in the room. When I walked through it, I found myself in a big bathroom. A tub with cast-iron lion feet sat in the middle of the room. There was a shower in the left corner of the room, and around a small wall near the door was the toilet. On my other side, were a sink and a mirror. A chair stood at the head of the tub against the wall. Leaving room for you to walk around the tub. The floor was covered in dark-grey tiles, with dark-blue tiles on the walls. There were golden accents, like the faucets on the tub and the sink, shining in the sunlight that filtered through the window.

"As, did you see this?" I yelled back at her.

"No, what? And hurry, I need to shower, too," she said as I heard her walking up beside me.

"Wow, did we die and go to bathroom heaven?" Her eyes were wide as she looked around.

"Not sure, but I don't mind!" I said while I pushed her backwards a little.

"Hey!" she protested, and I gave her a shit-eating grin.

"I was here first."

"Make it quick, Isa, we have to have lunch or breakfast," she said to the closed door.

A food heaven, that was my first best place on this world. My stomach agreed with that. We hadn't eaten in a long time. So yeah, it was quick.

I stripped, showered, and dressed quickly. I had grabbed clean cargo pants, a black sports bra with green frogs printed on them, and a black tank top. Astra moved into the bathroom as soon as I got out.

"Do you have some clothing, As?" I asked her, as I remembered her suitcases were still missing somewhere.

"Yeah, someone brought some clothing in when you were in the shower." I heard the tap being turned on. I walked over to the bed and pulled on my boots. I pulled my two swords out of my bag, placed two knives in each boot and one on my right hip. After that, I looked through the clothing for my leather jacket. Finding it, I pulled it on over my swords. It had a low hanging back, so the sword handles would stick out of it and move freely.

We'd had an amazing dressmaker at the school. He loved doing personalized stuff. And the jacket was one of his best works.

I opened the door to find Rayan still sitting there; I had totally forgotten about him.

"Hi," I said when I walked over to him. I saw his eyes scanning me, over my boots, the knife at my hip and the two sword handles that stuck out over my shoulders. I cocked my head to the side and placed a hand on my hip, pushing that one out a little, too.

"Something wrong with what you see?" I asked him. I could swear he swallowed before he turned a little red.

"Eh, I was only wondering, why so many weapons?" He waved his hand over my body.

"Many weapons?" We heard behind me. Astra walked into the room, wearing jeans and a t-shirt. Her blonde hair was loose and still a little wet. She looked perfect even in simple clothing. She was the kind of girl who had never needed much to look like a model. One of the Kings would have to fall for her. She chuckled when she said, "You think that is many? You haven't seen her in full armour yet."

I shrugged at the questioning look I got from Rayan. "I didn't want to scare you guys," I told him. That made them both laugh and had me looking dazed at them. "I mean it," I grumbled as I walked towards the door. "Can we get something to eat?" I looked at Rayan. He promptly got up from the sofa.

"You don't want to see the castle first?" he asked me.

"No, food is good," I said and pushed open the door.

"If that is okay with you, your Highness, we would like to eat first. We haven't eaten since yesterday morning," Astra said to him, remembering all the right things you needed to say to the King. If he hadn't been there, I would have slapped my head, or not because then I wouldn't even have talked to the King. That would be *so* much easier. I wouldn't have had to remember what to say or not to if they weren't around.

"Are you coming, Isa?" I heard Astra and turned towards her. She was standing in front of the door that led towards the Kings' Quarters, Rayan holding it open for her.

"Yeah, I'm coming," I said. My mind had needed a second to come back from the thinking trip it had taken.

"Why are we going that way?" I asked them both when I moved towards them.

"We are having lunch with all of the Kings, they wanted to meet us, properly I think," Astra answered while Rayan moved towards the stairs. I looked around when I walked through the door. To the left was another door, which went almost to the ceiling and also was made out of wood.

"They lead towards our corridor and our rooms," Rayan said when he saw me looking.

"We're sleeping next to you guys?" I asked, surprise in my voice. I hadn't wanted to be that close to them. I had assumed that behind that door would be another hallway and that they slept somewhere else. Like far, far away.

"Yes. And our private dining room is downstairs." He walked down, so we both followed.

"And upstairs, behind the big doors are our rooms and a small library. We also have an office, but you have seen that one. It is in the back of the throne room. And this is where we come to relax and be at home," he said as he pushed open the doors in front of us.

We entered a large room, there were high windows with their curtains drawn open, letting the sunlight in and giving an amazing view over the gardens that were placed between the wall and their living area. The room was spacious. To the left on a raised platform, was a dining table, where servants were currently placing plates and glasses. I had already smelt the food that some of them were walking in with.

I drifted towards the table without really noticing anything else.

"You want a napkin for that drool?" I heard. I looked to my right, finding Cian on one of the sofas that was placed around a glass coffee table. He looked at me with an eyebrow arched and a smirk on his face.

"Yes, please," I told him and sauntered past him. I looked back over my shoulder and told him. "Don't worry, I'll leave some for you guys." And with that, I grabbed a chair and sat at the table. The others were still looking at me, and I totally ignored them.

Food. Like a lot. Bread still steaming from the oven, baked chicken, and thinly sliced beef were the first types I noticed. Butter and other spreads were placed around the dishes. There were some salads, and more bowls filled with food. I was in heaven, that bathroom could suck it.

I had started filling my plate, with anything and everything, my eyes somehow even bigger than my stomach. And I was loving it. I heard the others pulling out chairs, and I continued to ignore them in favour of all the food. Then they walked in with pancakes.

"Ah, shit," I mumbled. I looked to my left and saw an empty plate. I picked it up and placed some pancakes on that plate.

"What are you doing, sweetheart?" I heard from next to me.

I looked up at the person to find Averey sitting there.

"What does it look like? My plate is full," I said and continued filling it with pancakes. When that was done, I placed it next to the other in front of me and started eating.

There was some laughter around me, and the others sat down, too. I noticed that Astra had taken the seat in front of me and next to me sat Cian. Astra had Flynn and Rayan next to her, they all started putting food on their plates. Even Averey did the same once he got a new one from the servants.

We ate in silence, and it was heavenly. The beef was cooked to perfection, and the salads were richly filled. The pancakes, oh those pancakes, there was a hint of vanilla in them, the light and fluffy bite to them made me moan. If I could have an orgasm from eating pancakes, I would have from those.

When I finished my second plate, I looked up. Flynn was watching me, and I gave him a smile. Still, I remembered what he had said in the car. I had talked to his little sister, his dead little sister.

With him seated this close to me, I could see the pain in his eyes, the sadness that stayed there. It must have been a painful moment or memory to have it still lingering in his eyes like that.

I saw his mouth twitching to one side and fist bumped inside my head for getting a small smile on his face. That was one good thing today.

Astra was in a conversation with Rayan, so I looked around the room. I found a fireplace and above it, a TV. My eyes lingered on it. They had a TV. We'd had one in the school, but that one was for movie night once a month. And even then, you had to watch with a lot of other people. Not a great thing. I needed to figure out a way to get back here and plan a movie night.

The sofas looked comfortable, there were some paintings on the wall and two chandeliers hanging from the ceiling. Behind me was a balcony, which showed doors.

That must be the rooms Rayan talked about. There were four doors facing me and one at the end of the hallway. That probably led towards another hall and stairs. That door looked more elaborately decorated than the others, more important. Before I could ask what was in that room, Averey interrupted my inspection of their living area.

"We wanted to talk to you two about what happened yesterday."

I turned fully towards him, looked that gorgeous male in the eyes, then told him what had been brewing inside me from the moment the Selection had began.

12

"First of all, you flying potatoes, I'm angry with you guys. You almost killed a lot of Witches yesterday. They could have died. I'm not even sure why you guys agreed to use Ilunias in the Selection test—" I started. Before I could go on Averey interrupted me.

"What did you say?"

"Are you deaf, mister? Listen good." I pushed my chair back a little, so I was looking at them better. "Three weeks before the Selection, the school got the message that you guys changed the test. Not the standard, touch the stone test or whatever it is you guys normally do. No, you guys wanted to know who was strong and smart and wanted to test the Witches in a fight. Against Ilunias. You know, dark-world creatures?" I waved my hands in the air, putting some power behind my words. All four of them were looking at me like I had lost my mind. Astra looked at her plate, she had almost been killed in that fight. It cooled down my temper a little. Made me realize that it would be a terrible memory for her.

"They were stronger than the Witches, which is something everyone could have told you. They stop learning how to fight when they reach the fourth year in the school, or something." I waved that away. "We Protectors had to stand watch, keep an eye out if something went wrong. And we could solely interfere if one of the Selection council would sign our instructor Lavina."

"We stood there, watching that fight go bad really quickly. And when the three Ilunias decided they had played enough, they blew up the inner shields the Selection held." I looked at Averey; my look must have been murderous from the way he flinched a little.

"They had one sort of protection, when they were knocked out or injured, and they were placed under a shield and pulled into a big shield under the box where the Selection and the teachers were sitting. It was the only thing that kept them safe for so long."

"Nuh-uh." I held my hand up towards Cian when I saw him opening his mouth. This got a chuckle from Flynn. I looked over at him, eyebrows raised. He quickly shut up. Good.

"The Ilunias were done playing your game, so they shattered the shields. That is," I swallowed, "That is when they attacked Astra." I looked over to the blonde figure in front of me, her eyes on me. And her blue eyes were filled with tears, ones she didn't want to shed, just couldn't stop.

"And if it wasn't for Isadora, I would be dead, with probably almost every Witch and Protector there. She saved me," Astra said softly

I was relieved that she had kept how I had done it out of it. They would probably find out soon enough. Still, it was not something they needed to know at that time.

"How did you save her?" Rayan asked me, keeping his own voice low.

"I killed the Ilunias."

"You did what?" Averey asked, shock sounded in his voice. And I knew for sure that if I had looked at him, his eyes would have been wide.

"I killed them, cut off their heads." I was still looking at Astra when I said that.

"All three of them," she said while a lone tear fell down, splattering on her empty plate.

"It's okay," Rayan said noticing the tear. He moved a hand to brush the next one away and gave her a napkin to wipe the rest.

"No, it is not okay, you guys wanted the strongest Witch." I pointed towards Astra. "And she sits there. She fought them the longest before they gave her a flying lesson."

I shook my head, removing the memory that had invaded my mind, her falling, screaming.

"But you killed them," Flynn said, it was the first time he had said something.

"Yes, I did what I had to do. If I could have spared them, I would have."

"Why didn't you?" Cian asked from next to me, his hand rubbing over his chin, and his eyes narrowed at me.

I swallowed and answered honestly. "Because if I did, they would have been used. Experimented on, used for another test that would probably kill someone. And it showed that the Selection couldn't handle them. They were better off dead." I looked at my hands in my lap. I was twisting them; shame had filled me for what I had done. Would there have been a better way?

"You did what you had to," Cian said, his hand landing on mine. He made me stop twisting my hands. My body started to react to his soft touch. It was so different from the big man that sat next to me. I looked at him. His green eyes were radiant and so full of comfort, it made me swallow. Another hand landed on my leg, I looked to the hand and followed it up to the person it belonged to. Finding that it was Averey, I heated up. Two Kings touching me. At the same time . . . I spaced out for a moment.

I jumped up and walked away from them, leaving them with their hands hovering in the space where I had been. I twirled around, using the lingering anger to suppress the feelings they had both awakened in me.

"I had to do it because you guys decided this was the way to go. You guys made me do it." I pointed at each of them. And that, apparently, was the wrong thing to say.

Averey got up from his chair. "Listen up. We didn't make you do anything. You swung that sword, you killed them. And no, we didn't decide that we wanted the Selection changed. It was fine for our ancestors, and it is fine for us. No, don't start blaming us." He moved closer with everything he said until he was right in my space. I wasn't short for a woman, but still he had to lower his head a little, so he could look into my eyes.

Oh, those beautiful grey eyes, now showing a storm of emotion, making them a place you wanted to disappear in. Be swept away in.

I focused on his mouth, wrong idea. So, the tip of his nose had become the next safe place on his face. He was too gorgeous to be real. And I wouldn't have believed it if he hadn't been standing in front of me, so close that if I had leaned in, I would have been touching his neck with my nose. I could have sniffed him. The idea formed in my head, and I had to use all my willpower not to do just that. I stepped back.

He breathed in for a second before he continued. "Look, we didn't know that they changed the Selection process. You two are the first to come to the Castle. Nobody else."

"You mean there are no other Selection members?" Astra asked from the dinner table, her hand in front of her mouth. I read what she was thinking on her face. And I wasn't the only one.

"No, we didn't hear of Witches being killed or turning up dead," Cian said. Relief flooded over Astra's face.

"Yeah, only, what if the Selection didn't tell you guys that, either?" I asked, the thought had popped into my head. Because if they didn't know that the Selection had changed the test, they wouldn't necessarily have known that there would be dead Witches.

"No, if a Witch dies in the school, the Head of the school is under strict orders to report that. We can't lose any Witch or Elemental," Rayan said, his happy smile was no longer on his face. He looked so much older with his face all serious–and so much hotter.

Astra and I both released a deep breath. "Okay, if what you guys say is true, and you didn't know about this, who arranged the tests, put the Ilunias in captivity, and made sure you guys were all in the dark?" I'd already had an idea, and that idea walked through the double doors behind the dining table.

Before I even moved a muscle, Averey's hand was in the air, pointed towards Icas Nox. Who now hovered above the ground, eyes wide.

"Was it your idea?" Flynn growled out, when he shoved his chair back and walked up to Nox.

Nothing came out of his mouth.

"Averey, loosen the air, man," Rayan said to the King in front of me. We all heard the breath of air Nox sucked in.

"What do you mean, your Highnesses?" His eyes moved fast over all of us, lingering on Astra. It made my blood boil. Then they moved to me, and stayed on me, giving me a creepy feeling. I shuddered a little. In that moment, Averey moved in front of me. Before my sight of Nox was blocked out by the back of Averey, I saw a smile creep over his lips.

I stepped around Averey as fast as I could and moved closer towards Astra. She was now next to Rayan who appeared to have moved closer to her, too. I stopped before the raised dais and looked at the man hanging there.

"You know what we mean. You are the high council member, you are the High Selection member. We want to know why you changed the Selection process, why you endangered those Witches," Averey said, his voice low.

Icas Nox looked again at me and then at Astra. "My Kings, I don't think it is a good idea to discuss that here." His eyes moved between me and Astra again.

"Oi, you pig of a bastard," I said and stepped on the dais, my own magic coming forth. "You start talking and fast, otherwise you will find out that I'm a real big problem," I told him. Fire had started licking my fingers and up my arm. His eyes followed the fire, and I swore I saw his eyes flash with something dark for a second. I blinked, and it was gone. Thinking I had projected it on him, I shook my head. He was still the blond-haired motherfucking A-hole that he had been from the beginning.

"Fine," he answered. With that, Averey lowered him to the floor. I looked at him, shocked that he would let him go. He shook his head as if he read my thoughts. I looked back, just in time to see Flynn hitting his face with a nice right hook. I looked back over my shoulder to Averey and gave him a big smile and mouthed 'thank you,' he nodded.

"What was that for?" Nox spit at Flynn.

"You don't talk to me like that," Flynn said, widening his stance, I moved before he could land another punch, grabbing his arm while it was in the air.

"Wait," I told him, "save some for me?" I looked up at the dark eyes of Flynn, the pain burned into me, and I took a deep breath. I wanted to take that pain away and make his eyes shine like his sister's had. He nodded and stepped back.

"You need to start talking, Nox," Averey said when he moved next to me and Flynn. Rayan and Cian also moved closer, Astra was still next to Rayan.

"We–"

I cleared my throat.

"I, decided that we needed a better way of testing the Witches, of knowing who was stronger, what they would do in an attack, and how they would use their magic. To find out which ones would fit best with the Kings," Nox started.

"And why didn't you talk with us about that?" Averey asked, his arms crossed in front of his chest.

"I didn't want to burden you with that decision. I'm

High council member and High Selection. That would be enough," Nox answered.

"And the others, did they agree?" I asked, wanting to know what role Bun Lady had in this all.

"No, they didn't at first. They needed some persuasion," he said, his white eyes focused on me, and again, they flickered black. I looked at the others. If they had seen it, they didn't show it.

"There is also the matter of finding Queens for all of you. I told the other members that. That it would be important to have the strongest Witches presented to you, so you could bond with them."

My whole body froze. 'Bond' with them? Before I could interrupt him, Averey did.

"Nox, we, indeed, need strong Queens, however not at the expense of Witches dying."

"Oh, no, your Highness, nobody died," Icas Nox said. "We kept them safe."

"Not that last time," Astra sneered at him, her fist clenched next to her. Rayan laid down his hand on her shoulder, which seemed to shake her out of her anger. She relaxed a little, and I turned back to the A-hole in front of us.

"Yeah, that was a mistake. We miscalculated some things." Icas dared to chuckle a little with that.

"You son of a flying potato's head," I said and moved, punching him in the face. My magic rose, filling the room. Icas turned white from the feel of my magic.

"Who are you?" he asked.

"None of your bloody business. If you ever decide that it would be a good idea to threaten any Witch, kill anybody again–"

"We didn't ki–" he started, and I punched him again.

The crunch of my fist against his nose was amazing, and when I pulled back, I finished what I was saying. "I will find out and hunt you to the end of this world and further. And believe me when I say, it will not be an easy death."

My magic pushed against him, he stumbled back. I had him pushed out of the hold Averey had on him.

"Isadora," Averey growled at me. My fist was in the air, ready for the third punch, but my name stopped me. "Stop." Averey commanded. And with that, I pulled my magic back, all of it, and the room took a collective breath. I turned around and walked towards Astra, took her hand and waited for what the Kings would do with this, this . . .

"Icas Nox," Flynn started. "You are stripped from your duties as a High Selection council. You will stay on as a Council member."

"Wait, what?" I asked him. Averey turned around and pinned me with his eyes, thunder storming in them. And I swallowed.

"We will have an investigation into this all. And we will send the other Selection council to the schools, again. To test the Witches, again, now in the old ways." Flynn turned around and moved to stand next to Averey.

"You will not come near these two women, you will not come near the Witches that will come here for the Selections. You are solely allowed into the castle for Council matters. Otherwise, keep to your house," Averey said, his voice filled with anger, not everything was for Nox. Most of it, though.

"You are dismissed," Cian said. And with that, it was over. No throwing into the cells, if they even had them.

"Wait, what? Is that all?" I asked the Kings when Nox left the room.

"Yes, that is all."

"Why? He did something behind you guys' backs, he almost killed people. He killed people!" I threw out, my hands flying into the air with my anger.

"What do you mean?" Flynn asked, he was standing next to me then.

"I was talking about the Witches, they could have been dead." I didn't want to tell them about the wives, about what Mara told me. It was not the time.

He narrowed his eyes at me and moved towards the sofas. The others did, too, leaving me standing. I started walking around, too pumped up to sit still right now.

"And we stripped him of being a High council member, and we removed him from the Selection. We can't do more yet, we need to follow the rules. And with him being an Heir to the house, he can't be shoved aside when we want to," Rayan explained. He looked up at me, his blue eyes understanding. It made me bristle, so I started moving around the room, around the sofas.

There was something wrong with Nox, and I needed to figure out what before things blew up. That was one thing I knew for sure. When I stopped moving, I stood in front of the fireplace, my fingers on my lips. Another thought entered my mind.

"When are you expecting the other Witches to come here for the Selection?" I asked them, my mind was running around with plans, things I needed to do. And I needed to find out how long I had before this castle would be too busy to sneak around.

"In four days, maybe sooner," Cian said.

Purple teapots, that didn't give me much time to roam around the Castle.

"Okay, and do you guys have a number that will accompany Astra in the Selection for Queen?"

"Isa," Astra hissed at me, I pulled up my shoulders in a 'yeah, what?' gesture.

"We normally have eight," Rayan said, there was a ghost of a smile on his lips.

"You have one now, and you guys need to find four in total." I held up four fingers to them. "So, you guys need seven more for you to choose the four from." I gave Astra a sad look, that meant less chance for her. She shook her head at me.

"We have enough for now. We don't need to choose now. The other Witches will come to the Castle, and we will see then," Averey said, the anger in his voice had remained.

"Nuh-uh. Not enough. We need to move this whole thing up. You guys need a wife," I told them again. Something was pushing me, rushing me. They needed to bond, that emotion was running through me and had clouded my mind.

"Isadora, shut up for a second, and listen to Averey," Cian said. I looked at him, an amused smile was on his face.

"We have time to find the Queen selection members, it isn't easy. They need to be bonded with us, we need to be compatible. And until the others are here, we have you two."

That left me with my mouth open, and my head cleared in seconds. They meant me.

"Oh no, hell no, shit, no, no, and no, no." I wagged my finger in front of them all and then turned around and stormed out of the room. It was time to get my stuff and leave.

13

"What do they think I am? Some stupid bimbo who they can woo or order to stay? They may be the most handsome men I have ever seen. Actually, they are some of the few men I may ever have seen. And they are Kings, but so what?" I said to myself in the otherwise empty room. I had rushed out of their private quarters as fast as I could after hearing that.

"Me in the running for Queen? Did they hit their heads when they woke up this morning?" I was almost done with my bags. I placed my last weapons in the right one and zipped it closed.

"I got Astra here, that was the whole point of this all. Now is the time to leave," I mumbled to the room again. I moved towards the bathroom, there was one thing I wanted to take with me from there. I grabbed the shampoo bottle out of the shower. I loved the smell of it, cedarwood and lotus. I popped the cap open and smelled it. "Mmh, the only good thing here," I said when I walked back into the room. My eyes were closed, so I could enjoy the smell even more.

"Are you sure?" I heard.

"Shit stickers! You should knock," I mumbled, and he laughed. I opened my eyes and found myself looking at

Averey. He stood in my door's opening, leaning against the doorframe, his eyes roaming over me, and then they moved towards the bags on the bed.

"What do you want?" I asked while I moved to my bags, placed the shampoo in it and picked them both up.

"We need to talk," he said while he moved towards me.

I side stepped around him and moved out of the bedroom. He grabbed my arm and halted me. His magic moved around me, it made me relax for a second, made me feel free. Almost as if I were running around in a lightning storm with the winds whipping around me. Air, his favourite magic.

For one second more, I breathed him in. He smelled like a storm, the electric of the lightning. I knew for sure if I closed my eyes, I would hear the thunder. Before I could lose myself in him, I shook myself loose and walked towards the door of the living room.

"Wait," he said. I didn't listen and pulled the door open. If I started listening, I would have wanted to stay, stay for the feelings he and the others had brought up in me. I had noticed them, that longing for them to be close. "You just met them, freaking donkey." I mumbled to myself when I walked into the hallway. Nobody was there, and I was grateful for that. If one of the other Kings would have been there, I probably would have caved. Who wouldn't? Maybe I was a stupid bimbo after all.

I walked down the long hallway, until I reached the main hall with the stairs, and then I walked down. When I reached the last step of the stairs, it dawned on me that he hadn't followed me, he hadn't called after me. My breath hitched, and I could feel my stomach turning. I swallowed, trying to moisten my suddenly dry throat. Tears welled up in my eyes at the sudden emptiness I was feeling. I shook my head, I hadn't wanted this in the first place. I wasn't going to cry about it then. I shook my head again and walked with strong paces towards the door. All the while, I was trying to convince myself that it didn't matter that none of them had come after me, that this was what I wanted, and that I needed to leave. I needed to leave.

When I reached the door, there was nobody to open it for me, nobody to say goodbye to, even if it had been a servant. My hand moved to the door handle, the iron cold against my clammy palms. I took a few quick breaths to calm my racing heart and pulled down the handle.

"Isa," I heard behind me and released the door handle; my hand shook a little when I placed my bags on the floor, so I could turn around and look at Astra.

Her blonde hair was pulled back into a ponytail high on her head, and she looked flushed, like she had run there.

"Yeah?" I asked as I placed a hand on my hip. I didn't want her to see that I was happy with her calling me out. "You came to say goodbye?" I asked her.

"No," she said and moved closer to me. "I came to stop you. You can't go." She placed her hands on my shoulders and lightly shook me. I let out a breath, and a small giggle escaped with it. I quickly shut down my emotions, not wanting to show her how relieved I was.

"We . . . I need you here," she started. "I don't want to go through this alone. I need you with me, Isa." Her voice lowered, and I could see her swallow.

That had me concerned. "What is it, As?" I asked her.

"I'm . . .," she started then dropped her hands from my shoulders.

"You can tell me, As," I told her softly. She looked at me, straight at me. Her blue eyes bright, and love shone through them. It made me smile a little.

"Tell me, As, I can't read minds," I joked.

"I'm scared," she said, and this broke my heart for the umpteenth time that week. I pulled her in for a hug. "Why is that, As? You are in good hands here," I told her.

I could feel her shake her head, so I moved back, looking at her.

"You need to tell me more then that , As. I can't stay

because you are scared. You are strong, I know you can beat what comes your way." I waited for her to answer.

She swallowed and nodded at me, and for a second, my heart sank into my toes, scared that she had agreed with me that I couldn't stay there, until she started talking.

"I'm scared of Nox." She shuddered with that name. "He talked about things when I was in his house. About magic, taking it and using it to destroy. I'm not sure what or who or why. He didn't say much when he found out I was listening. Isa, he scared me, I always found him creepy. But more now, with that. And you saying you saw King Flynn's sister there? That freaked me out more."

"Wait, you know about Flynn's sister?" I asked her, nobody had told me about that.

"Yeah, all the Witches and Elementals in the high societies know about that. I'm not going to tell you, though. It is his story to tell, not mine. And if you want to know, you have to stay," she said with a cheeky smile. I rolled my eyes.

"What you want, is that all? Is that the reason why you want me to stay? To keep you safe from Nox?"

She shook her head. "No, I want you to stay because I don't want to do this alone, like I said. I need my best friend here. I need my sister here. And I need someone that I can laugh with about all the other Witches that will arrive here for the Queen selection." She chuckled, and I knew what she meant. They would fall all over themselves trying to get the Kings' attention, it would be so much fun. For a second, I was mad at the idea of them trying to flirt with the Kings, and my jaw locked up when I grimaced for a moment. I released it and masked it all with a smile. I hadn't wanted Astra knowing I was jealous of the idea of another woman flirting with all the Kings, never mind just one of them.

"Look, if you go now, I will never see you again," she said, remembering what I had told her, about me living alone in the woods, hiding forever. "And I can't think of that, never knowing what happened to you. Never again talking about the simple things, like the new bath soap that came out or the new movie they made. Or what new weapon you got." She chuckled. I had never liked to talk about the next soap or the new make-up, like Astra always wanted. I got excited about a new weapon, jumping up and down excited.

"I need you here," she added.

I shook my head. "I don't know, Astra, I don't know what I would do here. I'm not a normal Witch, I'm a Protector. That is what I trained for my whole life. I can't change that, I will be looked at strangely, because of that. It is not something I want."

"Wait, you are afraid, that if you stayed, that people would look at you strangely?" Astra grabbed my arms and giggled at me. I arched an eyebrow at her.

"You, afraid of what people think? You, the girl who walked naked from the training hall to the other side of the school, to our room because Thalia stole your clothing. You didn't blush, held your head high and walked back to our room. The whole school was looking at you, yet you made the male teachers run back to their classes when they saw you coming. They gave you three months of cleaning the dining hall for that, even when it wasn't your fault." Her voice pitched a little higher. "And *now* you are afraid of what people will think of you?"

I nodded at her.

She continued, "You also lost that bet with Banu, the one about who could not laugh for the longest about something. Don't know what it was anymore." She waved with her hand in the air. "You lost and you had to walk around with a pink shirt dress on, even do your fight training in it. It kept moving upwards, and you kept pulling it down. It was hilarious." She laughed, and I smiled with her.

"Yeah, the good old days," I said. "Still, I don't like it. At school, it was different. We were all young, and, yeah, you know young." I had no idea how to go against that.

She was right, I had never cared about what others thought of me, not really. Merely what Astra or the others who I had let come closer thought of me. And that was it, I didn't care for the rest. It didn't mean I would harm them in any way, however I never cared what they thought of me. I'm me. If you don't like it, there is the door, see ya.

"Okay," I said to her. Her face lit up with her smile, and she hugged me close.

"We need to tell the Kings," Astra said and picked up one of my bags, Instead she dropped it back down. "What is in there, the whole arsenal from here?" she joked, fully aware that it was my weapons.

"Yeah, I wanted some new things. So, I thought, why not?" I said, holding my hands up. "They originally belonged to me, anyway," I whispered that to her.

"No, you didn't. You can't do that, that is stealing." She gasped. It was my turn to laugh out loud.

"I didn't. Those are my weapons, and that bag isn't that heavy." I picked it up, and she grabbed the one with my clothing. We both walked back to my room.

"What are you going to say to the Kings?" Astra asked when we were almost at the room.

"I'm going to tell them that I'm staying. Only, that there will be a but." I pushed open the door to my room. I didn't know when it had become my room, but it was.

"What is that 'but?'" she asked, when we placed the bags on the sofa and moved towards the hall.

"That I will stay, for you. And that I don't want to compete for Queen. I'm no Queen," I said to her.

"Yes, you are." Astra looked at me.

"No, As, I know what you are saying. But I'm not, look at me." I moved my hands along my body, indicating everything about myself. "I'm a Protector, I care more about my weapons than people."

"No, that is not true, you care a lot about people. That is why you are such a good Protector. You always want to keep the people around you safe." She gave me a warm smile.

I ignored her, not knowing how to answer that. It always sucked to hear things that you didn't want to admit to yourself.

"Like I said, I'm going to tell them I'm not in the running to become Queen. I will tell them that I'm here for you. As your Protector and that is that." I pushed open the doors to their private quarters. "Are you sure they are here?" I asked her when we walked down the stairs.

"Yes, I told them to wait for us here."

"You irritating blonde canary," I said to her. She knew full well that I would have stayed when she came after me. It lightened my heart a little, knowing that the Kings didn't come after me because Astra told them. We entered their living room, they were seated on the sofa, and as soon as they heard us coming in, their faces all showed a different state of relief. Only Flynn's face was closed off as always.

"You are staying?" Rayan asked, his smile already on his face.

"Yes. Only–" I started.

"I told you she would demand something, pay up Ray," Cian said and held his hand out towards Rayan. I chuckled, at that, and Averey pulled up his eyebrow.

"I would have done the same." I answered his unspoken question.

"So, here is the 'only.' I'm not going to be in the running for Queen."

"Why not?" Rayan asked, and his eyes widened.

"You don't want to date one of us?" Cian asked, he had his arms folded over his chest, his muscles bulging under his clothing. It almost made me say yes.

"No," I said while I looked at the wall behind him. *So pretty that wall.*

"Hear me out before you guys start asking questions." I moved towards one of the chairs and sat down. "I was raised as a protector, that is all I know." I held up my hand towards Averey. "And yes, I know how to use my magic, it is a natural thing for us, and yes that is it still for me." He nodded with that, his question answered.

"I'm here to stay for Astra. I can do a job here, protect her." I pointed towards her, she was still standing next to one of the sofas. "She is a handful," I joked.

"Only you are a Witch, sweetheart, a powerful one," Averey stated.

"Yes, I know that, thanks for the reminder." I almost growled the words out at him, but forced myself to level my voice before I spoke.

"Why do you guys want me in the running for Queen?" I asked them. This made them all look at each other, and none of them answered. It made me feel empty again.

"We, uh, you told us that you defeated three Ilunias," Averey started with that. "And your magic, we have felt it from time to time. It feels powerful." The others nodded with that.

"And we need to know for sure that you aren't bonded to one of us. If we let you walk away, we may never find someone to help us," he said. He had my attention then.

"What do you mean?" I asked him, sliding towards the edge of the chair I was sitting in.

"That isn't something you need to know right now." Flynn's deep voice sounded throughout the room, I looked up at him. I was a little shocked at hearing him talk but also happy to hear his voice again. I already liked his deep strong voice. If I was a bimbo, I would have swooned hearing him talk.

"Uh, what?" I looked back towards Averey, waiting for him to tell me what it was. He shook his head.

"Okay, save that for another time then. Still, I don't want to be a Queen," I said, now crossing my arms over each other as I leaned back.

Averey sighed. "Isadora, we didn't want to do this, but you will be in the running for Queen. We need to test you, too. We can't let you go without it."

I shook my head and licked my lips. Nothing had gone smoothly that day.

"Okay, let's do that now then," I said.

"It isn't that simple, and we only do it when the other Witches are here, too. It takes time to prepare, and we don't want to do it with one now," Cian told me.

I huffed out a breath. "Okay, fine, I will wait for that test. Still there are a few more things. One, I will not be introduced to the others as a Witch. Second, I will keep up with my training as a Protector. I hope you guys have room for me to train?" I arched an eyebrow in question to them.

"Yes. The other exit of this room, through the door on the other side of the hallway and then the last door right outside from there," Flynn said. I almost stared at him, he had said so much. I knew he had said that much at once already. Only, every time I heard him speak, he grabbed my attention.

"You can train there whenever you want," Averey added, and my head whipped to him and a quick smile spread over his lips. It had me blushing for a second, busted.

"And about you being introduced as a Witch, we have to inform the Council of this." Cian started.

"No." I answered back. "Look I'm going to stay, I'm going to go along with the whole testing thing for the Queen stuff. But no, please don't," I pleaded. If too many people knew that I was a Witch it would have led to questions. If there was one Witch or Elemental who knew my ancestors, it would mean that I would be screwed. And not the fun kind of way.

"We will keep it silent as long as we can," Rayan said. I looked at him, closed my eyes, and breathed out. I bowed my head a little to him and relaxed a little more.

"So, what are these tests?" I asked when I got my emotions back in line.

"You have to go on dates," Astra said. I looked at her, my eyes wide.

"Dates, you mean with them?" I waved my hand towards the Kings.

Rayan grabbed his chest and said. "Ow, the pain of rejection, it is too strong." And he let himself fall to the side on the sofa. It made me chuckle a little, and he winked from where he lay on Cian's lap.

"Yes, that is one part of the process. You go on a date with each of us, or more if we want."

"I thought it was a magic thing, like hocus pocus, poof, and you can see if we are a match?" I waved my finger through the air. "Why the dates?"

"We need to like the Witch, too, or at least see if we don't like them. And the test shows that if we aren't compatible together, we could still bond. Only, it wouldn't work as well. If we liked the Witch and we are compatible, we would bond, and we would be stronger for it," Cian explained, while he absentmindedly moved his hands in Rayan's hair. It looked sweet, I could have watched them all day long.

"And what if you are each other's soulmate?" Astra asked. I looked from her back to Cian, that was something I had wondered, too. What would happen if you were more than compatible, if you were meant for each other?

"Then you would be a Natural Bond to each other, you would be the person's other part," he explained. "It would mean that you would be not only stronger, you could become more powerful. It depends all on the person with whom you are bonded."

I looked at him and narrowed my eyes a little, not totally getting what he was saying. He saw my look and explained it again, this time differently.

"You have to look at it like this, you would become one. You would bring your magic to the party, and the other, your bonded, would bring hers to it. Meaning you could use double; your own and the amount the other has. It is almost like a rechargeable battery. However, one is the battery and the other the charger. But." He held his hand up, so I closed my mouth. I had wanted to place a joke in there. Come on, who wouldn't have? Charger, battery . . . two people.

"It works the other way around, too. You become more powerful than you already are. Only, that is when you have a Natural Bonded. Meaning that when you find your 'soulmate' as you called it, Astra, you would Bond without a ceremony; it would happen naturally. You will feel a pull towards the other person, or that is what the books say. We haven't had a natural Bond in years."

From the corner of my eye, I could see Astra looking at me, a question in her eyes, and I shook my head. It was not the time for it. I'd had the same idea as she had. Because if I ever found my Bonded, I would be even stronger than I was then, and the other would probably become Full-Blood level strong.

"Is that why you guys have this whole Selection thing? To find a Natural Bond?" I asked Cian.

"No, we have these Selections, so we can find the closest thing to a Natural Bond. That is why we have these tests, dates, and in the end, the Bonding ceremony."

"Okay, so dates." Rayan moved to a sitting position. "When do we start?" he asked. And I rolled my eyes. "You figure all that out, I'm going to unpack," I said as I got up, and for the second time that day, stepped out of their living room. I needed some time to think.

14

I reached the room, picked up my bags, and moved them to my bedroom. I needed to train and get my head back in line. And my emotions needed to be shoved so far in the darkest corner of my mind, that I could focus on what was important without distractions. And not on the dates, or the Kings. Definitely not the Kings.

I changed into a pink sports bra, a black tank-top, some sweatpants, and my sport shoes. I placed my swords on my back and left the rest of my weapons in the room. Before I walked out of the living room, I concentrated on my magic and pulled a little up. If I was to stay there, I needed to secure my room. I sent out my senses and pushed out my magic with it. Imagining it as a bubble, I began blowing it up bigger and bigger, so it would fill all my rooms with a small layer of magic. Some magic nobody would see and only the strongest would feel. I placed another layer over it, this one infused with a warning for me, almost as if I had placed a few strings around the room. I would feel the pull if someone walked into the room. That was one trick I had learned from Gran, she had found it important that I knew how to protect myself. I had never used it in school, too many people would have noticed.

When that was done, I left my room and went looking

for the long way around to the training rooms. I didn't want to walk through the Kings' quarters again, and I had wanted some peace to think and empty my head before I started my training. I walked left, reached the stairs and went down those. We had never gotten that tour from Rayan. I needed to ask the directions from one of the servants. He looked down his nose at me, then at my swords; after spotting them, he answered quickly. An Elemental, then; solely they and Witches acted like that around Protectors.

"Behind the stairs are double doors, they lead to the work area of the Castle, walk the first hallway out, go to the right and walk that hallway out. You will reach another double door to your right. Never go into that one. Those are the Kings' Quarters. You can't go in there, except when you are invited. The door to where you need to be is opposite their rooms," he said and moved away before I could thank him. Not that I had wanted to, still it would have been polite. I moved towards the doors he mentioned and walked into a hallway, the windows to my right showed the garden again, I loved the light they let in, lighting up the hallways. I reached the end of the hall and turned right, and kept walking. Coming past a lot of different doors. People walked past me, some gave me a small nod and others ignored me, or they were too busy to notice. I saw a few other Protectors walking around, they nodded at me.

When I reached the end of the hallway, and the double doors to my right, I turned left and opened the simple wooden door. I entered another hallway, this one smaller and darker. I heard the clashing of steel on steel. The grunting of people fighting and training. I was in the right area. I moved further, finding a door at the end in front of me and one on my right.

I opened the one to my right. I guessed correctly, this was the indoor training room. It was filled with men and women working out. Some were fighting together, the weapons smashing. Sounds reverberated through the room, the hard clanging made me feel at ease right away.

I looked around, they had climbing walls, boxing sacks, a wall filled with weapons on my right, and high windows that let in light to my left; I could see the outside training fields, ringed by a wooden fence. There were a few people out there, too. I wondered how many Protectors the Kings had in the castle. Today was the first time I had seen them or noticed them. That needed to change. If I wanted to know more about Nox, I would need help. I started to prepare myself for my training. When I looked around to find a good spot to train, someone interrupted me.

"Why are you standing there? Place your weapons there and get in line!" a male yelled at me. Three lines on his right arm showed me that he was a third chief. The third in line for chief and the fourth in line after the commander. And that would be Flynn. I arched an eyebrow at him and looked over the group of men and women standing behind him, all spaced evenly and with their hands behind their backs. They seemed to be starting a training session. I smiled at him; that would be a nice way to warm up. I removed my swords, placing them against the wall, and walked up to the rows of Protectors. Before I reached a spot, I found Lars—the Protector who had driven me to Icas Nox's house, He gave me a small nod and turned his head, indicating the empty spot next to him. He was standing in the second row, and I moved towards him. On the other side of me, stood a woman. I nodded at her, and she looked me over and then looked back to the front. I looked back at Lars and shrugged. He simply smiled and also focused back to the front.

"Are you done looking around?" the chief yelled from his spot.

I looked at the woman next to me before I realized he was talking to me. "Rookie," Someone muttered under a fake cough. Not caring, I focused on the Chief in front of us and gave him my biggest smile.

"Stop smiling!" he yelled again. Already wondering if he had an off switch for the yelling, I kept the smile on my face. "Rookie, quit smiling. It seems that you are new here, so try to keep up!" he yelled, a little lower than he had at first. I nodded at him and waited for his instructions.

Lars whispered to me from my side, "Don't provoke him if you want to keep walking at the end of the training. He always makes the new guys work harder. This isn't Protector school anymore, this is real." I arched my eyebrow at him. What did he think, that I was just a newbie, fresh from school? Did he already forget that he had driven me to Nox's house?

Before I could answer, the chief yelled again. "Keep it up!"

"You are now named Loud Mouth. LM for short," I mumbled at him, and I heard a chuckle from my left.

LM took a basic position and yelled over his shoulder, "Rookie, we will start slow for you." That earned a few more chuckles from the others. I didn't answer, why would I? It would be easy.

I mimicked his stance, feet apart, one to the front the other in the back, knees bent a little and arms in front of my face. Upper body a little turned, so I became a smaller target.

He started with punching, right, left. Then he kicked out, right, stepped to the front and kicked with his left. I followed the movements without thinking. Those were basics, I could do them with a blindfold on after the first two years of school. We moved through all the basics, each of them getting faster and faster after he noticed that I was keeping up.

I could see him working hard to make me falter. Still I kept up, sweat starting to form on my back. I followed his movements, I jumped when he jumped, I kicked out when he kicked. He jumped in the air and kicked out, landing in crouch, I did the same and added another kick to it before I landed.

The other Protectors were starting to breathe hard, and one of them wobbled when he almost landed wrong.

"Drink some water!" LM yelled at us. I got up and walked over to my swords. My tank-top was sticking a little to my back. I pulled it off and placed it next to my swords. I hadn't taken any water with me, so I looked around. A bottle of water appeared in front of me, I looked to the person holding it, it was Lars. I smiled at him and thanked him, then took a few sips. Before I could drink more we were called back again by the Loud Mouth.

The woman who had stood next to me still wore her tank-top, she looked me up and down again and gave me a smile. I winked back at her and walked over to the chief.

"We are going to fight one on one. Form a circle!" he yelled. Why did he yell so much? We could all hear him. I rolled my eyes at that thought. Still, I moved with the rest when they moved into a circle.

"Rookie!" He yelled at me. I looked at him as I waited for his instructions. "You first."

I moved forward into the ring. Someone whistled, and I swayed my hips a little and smiled sweetly towards the whistler. I pulled my hair band out and braided my hair quickly. So much easier than a ponytail.

"Are you done doing your hair?" LM asked me, his arms folded over his chest.

"No, give me a second." I answered and braided the last part, placed the elastic back and flipped it over my shoulder to my back. "Now I'm done." I gave him a smile and waited for further instructions.

"You will be fighting me. I want to see what you can do, Rookie!" LM shouted. Even though I stood in front of him.

"Are you sure?" I answered. I heard some of the others sucking in a breath, while others chuckled. The chief didn't react to it and said. "Take your position, a fight until I end it." He bent his knees and positioned himself in the basic stance. I loosened my shoulders.

"Take your position," LM said again.

"I have." I answered back, my hands loose next to my body, my knees a little bent, and still balancing on the balls of my feet. He smirked at me, thinking that it would be an easy fight.

"Are you sure, Rookie?" he asked again, mocking me, and the Protectors chuckled again.

"Yeah," was all I answered. He came at me, fast. Like all the Protectors, we were trained to be the best, fastest, and the strongest. We had been pushed to reach past our limits, and, obviously, so had he. He swung with his right, I turned my body. His fist flew along the side of my face, the wind of it kissed my skin. I grabbed hold of his upper arm and used his momentum to place my shoulder against his chest and swing him over my shoulder. He came down with an oomph. I turned around, and he got up fast. He took a new position as I relaxed back into my own stance. He started circling me. He kept his knees bent, ready for an attack. I waited. He kept circling, wanting to make me feel like his prey. Didn't he know that wouldn't work with me?

"What is it, Rookie, not wanting to start the fight? Are you too scared to do something?" he taunted. Or tried to, anyway.

"Why would I? This costs you more energy than me." I shrugged at him, it was true. That walking around me, it cost him energy, while I was preserving mine and still focused on him without moving around. He stopped moving, I could almost hear him thinking.

How had that guy made it to third chief? I looked at him, strong muscles, short brown hair and light-brown eyes. He looked smart, and he definitely looked like Protector material. There must have been something that made him third chief, or the standards had dropped terribly from what they had taught us in school. He cocked his head. "Why are you here?"

Ah, there were the brains. He then said, "Show me why you were selected to become a Protector to the Kings."

I gave him a smile, he thought I was there for the Kings. This would be fun.

"Okay," I answered. He charged me again, but I crouched low and kicked out my feet, sweeping his feet from under him; he dropped. He rolled with it and got up, close enough for him to start punching. He came close, but still missed my head. I gave him a punch in the stomach and one to his liver before moving out of the way, by dancing back. He moved with me, kicked out to my head. I blocked, grabbed his leg, and pulled him closer, then kicked out with my right and hit him on his jaw. He managed to block a part of it, still he would have had a ringing ear from that one. I dropped his leg, so I could punch his stomach and liver again and moved back. He moved with me. He faked a punch to the right to kick out with his right foot, it hit my shoulder. It wasn't as hard as what the Ilunias had hit me with, still I would feel it later. I moved with it and kicked out my leg, catching his. His other leg hadn't reached the floor yet, and he dropped to the ground like a sack of potatoes. I jumped on him, pinning him down with my feet pressed over his crotch and my arms holding his. If he moved, I would have squashed his balls, and he knew it.

"You need to learn to relax when you fight. You gave everything away, and you are more focused on making me angry than watching what I do."

"I still hit you," he said.

"Lucky shot," I answered, because it had been that, a lucky shot.

"Who are you?" he asked through laboured breathing, this time not yelling. So, I got up and stood next to him, offering him my hand to help him get up.

"I'm Isadora, chief," I answered, giving him some respect by adding his title.

"And she is part of the Selection," I heard Flynn from my right. I rolled my eyes and turned around. All the protectors bowed a little, it was more a bow with their head then an actual bow. Still it had showed a lot of respect for the King that was in front of them.

When I looked at him, his eyes bore into mine. He looked like he wanted to punch something, and honestly, I hoped it wasn't me. Before I could say anything more, to make the situation worse than it already was, I clenched my mouth shut. Because if they knew I was part of the selection, they knew I was a Witch. Only Witches could be in the Selection.

"And she is off limits!" he boomed out and looked around the room. His eyes landed on the third chief next to me. That had me speechless, and I knew my mouth was hanging open.

"Yes, Your Highness," they all said. Oh, hell no, he had not just ordered them all away from me.

"How am I going to train now?" I asked him while I walked over to where he stood.

His eyes roamed over my body, stopping on my pink sports bra and probably the breasts trapped in it. His gaze had made my breath hitch for a moment, and more things heated up. His gaze darkened, and he moved his eyes to my face. I needed a distraction, so I moved to gather my swords.

"Let's go," he said, his fingers ticked a rhythm out on his upper leg, distracting me. "Now, Isadora!" he added, his voice booming through the room. I cringed a little.

"I'm not some child," I said to him. I could hear people sucking in their breaths. Oh, purple canaries and more.

"'I'm not some child,' Your Highness." That had someone chuckling behind me. Flynn's head whipped to the person, and his gaze darkened more. This time not from the idea of sex, no, from the idea of murdering someone. I looked over my shoulder, one male was really pale. The third chief. It was my turn to chuckle a little then. Still, I didn't want to make things worse. I walked away with my swords and top in hand. I heard Flynn following me. When we reached the hallway, he grabbed my shoulder and turned me around.

It happened so quickly I stumbled a little, but he held me upright. His powerful hands were warm on my shoulders, the heat seeping further into my body, sinking low. Resting in the one spot I really wanted his hands. I blushed at the thought and looked at my shoes. I couldn't let him see what he was doing to me, I didn't want to see what he was doing to me.

"Isa." His voice was soft and low, the rumbling vibrated through me, and it did nothing to help the state I was already in. "Isa," he said again, his voice a little stronger; it made me look at him. His dark eyes looked black in the darkened hallway, an endless pool I had wanted to disappear in and not get out of, ever.

"It's good, that you are this good. However, you can't beat the third chief into the ground in a few seconds," he started.

"Why not? If he can't fight me, then he doesn't deserve to be a third chief."

"You are right and also not. A chief, no matter which one of them, isn't someone who fights the best, he or she also needs to carry the responsibility to keep the people under him safe. To know strategy and make the hard decisions." His voice was still soft, and his hands were softly kneading my shoulders, which had me almost moaning. I leaned a little towards him, his hands stilled for a moment before he continued.

"We chose him because he is good, he is smart and has insights that are needed." I looked up at Flynn, what he had said was vague.

Before I could ask why they were needed, he interrupted me. "No, I won't tell. You are still a Selection member, not a Queen," he said. His eyes moved to my mouth, and I lost all the thoughts I had. Just one came back up, *Kiss him*.

Before I could lean towards him, he had moved away.

"Give the chief the respect he needs, and remember, maybe he was toying with you today. He isn't bad or weak. You," he looked me over again before continuing, "have a unique style of fighting." He turned around and left. The lingering smell of burned wood stayed with me. Fire, that was his preferred element. The emptiness in front of me filled with cold, and I shuddered. I definitely needed a good shower and an amazing shower head.

Flynn brought me out of my fantasy of him and the shower head when he said, "Next time, fight with us if you really want a challenge." And with that he went through the door and left me alone.

15

I walked towards my room, when I entered, I closed the door behind me and stood still against it. Letting my head fall back my eyes closed, I breathed slowly for a moment, willing my mind to rest. It didn't work at all. I needed a shower. Walking straight towards the bathroom, I pulled off my clothing along the way. Turning on the shower head, I moved under the warm water. After a few moments, my muscles relaxed, but my mind still didn't.

"What did you do?" I heard from the bedroom.

"Nothing, As. Why?" I asked her. I heard her moving into the bathroom.

"I was talking with Rayan and Cian, about the whole date thing, and Flynn came in all gruff and angry."

That had me turning around, to face her. "How do you mean angry?" He didn't seem angry when he'd walked away. Maybe before that, he had looked angry.

"He didn't say much. It just rolled off of him," Astra said while she sat down on the chair in the bathroom.

"And why do you think I had something to do with it?" I folded my arms over my chest and looked at her.

"Because he was mumbling about you. He said something like this." Astra placed her hands by her side and puffed out her chest. It made me giggle. "That bloody woman. She just beat Monroe without breaking a sweat." Astra's voice was pitched low, almost like Flynn's. It made me laugh properly then.

"How? How did you know I was 'That bloody woman?'" I asked her, still laughing.

"Because you are the only person, I know who can beat someone without breaking a sweat," she answered.

"Not true, I think there are a few here who could make me sweat," I told her, my mind wandering towards the muscled bodies of the Kings. I was happy then that the glass shower wall had a wide blurred strip on it. She couldn't see my nipples harden. I didn't mind her coming into the bathroom, afterall, we'd lived together for years. However I didn't want her to see my body's reaction to the Kings. No, that wasn't something I wanted to share. She needed to become the Queen of one of them. The weird longing, I felt and the attraction I had to them needed to stay secret from her.

She giggled at what I had said. "Yeah." Was the only thing she could get out. Her mind had probably wandered around like mine had.

"What did the others say?" I asked her, remembering that she had told me that she had been talking with Rayan and Cian.

"They chuckled and told him that he doesn't need to worry." Astra pulled her leg up and placed her arm around it, so she could rest her chin on her knee. "What did you think they meant with not worrying about it?"

I held my head back under the warm water to start washing my hair and thought about what she asked. I had unpacked the amazing-smelling shampoo, still Flynn was right, I had undermined the third chief they chose. It could have meant trouble in the hierarchy of the Protectors. We may not have liked Witches that much, but the way they ranked their people was a great system. We used it, too, testing your strength, fighting skills, and level of intelligence to see where you would be placed. Where your strengths would be used to the fullest. Like Flynn had already said, LM was chosen because of his full skill set.

"I think I need to resolve something, I beat the third chief today. To be honest it wasn't that easy. He got a good punch on me, and that hasn't happened in a long time." I moved my hand over the bruise that had started forming on my shoulder. "That aside, I think I also need to apologize for not talking respectfully to the Kings." I looked at the water that pooled around my feet.

"What did you do now?" Astra asked, her lips thinned out, and she rubbed a hand over her neck.

"I, kind of, sort of, forgot to say 'Your Highness' to Flynn," I told her. I knew I didn't say it all the time, but I was undermining him and his position in front of the Protectors. She laughed and the frown on her face disappeared.

"That is all?" she asked. "You have never said 'Your Highness' to them or bowed to them. I think you are the only one in this whole world who doesn't say that or doesn't bow to them and gets away with it." She placed her foot back on the floor and looked at me seriously.

"Isa, if they don't mind that you don't say it, it is fine. Only, you need to start acting like a Selection member, like a Witch. Because that is what you are, and that is what you will be from now on. And you really need to start using the right words around them."

I turned off the shower, it suddenly wasn't that heavenly. When I opened the door, Astra stood there with a towel in her hands. I took it, giving her a small thankful smile.

"I know, As, I know. Only, I don't know how," I told her while I wrapped the towel around me. "Like I said to the Kings, I don't want everyone to know that I'm a Witch. And they agreed on keeping it silent for now. Let me be a Protector for as long as I can be." I moved towards the bedroom, the towel still around me and still dripping water from the rest of me.

"As, I'm . . ." I started. I wasn't sure what to tell her. That I was in a place I shouldn't be, that I was in the house where my Great-Grandmother had ruled the world, where my Gran had grown up. Where they had murdered my ancestors.

"You're what?"

"I never planned on coming here, I never planned on being here." I waved my hands around. "I planned on going to my home, to stay away from all of this. You know what I am. You know that if the wrong people knew, I would be in trouble." I had never told her why going here would be such a problem, why it was dangerous for me that people knew I was a Witch. If there was someone out there that knew what my Great-Grandmother, the last Queen, looked like, they would have connected the dots. Gran always said I looked like her, I had reminded her of her mother, in almost every way.

I was lucky that I hadn't found any paintings of Seraphine hanging around. I had no idea if she truly looked like me or I like her. I still didn't want to test it out.

"I will do my best to be better, different," I told her, while I started drying my body and hair. Astra had moved out of the bathroom with me, she was sitting in a chair.

She looked at me and nodded. "Okay, good. Now the reason I really came to see you." I turned around and looked at her. "The other Witches will be here in a few days, they hope. They will be starting the test tomorrow at the schools. Depending on where the schools are, they will take between a few hours or days to get here. They gave us two days free, to make sure they kept it fair to the others. And that we didn't get more 'Date time' with the Kings than the others."

"Okay, sounds fair. And what will we be doing for those two days?" I asked her, happy that we didn't have to date the Kings right away. That we could look around in the castle a little bit before it would be full of irritating

Witches. We would be having a few more days of peace, a few more days to explore.

"That is for us to decide. They said if we wanted to go out of the Castle, we needed to inform them, so they could send a protection detail with us."

I rolled my eyes at that, then pulled on some underwear and a new sports bra, my black cargo pants, and a black tank top, I picked up my swords and placed them on my back. Next came my black leather jacket. With my boots in hand, I moved to the bed to pull those on, too. Finally, I pulled my hair into a ponytail and looked to Astra.

"Okay, what do you want to do first then?" I asked her.

"Let's explore the castle some more?"

"Yeah, sure." I got up and walked towards the living room. "Where do you want to start?"

"Let's start in the main entrance and go from there, we can walk in a circle. This castle is a square, so everything is connected, and I would love to see the garden finally."

We moved into the hallway. There was a Protector at the door of the Kings. He looked at us and mumbled, "Chief." I gave him an arched eyebrow and moved away.

"Why did he say 'Chief?'" Astra asked when we were far enough away from him.

"Nothing," I answered back, not wanting to explain it to her, not wanting to tell her that being called Chief is a way that a Protector tells another that he or she is better then them. When you become the Chief, it means you are in command of all the Protectors. You are the best. It is a way of showing respect.

"So, where do we go first?" I asked when we walked into the main hall. We looked over the railing downstairs.

"Uhm, let's go to the ballroom first, then from there to the halls next to it and see where it takes us?" Astra said while she waved her hand towards the big doors that stood open.

"Yeah. And then find a kitchen for some food. I haven't had lunch yet," I told her.

"We can do that first if you want," she said when she walked towards the stairs.

"No, I'm fine, we can do the exploring first, we don't even know where the kitchen is."

"Oh, I think you can find that fast enough." Astra chuckled.

I shook my head and walked after her. We moved towards the ballroom. It was a big room with high ceilings. Chandeliers hung in a row reflecting the sunlight and projecting colours on the walls. Then there were the arched windows to our right and a big glass door at our left that showed the garden. There were dark-red drapes hanging next to the windows. They hung from the ceiling to the floor, where they rested on the polished marble; it almost looked like a mirror. At the end of the long hall, was a raised platform. That was probably where the musicians played and the place where the Kings' thrones sat, if there was a party in here. The walls were a soft white and covered in golden ornaments. The sunlight made it all seem more golden, almost if we stepped into a fairy tale.

"It is amazing," Astra said, she walked in front of me and twirled around.

I walked up to her and bowed. "Can I have this dance from you, my Lady?" I joked, holding out my hand.

"Of course, my good sir," Astra answered, and she placed her hand in mine. We started moving through one of the dances we had been taught at school. We laughed while we twirled around, dancing throughout that big room and just enjoyed it. When we reached the other side of the room, we were a little out of breath and still laughing.

I wiped away a tear that had escaped my eyes. "Thank you, my Lady," I said and bowed to her, she pretended to hold her skirt and bowed to me, too. We started laughing again. The tears rolled down our cheeks as we caught our breaths.

"My Lady, let's escape these prying eyes and go for a

stroll in the garden," I said and tried to keep my face straight, which didn't really work.

"Yes, good sir," she answered, and I turned around then froze. Averey was standing in the door opening. His eyes roamed over me slowly. I looked down to the floor before he could see me blush.

"Your Highness," Astra said when she noticed him, too. "We were just looking around."

"That is fine. I was just wondering who was laughing so much in here." I looked up at him. His eyes were still focused on me, though he spoke to Astra. "We haven't had that much laughter in this room in a long time."

"Maybe you should have a party then," I said. "Eh, Your Highness," I added quickly.

"Maybe we should, Isadora." He said my name slowly, almost as if it meant something more.

"Come, As," I said and pulled her along towards the garden doors.

"If you two want, you can also check out our library," Averey said when we reached the glass doors.

"Yes, thank you," I said and pushed them open not knowing what else to say.

We walked into the inner garden, where we were greeted by the smell of flowers, earth, and grass. I breathed in deeply, feeling connected to the garden right away. It would quickly become one of my favourite places in the castle. We moved around, walking over the small paths that wove through the gardens. Surrounded by rose bushes and other flowers, we walked in silence. Both of us were lost in our own minds. Sometimes, when you were friends that long, talking wasn't necessary, I enjoyed her company and silence. It gave me the time to think about Kings, no, things. Other things, nothing that had to do with Kings. Not thinking about the Kings just other things, not their things. Just other things, a tree, yes, I thought about trees. Long hard trees.

"Purple canary," I grumbled. Luckily, Astra hadn't heard.

"Who do you think will be the other Selection Witches?" Astra asked. Thank you, Astra, for speaking. My mind had needed to go back to normal things.

"I don't know. I think we will find out soon enough," I told her while we kept on walking. We were almost back to the glass doors, instead these were the glass doors that led towards the main hall.

"Come, let's go to the main hall and move towards the other side of the castle. I think the kitchen is there," I told her. We moved through the main garden doors, which were open. After looking around, we found a double door to our right that seemed to lead us towards the other side of the castle. We walked through it and entered a hallway, it was amazing to see how everything was opened up on the lower levels of the castle. Instead of making it a stuffy dark place, it was filled with natural light. The garden, which seemed to be the heart of the castle, was visible from almost everywhere. We walked around the corner, and the doors changed from elaborate to simple. I hadn't noticed that this morning.

This hall was full of servants who were walking around, carrying trays and other things, they all greeted us with a smile. Some of the Protectors we saw nodded at us, and I gave them a smile. We reach a door that was standing open slightly. And the smell of fresh baked bread made us stop.

"Kitchen?" I asked Astra and pointed towards the door we had both been sniffing at. How I missed this door this morning I have no idea.

"Yes." And she walked into the room. I followed quickly. The kitchen was filled with people, some wearing white shorts, while others wore the full black suits indicating they were servants. They all walked around quickly, almost like a nest of worker ants.

"What are you ladies doing here?"

I looked towards the voice, my mouth falling open when I found Rayan sitting at the table in the corner.

"What are you doing here?" I asked him, totally forgetting the question he had asked me.

"We may be Kings, but it doesn't mean we don't know where to find the kitchen." He laughed and motioned for us to take one of the empty chairs. I sat down next to him, so I could look towards the kitchen, watching them all work. Astra took a seat on the other side. I was looking at a big round bellied man. When he noticed us sitting next to Rayan, he placed his spoon on the counter and moved towards us. The man's round belly covered was in flour and other food products. His moustache covered his upper lip and curled down to the sides. Grey hair peeked out from under his hood and his rosy-red apple cheeks smiled down at us.

"I would like some food for the beautiful ladies," Rayan said.

"Yes, my King. What can I get for you two?" the cook asked.

"Whatever you are making," I told him, the saliva was already filling my mouth. The smells coming from the pans that stood on the stoves on the opposite of where we were, were mouth-watering. The big wooden work table in the middle was full of herbs and spices, chopped vegetables, and other things. People were stirring pots, chopping things, or tasting foods. One person pulled bread out from an old fire oven in the left corner of the kitchen, the smell made my stomach growl.

"It smells amazing in here," I said to the cook.

"I'll get you girls something." He walked away, his voice booming over the noise in the kitchen, ordering plates for us. In a few minutes, the table was loaded with food.

I started picking out things and started eating. "Mmmmh, oh, yeah," I mumbled when I took a bite of some chicken.

"You really like that chicken, don't you?" Rayan asked me. I nodded at him, my mouth full of chicken.

"What are you two going to do tonight?" Rayan asked us.

I shrugged. "Probably sleeping," I answered him when my mouth was empty.

"I think some reading, or walking in the garden," Astra answered.

"Okay, and what will you two be doing after you have finished this late lunch?" Rayan waved at the food on the table.

"Eat dinner," I said to him.

This made him laugh, and Astra gave me a smile and said, "We were exploring the castle, so going on with that."

"Okay, okay. And after that?" Rayan pressed on.

"We have no other plans after that," I told him when my plate was empty, I was still nibbling on a piece of bread that tasted like heaven.

"What have you already seen?" he asked us.

"We have seen the ballroom, the garden, and this side of the ground floor of the Castle," Astra answered. I took a sip of the water that was in front of me and studied Rayan. He was leaning a little back in his chair, relaxed. He looked at home here, his arm slung over one side of the back of the chair and an easy smile on his face. Astra told him about the garden, how she had liked it and would be going there a lot. His mouth moved, and he said something. His lips formed words I didn't hear; my mind was already on kissing those lips. Some fingers snapped in front of me.

"Huh, what?" I asked when I refocused on the world around me. Rayan's blue eyes twinkled with mischief, his smile sultry. His eyes turned darker when he looked at me. Heat flared in them, and my body reacted. I took a sip of my water again, remembering I still held the glass between me and the table; floating.

"I told Astra about the other parts of the Castle, that they are kind of the same and boring."

"Oh, what is with the other end of the castle?" Astra snorted at that, and I looked at her.

"He was telling about the rest of the castle, that the other side of the building houses the guest rooms, they're where we sleep. On the ground level, we have the council rooms and more offices. And on this side, they have the rooms for important staff members and other important permanent guests. And then on the ground floor the, kitchen and other rooms like the laundry room and the training areas."

"Oh, we don't have to go exploring anymore." I arched an eyebrow at Rayan.

"Yes, now you both can come with me," he said and got up from his chair. I looked at Astra. She shrugged, got up, and followed.

"Thank you, cook," Rayan said when he walked past the cook.

"Yes, thank you," Astra said, too.

"It was amazing, thank you so much," I told him before walking after the other two.

16

I followed Rayan and Astra through the long hall. We reached their double doors, and for a moment, I thought we would have gone into their quarters again, except for Rayan to go through the left door. My mood lifted right away. It was the hall that would lead towards the training rooms. We moved to the end where he held open the door that led us outside. There were Protectors training on the fields outside. The sun stood high in the sky. Luckily for us, it was already on its way down. The heat would be replaced by cooler air soon. I looked around at the high walls with the Protectors who kept everyone safe. Trees that were scattered here and there that would provide some shade during the day on the training fields. It was hard to believe that it was only our second day there. So much had happened. The Ilunias, Astra being kidnapped, and now me being part of a Selection, meeting sexy-ass Kings. The one good thing about it all was that I could use my magic again; didn't have to hide anymore who I was. Okay, maybe I was still hiding, sort of, and still used my Protector training more. Only, I was freer than I had been in school.

"Where are we going?" I asked Rayan when I moved to

his side. Astra walked on his other side, she was looking around, too.

"You'll see," he answered with a wink to me.

I rolled my eyes at that. "I'm not a big fan of surprises."

"No, she isn't," Astra chimed in.

"Oh, why is that?" Rayan asked, a twinkle in his eyes, which made my stomach flutter with excitement and more.

"One time, we gave her a surprise party, when she was younger–" Astra started, her face had already lit up with the memory of the story she had started telling.

"No, As." I stared at her, trying to glare. Which made her to laugh.

"You have to hear this, King Rayan," Astra said. I didn't know how she remembered to say King every single time. She laughed again at my expression. I rolled my eyes and placed another glare on my face. If looks could kill, she would have been totally dead by now.

"Oh, now I need to know," Rayan said when he saw my face.

"No, you don't, either. Astra, shut up." I pouted at her.

"It was the first year of school, or second. Not sure. But we were young, keep that in mind," Astra added that, and I gave her a sour smile. At least she had told him we were young.

"And we gave her a surprise party. When she entered our room, we jumped out and yelled surprise. She . . ." Astra laughed. "She . . ." Her laughing kept interrupting her, so I finished.

"It scared me so badly I peed in my pants." I looked at the ground and listened to the laughing of Rayan and Astra.

When Rayan got his breathing under control, he said, "You, the one who stormed into this castle, fought three Ilunias, and sort of got Astra back all by herself, were scared of a surprise party?" He chuckled, Astra was still laughing, tears streaming down her face.

I stopped walking, held out my hand with one finger out and said, "First, I did save Astra. You guys barging in wasn't my idea. And we were perfectly fine without you. Second." I held up a second finger. "I was nine or so, and they scared me. I wasn't expecting them there. I hadn't had a birthday party in a long time. And third, that was before I knew I was this amazing person," I told him, adding a third finger to the two already in the air, my face blank. I heard Astra snicker next to him.

And with that, Rayan's face broke into a big grin. "My apologies. You *are* amazing." His eyes twinkled when he said that. When his gaze darkened, my breath hitched. Shitting baseballs, I needed to get away from them. They kept doing that to me, making me want to jump them. How could I want to jump four people at the same time? How could I want them all? I think one of the Ilunias had hit my head harder than I thought.

I collected myself and bowed to him and said, "Thank you, thank you." He laughed and started walking again. Astra and I moved next to him. "Where are we going?" I asked him again.

"You will see, we are almost there." He pointed towards a small Greek temple-style building.

"What is in there?" I asked him.

"You will see. Are you always this impatient?" He chuckled.

We reached the building made from white marble. The stone columns carried a simple roof, and there were no windows that I could see. Except for the small wooden door. Rayan opened it and moved into the building. He needed to bend a little, whereas I just walked through it, skimming the top of the doorpost. Astra fit perfectly through it, too. We entered a moist area; the lights were off. Everything was dark, and for a second, it reminded me of the surprise party we were just talking about. Then Rayan switched on the light, and we were standing in front of a pool. The pool was surrounded by a mosaic, portraying different things from flowers to creatures that didn't exist anymore. The walls were also decorated with mosaics. It was beautiful. We both just stood there, looking around in awe.

"You girls can change there. You will find some bathing suits in the small cabin in that room, also a few towels. Feel free to stay as long as you want." Rayan motioned towards the pool in front of us. The steam rose from it, a few underwater benches lined one side of the pool. He walked back towards the door.

"You aren't coming in with us?" I asked him, when he walked past me.

"No, I thought you two needed some time alone together and relaxing." He looked to the door. "And I have work to do." With that he left us alone.

I looked at Astra, to see a twinkle in her eyes. My face lit up from the idea of a relaxing swim. We both moved towards the dressing room. We pulled open the cabinet with the bathing suits. Astra pulled out a triangle top and some bottom with strings on the side, in a deep dark-red colour. I looked around, finding a black triangle top with simple black bottoms. We both changed, and I grabbed two towels from the cabin before I walked after Astra towards the pool. I dropped the towels on one of the stone benches that lined the walls and dove into the warm water.

I felt everything relax almost immediately. The warm water washed away the stress and tension inside my body. When I came up, Astra jumped in next to me, spraying me with water. I laughed. When she came up, I splashed her with water, and we played like that for some time.

"Come let's–" I started saying, only to be sprayed with water. Coughing, I looked at As. She giggled. "–relax." I finished what I had wanted to say, and moved towards the underwater bench in the pool. I sat down, placed my arms on the ledge behind me, and looked around. The ceiling had one big mosaic scene on it, showing a night sky dotted with flying dragons. Those were a myth. Still, it was amazingly made. We both sat in silence, and I closed my eyes, letting the water relax me even more. I heard water splashing next to me and opened one eye to look at Astra. She was using her magic to make animals out of the water. A few horses ran past me over the water, they looked good. It had my full attention. She let them run all over the pool. When they reached her again, she formed them into dolphins, swimming in the water, jumping up out of it.

"It is good that you are here," I said to her, my eyes on the next group of animals she made, elephants. They walked towards me, lifted up their trunks and sprayed water in my face. I laughed, Astra did, too. It sounded relaxed.

"Yeah, I'm happy to be here, too."

"Did you tell your parents that you are here?" We hadn't really talked about her parents or Icas Nox.

"No."

"Are you going to tell them?" I turned a little, so I could look at her. I let my arms float on the water, slowly moving them around.

"No."

With that I stopped moving my arms and fully focused on her. "Why not?"

She turned to face me, too.

"Then what? Tell them I'm in the Castle, part of the Selection to become Queen. Because my best friend brought me here?"

I cringed a little at her words. "As, you got yourself here. You are the strongest of the whole school. You mastered three elements, *three*. That is a lot."

She looked at her hands in the water.

"Look Astra, you are strong, beautiful, and you have a good heart. You can do this, you can become a Queen to one of the Kings," I told her.

"No, I can't," she said, her voice soft.

"Why not?" My eyebrows pulled together, worry seeped into me.

"I can't. I can't give them what they want." She now looked at me, her bright-blue eyes bore into mine, willing me to read between the lines. She stayed still for a few seconds longer making me fidget in my seat. What was pressing on her that she turned from a happy and relaxed woman to this somber person?

"Astra, what is going on?" I asked her. She moved in the water, hugged herself.

"As, please tell me. You know you can tell me everything," I told her, while I moved to grab her hands. She looked at me, tears formed in her eyes.

"You know . . ." she started, her eyes moved back to the bottom of the pool.

"What do I know?" I squeezed her hands. She sighed

"You know how my parents are. How they want the best of the best. How they want me to produce a strong and healthy bloodline. They married me off to Icas Nox because of that idea."

"Yeah," I answered, not knowing where she was going with this. She kept silent again. "As, you are here now. You will win one of the King's hearts, and you will live happily ever after." A surge of jealousy entered my heart. As much I had wished everything good for her, the idea of someone else with the Kings nauseated me. I pushed the feeling down; she needed one of them more than I did. It would give her peace from her family, a way to truly escape Icas Nox. All I could think at that time was if she didn't become a Queen, who knows what he would do to her?

"That is the problem. I can't." She swallowed. "I can't make them happy. I will never make them happy, or get children or a happy ending," she told me.

"What do you mean, are you infertile?" My eyes were focused on her.

She shook her head. "No. I'm . . . I'm gay," she said. A laugh burst out of me. Astra pulled her hands away so fast, she had pulled me a little forward. "That isn't funny, Isa!" she yelled at me, her hands splashing up water.

"Yes, it is, As." I contained my laughter, swallowed it in, because I was imagining the worst.

"No, it isn't. My parents will hate me even more for not continuing the family line, for loving another woman. For being different." She was shaking. I pulled her in for a hug, and she hiccupped the moment she was sitting in my arms. A haggard breath followed, and I knew she was crying.

"It will be fine, Astra. I will be there to protect you from all that. You can always come and live with me. And we will find a woman for you to love and be happy with." I stroked her hair.

"Are you sure?" she asked me through her crying.

"Yes, As. It isn't a big deal, not for me. And we don't have to tell your parents. But we have to tell the Kings. They need to know that you don't swing that way," I joked at her, it made her chuckle.

"You are right," she said and pulled a little away.

"Why didn't you tell me this before?' I asked her. I had never noticed anything about her that may have suggested she liked women.

"I never knew how, and I never needed to," she said to me.

"Okay, now the most important question," I said to her, a smile on my face. Her face was puffed up from tears, and Astra tilted her head a little. Almost asking me, 'yeah?'

"Who do you like?" I giggled it out. "Oh, and why did we talk about all those male teachers when we were younger?" I asked her after that. She laughed. She was the one who always wanted to talk about the male teachers we had. "Yeah, I'm sorry. I didn't know how to share it with you, so I kept it inside. And for the girl I like; I like Banu." She said it softly while a blush crept onto her face.

"Not even me?" I asked her and placed my hand in mock offense on my chest.

"No, not you. You are my sister. That is enough of you in my life," she answered.

"Okay, fair enough. So, what's next? Does Banu know?" I asked her.

"I'm not sure," she answered. We had both known that Banu was a lesbian. She had told us when we were fourteen. Her parents were all okay with it, the Nulls didn't care about bloodlines. They cared about living every day to the fullest.

"We need to make sure she knows. I think she wouldn't mind that you have crush on her." I winked at her.

"Who has a crush on who?" we heard a woman's voice ask.

I looked towards the door, finding Violet there, a towel wrapped around her body and a sneer on her face.

"None of your business," I told her and focused back on Astra.

"It is, when it will be important to the Kings," Violet said as she moved closer to the pool's edge.

"Still, it is none of your business. Go irritate someone else." I waved my hand at her.

"No, you two need to go," she said, while she unwrapped her towel. She was a woman without many curves. She had an ugly green swimsuit on, one that made her look like a plant. Her hair was still in a bun on her head, I almost wanted to ask if she ever let her hair down.

Only, I was stopped when Astra to started speaking, "Why?"

"Because this pool is explicitly for people who have permission from the Kings to be here." With the last words, she had pushed out her chest a little.

"We have permission," Astra answered.

"Oh, and from who?" Violet asked and placed her hands on her hips as she looked down at us.

"Rayan," I told her.

"It is 'King Rayan' to you." Her eyes narrowed at me, and I smiled back at her. "I have seen scarier things than you," I told her. This made her blink a few times before she grinned.

"Are you sure?" And with that she lifted her hands, the water around us rose up into four walls, enclosing us.

I looked at Astra, and we both laughed, a full belly laugh. That woman forgot who she had in front of her. Astra stood up on the bench, I did the same. The water in the pool had dropped, leaving half of it filled. The other half was surrounding us. Astra moved her fingers a little, forcing a part to open. We both stepped out of the pool.

"You two think you can go against me?" Violet sneered.

"No," I answered. "She can beat you without much problem." I added while I pointed to Astra.

"Yeah, not tonight," she said, and with a movement of her hand, the water dropped back into the pool.

"You would think that the people in the council would be stronger than this," I told Astra, while we walked past Violet who looked at her hands.

"Yeah, you would think so," Astra answered, grabbing the towels, and we moved to the door.

"I will get you two, and I will find everything out!" Violet screamed to us. We both chuckled when we reached the dressing room. We wrapped the towels around our bodies, picked up our clothing and moved outside. We had stayed longer in the pool than I thought. When we walked out of the door, the sky was turning darker, a few stars even shone. We walked towards the castle, barefoot, the grass tickling them.

"She was really weak, wasn't she?" Astra asked me, when we were almost back to the castle.

"Who do you mean?" I asked her.

"Violet, that woman, who threatened us?"

"Oh, her? Yeah she was. Maybe she didn't rest enough?" I answered her when we entered through the small side door that would lead us towards the training halls and then to the servant's area of the building.

"She looked surprised when I cut through her magic, though, like she didn't expect it."

"Maybe you are stronger than you thought?" I said to her. I pushed open the door and let her in. We were both headed towards the bigger hallway when we walked into Averey.

"Hi, ladies," he greeted us. His eyes moved over my bare legs and up over the towel and then settled on my eyes. "Had a nice swim?"

"Yes. Oh, and Astra needs to tell you something," I said while I nudged her a little.

"No, Isa, not now," she grumbled.

"Yes, now. It will be easier. You don't know what Violet heard," I told her, giving her a pointed look.

"No," She grumbled and walked away.

"What's going on?" Cian asked when he opened the door. He looked at Astra, who had stormed away and then focused back on me. His eyes trailed the same path as Averey's had done.

"She doesn't want to be in the Selection to become Queen. Because she doesn't like your hanging bits," I told them. Their eyes went wide for a second.

"Oh. That is fine, we knew already," Cian said. This had me blinking stupidly. "Wait, you knew?" I stumbled out.

"Yes, we figured something from the first moment we met her. She wasn't checking us out as much as others do," Averey said, while he looked at me. His eyes narrowed, and a blush crept onto my face.

"Why are you keeping her in the Selection then?" I asked them.

"Because if she is part of the Selection, she will be safe from Nox," Cian told me.

I looked at him. "Okay, keep her in the Selection until it is solved or I can get her away," I told them and turned around after Astra. Before I could crawl into my bed, I needed food. I called for a meal and while I waited for that to come up. I took a shower and changed into my pyjamas.

When the food was brought up, I started eating at the small table, while I looked out of the window. The night sky turned darker with me watching it. When my plate was empty, I moved to my bed, it was time to put this day behind me. I wondered what tomorrow would bring, and with that I fell asleep.

17

———

"**G**et up." Someone pulled the blankets away, making me shiver when the cold air rushed over my skin.

"As, shut up." I tried to reach for the blanket, instead to feel a leg next to my bed. A very muscular leg. This had my eyes flying open. I looked at the person who was standing next to my bed. And for a second, I had hoped I was dreaming.

"What do you want, Flynn?" I grumbled at him. I moved to grab the blanket out of his hands, but he pulled them away again.

"Training, five minutes," he said and threw the blanket back on the bed.

"What are you talking about?" I asked after him.

"Training, in five minutes. Get your butt out of bed." He glared at me.

"Or what?" I asked with a smile on my face. I liked the bossy version of Flynn.

"Keep on going, and you will find out," he said, while he folded his arms in front of his chest. It distracted me from what I had wanted to say. His arms bulged with the movement. Before I could react, he moved towards me, picked me up, and threw me over his shoulder.

"What the duck?" I yelled at him and hit him on his ass, I kept hitting him, slapping his ass. His well-formed ass.

"Don't." He growled out, the rumble of his voice vibrated through me, making my body react. I hit him again, just to see what would happen. He smacked me back, his hand hitting my butt, and I squealed. I never squeal. Flynn bent down to pick something up, I couldn't see what it was. I slapped his ass again.

"Do it again, and you won't be sitting for the next few hours," he said when he started moving. He walked out of my room with me bouncing on his shoulder.

"What are you doing? I'm not dressed for training." I told him, he ignored me. "Flynn, put me down." I hit him in his side this time, but he didn't react.

"Come on man, put me down." I said and smacked his ass again. He smacked mine back. "Ouch," I mumbled. Only, everything inside me heated up. Never knew I would have liked getting spanked.

"I told you." His voice was low, almost husky.

"You like doing that." I grumbled at him. I knew he was laughing, I could feel it vibrate through me. I crossed my arms as much as I could in front of my chest and pouted the whole trip to the training grounds.

It was still dark outside when we reached the empty training field. The lights didn't really reach the centre of the training area where we were standing. Flynn moved the arm away that was holding me onto his shoulder. It made me slide a little down his front, and for a second, I expected to be dropped to the ground. But a hand held my ass, slowly letting me slide down his body. His hand moved up towards my back, while I moved down his body. When my feet reached the sand, I just stood there. My body was pressed against his, feeling all the hard muscle of him. I pushed away a little and looked around in the dark. I made some Witch lights and pushed them out into a circle around us, letting them float a little above the ground. Flynn looked at them, rubbing his chin when he slowly circled around. He shook his head, when he faced me his eyes narrowed, and he said. "Your Light. It isn't blue."

I shrugged in answer, not really knowing how to explain that one, I changed the subject. "Where are my weapons? I can't train without my swords." I placed my hands on my hips. Flynn pulled two swords from his other shoulder. I looked at him, stunned. "How the canary did I miss them?" I mumbled at myself.

He still answered me, "You were giving my ass attention." There was a half smile on his face. And for the first time, I saw a twinkle in his eyes, they were there for a second and then gone. Still, it made my breath hitch, and I forgot to move. Flynn moved towards me, my swords in front of him. I mentally slapped myself, and grabbing my swords, placed them on my back.

"Ah, not naked anymore." I sighed.

"Naked?" he asked me.

"Oh, yeah, you know." I moved my hands towards the handles of my swords. He pulled up his eyebrow in response.

"You know, naked without your weapons."

"Wait, you felt naked without your weapons and now you're not? You are half-dressed you know that, right?" He looked me up and down, his eyes skimmed over my stomach and then dropped to my sweatpants that were hanging on my hips, to end on my bare feet in the training sands.

"Yeah. Let's train, Flynn." I told him as I moved a little away from him. I stretched first, reaching my arms over my head, making myself as long as I could, and stretching my back. I kept my breathing even, slow. I bent forward and stretched more. I heard Flynn moving, he was stretching, too. I went through my standard routine, stretching everything. When I was done, I pulled out my swords, their ring sounded through the air. The hilts were wrapped in leather, smoothed down from use. I gripped them and took up my first stance.

"You want to warm up first?" Flynn asked me. I nodded and started moving. Flynn stayed on the other side of the ring, and he started moving, too. I kept going through the basic moves of the Protector training, flowing through them as water flows through a river. Dancing around the circle, while Flynn moved in rhythm with me. We both worked through the basics, and when we were done, neither of us was even out of breath.

He started moving again, now he used his magic. All four Kings were masters in all four of the elements. And Flynn used them all, almost if he was dancing with them. You could see when he made it through to Fire, that it was his favourite. His whole body moved easier, and the Fire flirted around him, as if she was a lover of his.

I stepped back to watch, my eyes focused on him. His movements, his strong legs that kicked out, his arms that punched a non-existent person. He jumped in the air, kicked out, and landed in a crouch. I knew my mouth was hanging open, and probably reached all the way to the floor. The fire lit up his face, casting shadows over him. His dark eyes shone bright while his whole body seemed at peace.

He moved again, twisting and kicking out over the floor. He moved onto his hands and jump up in one smooth movement; sand flew up with him. You wouldn't have guessed that, a man like Flynn, with a body like Flynn's, would move that smooth and fast. He was all muscle. Well-defined muscle, and that was only what I had seen through his shirt. Why was the man wearing a shirt? I shook my head. I needed to get back into training myself. So, I moved into the ring again and took a stance. I closed my eyes and brought out my magic. I wanted to try that, I wanted to see how it was to train with my magic, my excitement getting the better of me. I stuffed the warnings from Gran towards the back of my head.

It would be the first time I would use magic in training. The first time I had used magic in a fight was with the

Ilunias. I wanted to know what I could do when I used it in training. Could I use mine almost how Flynn had used his? I wanted to dance with mine, too.

I started to move, swinging with my swords, blocking, cutting the air in front of me. I danced around, pulled at the earth, fire, water, and air around me. Made them dance with me, used them to speed up my movements, to make my swords deadlier and my kicks stronger. I used all of my magic this time. It was easy letting myself go around Flynn. I had started to trust him, his silent presence a comforting place for me. I noticed I could be me when I was with him easier than with the others.

I twirled around, my hair was loose, so it moved around with me. I kicked, stabbed, and sliced. I went from one position into another, jumped up high, and crouched down low. My breathing had started to pick up, just like my heartbeat had done. It was amazing, the feeling of being free, free to be who I was. My mind calmed down, while my muscles warmed up. I moved faster, became stronger, and my magic moved around me. I felt so much more: the fox at the edge of the training field, the Protectors that walked the walls, the people inside the castle. Most of them were asleep. I stopped suddenly. I had felt Flynn, his heartbeat. It was steady, not out of breath like mine. I stood still, my swords still in position, still in the air. My eyes were closed, and my breath came fast out of my mouth.

I relaxed my stance, all the while keeping my eyes closed. I wasn't ready to look at Flynn. Not after knowing he had been watching me. I didn't want to see the judgement that would be in his eyes. I may have started trusting him, but I couldn't handle the hatred if he had figured out what I was or who I was.

The only thing I had wanted to do was to run away. Because if he knew what I was, he would tell the others, and I would be killed. Why in purple canary's name had I used my magic? Why didn't I listen to Gran and keep it all a secret? That was it, it would be the moment someone found out. It would be the end of me. Panic surged through me, my breathing became shallow. I stepped backwards, my bare feet moving in the sand. My swords touched the ground, slicing through the grains. I could hear them move along my swords. I moved my other foot where I could feel the edge of the circle, the edge of my magic. I still kept my eyes closed, I didn't want to see him, didn't want to know.

"Are you running?" someone asked, it wasn't Flynn. I recognized his voice. Averey.

A tear had slowly made its way down my face, I still had my eyes closed. He must have seen my magic, too.

"No, she isn't," Flynn said, his voice commanding, and I opened my eyes. I was outside the floating lights. Flynn stood in the middle of the circle, looked straight at me. His dark eyes were even darker then normal, his face showed nothing of what he had seen. It didn't show if he knew what I was. His smouldering dark eyes were the only indication that he had seen something. I didn't find out if he liked it or not, because his gaze had shifted to the person behind me.

"Averey," he said in greeting. I felt him moving towards me, his body heat brushed against my arms when he stopped next to me.

"You didn't tell us you had this much magic." Averey looked down at me, I felt his eyes burn into me. I didn't look at him, I kept looking to the ground, to my toes in the sand. I moved them through it, wiggling them around.

"No," I whispered.

"Why not?" he asked, his voice calm and even.

"Because I can't," I said and turned around and ran back towards the castle. I heard them yelling my name, I kept running. Back to my room.

I slammed the door shut and ran through to my bed. I dropped my weapons on the floor where they clanged on the stones. I didn't care.

I had just blown everything, I had just made things

worse. Why did I do that? Why did I show them my magic? They would never let me go, they would kill me if they knew who my ancestors really were. Sobs wracked through me. I hugged my knees to my chest and cried. With every sob I heard Gran's voice.

"You need to keep it a secret."

"You can't tell anybody."

"They will kill you if they know."

"You aren't safe in that world, Isa girl. They will hate you."

"You are a threat to them."

I sobbed again as her voice filled my head. All the things she had told me, that she had warned me of, ran through my head.

"SHUT UP!" I yelled at the empty room, I yelled at her, I yelled at me. I lay there for some time, tears streaming over my face.

Nothing had happened yet, I was alive, maybe he hadn't known after all. I looked up through watery eyes to see a man standing in my doorway. My eyes widened when I recognized him. I started crying again. Strong arms wrapped around me, pulling me into a hard body. "What's wrong sweetheart?" Averey asked softly. I didn't know what to say to him then. What do you say to the ruling King? That you are the last Full-Blood Witch, that you are the heir to a throne he had? That his ancestors had killed mine, that they had hunted my grandmother, that they had taken away her freedom when she was forced into hiding. That they had taken away mine.

Sobs wracked through me again, making my breathing ragged. He pulled me closer, his body heat wrapped around me, the scent of thunderstorms filled my lungs as I breathed him in. It calmed me, so I moved even closer, placing my head in the crook of his neck. I cried some more, letting it all go. Letting the stress of it all go. Not caring for a moment that it would probably be the last time I would see him. Because if I wasn't killed, placed in a dungeon, or something else, I needed to leave. If they hadn't figured it out, they would have with what they just had seen, I was a stupid woman.

I hugged him closer, moved my arms around him, and buried my head even further into his neck. His arms were around me, his hands slowly moving up and down my back. I had calmed down and my breathing had become easier. I pushed him away from me, so I could face him. There was a wet spot on his shirt, the stain of my tears.

"Sorry," I mumbled at the sight of the dark spot, I tried to wipe it away. He grabbed hold of my hand and brought it down. He kept my hand in his, his thumb stroking the back of mine.

"What is going on?" he asked, his voice low, and his eyes full of concern.

This had my breath hitching for a moment. I had expected something else, hatred. Who would comfort someone if they hated them? I shook my head, trying to clear the still fuzzy feeling of the crying.

"I need to leave," I said when I knew I could trust my own voice; that there wouldn't have been any more tears. This had him narrowing his eyes at me. "You aren't telling me something, sweetheart." I looked at him, his grey eyes were soft and focused on me. I looked down at our hands.

He hooked a thumb under my chin, slowly lifting my head up, so I would look at him again.

"There is something you aren't telling me. You don't cry like that after a training session. Not you." His thumb stroked my chin, almost touching my bottom lip. I parted them a little, too focused on the feeling of his thumb slowly moving over my chin. The heat it had awakened inside me felt as if someone had lit a fire inside. My body's reactions to them kept getting worse, becoming stronger. I didn't want to leave. I didn't want to go away and never see them again. Never stare into Averey's grey eyes, seeing the storm that lived inside him. Never see Flynn dance with his magic, never hear Cian's voice, or see Rayan's smile.

My mind had gone blank for a moment, when his

thumb started to move over my parted bottom lip. His fingers were rough from working with his hands, from fighting with weapons. It made the sensation even better, the roughness that touched my soft lips. He watched my lips, and a shiver ran through me. I hated what I was going to do. I needed to leave and not go any further with it. However if I planned on leaving, I could give myself this, right? Give myself this one moment with him.

I reached out with the tip of my tongue and licked my lip just where his thumb was, and watched his eyes turn darker; two silver pools swirling with heat. His breathing became shallower. His thumb inched up a little more, touching my lip with more intensity. It made me shiver again. His other hand moved slowly towards my knee, where it kept steadily inching upwards. He started making small circles on my leg.

"What you do to me," he grumbled out, his face inched closer to mine, his eyes still focused on my lips. My eyes lowered to his, those lips, full and soft. They had looked amazing to kiss. And he would have been my first kiss. I could feel his breath on my face as his thumb caressed my cheek. I had wanted to close my eyes and move forward, to touch his lips with mine. Instead, I pulled back, moved from the bed. His hand still hovered in the air, almost if he could still touch me. He dropped his hand and looked at me.

"I need to go," I said to him, before I looked too deeply into those eyes, eyes that would haunt me for the rest of my life. I moved out of the room, still barefoot and in my pyjamas. I moved out of the room, away from him.

Averey

I got up after her, wanting to keep her there. To pull her back against me. I stopped when I saw her swords still on the ground. She wouldn't leave without her swords. A heavy weight had lifted from my chest, and I breathed deeply. I moved out of her room, the feeling of her magic still lingered in the air. The memory of her lips so close to mine haunted me all the way back to my Quarters. When I walked in, the others were sitting inside. And from the looks they had given me, I could see that Flynn had told them what he had seen.

"Is it true?" Rayan questioned, his eyes lighting up.

"Is what true?" I asked him. I knew who Isadora was. From the moment I had seen her, I knew she was my Natural Bonded. And the morning had confirmed another thing I had suspected. She was the Great-Granddaughter of Seraphina Savill Royal; the last Queen of this world, the one our ancestors had murdered. No wonder she had wanted to leave. I wanted to know what they thought, if they had connected the dots.

"That she has four elements. Can control them like we can?" Rayan asked, he was almost bouncing up and down in his seat. I looked at Flynn, the big silent King, he shook his head slowly. Letting me know he knew, too, and that I didn't need to tell them more. Not yet.

"Yes," I answered.

"Is she leaving?" Flynn asked, his voice was low and sad.

"No. I don't think so. She walked out of her room when I was there, but she left her swords. She wouldn't leave here without her swords. Or without telling Astra," I answered while I walked back towards the stairs. I needed a cold shower and a lie down. I needed to think about what we had to do next, how to keep her there, with us.

"I'm going to my room, I've got a headache," I told them over my shoulder, I heard Rayan chuckle.

"Make sure the shower is cold," he said, and I heard Cian laugh, too.

I shook my head when I walked up the stairs.

"Averey," I heard behind me. Flynn had walked after me.

"You know who she is?" he asked me. I nodded. "Good," he answered and moved back towards the room.

I moved towards mine, getting that cold shower. I laid

down on my bed afterwards. I wasn't sure how to handle it all, how to tell the others of the plan that had started to form the moment everything fell together. I knew they would agree; the biggest question was, would she?

I closed my eyes, feeling myself drifting away. I thought of her. Of Isadora. Her body against mine, her soft moans escaping those lips I had touched. Her hands roaming my body, strong and powerful. My hands sliding across her hips, kneading her ass. Her breasts bouncing up and down while she rode me, her hair falling around her, and her face filled with pure bliss.

I opened my eyes, sighed, and got up to get another cold shower.

18

The stone floor was cold under my feet as I moved aimlessly around the Castle, not really knowing where to go. I really wanted to leave and go back to the forest, go back home. It would have been so much easier to leave. It would have made things so much easier just ignoring my feelings. Where there was nobody who made my body feel like it was on fire, nobody who wanted to know me, kill me, or whatever else they thought of. I would have been free, free to do what I wanted.

Free to be alone.

That made me stop in my tracks. I breathed in a hesitant breath. I would be alone, free but alone. Would it have been worth it? I would have been safe from the Kings, from the people who might want to harm me, but still, would it have been worth it? Before my thoughts could think that over, I heard something. I looked around, finding myself in the servant's side of the castle. The kitchen noise sounded through the open door next to me. It wasn't what I had heard. I heard a voice. One that would forever grab my attention, a voice I had hoped not to hear again this soon.

"She needs to be dealt with," Icas said. I moved towards his voice, the door of the room he was in stood on a small ledge. I couldn't look inside, but it was enough for his voice to reach me. I moved to stand next to the door, looking like I belonged there.

Goosebumps flew over my skin, the hair on my neck stood up straight. The voice that answered him wasn't from here. The low hissing sound that followed every word it spoke slithered around me, crawling up my spine. It made me go stiff, and I wanted to wash it off me, get rid of that feeling.

"Some things take time. You know that. Don't act harshly," the voice said. I resisted the urge to hug myself and move away from that voice. "You said you don't know who she is. Except that she is powerful. We need to be careful if we want this to succeed." The slithering voice kept on talking, kept on giving me the shivers, made the goosebumps on my body rise even higher. "We will contact you. Someone is listening."

And with that I turned around and opened the first door I could. My heart was racing. I hadn't known who that was, what it was, or why it had talked to Icas. The one thing I knew was that they had been planning something. Something that needed to be stopped. That had made up my mind, I couldn't leave then. I needed to protect Astra and the Kings. Yeah, they needed protection, too. That was my job after all, what I had trained for my whole life. I fist pumped the air and murmured, to the dark empty room. "I'm a Protector, and I need to protect the shit out of this." I giggled with that, my nerves running all over the place after hearing that voice.

My eyes had adjusted to the dark room, and I found myself in a storage closet. I leaned back against a cabinet and thought about what I had heard, what I knew about Icas. One more point against him. The list just kept on getting bigger. I closed my eyes, so I could think. What next? Should I tell the Kings even though I didn't know how? They knew I didn't like him. And what would I tell them? 'Hi there, I just heard Icas talking to some creepy guy in a room in the servants wing.' And what would they say? 'Oh yeah, okay he's bad, so let's kill him.' Nope. That wasn't going to happen. I shook my head. I needed proof. I needed that badly, and that was what I would be looking for. I needed something that could show them what kind of guy Nox was. What he had been doing with his wives, what he had wanted to do with Astra. And I needed to figure out who or what that creepy thing was. That was why I stayed. After that, I would leave. I nodded to myself, that was the plan.

I heard the door open, and I looked at the person standing there. My heart had started beating fast, and for a second, I thought it would be Icas. Only, I saw a girl standing there, a confused look on her face.

"Oh, hello," I said and waved at her. "Just looking for my room." I looked around. "I don't think this is it." I walked past her as fast as I could. She didn't utter a word, instead she kept staring at me. I didn't look back and walked to my room. I didn't see Icas anywhere which was a relief. When I got back to the door to my room, my mind went back to why I had ran away from it in the first place. I stood still in front of that door, the door that led me to my room, to the place where Averey had almost kissed me. I touched my lips. I still felt the ghost of his finger on my lip. I closed my eyes, letting myself relive the memory. I was pulled out of it by a voice I wished I could punch right then.

"Still here?"

I sighed and turned to look at Thalia.

"Yes." I placed my hands on my hips and raised an eyebrow at her.

"This is your room, Miss." The male servant that stood next to Thalia with her bags in his hand motioned to the door he was standing in front of. She looked at him and waited. I heard the man sigh as he placed a suitcase on the floor to open the door for her. I rolled my eyes at her when I turned back towards my door.

"Chief," someone said to my left, before I could open

my door. I looked at the Protector at the door to the Quarters of the Kings. "The Kings wanted you to know that you are allowed into their Quarters when you want. And that you are welcome to train with them if it pleases you." He bowed his head. I was still looking at him, my mouth hanging open a little, my hand on the doorknob and the door slightly opened.

"You already spoke to the Kings?" Thalia asked.

"Yes."

"What would they want to talk about with you? You aren't even a real Witch." Her voice pitched higher. I turned around to look at her, her nose had wrinkled up, and her eyes bore into me. I really didn't like her, she was so exhausting.

"You don't even agree with yourself, Thalia. First, I was a Witch in the Arena, now I'm not. Make up your mind. I'm not here to do it for you. I know who I am, and I don't care what you think. And yes, they talked to me. Go unpack your shit, Thalia, and leave me alone," I told her and turned back towards the Protector at the door.

"Thank you, let them know I got the messages," was all I said and moved into my room before Thalia could start talking again. Someday, I would do more then punch her nose. I moved towards the bathroom, I still hadn't showered after the training with Flynn, and I still smelled like sweat. I undressed and moved towards the shower, turning it on and letting the warm water relax me.

Cian

"Sirs, I relayed your messages," the Protector said when we called him in to enter.

"What was her answer?" Rayan asked him, sitting up straight in his chair. We were in our Office, things still needed to be taken care of when you ruled a whole World. And with the Gate, it wasn't always easy. I looked from the papers that lay in front of me up to the Protector standing in the office.

"She thanked me and said to let you know she received the message." His arms were behind his back, the same stance Isa had taken the first day we had met her. She had been the best thing to walk into those doors for the first time in years. The thought of her made me smile, the way her eyes moved over us the first moment she had met us. The way she went against us, almost bossed us around. The way her brown eyes lit up, with intelligence swirled in them. A woman after my own heart. I wondered if she liked to read. She carried a lot of weapons on her body. It made me doubt if she would care for reading and knowledge. Things I loved, fighting was one thing, knowing how to protect yourself another. However the bigger fights, they were won with knowledge, that was the real power.

Rayan pulled me out of my thoughts. "That was all?" He threw his hands in the air, which made the Protector smile a little. Almost as if he had known our secret; that we really liked her, that she was my Natural Bonded. I had felt it the moment my eyes found her. The pull towards her, my magic that had wanted to wrap around her and keep her close. I had wanted to wrap my arms around her and keep her against my body and more. I needed to focus.

"Thank you, you can go back to your post," I told him and focused on the papers in front of me.

"Uhm, excuse me, Sirs," the Protector said instead of moving out of the room. We all looked up at him again.

"Yes?" Averey answered.

"The other Witch who arrived today. I forgot her name, ugly girl."

"Keep the language nice," Averey said.

"Sorry, Sirs, she is just a handful. She insulted the Chie . . . Miss Isadora, in the first minutes she saw her standing in front of her room." He looked at us all.

"Okay?" Rayan asked, his eyebrows pulled up high, a questioning look in his cute blue eyes. I chuckled at my own thoughts, I had told him that once. He got mad at me, didn't want to be cute.

"They seemed to know each other, and Miss Isadora kicked her butt."

We all stood up at once. The Protector chuckled and held his hands up. "No, not literally. She told that lady. What's her name?" He placed a hand under his chin.

"Thalia Ranteau," I said.

"Yes, that girl. She told the girl to stick it. Sort of, not in those words." The Protector was now rambling.

"You can leave," Averey said and moved his hand in the direction of the Protector, indicating he really should leave.

We all sat down on our chairs, I looked towards Averey.

"That means she is staying." I held up my hand to him, stopped him from speaking. "Yes, I know you said you didn't really think she would leave. Only, knowing it for sure made me feel a hell of a lot better." The others had nodded at what I had said.

"Okay, did you find something out about her?" I asked him. He chuckled and shared a look with Flynn.

"I know you and Flynn know something that Rayan and I don't know." I narrowed my eyes at them, showing my displeasure in not knowing what had been going on. I had always known what was going on. I was the smart one, most of the time.

"I thought you would have figured it out by now," Flynn said with a smile on his face. It made me forget what we were discussing. Flynn hadn't smiled at all in the years I had known him, and it made his face light up. My brother was changing. And Isadora was the source of that change.

"I have an idea. But I need to look it up in some books. Something I will be doing tonight," I told them.

"Good. If you know who she is, we let Rayan in, and then I need to discuss something with you guys. Something huge and important for the World and the fight against the Dark-World creatures," Averey told us, he looked back at the papers on his table. He was searching for new Protectors to enlist in the castle. We needed as many as we could get then, since the Gate had started opening more. We needed our Queens, we needed more magic to close the Gates further.

We had never closed it fully, we didn't have the power for that. And we had been searching for a way to find that power. I looked at the spot where the Protector had stood, my mind drifting back towards Isadora. Maybe we had found that power.

I got up from my desk and moved towards the door, mumbling to the others about the library. I heard a chuckle from Averey as I closed the door behind me and went in search for the books. I needed to find to figure out just who she was, to find out what Averey and Flynn seemed to know.

Isadora

I showered for a long time, wanting to wash off the feel of that slithering voice, from meeting Thalia again–all of it. Just a few days earlier, we had been in the same school. Only, it had felt like I had left there years ago already. I was more at home at the castle than I thought. Whether it was because my ancestors had lived here or because of four handsome Kings that kept bothering me in the most perfect ways.

I stood there, the warm water cascading down my body. My mind lingered on the Kings and what they did to me. I felt my nipples harden, and my mind drifted off. Them naked, seeing their muscles, their sculpted bodies, feeling their strong hands going over my body, followed by soft lips kissing me. I rubbed my upper thighs together, trying to release the pressure that had started building in my center. I opened my eyes and looked at the shower. It had another showerhead, a smaller one that was connected by a hose. This one had an adjustable head. I grinned and grabbed it, turned the shower over to this head, which ended the water that came out of the over-hanging rain showerhead above me.

I switched the water jet on the head in my hand to a strong focused one. And held it down between my legs, the jet hitting my clit, and I moaned at the feeling. I moved it around in small circles, hitting the right spots while I imagined it was one of their hands. My other hand moved to my breast, and I started kneading, rubbing over my nipple. All the while thinking of them, naked and hard; thinking they were the ones touching me. My breathing became shallow, and my center started to tingle, the pressure built. My toes curled inward, and I pinched my nipple at the moment I reached my high. I shuddered when I came. I kept the showerhead there a little longer, riding out my orgasm. Finally, I moved it away and opened my eyes. After I had caught my breath, I placed the showerhead back and turned the Rain shower back on. I smiled at the showerhead, happy to know that this one was even better then the one we had in school. I turned the shower off, all the while smiling. Maybe I could handle all those heated looks I got from them, with this shower.

When I stepped out of the shower, I dried myself off and got dressed. After that, I sat down on my bed. I needed to think things over.

I needed help, except from whom? I hadn't wanted to involve Astra in this. My mind thought back at what I knew from Icas and his house. Then it landed on Mara. Would I have been able to summon her here? I had never used my powers for that, or known if I could do it. I had seen her, she was there. Meaning that she would be in this world.

"Okay, Isa, let's do this. You need answers, and you need help," I said to myself before I closed my eyes. I needed to focus and relax. I breathed in deeply, held it for a second, and let it go. I continued until I felt myself slip into a light trance. I was never the best meditation student, but that was the best I would reach for now. Hopefully, it was enough. I reached inside, to that spot where my magic was. The light that filled me and allowed me to use the elements how I wanted, to use the magic around me. I pulled a small line, pulled it up and up, towards my hands. Letting it float there, concentrating on it. I called out.

"Mara," I said first. Nothing happened, I focused more on her, on the feeling she had given me. The twinkle in her eye, the way she had looked like her brother. How tough she was, how she had wanted to help and save Astra. I focused on her energy I had felt from her that night.

"How did you do that?" I heard a little voice say. When I opened my eyes, there she was.

"What do you mean?" I asked her. She looked around confused.

"You pulled me from the house, I could never leave the house before," she said, and a smile crossed over her face, lighting up her eyes.

"Did your uncle capture you?" I asked her, concerned about her.

"Yes. I don't know," she said finally, after she had focused back on me.

"Mara, can you help me?" I asked her, I had really wanted to ask her how she was doing. However, I didn't think you should ask a ghost that, especially a ghost that was still twelve years old.

"Yes." She nodded her brown curls bouncing around.

"Good." I gave her a smile and told her my plan. When she got it, she disappeared, and I let my magic go. It was then time for me to go and find out more; time to go to the library and see if I could find some things that would be helpful.

With a newfound energy, I then picked up my swords and walked out of the room.

19

I walked out of my room to see more women in the hallway. I didn't glance their way, not wanting to notice them or be noticed by them. Before I could sneak past them, Thalia had spotted me.

"Isadora, why not meet the rest of the Selection?" she asked, with a sneer-filled voice.

"No, I'm good," I said and strapped my swords on my back.

"You said she was a Witch. Why does she have weapons?" a voice asked.

"Because she pretends to be a Protector," Thalia answered the person.

"Why would she want to do that?" another asked.

"Because she isn't strong enough to only be a Witch," Thalia mocked. I wanted to stop walking and kick her ass again. She knew how strong I was. She had seen me fighting the Ilunias. But I knew that was exactly what she had wanted from me. I walked towards the door of the Kings' Quarters. Another Protector stood in front of the door, this time it was the woman who had stood next to me in the training. Her eyes focused on the Witches in the hallway, her brow pulled low and her mouth pulled even lower. Smiling upside down, a trick I never could learn. It had me chuckling, and then her eyes moved towards me. They widened when they landed on me.

"Chief," She said softly.

"Don't, not a Chief," I told her, standing next to her with the big doors still closed.

"Where do you think you are going?" I heard Thalia demand, her voice much closer. I turned around and found her standing a few feet in front of me, her arms crossed in front of her chest.

"The library," I answered back. I looked at the other women that stood behind her. None of them were people I recognized. Some looked at me with disgust written on their faces, others just stared. There were seven in total. That meant they had reached their eight, with Astra included. They were fast getting them here. Disappointment filled me with the thought that the Kings would be spending time with those other Witches. Some were beautiful, a redhead with hair that curled down her body and green eyes that sparkled. Another with short brown hair, a face that was heart-shaped, and lips that every person would have wanted to kiss. They were all beautiful, and that got to me, the Kings would definitely find a Queen amongst them.

"You aren't allowed in there, those are the Kings' Quarters," one of them pointed out. Her blonde hair was pulled up into a bun, high on her head. She wore a light-pink dress. Her grey eyes bore into me—they weren't like those of Averey, hers were grey like the stone walls of the castle; boring and dull.

"She is allowed," the Protector next to me said, I looked at her. Her eyes softened a little towards me.

"Why?" Thalia asked.

"That is none of your business," the Protector told her. She turned around to open the door for me.

"You their whore?" Thalia sneered as she moved two steps closer.

"Sorry?" I asked and turned around to face her again.

"That is the only explanation for why they would let you go into their Quarters. You slept with them, you are their whore." She pointed at me, bringing me right back to the fight in the Arena.

I heard others whispering, I heard them saying whore.

"Thalia, are you sure you want to point that at me?" I asked her while I let my power fill the hallway.

"You are a whore, Isadora, a common, plain whore who hoped to get something out of this. You will not. I will become Queen, and I will see to it that you are placed by the Gate. And—"

"You really want to go there?" I asked her, I knew she wanted to say 'be killed right away.' Her face had turned red from the anger, her eyes spewed hate to me. I saw the others reacting to my magic that had filled the hallway. I saw some of them swallow, while others stepped back a little. Except Thalia hadn't noticed it, or she was just stupid enough to ignore it.

"I will be Queen. And I will make sure that you will disappear from this world. And that little friend of yours, too." She gave me a smile, showing me that she believed she had won.

"Oh, girl, you are so stupid," I said and let go of my magic, I pushed her to the other end of the hallway with my air. She didn't even have time to scream, it happened so fast. I set my hands on fire and walked through the group of Witches, which scrambled out of my way. "You can hate me, wish me dead, or even try to kill me. Only, you will never ever touch Astra," I growled out. She hit the wall at the end, I pulled at the stone and cuffed her around her arms and legs. Her face was white, her eyes wide open in fear, and I could almost have seen her heartbeat beating out of her chest.

"You. Will. Stay. Away. From. Astra," I growled the words out one by one. She needed to learn, she needed to understand that you didn't threaten what was dear to my heart. And Astra had a large part of that, she was my family, my chosen blood, and she was my sister. The fire around my hands licked towards my arms. I fueled it, letting it move over my arms like a lover would; kissing his way up them.

"And if you don't," I said to her when I was right in her face, "I'll make sure that what you have seen now will be nothing compared to what I will do to you then. Got it?" I smiled and looked at her. She nodded, her eyes still wide. "Good," I purred out and started moving back. She was still in the stone shackles I had made. When I had gotten halfway down the hall, she said one more thing.

"I know Astra is gay!" she yelled. I spun around quickly, using the air to fly towards her. My swords were already out, I crossed them in front of her throat. I saw real fear in her eyes as a tear streaked down her face.

"And what are you going to do about that?" I asked her, my voice low, cold, and unforgiving.

"No-no-nothing," she stuttered out. I smelt the urine that had flowed to the ground.

"Good," I said and pulled my swords back, making them slide over each other. The sound of steel on steel cut through the air. I placed them back in their sheaths, the sound followed by a deafening silence that had filled the hallway. I walked back towards the Kings' Quarters, the Protector stood there, her own weapons in her hand. She was holding knives, and I nodded at her in thanks.

Most of the Witches had moved out of my way, a few of them even bowed to me. I rolled my eyes at them, stupid girls. When I reached the door, I turned around and looked at Thalia, at that moment, I had felt sorry for her. Until she looked at me, and I saw the hate in her eyes. I flicked my wrist for show and let her go from the wall. She stumbled down towards the floor. One Witch had moved towards her to help, the others had just looked. When I pushed open the door, the Protector bowed. I arched up an eyebrow at that. "Don't," I whispered. She stood upright. "What is your name?" I asked her.

"Liv," she answered me.

"Thank you for having my back, Liv," I said to her and moved through the door, letting it go after me.

"You will regret this!" I heard Thalia scream. I sighed, and the doors closed behind me. I walked towards the library, my shoulders slumping a little, the weight of what I had done hung heavy on them. That would have consequences, I had threatened another Witch, in the house of the Kings. And I would have done it all again, and I would take the punishment with my head held high. I pulled my shoulders back and walked into the library. The smell of books and wax filled my lungs when I breathed in. It was darker here, to protect the books from the sunlight. A few windows had their curtains pulled back. It was silent; just the place I needed to be, my escape.

I would wait to see if Thalia would go to the Kings, something inside me told me she would. The moment I had rushed to her, I knew that this would come around in a bad way. There were a lot of things you could do to me and say to me, but threatening Astra–that's the one thing you didn't do. I looked down to the floor, letting my head hang.

"Hi there," I looked up from the floor and stared at Cian. He sat at a big table filled with books around him.

"Oh, um, hi," I said and moved towards the table. I looked at the books that were displayed. All of them were about the history of the World, the Queens that had ruled the world and had lived in the Castle. I felt all the blood drain from my face when I saw what he was reading.

Seraphina Savill Royal. My Great-Grandmother.

"Oh, shit," I mumbled, and started moving towards the door again.

"Don't go, Isadora," Cian said, and I looked at him. I expected to see hatred in his eyes, I merely found compassion. His hand was in the air as if he had wanted to stop me that way.

"Why?" I asked.

He looked at the book in front of him and closed it. He swallowed before he answered, almost as if he had been nervous. "Because I like your company." He stared at me, his eyes focused on mine. I gave him a small nod and moved towards the table again, taking the seat across from him.

We sat there, watching each other for a few minutes before he spoke. I expected him to say something about my family. I needed to see where this would lead. I knew that he knew who I was the same way that I was sure Averey and Flynn knew. My nerves had kicked in, and worry filled me. I wondered why they still hadn't reacted to it, why they still hadn't killed me or banned me.

"What is your favourite food?" he asked me, and my mouth fell open.

"Sorry?" I asked him. He chuckled, knowing full well that I hadn't expected that question.

"Your favourite food. What is it?" he asked again, and I picked up my jaw from the table and answered.

"I like almost everything, but you can wake me for pancakes, pie, steak, pasta, chicken soup, ice cream, cook-ies, chocolate, don't forget that one–" I had wanted to go on, but I was interrupted by Cian.

"Okay, I believe you when you said 'everything,'" he said whilst laughing softly.

"Oh, I totally forgot the bacon, on bread with an avocado smash." I had almost drooled with the idea.

"Okay, I get it, you like food." He chuckled. I relaxed a little in the chair, still not totally comfortable. There were still books about my ancestors on the table, I kept glancing at them, and he noticed.

"Why didn't you tell us?" he asked, his hand moving towards the cover of the book he had been reading. In golden letters was written, Royal.

"So, you guys could kill me?" I asked him. He sucked in a breath through his teeth.

"We would never," he answered before he pressed his

lips together, almost as if he had remembered that he couldn't say more.

"No, that is what my great-Grandmother thought when she was murdered, here in this castle. She was betrayed by her own people, her own High Houses." I looked at him. "By your families."

He shook his head. "No, not all our families. We aren't all from the original High House. Only Flynn and Averey," he told me. I cocked my head to the side and looked him over.

"What do you mean?"

"Only Flynn Nox and Averey Thorne are from two of the High Houses who killed the Queen."

"Still, you sit here on this throne, you are the King of this World." I waved my hand out, indicating everything around us.

"It wasn't by choice," he said, while he folded his hands on his lap and leaned back into his chair. His voice was low and soft, and what he said had caught my attention.

"How do you mean, not your choice? You fought for it, you made the decision to enter the competition." My voice held an edge of anger.

"No, Love." He shook his head; a smile ghosted his lips when he said the last words. My body had reacted to it, heated up, and I felt my face flush. I mentally punched it down, didn't want it, didn't need it. I'd just had an amazing shower, didn't need another so soon.

I kept waiting for him to tell me why. "We were forced into it, we all were. When they found out we were strong, they pushed us harder, trained us harder. The schools are brutal for the Elementals. And for ones as strong as us, our families solely saw the power they would gain."

"And now that you have it, now that they have it. Everything is better," I said to him, disgusted at what their families did. There was still the anger I held towards them, the anger I didn't want to recognize and didn't want to feel, either. Only, it was hard to ignore it when you were in the house where you should have grown up; where your mother should have had a happy life. Where she would have been Queen.

"We cut them off," he answered.

That had me silent for a moment. "You cut them off?"

He leaned forward, almost if he would be telling a secret.

"Yeah, we did. They expected us to be puppets for them, that they could rule through us. Instead they forgot one thing." He paused for a moment, and I was totally hanging onto every word that spilled from his lips.

"We bonded in school, we became friends, brothers, and we decided that we needed to rule because we needed to help the world get rid of people like our families." He leaned back. "And that is what we do now, what we are looking for. A solution to the problem they helped create."

"Okay, but why are you looking up *my* family?" I asked him.

"Because Averey and Flynn found out who you were. And they told me that I needed to figure it out by myself."

My breath hitched a little with the confirmation that they also knew who I was.

"And now, that you know it?" My voice was low and soft, almost a whisper.

"Now we plan ahead," he answered me, I stared at him.

"Why would you? And what has that got to do with me?"

He shrugged. "No idea, except Averey has a plan." With that my stomach had twisted a little. I wasn't happy with the idea someone had a plan, and I didn't know that plan.

"And what is that plan?"

"I have no idea. He just told me to find out who you were," Cian said.

"Am I safe here?" I asked him, while I looked him in the eyes, his green eyes which were vibrant in the soft light of the library.

"Yes, you are and always will be. To be honest, this is your house more than ours."

I nodded at that.

"I have a question for you," he said while he got up and picked up the book that was in front of him.

"Why haven't you told us that you were the last Full-Blood Witch alive, that you were the last Savill Royal?"

I swallowed. "Because I promised Gran."

He nodded at that, accepting what I had said. He laid down the book in front of me and opened it to the family tree of my line. It was a long list of names; most of them I had never heard of, all of them were related to me. He pointed towards the bottom of the list, my Great-Grandmother's name.

Seraphina Savill Royal.

Under that was my Grandmother's name. Lina Savill Royal, but beneath that, it was empty. My mother's name should have been there. Isla Seraphina Savill Royal.

I swallowed tears I didn't know had threatened to fall. "Love, your name should be in here." He picked up a pen and handed it to me.

"No, not only my name. My mom's, too." I took hold of the pen and wrote down her name. The name of the mother that I had never known, just heard of. My mother had left me with Gran the moment I was born, she just left me. I wrote down her name, my hand shaking a little from the emotions I had always kept at bay. From the anger, the hate, and the hurt that had ran through me in full force. That now came rushing out, at seeing my Gran's name and hers under it. I may hate her for leaving me, but she was family.

"It's okay, Love." Cian placed his hand over mine and stroked slowly with his thumb. With that, the tears flowed. "Let it out, my Love. It is fine. You are safe."

And I cried. I poured out all the hate, the pain and everything else out of me. At some point, Cian had sat next to me in the chair, and he pulled me onto his lap, close to his strong body, holding me tight and letting me cry. I had never cried this much in my life. This place and them, they brought so many emotions up to the surface; the ones I had stuffed away throughout the years.

His hands slowly moved up and down my back, soothing me with the easy rhythm he had created. I moved away from him, wiping at my tear-streaked face. I moved further away. I had wanted to get out of his lap, only for him to hold me tighter.

"I–" I started.

"No Love." His chest rumbled against my hands. "You don't have to go away." His voice was soft, and his eyes pierced mine. The meaning was clear. I didn't have to go, not from his lap or from here.

"Why?" I asked him. I wanted to know why they had wanted me to stay, was it because of the pull I had felt towards them?

"Just stay." He almost begged. I could feel he was hiding something, and for a second, it had made me want to leave even more. He must have seen the panic that was setting in because he leaned forward and kissed me. His soft lips touched mine, hesitantly at first, until he noticed I hadn't pulled away. I wanted to, I wanted to move away and not start that. It had felt so right, his lips on mine. I slowly relaxed, and he pressed harder, kissing me harder. I sighed and gave in.

He nibbled on my lip, softly biting and kissing. Then pushed a little with his tongue, and I opened my mouth a little for him, letting him in. His tongue danced around mine. His hands roamed over my body, slowly moving from my back to my ribcage and finally to my ass. His hands kneaded my ass, and I sat up a little with the move-ment. I felt his hard erection in his pants, and I moaned when I pushed down a little. The friction was amazing against my core. He sighed into my mouth when I did the movement again. And that was when someone stormed into the library.

"We have a problem."

I jumped up to see Averey looking at us, an amused smile on his face.

"You know?" he asked Cian, who nodded.

"Good," Averey said. I looked from him to Cian, embarrassed by him finding me like that on Cian. And a little flustered at the idea that he had seen us.

"What is this problem?" Cian now asked. And I knew what he was talking about the moment I looked at Averey again. I groaned and waited for him to speak.

20

I had braced myself for the yelling and cursing that I assumed would come.

"You attacked another Witch in our house?" he asked. His voice was low and it held an edge of something, almost as if he had wanted to laugh. Pride? Was that what I had heard?

It confused me, so I said, "Yes." There was no point in denying it.

"Do you know what kind of trouble you've placed yourself in?" he asked, while he moved closer, he was focused on me.

"No," I answered him. Cian was still sitting in the chair, looking at me and then back at Averey. He didn't say anything.

"No. Are you that stupid?" His voice had really turned low, and anger filled it, I didn't know why he would be angry at me. He flexed his fist and clenched his jaw, before he spoke again. "You just attacked another Witch."

"Yeah?" I shrugged, that was something I had already knew, I was there, I had done it.

"You attacked Thalia Ranteau. She is the daughter of the family who started all this." He moved his arms in the air, swinging wildly. "She is the daughter of the most devious man in the world, the family who opened the Gate. The ones who killed the Queen," he said, almost frantic.

"Wait, what the actual fuck?" My heartbeat picked up, and I look at Averey and then back at Cian.

"Yes," he answered simply.

"What do you mean with 'yes?'" I needed to hear him say it.

"The Ranteau was the strongest family in the last reign of Queen Seraphina. They came close to the Savill family. Only, they never matched what the Queen had. They wanted more power and started the uprising. They opened the Gate, to have access to creatures for their army against the Queen. They murdered her."

I could feel my heart beating out of my chest, my fists trembled at my side.

"That stupid cunt! Her whole family is the reason why I never knew my mother, or my Great-Grandmother. Why I never had a normal youth."

"Yes," Averey answered.

"That is true. But—" Cian started.

"No not 'but.' She got what was coming to her, and knowing this . . ." I moved forward, going to hunt down that stupid Witch and make sure that her family knew how it felt to lose something close to their hearts. A pair of strong hands grabbed me, I was pulled against a solid chest, and the smell of a thunderstorm hit me. I tried to get free, tried to escape him.

"Isa, sweetheart. You can't go after her. They have a lot of influence right now. And the chances are, they know who you are just by looking at you. We didn't know, I figured it out when I saw you train with Flynn. Cian." He turned me around, so I was looking at the man he spoke of. I could still feel the anger in the way he held me. However now, I wasn't sure if it was truly anger. The way he held me was almost if he was protecting me.

"Our scholar, found out when I directed him towards the books."

"How?" I asked him, not wanting to know how he knew, what had triggered it for him. I had wanted to know why only her family knew who I was just by looking at me.

"Because they were close to the Queen. Being the second most powerful family in this world, she kept them close. They hated her for her whole life, and while most of the old High Houses died out in the battle that followed her death, they kept to themselves and saved most of their own."

"That doesn't explain why they know who I am when they see me, merely that they are cowards. Wanting power and not fighting for it, lazy turdfuckers," I sneered at them, my anger still fuelled my body.

"One of the first four Kings was from their family. He passed information down to the other Kings, and then that information came to us. They always knew that the daughter of the Queen escaped. They never found her, and we never looked. We didn't expect her to be alive now, or to have a grandchild." Cian looked me over, indicating he meant me, I was the grandchild.

"She's dead," I told them, I felt Averey freeze behind me. The anger drained out of me at the memory of feeling my Grandmother die, I had woken up that night. I had felt her go. That was why I had known my parents were still alive, because I hadn't felt them go. And Gran would have told me.

"Who?" Cian asked. For a scholar he was really slow that day.

"My Grandmother."

"Oh," he answered. I felt Averey's hands moving over my arms, sliding up and down soothing me.

"When?" he asked me.

"A few years back, almost five now," I told them. They both looked at each other.

"Five years?" Cian asked, while he got up from his chair.

"Yes," I answered, I followed him with my eyes. "Why?" I asked when I didn't get any more reaction.

"Because something changed five years ago," Averey said, his breath hot in my ear.

I shuddered a little, with the feel of his breath stroking my ear. His warm body was behind me, and his hands still stroked my arms. I leaned back a little, my back against his chest. Cian walked back towards us, a few books in his hands. My eyes caught on a small black one. He saw us standing like that, and a small chuckle escaped him. I started to move away, suddenly fully aware I had just kissed him, and I was almost rubbing up against Averey, however for him to pull me back and move us both towards the chair Cian and I had sat in. He sat down and pulled me on his lap.

For a second, I froze. What was he doing? But then his hands moved over the sides of my legs, comforting and soft. I breathed out a soft moan and leaned back into him. Those men were driving me crazy, and secretly, I liked it. I would not be admitting it to them, though.

Averey

The way her soft moan came out of her mouth, almost if she had wanted to keep it inside but couldn't, made me stir, but I willed it down. I didn't want to scare her. I wanted her relaxed. We still needed to talk about what she did to Thalia. Even if it was funny, and I was proud of her.

But first, Isa. I kept moving my fingers over the sides of her legs, I wanted to keep touching her, needed to. It felt too good to stop. Cian had sat down in the chair in front of us, his eyes moving over her body, to end on my hands on her thighs. I saw the hunger in his eyes. We were used to sharing women, had done it before. And my brothers, they weren't bad to look at, either. He looked at me then, and I knew he had read the heat in my eyes, because he moved in his chair. Getting more comfortable since his cock was probably straining against his pants. He liked what he was seeing. Maybe, hopefully, next time, because now wasn't the right time to do this.

"When the first Kings died, they made sure that the strongest Elementals would be the next Kings. They started the Competition. When an Elemental wants to become King, they need to show that they are the strongest. Because . . ." Cian looked at Isa, his green eyes focused on her.

"Because they knew that they weren't strong enough to close the Gates, they managed to close it partially." Cian told her.

"That is why there are still creatures coming through," she said.

"Yes. And that is why we need strong Witches at our side. The last four Kings married the strongest, and it made a little more difference." He stopped talking when he pulled out a book.

"It didn't close the Gate, right?" she asked softly.

"No, they weren't strong enough. From the moment we won the Competition, we searched for a solution to close the Gate, to make this world safe again." He picked up another book, looked it over and placed it back. Isadora was looking at the books on the table as her magic moved around us slowly. I closed my eyes for a second, feeling her magic around me. She reminded me of an easy summer's day at the beach. The warm sand between your toes, the soft sounds of the ocean, and the breeze that let you cool down. There was also something else. Her magic held an edge, something raw and powerful. Almost as if you could fall into it and keep falling, an endless well of magic.

That was probably how every Full-Blooded felt, raw and powerful. It made me feel small and insignificant. That thought made me chuckle.

"What?" She turned around to look at me.

"Nothing," I said, I knew the smile was still on my face.

"Yes, you laughed at something. And what Cian is telling me isn't funny. Tell me." She arched an eyebrow, her brown eyes stared into mine, and all I could think of was kissing her. My eyes drifted to her lips, and I felt her stiffen in my arms. Quickly, I looked back at her eyes.

"Okay." I smiled at her. "You are the strongest woman alive and sitting on my lap. It made me feel small and insignificant." I kept looking at her, waiting for her reaction. Hoping she would understand what I had meant. And then she laughed, a full laugh. The best thing I had ever heard.

"Dude, have you seen yourself in the mirror? You are big, huge even." She looked me over, her eyes heating up a little with what she saw. Making me, again, punch down the longing to kiss her. I felt her relax even more, when she turned back to look at Cian. He pulled up an eyebrow at me and continued talking.

"We found this journal." Cian picked up the black leather book and gave it to Isa. I bit my lip as I held back a moan when she moved forward to grab the book, her ass moving over my cock. She needed to get out of my lap before I jumped her. I looked at Cian and saw him smirking at me. He knew what she was doing to me. Luckily, she got up to look at the book Cian gave her.

Isadora

I got up from Averey's lap, grabbed the book Cian was holding, and moved away a little. I needed space and room to think. I had felt more of Averey then I had wanted, and it had me hot and bothered at that moment. *I needed another shower*. Luckily, the book was the best excuse to move away.

"It's the journal from Seraphina Savill Royal," Cian said to me. I opened it, finding a feminine handwriting. I flicked through it, not really reading anything.

"You can take it to your room, Love," Cian said. I turned to him and nodded.

"And those other books?" I looked at the pile next to him.

"I need to read those first. When you told us, your Grandmother had died five years ago, something clicked in my mind. Something changed in the power balance in the Gate. And we think it was connected to your Grandmother. We need to be sure." He opened a book and started looking through it.

"And while Cian looks into that. We need something settled," Averey said as he looked at me from the chair. I was reminded about his hard length that had been poking against my ass moments before.

"Sorry, what?" I asked, my mind flushed with the thought of him naked, all that glorious male in front of me, his skin against mine. I breathed out a sigh.

"You attacked a Witch," he said as he got up. "Come." He motioned for me to follow him.

"I'll make sure the book gets to your room, Isa," Cian said, and I handed him the small journal back. Averey was now by the library door, and I rushed towards him. Not really wanting to hurry.

"Averey," I said to him before he could open the door. "What are you going to do with me?" I asked him. I hoped he understood that I had meant, me being Royal, being the heir to a throne that was theirs.

"Nothing," he said, a smile on his face. I didn't believe him for a second, the twinkling in his eyes told me he was up to something. Before I could ask, he moved through the door. I followed him down the stairs and towards their Quarters.

Flynn and Rayan were sitting on the sofas, talking softly. They stopped the moment I entered.

"Send them in!" Flynn bellowed to someone behind the door. I heard the doors open and looked at the people who walked in. Anger soared through me the moment I recognized who they were. I closed my fist and kept my magic buried deep down inside me. Because if I lost control then, it would, for sure, have meant my death and theirs.

Thalia stood in front of two older people. They must have been her parents, they looked similar. Her mother had the same strawberry-blonde hair as Thalia. And Thalia had her father's eyes, a simple blue–no spark to them. Their eyes moved towards me while Thalia sneered at me. Both of her parent's faces turned white. Hatred filled their eyes and the room around them. I didn't think Thalia had known who I was, her parents had, though. I heard someone move around, I noticed his magic before I found him standing next to me. Rayan. Another person moved to stand next to me I knew it was Flynn because Averey still stood in front of us. He moved towards me, too. They all stood next to me, and I smirked at the Ranteaus.

The door opened, and Cian walked in, almost as if he had been summoned by me, by the power that was gathering in this room. Thalia was strong, it would mean her parents were, too. He looked at them and then at me and the others. He moved towards me, standing next to Rayan. When I looked back towards the Ranteaus, cold entered my veins, and hatred filled my body. It consumed me, there was one thing keeping it away, the feeling of my men around me. They kept me grounded. Because this was a part of the family who had made sure mine was destroyed.

"She needs to be dealt with." Thalia pointed at me.

"And why is that?" Averey asked. I hadn't explained my side of the story, and I didn't know what Thalia had told them. I looked at her, focused on that bitch.

"She attacked me," Thalia spat out.

Averey looked at me, "Why did you attack her?"

"She threatened Astra," I told him, folding my arms over my chest and looked at him straight. I didn't care anymore, the hatred dug deeper into me, consumed me more and more.

"I did not," Thalia said, her voice pitched higher with her lie.

"Oh, girl, please don't. You know you did, and you know you peed yourself," I growled out.

"Don't talk to her like that," Thalia's mother sneered.

"Why are you even here?" her father asked. I looked at the man.

"Because I belong here," I answered. It wasn't totally a lie or the truth. However, they didn't need to know that.

"No, you are a Protector, the bottom of the food chain, you are nothing," Thalia said, she looked at Averey. Her face had changed in a blink, her eyes started to water.

"Please, my King, send her away. She is a disgrace, she doesn't belong here." She even sniffed when she said that. Averey looked at her, not reacting at all to what she said or did. It made me breathe a little easier, made the anger pause for a moment, only to start swirling in full force the moment her father started speaking.

"My King," her father started, he didn't sound honest when he said that, "you need to remove her." He didn't say 'from the castle.' The threat was clear as glass.

"Why?" Averey asked. Flynn and Rayan moved a little closer to me.

"Because she is a threat to your thrones," the man said. This made Thalia turn around.

"Why's that, daddy?" she asked, her voice sugar sweet, he looked at his daughter. A cruel smile appeared on his face when he said.

"Because she is the last Royal, the rightful heir to the throne they are sitting on."

Thalia spun around to look at me, her eyes wide.

"Hi, I'm Isadora Seraphina Savill Royal." Since the cat was out of the bag then, why not do it right? I cocked my head to the side and smiled at them, giving them a wave. I could feel Rayan freeze for a moment. He hadn't known yet. That had to wait for later.

"You . . .?" she started, her eyes getting wider as all the colour drained from her face, "You are?"

"I'm what?" I asked her.

"Full-Blood."

"Yup, no drooling please." This was the last thing I could say, apparently. Her parents had both pulled magic around them, their eyes focused on me.

"STOP!" Averey commanded. He was holding up his hand, and I could feel the magic coming off of him. Thalia looked at Averey, her eyes moving towards the ground. Her parents' eyes were still focused on me. I shook my head at them and made a tsking noise. "I wouldn't do that. You know who I am, you know what I am. Do you really want to test your powers against mine?" I asked them. I let go of my magic, wrapping it around them. Thalia stumbled backwards, practically falling against her mother. I pushed and pushed more magic at them, making them suffocate on it.

"If it is power you want," I growled out and stepped closer to them, forgetting all about the men in the room, forgetting all about the balance they had kept around me. Because the people in front of me, they had a hand in the murder of my Great-Grandmother, the last Queen. They were the family who had wanted more power, took whatever they wanted without thinking about the cost. The hatred finally fully consumed me.

"Take it," I said to them. I was almost upon them, my hands engulfed in fire. The air around me moved faster, whipping my hair around. The castle rumbled around us when I pulled at the earth, and water started to flowed around my feet.

"Isa, Sweetheart." Averey spoke softly to me. I had totally forgotten they were there. The anger had made me forget. A hand touched my shoulder, pulling me back against something solid. The smell of burning fire reached me, strong arms folded around me and held me there.

"Guerrero, stop," he whispered in my ear. "You have to

stop," he said again when I kept pushing my magic. A pair of blue eyes came into my view.

"They aren't worth it," Rayan said softly.

"They are responsible for all of this," I growled out at him.

"Maybe and maybe not, Babe," he said, his eyes pleading with me to see that what I was doing wasn't any better than what they had done to my family.

With that realisation, I stopped and pulled my magic back quickly. It left me breathless. I looked at the three people now huddled together. "You aren't worth it," I whispered. I could feel Flynn tighten his arms around me, and Rayan let out a breath, he turned around and looked at the family on the floor.

For the first time, I heard him talk like a King.

"You are banished from this Castle, all three of you. Nobody threatens our girl. And." He looked at Thalia for what he was about to say next. "Nobody threatens someone in this castle, without us knowing, and if you do, you don't lie about it. We will find out," he said. They stood there not reacting at all until he yelled. "OUT!" They scrambled and moved.

I looked at him when he turned around, finding his blue eyes.

"You guys didn't believe her?"

"No, the Protector . . ."

"Liv." I filled in.

"Yes, Liv. She told us what happened even before Thalia came along. We told her she needed to stop. Only, she ran to her parents. They think themselves really important. Being one of the last Original High Houses." Rayan rolled his eyes with that.

I was still in Flynn's arms, leaning against his chest.

"So, Full-Blood," Rayan now said.

"Yeah. Sorry I didn't tell you guys," I said while I looked at the floor.

"Don't ever turn your eyes down to us, Babe." Rayan

said, his hands soft on my chin, his blue eyes glinting with excitement. I nodded slowly.

"What now?" Cian asked.

I looked over towards him.

"What do you mean, 'what now?'"

"They will not keep their mouth shut. The whole world will know who you are, Isa."

I groaned at that.

"We will have a ball in three days. We will still go through with the plan we had," Averey said, taking the lead as always.

"A ball?" I asked, eyes wide.

"Yes, a ball. That is the place where we introduce all the Selection members to the world. Where we show them, who will be in the running to become the next Queen."

"Come." Rayan held his hand out towards me. I gazed, confused, at him and his hand. "It is late, I'll take you back to your room." I looked outside, to the window where there was no daylight. Solely the silver glow of the moon. I placed my hand in his and moved with him towards my room. I didn't speak at all to him, not knowing what to say. I was relieved that they all knew now, that I could be me. The silence between us lasted until we reached my door.

"It is okay, Babe. I sort of get it," he said out of the blue. "Goodnight, sleep well, don't let the bedbugs bite," he joked to me and squeezed my hand before he turned around. I smiled at his retreating back and went into my room. I went straight to bed, I needed sleep. And luckily for me, it came fast.

21

I woke up slowly; the room was dark around me, and for a second, I had thought I was back in the school. Until I reminded myself that I was not. I was still in the castle. And a lot of shit had happened the day before. I looked over at the night stand, finding the black journal that Cian had showed me. I made some light and reached for it, opening it to a random page and started reading.

We always knew there were other worlds, that there were Gates you could go through. My adviser Ulrik Ranteau–That must be Thalia's Great-Grandfather–*was obsessed with them; wanted to know how they worked and if we could open them. He was a really powerful Full-Blood, and after years of searching he found out how to open a Gate. Using dark magic, using his own soul, he opened the Gate to the Dark-world that now invades our lands. The creatures that come through aren't the same as we have here. Some can be good, others are here to hunt, to find magic, or just to kill people. I can't let that happen.*

We, my men and I, decided that we needed to fight against them, protect the people, and make sure that the Gate closes. We don't know where Ulrik is, I think he lost his way when he opened the Gate and entered that world.

With my four men, I know I'm strong enough to close the Gate. I hope I'm strong enough to fight the houses on this, too, because they don't want me to sacrifice myself and my men, not to save them.

I looked up from that. Seraphina had planned on sacrificing herself and her four men. Four. She had *four* men in her life. And she had wanted to give them and herself to close the Gate. It had given me more questions. I kept on reading.

I told the ten High Houses my idea, told them that my daughter Lina would rule the world after me, and that she would find her own men. They shot down my proposal. They didn't want to hear anything about it, not even the plan I had to sacrifice myself to save them all. They rejected the idea, there aren't any more Full-Blooded men around. So, how could Princess Lina find powerful men, to be hers, to help her rule? They wanted something, I knew what, however I could never act on it.

I read the last sentence again. It sounded like she had known what would happen to her. I kept on reading.

I told them that Lina would find her men, the ones she was meant to find. The men that would bond with her and that she already had one. The last Full-Blood male that didn't go into hiding. Nobody knew of him, except for me. Before I sent them away to a safe place, I married them, making sure she knew I loved her and approved of her choice. He stayed with her through everything. He truly was her Natural Bonded. He loved her, and I knew she loved him just as much. And along with him, she would find the other three she needed. They didn't need a Full-Blood, only someone powerful enough and bonded to her to rule. That was the most important thing. The Full-Blood pulls at the ones she needs, she finds the ones who will complement her, enhance her powers, and who will help her build and grow. It doesn't matter how powerful they are. Merely that they stand by her, trust her, and love her. Lina will find them, I know.

I said goodbye to her, when I sent her away, telling her to only come back when it would be safe. When the Gate would be closed, and the houses would accept her and her men. No matter who she chose, who she bonded with.

Gran had never told me about other men. Except about

Grandpa, who had died a few years after my mom was born. She had never found the other men she needed. *That was why she never went back.*

"I'm sorry, Gran," I whispered to the empty room. She had lost her mother when she was just a young woman, lost her other half, her bonded, too soon and had never found the others. Almost as if without one, they couldn't be whole. I had been staring at the wall for some time, thinking it over. She had talked about bonded. Natural Bonded. A pull from a Full-Blood to the persons they need. The pull I had been feeling towards the four Kings, could it be? Could they be my Natural Bonded? The ones who were meant for me? I shook my head; crazy ideas weren't things I needed right then. I looked back at the journal. After flipping through a few pages, the words *coming for me* caught my eye, and I started reading again.

I know they are coming for me, the houses turned against us. Wanting more power, four high houses killed the other families. I have seen what will happen next. I know I will die tonight. They will kill me, before I have a chance to close the Gate fully. We managed to put in almost all of our magic and closed it as far as it is now. But we are weak, my men and I. We don't have much left.

Then the text blurred out a little. Almost as if she had cried at the last part. The page stayed empty, nothing followed. I turned it, and a folded piece of paper fell out of the book. When I picked it up, I opened it, the paper had faded to yellow, and the ink had been fading, too.

Dear Great-Granddaughter, I know you will exist. I have seen you. My beautiful great- Grandchild, you will not be the last. Believe me, I have seen the others, too, standing at your side. You and your men will fight the last battle, the battle we couldn't finish.

I regret every single day, after seeing this vision, that I will never meet you, that you will grow up in a world not meant for you. That you need to fight for what you want. I'm sorry I left this to you. I'm sorry that the world didn't understand that my sacrifice had to be made. That they killed me before I could save us all.

If you ever read this, remember that you are in the right place. That you need to be here, that you need to make the worlds better. The Dark-World isn't what you think it is.

You, my beloved Great-Granddaughter will be the most powerful Full-Blood ever to live. You aren't there yet, you need to dig deep, fight hard, and trust your men. I have seen more than you, seen the battle that will come. Trust yourself, your instincts. You are a Savill, the oldest bloodline alive.

I love you. Seraphina. Your Great-Grandmother.

Tears welled up in my eyes as I folded the letter back. The Queen had told me to trust my instincts, my men. I looked to the window, the soft colour of the morning showed through the crack in the curtains. It was early, and the perfect moment to go and train, to let my mind work on what I had just read.

I moved out of the bed, pulled on my purple and black sports bra, easy training pants, and my sport shoes. Picking up my swords, I placed them on my back and some knives on my upper thighs. I looked at the journal on my night-stand, and for a moment, I became scared. Because if what Seraphina had said in that journal was true, it would mean that those Kings were mine. Somewhere deep down, the butterflies had started moving, they took away the fear. And a grin spread over my face. If they were truly mine, then maybe I needed to let them know I was theirs, too. Screw the Selection or the other Witches, I needed to find my men. Happiness had swelled up around me, and I knew I looked stupid with that grin on my face. But it was such a relief, acknowledging the feelings I had felt for them. Finally letting them in, reacting to them for the first time, and not feeling held back because I couldn't be with them because of who I was. They had known, they hadn't seemed to care. And if the Natural Bonding thing was real, it would mean that the pull I had felt towards them was real, too. I almost skipped out of my room and moved towards the training field outside, happy to find out that I hadn't been going totally going crazy towards them.

————

I pushed open the door to find the summer warmth already in the air. The Kings were there already, they sparred with each other. When I moved closer, I could see the sweat on their naked upper bodies. It made them glisten in the sun. Their muscles rolled over their backs with their movements. All four of them looked at me at the same time. Almost as if they sensed me coming.

"Hi. Can I join?" I asked, my voice came out low and breathy. I swallowed around the lump that had formed in my throat after looking at them.

"Yes. Warm up," Flynn commanded. I moved towards them, placed my swords on the ground and started my warm up. Moving through the movements I knew by heart. When that was done, Flynn paired me up with Averey. His silver-grey eyes moved over my body, stopping on the skin of my stomach. I did the same, checking him out. His muscled chest, his powerful arms holding the sword in his right hand. He wore simple shorts, showing me his powerful legs. The full summer heat of the day wasn't there yet, but you would think it was.

Not wanting to fan myself, I moved into a standard position, holding my swords out.

We both started to circle each other. I could hear the sound of steel on steel somewhere behind me. Knowing that the others were training, too, I focused back on Averey, and right on time. He had moved fast towards me. I blocked and spun away, slicing with my swords through the air, wanting to hit his. The clang of steel vibrated through me when my swords hit. I looked into his eyes, my heart rate picking up a notch at the heat in his. Smouldering me from the inside out.

I spun back, breathing harder. Not just from the fight.

"What are you going to do?" he asked me, when he moved towards me again. Now slicing towards my head. I ducked and swiped with my feet, but he dodged as he jumped over them.

"About what?" I asked him, when I got up and moved around him.

"That the whole world will know who you are."

I slashed at his side. He blocked again and pushed me off. I stumbled back from the force he had put behind it.

"It is what it is," I answered him. He pulled up an eyebrow.

"You were against it a few days ago, really against it," he said and moved towards me, I blocked his sword and kicked out with my feet. I hit him in the ribs, causing him to grunt a little.

I shrugged at him. "That's the past." And it was true, it was the past. And I had needed to let go of a lot of things that were in the past. The thing that mattered then, was finding out if they wanted me as much as I wanted them. Finding out if we could build something.

And finally, finding out what that Nox fellow was doing. And hopefully, finding a way to close the Gate without sacrificing myself or them, because I couldn't do that. *What a freaking to do list.*

A smile played over his face at my answer. "It is," he said and moved towards me. He moved around me, and I blocked his sword coming low for my legs. He head butted me, and I groaned.

"It's on," I grumbled at him.

I swung with my swords in a circle, and he stepped back. I moved towards him, letting my senses spread out, used my magic to see more. His eyes lit up when he noticed, and I felt him doing the same. Swirling away from his sword, I moved down to the ground, kicking out with my feet and getting back up in one motion. He had found a way to move around me, and kicked me in the back. I almost fell, but I used the air to keep me from falling to the ground, pushing myself back up where I gave him a cheeky grin. He smiled back at me.

I moved in again, swinging my left sword high and my right low. He held one sword, he needed two to block this move. But then, he began to pull up earth and blocked my right sword. The earth dropped back, and he kicked at my hand holding my right sword. I lost its grip, and it fell to the ground. He then swung with his, I ducked again and ran into him, hitting him square in the stomach as he grunted from the impact. He pulled me up and lifted me over his shoulder, the sky flashed before me before I used the momentum to throw my legs over his shoulder, too, and landed behind him, I grabbed his shoulders and pulled him down to the ground. He landed hard, and I moved over him, using the earth to capture his sword arm. I sat with my legs over him, his breathing hard enough that it moved me up and down a little. The thought made me blush.

His other hand moved slowly to my leg, almost as if he knew that I had changed, that something in my mind had clicked after reading Seraphina's journal. Something *had* clicked, or my stubborn streak didn't want to hide my feelings for them after yesterday. They had stood beside me, like Seraphina said they would. I breathed out slowly, getting my own breathing back under control. I smiled down at him.

"You lose," I said. His hand was now on the inside of my leg, and I could feel more than the rising of his laboured breathing against my core. Heat flooded me again, and I knew that he had seen it in my eyes, because his darkened. My mouth opened on a soft sigh.

"Up," I heard Flynn growl. I looked at him.

"Why? I'm comfortable like this." I wiggled my ass a little, and it made Averey move under me. His length pressed against my ass. And I was loving it, so freaking bad.

"Training isn't over," he said.

And I pouted at him. He pulled me up from Averey. I gave him a smile not wanting to drop my gaze to the erection in his pants. There were a few things I had done and some I had not yet. That was one of them. It was fun to tease him, but going so far was enough for now.

Flynn pulled me flush against him. He lowered his mouth next to my ear and whispered, "Guerrero, don't tease Averey so. That isn't nice." I looked up at him, when he pulled away. My face turned red with that, and I looked at the ground. Did he know I was a virgin?

He placed his hand under my chin and lifted it up, so I looked at him again. I saw it in his eyes, he knew, despite my flirting, that I was a virgin. "Don't worry, Guerrero, we will be gentle," he said and kissed me, his soft lips moved slowly over mine, teasing and tasting. I pressed closer to him, and he chuckled against my lips before he pulled back. "See," he said, arching an eyebrow at my flushed face and my faster breath.

"Fine," I growled out, getting what he was saying. Hot and bothered, I moved away from him. Luckily for me, I wasn't the only one; his pants showed some straining in the front. It made me flush even more. I was so out of my league there. I needed to keep it in my pants, though not for long, I hoped. Because the idea of them with me, naked and all sweaty, was a real appealing thought.

"Go train with Rayan," Flynn said when he walked over towards Averey who was still laying in the sand.

"Come, Rayan," I said and pulled him by the hand a little farther away from the rest, "let's get some space." More, I needed more space from Flynn and Averey. It wasn't any easier with Rayan in front of me, his lean body taunting me with every move he made. His honey-blond hair, now golden in the rising sun, his blue eyes full of mischief.

"So, you want us," he said, a grin on his face. "You want this gorgeous body." He motioned to himself. The twinkle in his eyes came out more with the teasing he was doing.

"No," I lied and crossed my arms over my body. If he could tease me, I could tease him.

"Okay," he said and sat down. "Then we don't train." I looked at him on the ground, shrugged, and moved to sit next to him. He was looking at Cian and Flynn fighting. Their movements flowed into each other, no moments of hesitation like some new fighters had. It was mesmerizing to watch.

"Why didn't you tell me?" Rayan asked, his voice low and soft.

"What?" I looked at him. He was looking at me, his blue eyes missing the twinkle they had a moment ago. I missed them already.

"That you were a Full-Blood, that you were a Royal."

I swallowed at that. "I couldn't, and then, I didn't know how." It was the truth; from the moment I had seen them in the throne room, they had pulled at me. And I hadn't known what to do with that until the journal.

"We would never have killed you, if you thought that."

I chuckled at that.

"I swear, we couldn't," he said almost as whisper.

"Why?" I turned in the sand, so I could look at him.

"Because you are our Natural Bonded." He was now looking at me, his face fully serious. His everlasting smile was gone, and I could see the uncertainty in his blue eyes. He was scared.

"I know," I said to him. I had known from the moment I met them, felt the pull. I knew then for sure that it was okay, that it was something good, and I wanted to relish in it. I wanted to know them, be with them, even when it was destined by the Natural Bond.

"You aren't scared of that?" he asked me.

I shook my head no. "Why would I be? I'm meant to bond with four amazing people. In the short time I got to know you guys, you saved me and Astra."

"You finally admit we saved you." He chuckled, some of the twinkle making it back in his eyes.

"Yes." I groaned out. "You let me stay even when most of you already knew who I was. You kicked Thalia out of the castle, thank the piggies for that. And you didn't mind leaving Astra in the Selection. You protected her." I bit my lip. Not knowing how to say what I had wanted to say, I blurted it out in a rush, "And my Great-Grandmother had seen you guys. So, yeah, with the pull and so on. I trust my instincts, and they are screaming for you." I looked at my hands and the sand that was moving through it on the ground.

He laughed at that. "So, you trust your dead Great-Grandmother?"

I nodded at that. It sounded silly, but it was true. She had known what it was like to be Naturally Bonded. "And my instincts, mostly those," I told him.

It was silent for some time, and we both looked at the others training.

"You know," Rayan started. "I loved someone a lot. I thought she was my Natural Bonded, she made me believe it. And then she dropped me."

"What happened?" I asked him, while I focused back on him.

"Not now, please?" he asked me, his eyes were downcast, and his voice was softer than ever, almost a whisper.

I looked at him, seeing him in a new light then, it explained so much about him. His flirting, his always laughing. Showing the world, he was okay. Yet, it was only on the outside. On the inside, he wasn't; it hurt me to know that someone had done that to him.

"I can't promise that I won't hurt you, Rayan. I can promise that I won't let you fall." I grabbed his hand and squeezed.

"Thanks."

We both looked back towards the others. It was decided, I trusted my instincts. It still didn't mean I would jump them right away, and become their bonded. I wanted to find out more about them, learn more and see if I really would like them. Not just because of the pull I felt towards them. I would, maybe, date them. That thought had made me nervous.

When the others were done, we got up and moved towards their Quarters. Breakfast had been served already, and we all started eating. They joked together and laughed, and I looked around at them, enjoying their company and their easy going way around me. It made me feel I was at home. I joked with them, we talked, and we ate, it was nice.

22

———

"We need to tell the other Witches about the ball," Rayan said, he was sitting next to me. Every so often, he would lean over me to grab something, his hands casually touching my arm or leg. It made me squirm in my seat every single time. The others had glanced at me every so often, too.

They could tell that something had changed in me, it was true, I had come to terms that the pull I felt towards them, was normal. It hadn't meant I would roll over and lay on my back for them. Okay, maybe I would have, still didn't mean they owned me, or that they could tell me what I wanted or needed.

"Okay?" I asked him.

"We need to introduce them to the rest of the world," Cian told me. I looked over at him, sitting across from me.

"You guys will still go through with the Selection?" It came out as a growl; jealousy and I weren't good friends.

"Yeah," Rayan said, and I snapped my gaze back to him. His eyes held the twinkle I had started to like.

"We have to," Averey said. I looked at him and narrowed my eyes. "Sweetheart," he started, only for him to stop talking. He didn't know what to say, the air had become thicker, the tension rising.

"We have protocols to follow, love. We can't just abandon everything," Cian said, his hands folded on the table. His green eyes were soft.

"We have a plan, Sweetheart," Averey finally said. I looked at him, waiting for him to say more.

"What plan?" I asked when nothing came out.

He closed his eyes with a sigh. "We can't tell you," he said. I held up my hands and pushed myself and the chair away from the table. The Queen had told me to trust them, and it hadn't started that well.

"Do what you want," I said and moved towards the door.

"Love–" Cian started.

I turned around and held up my finger, waggling it at him. "Nah, don't," I said and turned around again.

"Isadora," Averey said, his voice low as it sounded through the room. I stopped before the doors and waited for him to speak. It was a command from my King and not the man I had started to like. Maybe even more than, like.

"You need a dress; there is a dressmaker in the castle. Servants hall, two doors left from the Kitchen. Go to her."

I started moving, only to be stopped again.

"And you will be at the ball, as a Witch." He didn't have to add anything more to it. The silent command to leave my weapons in my room was there. I nodded, pushed open the door, and moved towards the hall. I breathed out for a moment, just leaning against their door. When I pushed myself off of the door, I started walking towards the servant's hall. I had walked out on the left side of the castle, the council's side. It meant I had to walk the long way, but I didn't mind, it calmed me down a bit with the walk. I found the right door after asking a servant. These doors looked so much like each other. I knocked one time.

"Yes?" I heard a voice from behind it. When I pushed open the door, I entered a small room filled with fabric and a high window that let in light. The sun was fully risen then. Everywhere I looked, I found fabric, piled and piled on top of each other.

"Hello," I said, though I couldn't find anyone. I was sure I had heard someone answering my knock.

"Yes, here. Hello." I saw a hand waving above me. I looked up towards a high closet, finding a young woman on a wooden ladder.

"Good, can you take these from me?" She lowered two dark-blue rolls of fabrics. I grabbed them and stayed next to the ladder. She picked out another roll of fabric—that one silver—and climbed down. Her brown, curly hair reached just above her shoulders, and while she climbed down, it bounced around. Her brown eyes were darker than mine, and her face was filled with freckles. A small mouth and a petite nose all on a soft round face greeted me, smiling.

"Hello," I said again.

"Hi, thank you. You can place them there." She pointed towards a table against the wall next to me.

"And you can tell me which fabric you liked the most." She had a soft and sweet voice, one that easily reflected the person standing before me.

"What do you mean?" I asked her, still holding the fabrics.

"You are here for a dress for the ball, right?" She pointed again to the table, placed the silver fabric on it, and I moved to do the same.

"Uh, yes. That is right. How did you know?" I pulled my eyebrows together at her, wondering.

"Oh, girl." She giggled sweetly. "I know a lot." A twinkle had appeared in her brown eyes when she said that, and for a moment, I was taken aback.

"And you aren't the first one to walk in here today." She giggled again. Then it hit me, she was joking with me.

"Oh," I said, and a soft laugh escaped my throat. Something I had needed then more than I thought.

She giggled again. "Come on. Pick the colour you like. I

know that one of these two was made for you. One of them will go with the silver," she said while she stroked the silver fabric lovingly. It was beautiful, the same silver of moonlight when it hits a lake, breathtaking.

I looked down at the two blues on the table. One was a dark navy-blue, almost midnight. The other was a darker blue that flowed over into a lighter blue. I looked at them both, but my eyes kept going back to the midnight fabric.

"This one." I touched the navy blue.

"Yes, that will do perfectly, pairing it up with this silver one." The woman was still stroking the silver fabric. "You will have a dress fit for a Queen," she mumbled.

"Sorry?" I asked her. She ignored me and grabbed the navy blue and the silver fabrics, moving them to another table, one that was holding a sewing machine. She placed them next to it and turned around. Her eyes moved over my body, one hand moved towards her lips, and she nodded at me.

"Easy dress, but it needs to move around you and with you. Not against," she started, her eyes still moving over me. It made me nervous.

"Long enough to flow behind you. You will wear heels, right?" she asked me. The question had totally come out of nowhere with her rambling.

"Yes," I answered quickly.

"Good, a bare back and support for the front. Do you mind silver or gold?" She was now looking at the fabrics.

"No, I don't mind. Why?" I asked her.

"Don't worry," was what she answered.

"Who are you?" I asked her, I had never heard her name, and she kind of freaked me out. I liked to know the names of the people who freaked me out.

"Oh, girl, sorry. I'm Stella." She held out her hand to me, and I reached over and shook it.

"You are Isadora." She winked at me before she dropped the hand.

"You heard?" I asked her, curious about what she had

heard.

"Some things," She answered while she turned around to the sewing table. "Other things I have seen."

"What do you mean, seen?"

"Seer," She answered shortly, when she sat down.

"Why are you here then?" I asked her, my arms folded in front of me. I didn't understand why the Kings would have had a seer working as a dressmaker. It was one of the things I couldn't do, see into the future. It was something you were blessed with, or cursed, depending on how you looked at it. Always knowing things before they happened, it must not be great.

"I love making dresses." She pulled out needles and scissors, having already started to work.

"Wouldn't your powers be more useful advising the Kings?" I still hadn't wrapped my mind around her.

"Yes and no. I'm not that strong, and when I get them, I inform the Kings. We seers can't see on command, girl." She'd answered my next question, too.

"Okay." I pulled up my eyebrow at her and started moving towards the door. Before I reached it, something popped up in my mind.

"Don't you need my size and stuff?" I asked her while I turned back to look at her.

She giggled, and shook her head. "No, silly girl. I already have them. I'm the best you know. That is why I make the clothing for the Kings and their Queen." She smiled at me.

"Don't you mean 'Queens?'"

"No, no, girl. I will deliver the dress to your room. And yes, there will be slits in the sides, so you can access your knives." She winked with that, and my mouth dropped open in a silent *o*.

"Thank you," I stammered out and walked out of her room.

"Chief," someone said when I stepped outside Stella's room.

I looked up, finding a Protector in front of me. "Don't call me chief," I grumbled out at him.

"Yes, chief. Miss," He answered. "I was sent to get you; the Kings are announcing something in the Throne room. All the Selection members need to be there." He had started to walk away with that. There was one option and that was to follow, the Kings had summoned, and we would go.

We walked towards the main hall and then into the Throne room. It was already filled with the Witches of the Selection. I saw some Council members standing at the side of the raised dais. Violet was one of them, she saw me entering and lowered her eyes. It made me smirk, I moved towards Astra who was standing a little to the side. The other Witches were all huddled together in the centre. The Kings weren't there yet.

"Do you know what this is about?" Astra asked me when I reached her.

"Yes," I grumbled out.

"What?" She arched an eyebrow in question.

"You will find out soon enough," I answered her when I saw the Kings walking into the room, they had walked out of the office from behind the dais.

"Hello, ladies," Rayan said, he winked at some of them. I heard them swoon. It made me roll my eyes.

"Where is Thalia?" Astra whispered at me. She had distracted me from the jealousy that came rushing up at seeing Rayan flirt with them. I looked around the room. She wasn't there, indeed, and I hadn't expected her to have really left. I had expected her to make a bigger scene out of it all.

"Gone," I said to her. I didn't try to keep the smile off my face. I looked back to the dais. The four Kings stood in the centre then.

"We will be having a ball in three days." The girls all giggled at that. Averey held his hands up to motion them to silence.

"There, we will introduce the Witches for the Selection to become Queen." His eyes moved towards me, and I stared back.

"Also, that Protector bitch?" one of them said. I recognized her as the one who had helped Thalia.

"Don't speak about her like that," Flynn growled out. I saw the Witch's face pale.

"Everyone here is a Witch, and you will treat all of them like equals," Averey said to her, causing her to nod back.

"In three days, we expect you all to be dressed in your best dresses and on your best behaviour. This will be sent out live to the rest of the world, everyone will know who you ladies are."

Some of the girls giggled again, making me roll my eyes. Again.

"Then, there is one other thing, we will add new Protectors to the castle's defences. They will help with the protection of the ball." Averey moved his hand towards the row of Protectors. I scanned them, I hadn't noticed them at first. I squealed when I saw three faces I knew. I ran towards the girls.

"Banu, DeeDee, Lena. What are you girls doing here?" I asked while I hugged them all.

"We passed our test and were chosen to come and work at the castle." Banu lifted her eyebrows at me, the question clear.

"No, it wasn't me."

"I did," Astra said, and I turned to look at her. Her face was a little flushed.

"What do you mean?" I asked her.

"I found out that they passed their test. I asked the Kings if they could be brought here. It would make you happy," she said. She didn't add that it would have made her happy, too. She kept glancing at Banu.

"Girl, you are the best," I told her and hugged her.

"We will start with the dates today. We want to begin

the Selection process as quickly as we can," Averey said, interrupting my happy reunion.

He explained to the Witches, that the dates were to find out if they would be compatible for a Bonding ceremony. It had me fuming inside. They thanked the Witches and told them they would inform them when their dates would be and with whom. Some of the Witches had started whispering to each other, glancing over to the Kings. Rayan moved off the dais, towards us. I looked at him. He gave me a wink and still smiling, he said, "We have a date tonight."

"Oh," I answered. I wasn't sure if I had wanted to go on a date with him then. He must have seen my doubt.

"You want to, right?" he asked me.

"Uh, yeah. Okay," I answered, I really didn't know. I knew that it would have given me a chance to be with one of them that night. Maybe I could ask him more about the flirting. I knew he was hurt when he was younger, but it hurt me when I had to watch him flirt with others. I so hated jealousy.

"Okay," he said slowly. "I'll pick you up around six." He moved back towards the other Kings who were still on the dais. They all looked at me when Rayan had probably relayed the things I had said.

"What was that about?" Banu asked me. I shrugged at her. I looked to the Witches, they all were silently watching us.

"Come, let's go to my room." I told them, I didn't want to stay there any longer. And those Witches, they hadn't looked too happy. I showed the others the Castle as we walked back towards my room. We talked about what had happened after Astra and I had left the school. They had passed their exam without any problem. Banu even joked that it had been too easy. Banu was the best Protector after me, DeeDee and Madalena came close to her.

"Nice room," DeeDee said when we entered the small living room.

"Thank you." I waved at the sofas with my hand, indicating they should sit down.

"What was that with the King?" Madalena asked, Astra nodded at me.

"Nothing," I grumbled back. What could I have said? They were my bonded, we had this pull, or I couldn't seem to resist? I totally hated it when they flirted with someone else. Astra had noticed it and saved me from more questions.

"Thank you for coming," Astra said.

"You know, we couldn't say no to an invitation to the Castle, to be part of their security," Banu answered Astra.

"I know you girls all wanted to do something else after graduating. Still, I'm happy that you are here," I said to them, giving them a smile. I was really happy they were there. I needed some more help with finding things out, and they were perfect. It also meant I didn't have to ask Astra for it all the time.

"Girls," I said, because it was time that I told them a few things. They would find out soon enough, and I'd rather have them finding it out from me than one of those Witches.

They all looked at me. I was still standing behind one of the sofas, my hands resting on the back. "I need to tell you something. Important," I said. It took me a moment to gather my balls together and say it out loud.

"You need to keep this a secret," I warned them, before I blurted out. "I'm Isadora Seraphina Savill Royal." I squeezed my eyes shut, didn't want to see their reactions. It was silent for a few minutes until one of them said something.

"Okay."

I opened one eye and looked at them, then opened my second. All four of them were watching me, nothing but love reflected on their faces.

"Uh, you know what that means?" I asked them.

"Yes, that you are a Full-Blood, the rightful heir to the

throne," Astra said.

I let out a breath and moved to sit on the sofa.

"Yes, and there is more," I told them. I explained the pull I had felt towards the Kings, that I was reacting to it and hadn't known how to handle it. I told them about the night Astra was kidnapped, how I got her back, and about the little sister of Flynn.

"I haven't heard from her yet." I bit on my lower lip, worried for her.

"Isa, she will be fine. She is a ghost, after all," Lena said.

"Yeah, you are right. Still." I looked absently towards the fireplace, almost if she would be standing there.

"What do you want us to do?" Banu asked, back to business as always.

"I need you girls to protect Astra at that ball. And before that, I want you to find out as much as you can about Icas Nox and the Ranteau family." They nodded at that. I was happy that Astra hadn't gone against having protection.

"Who will protect you?" DeeDee asked me, and I rolled my eyes at her.

"You know who you are talking to." I smiled, and she laughed. "Okay," I said. "I'm going to take a quick shower, and then we talk some more." When I got back all clean and in a new outfit, I sat down, and we talked, a lot. You would think we hadn't seen each other for years and not for just a few days.

We ordered some food and had a great day. Then, someone knocked on the door. I knew it was Rayan, I could feel his magic behind the door. I sighed and walked towards it to open it.

He stood there, his face in that beautiful smile, his eyes twinkling. "I'm here to pick you up for our date," he said, and his smile got even bigger.

"Okay," I said, I waved at the others, grabbed my swords, and moved with him, still unsure if I should have been happy with it or not.

23

We walked towards their Quarters where he gallantly held open the door for me. I waited for him, not knowing where we were going.

"This way," he said, and we moved towards the library. He held those doors open, too, giving me a soft smile, not his cheerful happy one. It made my jealousy and anger lessen a little. I had it all cropped up inside me.

"Where are we going?" I asked when he grabbed my hand and started moving to the back of the Library.

"You will see," he said and kept pulling me softly along. I kept silent, not knowing what to say and too curious about where we were going. We walked to a door I hadn't noticed the first time I was in the library. He pushed it open, and it revealed a stone staircase. I looked up, not seeing anything at the top. He held out his hand, and a light appeared. He held it out in front of him, and we moved up the stairs. Eventually, I saw a door. He let go of my hand to push open the door, it creaked a little. We entered a small balcony where I looked around. I saw that we were on the roof, I could see the whole castle's roof, the forest that stretched behind it, and then the city.

There weren't many tall buildings. It gave us a perfect view of the sun which hung low in the sky; it was ready to go down. I looked towards Rayan as he moved to a table against the balcony's railing. It was set for two people.

"I thought, we could have a private dinner, while the sun was setting?" He motioned to the table, a shy smile on his face. I nodded at him and moved towards the chair he had held out, I sat down and he pushed me towards the table. That was when I noticed the maid standing next to the door, we had come in. She smiled at me.

"She will be serving us." He motioned for her to come closer. She was holding a bottle of wine. Rayan started talking while she poured a generous amount into my glass.

"How are you?" he asked, his voice soft, and doubt had seemed to seep through it.

I chuckled a little with his question. "I'm okay," I said to him, waiting for the servant to go away. When she did, and the door closed with a soft thud, I looked at him.

"Why did you flirt?" I asked him, he seemed to be taken aback by my sudden change in mood.

"What do you mean?" he asked.

"Those Witches, you flirted with them," I growled out, I would become a bear if I kept that growling up.

"I would never," he said, while he held his hands up.

"You winked at them," I told him.

"Babe, it doesn't mean anything."

"Yes, it does." I cringed at my own whining voice. I really hated the jealousy, it wasn't me, and I had wished I could push it away.

"Babe, listen." His blue eyes totally focused on me, a soft twinkle lighting them up. "I'm here with you, not them. I don't like them, I'm . . . I'm pulled to you." He ended on a soft breath.

"I am, too." I answered him. It was the first time I had admitted to the pull in front of one of them, and his face lit up with that. Before he could say anything more, the door opened, and the servant walked in with a plate of bread and some butter. She placed it on the table and walked away again.

"Can't she knock?" I said under my breath.

"She did," Rayan answered, that everlasting smile back on his face.

"Why do you flirt with everything?" I asked him, while I took a sip of my wine. I looked at the glass in my hand. It was really good wine, not that I'd had much in my life till then.

"It is who I am," he answered. "It is not something I can do anything about. It is my personality." He leaned back in his chair.

"Okay, I can understand that. But, if what you say is true, with the pull and all," I waved my hand in the air, "then why still flirt with them?"

"Babe, I flirt with you more." He gave me a wink, and a soft blush appeared on my face. "You never notice it." He laughed at what he said.

"Oh," was the only thing that I could say.

"Now it is my turn."

I pulled my eyebrow up in question.

"You asked me something, now I can ask you something. That's how it works, right?" He winked again though he didn't let me answer before asking me. "Why were you trained as a Protector and not a Witch?"

I took another sip of my wine and thought about it.

"Gran told me to." It was the only answer I could have given that was the truth. I was eight, what the hell did I know then?

"Why did you agree to it?"

"Nuh-uh, it is my turn." I gave him a smile.

"You told me you were hurt, when you were younger." His face fell a little with that. "Can you tell me more?" I added softly.

He nodded, still, he stayed silent for a moment.

"It was a few months before I became King. There was this girl I had met. Sweet and funny. I met her one weekend when the guys and I were out in the city near our school. We were in a club, so we danced, talked, and after that we decided to see each other again." He drank some wine before he continued.

"We were together from that moment, when I wasn't in school, I was with her. I was in love, totally in love. Thought she was my Natural Bonded." He looked up at me.

"I know now that it wasn't true. It never felt like this." He motioned to me. I remained silent listening, while eating the bread.

"Then the trials for King came, and we entered. She cheered us on, became really fanatic about it. She pushed us, and me, to become better. She turned into something else." He looked towards the setting sun, his mind in the memory.

"We were close to winning, there were four other guys who were strong, too. One day, I wanted to surprise her." He looked at me, a sad smile on his face. "I went looking for her, except I found her in bed with one of the other contestants. Do you know what she said when I found her?" I shook my head.

"Sorry, honey, you aren't good enough to become King and get me as your Queen. She just turned back to the guy she was riding and went on." I grabbed his hand and squeezed.

"What did you do?" I asked him, while I rubbed my thumb slowly over his hand.

"I became a King." He laughed at that a little.

"What did she do?" I really wanted to punch her right then. Nobody hurt one of my guys and got away with it.

"She came crawling back to me, saying it wasn't her fault. That they had forced her to do it." He looked back to the sun. A knock sounded on the door.

"Come in," I said absently. The servant walked in, holding a plate with food for both of us and set it down.

"Everything alright?" she asked us. I nodded and waited until she left.

"Do I need to kick her?" I asked him.

Rayan looked at me. Seeing my serious face, he laughed.

"No, it is fine. I told her she could suck it. And decided that I would never fall for anyone again."

I squeezed his hand before I started pulling away. He grabbed it. "Until I saw you in that throne room," he whispered, and that made me freeze. His blue eyes had moved towards my lips. I knew what he had wanted.

Instead, I said, "Let's eat, before it gets cold." I speared a piece of meat on my fork and started eating. He was silent as he ate—the opposite of me, I was moaning.

"This is so good," I told him with my mouth full. He chuckled at it. The air around us changed, becoming cooler while the sun slowly set.

"Do you like being a Protector?" Rayan asked me when I had finished my plate.

"Yes. But to be honest, I haven't been much of a Protector yet."

He pulled up an eyebrow in question.

"First, we had the Selection going wrong thing, then I came here, and, yeah. Now I'm going to be a Witch."

"What would you want to be?" he asked me, his eyes roamed my face.

"I don't know. I'm grateful that I can defend myself with more than magic, that I have these friends around me who like me for me." It was my turn then to look over the railing, the night was almost full, and the stars were already shining in the dark of it. Rayan snapped in his fingers, and a few lanterns started to burn, coating the roof in a soft golden light, very romantic.

"I love to protect, to help, and to make things better," I finally said to him. "It is what I want to do, and being a Protector makes it much easier." I looked back at him, his blue eyes had seemed to light up more in the soft night sky, the lights reflecting in it. Almost if the stars were in his eyes.

"You could do that as a Witch, too," he said.

"No, you value a Witch too much to let her go to the

Gate. If I were a Witch you guys would have never let me go there." I shook my head at him.

"We do, they are the strongest in this world."

"That isn't true. The Protectors who fight by the Gate, who keep us all safe. The families who sacrifice themselves, so you guys can sit here, up high and safe. They are the strongest."

"Maybe, but they can't keep the Gate closed," he said. That had me taking in a sharp breath.

"No, and it seemed none of you four can, either. You can't say to me you believe that the Nulls are lesser than Witches or Elementals." I shook my head wildly.

"No." Rayan looked down at the table. "They aren't lesser then us." He looked up at me and continued. "But they don't know how hard it is to keep it as closed as it is."

"Tell them." I crossed my arms. "Tell them, that you guys do everything to save them, too. You guys hoard magical people up here, keeping them away from the fight. It has made the Protectors angry, even in the schools they were divided. You must have known that?" He nodded slowly at that.

"You can't do this without them, Rayan." My voice was soft and comforting. I didn't want to be mad at him.

"That is true, there are so many things we need to do. Being a King isn't easy, either." He looked at me.

"Poor baby." I pouted at him, and he chuckled.

"I'll tell my brothers what you said. We will change things." He nodded at me, or himself, and determination moved in his eyes.

"It is beautiful up here," I said. I'd needed to change the conversation. I didn't want to ruin our date.

"Yes, it is." I looked at him and found him staring at me. It had me blushing. A knock sounded again on the door, this one was different from the servant girl. We both looked at the door.

"Yes?" Rayan said, the door opened, and Averey walked out. He nodded at me and looked then at Rayan. "We need you." And with that, he turned around, not saying sorry or anything. Rayan got up from his chair and moved towards me.

"Sorry, Babe, you can stay here if you want. Enjoy some more of the view." He looked at my mouth again, merely for him to kiss my cheek. He smiled at me and moved away.

"Thank you," I said to him before he could close the door.

"It was all my pleasure." He winked at me, and I shook my head laughing at him.

I stayed there for a while, looking out over the railing to the forest and listening to the sounds that came from it. Then up at the sky, all those stars that looked down at me, it was gorgeous and peaceful.

I was interrupted by a soft knock on the door, I looked at it and waited for the person to open it. It was the same servant girl that had brought our food the whole date.

"Oh, sorry, I didn't know you were still here." She looked around. "Where is the King?" she asked me.

"He needed to leave, the others needed him," I told her. She nodded at that and started collecting the plates. I moved to help her.

"Miss, no. You don't have to." She laughed softly.

"It is no problem, it is faster cleaned up this way." I told her and grabbed the glasses.

"Thank you, Miss," she said when she started walking towards the door again.

Before we reached the door, I felt the air move behind me, something rushing through it. I dropped the glasses I held when something embedded itself between my shoulder blades, the glasses shattered on the floor. The servant girl turned around, except it wasn't the same girl anymore. One side of her face was missing, her only eye glazed over.

"Purple ducks," I grumbled at her, pulling the dagger out from my brace at my hip. I couldn't reach back to my swords, there was still something sticking out of my back. I felt the warm blood slowly trickling down. I crouched a little and waited for her to move. She didn't do anything, she kept looking at me, the plates still in her hands, which were missing some skin.

"Hello, my dear," something chuckled behind me. I didn't dare to turn my back towards the servant girl. I moved to the left, trying to get my back to the roof of the Castle, instead I was pulled back. I clenched my jaw, and tried not to scream at the pain in my back.

Something tsked me. "You aren't going anywhere."

"Dear, would you please?" the voice said to the servant girl. She dropped the plates, where they scattered on the floor. Her hands moved towards my knife. I tried to slice her, again I was yanked back. That made me grunt out of pain, I lost my balance and fell down on the floor. The servant girl bent to pick up the knife that had fallen out of my hands.

I looked up to the thing that was holding a chain, which fell from his hands towards my back. I found a person looking at me; dark eyes stared at my face. His hair was chopped short, black and messy. His face might have been handsome if he would have stopped sneering at me. He wore a long coat made out of some kind of leather. His black pants and shirt added to the whole creepy style he was wearing.

"What do we have here?" he asked me. I arched an eyebrow at him.

"A Protector, sir," the servant girl hissed out. That meant they hadn't noticed my magic, I stuffed it further back into me, making it disappear. I saw his jaw clench for a second, and his eyes flicked over my face.

"Why is a Protector on a date with a King?" he asked, his voice strong and demanding.

"I wasn't–" I started.

"She was," the servant hissed out. I kicked towards her,

hitting her in the legs, and she dropped to the ground with a sickening crunch.

"Please don't do that," he said and gave a small tug at the chain.

"Why? You need her for something?" I gritted out through my clenched jaw.

"Yes, I had. Now she is useless." He looked over at the girl at my feet, crawling around, her legs broken. He flicked his hand towards her, she screamed and then went lifeless.

"Look what you made me do. Now I need to find another one." He pouted at me and then laughed.

"What do you want?" I asked him. I needed to distract him, find a way to get that chain out of my back.

"It doesn't matter what I want." He cocked his head to the side, reminding me of an animal on the hunt. A shudder ran through me. "I will take you as replacement for her," he said and got up from the railing he was leaning on. He yanked at the chain, and I gritted my teeth harder.

"Come on, stand up," he growled out. I moved, standing up slowly. He was before me, and I had to look up, to look at his eyes. I had first thought they were black, instead I found them more blue than black. They reminded me of the dark-blue I had chosen for my dress.

Before I forgot that he had a knife with a chain in my back, I punched him in his kidneys, causing him to grunt a little, only to chuckle after it. I punched him in the face, hard. Still he kept chuckling. My back was hurting with every move I made.

"My dear, that tickles," he said, still laughing.

"Oh, it does, does it?" I said to him, and I moved closer to him, doubting myself for a second before I slammed my mouth against his. He froze, his lips tense. I moved my hands behind him, searching for the knives the servant had forgotten on the table. When my hands reached the metal, I snatched it up. Then I felt his mouth move a little, softly against mine, and it was my turn to freeze. With the knife in my hand, we stood there. His tongue darted out, and I moaned a little. I freaking moaned. This had me snapping out of my haze, and I slammed the knife between his shoulder blades. He grunted against my lips, and I stepped back. Wiping my mouth, I reached back towards the chain and yanked it out, a growl of pain escaped with it. I had to take in a few breaths before I could do more.

"Sneaky bastard," he grumbled. Still his hands moved towards his lips, and I shuddered at the look he gave me. I didn't spend too much time analysing what that shudder meant.

"Don't fuck with me," I snarled out at him and threw the chain at his feet.

"Mmh, don't tempt me," he said and pulled at the chain; it wrapped around his arm, showing me muscles, where the chain wrapped around, turning into black ink on his skin. I grabbed my swords from my back and looked at him, the weight of them a comfort in my hands. I crouched low and shifted my weight, ready to attack him.

"Later," he saluted me and jumped backward off of the balcony. I ran over and looked down, I saw nobody. And seconds after, the door opened.

"What is going on?" Averey's low voice washed over me, and I relaxed.

"Not sure," I answered him. I was still looking for the man who'd attacked me. I sighed and turned around.

"Why is there a dead servant on the floor?" Flynn asked, looking a little closer at the girl. "And why is her face almost gone?" He looked at me.

"Not sure," I answered him now, I cringed as I placed my swords back.

"Are you alright?" Averey moved towards me, his face full of concern.

"I will be, need to clean it."

"Clean what?" Flynn stood up and moved towards me, he turned me around, and both men were silent for a minute.

241

"Who the fuck did that to you?" Flynn growled out.

"Not sure," I said again, feeling like a broken tape recorder.

"What do you know?" Averey asked when he moved into my line of sight.

"I had the date with Rayan, you came in and took him with you. Then this servant girl," I pointed at the dead body on the floor, "came in and started cleaning the plates. I offered to help, and when we moved towards the door, something buried itself in between my shoulder blades. The girl turned around and was like that." I nodded again to her, and then I realised something.

"Ew, gross she touched my food." I shuddered at the thought, then continued talking.

"Then there was this thing"–I wasn't sure what I would say to them. I kissed it, and to be honest, I had liked it. – "with a chain, which was attached to the knife in my back. I scared him off. I think." I pulled down my brow. "And then you guys came in."

"Why did you come in?" I asked Averey. Flynn was still at my back, holding something against my wound.

"We felt magic, something breached our defences." Averey now looked behind him towards the forest.

"I don't know what it was, except that it's gone now." I moved away from Flynn and started towards the door. I wanted to shower and sleep.

"Where are you going?" both of them asked at the same time. I turned around, my hand on my hip.

"Taking a shower and going to bed," I told them, then turned around and walked towards my room.

24

I woke up slowly, my shoulder was still sore from the encounter the night before. It had hurt when I got under the shower and washed it clean. After that, Flynn had stopped by with bandages. He helped me dress it, and it was really sweet, but I made him leave fast. I wanted to sleep, wanted to forget that kiss.

Now that I was awake, the only thing I could think of was that damn kiss. I had convinced myself that it had been necessary; if someone liked pain, it wouldn't help kicking them. Meaning, if I had wanted to get close enough to grab the knife that was behind him, it was the only way. I threw the covers off and hauled myself up. My shoulder blades burned a little at the movement. Being a Witch meant fast healing. Still, we weren't immortal, and things still hurt. And a knife between your shoulder blades wasn't something that one night of sleep would fix.

"Can I come in?" I heard someone ask and looked up to find Banu standing there.

"You already are." I chuckled at her.

"What happened?" She motioned to my banded back.

"Was attacked." I got up and moved to my clothing.

"What are you doing?" she asked me and moved more into the room.

"Training," I said while I pulled on a tank top. I hadn't wanted to change into another sports bra, it would have taken too much time. I pulled on my sweatpants and training shoes, grabbed my blades, and walked past Banu.

"I'll get the rest, we can train together," Banu said while she kept walking behind me.

"Sure. I'll wait," I told her. Shortly after she left, Flynn walked through the door.

"Why are you out of bed and dressed like that?" He looked me up and down.

"Training," I answered him as Banu and the others walked up to us. "You ready?" I asked them and started walking away, just for Flynn to follow us.

"My King," DeeDee started, "can we help you with something?"

"No," he answered.

"Okay," she said and gave me a lopsided smile. We kept on walking in silence after that. Flynn stayed close to my back. It was comfortable, having him there. We reached the training rooms, but it wasn't as busy as the last time I had been there.

We moved to the back of the room where there were mats on the floor. We started our warm ups. Flynn stayed and watched, leaning against the wall next to us. I ignored him and stretched. It was hard, I could feel his eyes roaming over my body.

"Let's spar together," I told the others. I paired up with Banu, and DeeDee and Lena paired, too. We started standard training, moving around each other. Kicking out, slamming our fist at each other, ducking and moving again. I started breathing harder, feeling the pain in my back quickly. I pushed myself harder, wanting to forget the pain, the memory of his kiss. I was distracted when Banu kicked out, sweeping my feet from under me. She jumped on me and smiled.

"You're dead," she said. I breathed out slowly and nodded at her.

"You are distracted by something or someone." Before I could say something to her, she looked over at Flynn. I nodded, knowing it was better to have her thinking it was him; well partly, it had been him, all of them. And I had gone and added a fifth. I groaned a little because the idea of fifth man around was great, heavenly, amazing, and terrible all at the same time. Flynn had moved towards us when he heard me groan. His hands were by his side, flexing, and his jaw was taut; his eyes moved over me.

"You are done," he gritted out. Banu got off of me and held up her hand, instead for Flynn to bend down and pick me up, holding me against his chest as he started moving.

"Uh, what?" I protested at him.

"No," he growled out. I sighed and placed my arms around his neck then laid my head down against his chest. I waved at the others who now laughed at me.

"Where are we going?" I asked him when we were in the hallway.

"My room," he said softly and moved towards their Quarters. My heartbeat picked up.

"Why?"

"I need to clean your wound. I have supplies," he said, and he pulled me closer to him. I breathed in his scent, the lemon and burned wood, which made me think of home, filled my nose. We reached their Quarters. Only Cian was in the main room when we walked in.

"Flynn, what are you doing?" he asked when he saw me in Flynn's arms. Flynn growled, so I answered for him.

"Helping." And I gave him a soft smile and winked before we made it through the door that led to the staircase and their rooms.

When we were in the hallway, he walked into the third room. He gently placed me down on a large bed to the left.

"On your stomach," he demanded. I did what he asked, my head on my arms as my eyes followed him around the room. His room was simple, a cabinet, two chairs, with a small coffee table between them. Bookcase to one side of the room and windows that let in a little light. There was another door, probably leading towards the bathroom. He moved towards the small cabinet next to the door we had come in. It was full of bottles with labels on it. He grabbed a few, placed one back and then moved towards me. He placed the bottles on the nightstand and looked at me.

"Shirt off," he said.

"Yes, Sir," I joked at him. I needed something to cut the tension in the room.

"Isa, please," he said, and I looked up at him where his eyes pleaded with mine. I wiggled myself out of my tank top. My sports bra fell just next to the wound, which was lucky for the guy who had done that to me. I had been wearing my favourite one, if he had hit it . . . oh, he would have burned.

"Thank you," he said. The bed dipped when he sat next to me. Softly, his hands started to take the bandage off. I hissed a little when I felt it sticking to the wound.

"You should have let me treat it yesterday, not only bandaged it," he scolded me. He opened a bottle, and the air filled with a strong smell, I scrunched my nose up at it.

"What's that?" I asked him when he moved to put it on my wound.

"Healing salve, Cian made it for me. It helps speed up our healing even more; it closes the skin and kills all the bad bacteria." He placed it softly on the wound, rubbing it in with easy and slow strokes. I closed my eyes. When he was done with that, he moved to grab another bottle.

"When did you see Mara?" he asked me, when his face was turned away from mine. I swallowed. He had caught me off guard.

"In Icas Nox's house, when I was hiding from him. She found me," I told him. "I thought she lived there. She seemed so real," I breathed it out, the memory had still been close in my mind.

"She did, we did," he said when he turned around with a new bandage. "This has some cream on it, keeps the bandages away from the wound and still allows it to heal." He placed the bandage on my wound. When he was done, I turned onto my back, so I could look at him.

"What happened?" I asked him. He looked at his hands, that big guy suddenly looked so small with the way he sat there. I got up and sat on his lap, wrapped my arms around him, and held him close to me.

"We were young. One day we were playing in the woods. Our parents had told us not to go there, still we went. I dared her to go with me." He swallowed with the memory. "Mara was always the toughest of us. She knew what she wanted even when she was just twelve." He looked at me and gave me a sad smile.

"We played hide and seek, it was my turn to find her."

I moved my fingers over his neck, circling them softly.

"She hid." He swallowed. "And I counted. The moment I heard her scream, I ran. She screamed so hard, I moved harder. When I reached her, she was cornered by a Dark-world creature. It had wings, big wings. Claws for nails and more of a dog's nose than a humans. It snarled at her, licked with his long tongue at her." He shuddered at the memory. "When I moved into view, he looked at me, and I could swear he laughed. Before I could do anything, he speared her on his claws. Right through her chest." A sob racked his body. "She looked at me, did you know? She asked me to help, and I was too late." Another sob racked his body.

"I saw her eyes turn lifeless, her body fell down to the ground, blood all over her. And that creature, it just laughed and flew away." He looked at me, the pain so overwhelming in his eyes, it made me choke up.

"Babe, it's okay. It wasn't your fault. You couldn't have known that there would be a Dark-worlder."

"I could have," he said and pushed me away to get up.

"No, Babe," I said, my voice was strong even with all those feelings going through me.

"Yes, our parents told us. They said not to go there. Not

to go into the forest, don't go too far. And still we did, I did. And she came with me."

"No," I said to him, following him. I placed my hands on both sides of his face. "Babe, no. You didn't know it was there, in that spot she would be hiding. Yes, it is terrible that it happened, that she died. Only, you were a child, too, young and a little foolish. Please don't blame yourself." As if his sorrow had summoned her, Mara appeared next to us.

"It wasn't his fault. It will never be his fault," she told me. I nodded at her. "Please tell him I love him. He is the best big brother I could have."

"Flynn." I made him look into my eyes. "She is here."

He sucked in a breath, and he moved his head around, making my hands fall from his face. "Where?" he asked. I pointed next to him, he turned and looked.

"She wants you to know that she loves you. That it isn't your fault. Wrong moment and wrong time. You were a child." Mara nodded at me, she reached out towards Flynn, brushing his hands, his fingers twitched.

"She is really here?" he asked me, his voice pitching a little higher.

"Yes. Flynn, you were young. You couldn't defeat a Dark-world creature by yourself. It is hard, I'm sorry. But she is fine, she is happy."

"I'm so sorry, sis," Flynn said, his face wet from the tears he had never cried till then.

"It is okay, brother. I love you."

I repeated what she said, and he looked over at me. A soft, sad smile on his face. "Thank you," he said.

Then Mara turned towards me. "I haven't found anything yet," she said and disappeared.

I moved back towards Flynn, hugging him close. "She is gone, Flynn. She is fine, and you did your best," I told him again. He looked at me and his hands moved towards my face. He lowered his head and kissed me softly, a brush of his lips against mine.

"Thank you," he said again.

"It's fine," I told him and held him again, placing my head on his shoulder. We stood like that for quite some time. "Mourn now, but leave it behind you, Flynn. Holding onto it is never good, she is happy now. That is the most important thing there is," I told him. He nodded to me. "I need to go take a shower, okay? I can shower with the bandages, right?" I asked him while I touched it.

"That is no problem." He moved towards my shirt that was still on the bed. Picking it up, he handed it to me. "You are amazing, Guerrero," he said and kissed me again, his lips more demanding, moved over mine. I leaned into him, deepening our kiss. His tongue darted out, and I greeted his with mine. We kissed until we were gasping for breath. I pulled away. His dark eyes were full of promises and sorrow. How I wanted to react to the promise, but he needed to mourn; he needed to give that sorrow a place.

"It will be fine," I said to him and touched his chest for a second before I moved away. I walked out of his room and back towards the hallway that would lead towards my room. I still had my shirt in my hands, walking around in my sports bra.

"Look who's here," someone said when I walked through the door. I looked up, seeing the other Witches standing before me.

"Getting lucky?" one of them asked, pointing at my shirt in my hand.

"Move," I grumbled at them, totally not in the mood for them then.

"No," one of them said.

"Yes, girl. I'm not in the mood to play," I told them and started moving past them.

"But we are." I looked up at the one talking. It was the same Witch that had helped Thalia, she had brown hair hanging loosely around her. She was skinny without any womanly curves; her eyes slanted a little at the edges, and her nose was a little too big for her face.

"You are spending too much time with them, getting too many privileges, and you have been here longer than us. It isn't fair." She folded her arms in front of her. I waited for her to stamp her foot on the ground, just to be disappointed when nothing happened.

"That is up to them. Please move now." They blocked my way to my room.

"No," a redhead said.

"Oh, come on, girls. Why today?" I asked them with a growl.

"Why not?" someone in the back asked. And with that, the air slammed into me, totally unexpected as I flew against the door. Hitting my shoulder hard, I grunted out.

I pushed the Witch's magic down, and I dropped to the ground.

"You ladies have chosen the worst day to be mad at me. I'll give you one more chance. Move," I said.

"Only if you promise not to talk to the Kings anymore," the first Witch said, her hands now flickering with Fire.

"Oh, Babe–" I started.

"I'm not your Babe," she sneered.

"That isn't up to you to decide," a voice boomed from behind them. I looked around, finding Averey standing there, his hands crossed in front of his chest.

25

His eyes moved over the girls in front of me, and he looked sexy as hell standing there.

"Your Highness," some of the Witches muttered.

"Hi," I said, which got me a glare from Witch Bitch number one.

"It is 'Your Highness,'" she said and turned around to look at Averey as she bowed low. "My King," she purred. I rolled my eyes and started moving towards my room.

"Where do you think you are going?" Witch Bitch said, when she noticed me moving.

"My room." I pointed at my door, she cocked her head to the side. "No," was what she said next. It made me laugh, and her face reddened. "Why do you think that is funny?" she asked me.

"Isn't it?" I laughed.

"You need to bow to your King," she said instead.

"Nah, not today." I told her and moved to open my door.

"You can't act like this, you aren't the Queen here. You are nothing!" she screamed at me. I looked at her and then to Averey. One side of his mouth had curved up when he saw me looking at him. I rolled my eyes again and looked back at the Witch.

"Girl, I don't have time for this. My back hurts, and I really want a shower."

I moved again to push open the door, the Witch moved even closer to me and said in a low voice, "You need to leave. You don't belong here."

I was so sick of them; my temper had risen higher with everything that had come out of her mouth.

"You think I don't belong here? Do you even know to who you are talking to?" I started, my hands on my hips as I glared at her. "I am Isadora S–"

"That is enough! Inside, ladies!" Averey's voice boomed over us. I looked at him, the rest of my sentence died when he shook his head at me.

"Yes, My King," the Witch Bitch said and moved to the end of the hallway.

I finally opened my door and threw it closed when I was inside, except the satisfying slam never came. I looked back at the door, Averey stood there with his hand holding the door open.

"What?" I asked him.

"Don't tell them," he said while he walked into the room, closing the door softly.

"Why? I'm sick of them yelling at me and of the looks they give me. And they came only two days ago. How will it go after the ball, the dates? When you guys . . ." Words stopped flowing out of my mouth with the idea that they would be picking other Witches, too. The world expected them to have four Queens, not one–not like my Great-Grandmother.

"Ah ducks." I threw up my hands and turned towards my bedroom.

"Isa, you can't tell them. If you do it now, they would hate you even more. For being better than them. You already are, they can see that," he said to me. I swirled around.

"I don't want to be better than them. I want to be me,

Protector and Witch. I want to be Fucking Isadora Seraphina Savill Royal. And nothing more. I want to be me."

"And you are. That will not change." He moved closer towards me, and I took a step back.

"I don't know. I was always Isadora, solely that. Nothing more." I looked at the ground, my hands fumbling with my pants.

"That's not true, sweetheart, you were always more. You are a Protector." He moved his hands towards me, and I stepped back.

"What did you want?" I asked when I looked at him, his silver-grey eyes focused on me.

"I came to ask you something," he said calmly.

"That is?"

"What happened on the roof last night?"

"I already told you guys." Again, I threw my hands up in the air and moved towards my bedroom.

"You didn't tell me, us, everything. There is more." I whirled back around. His arms were folded in front of him. It made him look so yummy, I wanted to lick him all over. I shook my head with that thought, just for Averey to react to the movement.

"You need to tell us." His voice was lower, it made me shiver and be angry at the same time.

"No, I told you. The girl was more dead than alive. He controlled her and was angry when I broke her legs. He killed her, and I fought him off, and when he was gone, you guys came running in."

"Him?"

"That's all you took from it?" I placed my hands on my sides, and Averey moved closer.

"You didn't tell us it was a him. Was he an elemental? Human?"

"He killed the servant, he used some kind of magic. And he looked human." I didn't tell him that his lips definitely felt human. The anger that radiated from Averey would have exploded the moment had I mentioned that I had kissed the Dark-worlder and liked it. Especially the *liked it* part.

"What else?" He looked at me, his silver-grey eyes full of storms, the ones I didn't want to be in right now.

"Nothing, I attacked him, scared him off, and he left. Like I said, you guys came running in." I folded my arms over my chest, which pushed up my breasts. I was still wearing my sweat pants and sports bra. His eyes flickered to them, and his breathing stopped for a second before it sped up.

My cue to leave the room.

"I'm done with this, I told you what happened. I need a shower," I told him, then turned around and moved towards my bedroom.

"Why didn't you use your magic?" he asked, while he followed me.

"Can't you just leave?" I motioned to the bedroom we were standing in.

"It's my castle," he answered.

"Not technically." I narrowed my eyes at him.

"Oh, yes, as long as you aren't Queen, it is mine. I'm free to enter every room I want, without permission from anybody. Not even yours." He looked smug at that, one side of his mouth pulled up.

"Fine, feel free." I started pulling off my shoes, indicating I still would go and take that shower.

He moved to stand differently, it made me notice the growing bulge in his pants that seemed to grow even more when I started looking at it.

"Why didn't you use your magic?" he asked again, his voice was low and coarse and not angry.

"He thought I was a protector. I went with it." I was now barefoot and looking at him.

Averey cleared his throat and asked next, "Why did you let him escape?" He tilted his head and kept looking at me, waiting for an answer. I didn't even know why I had let him go. I was strong and fast enough to get him. The kiss had surprised me as much as it did him, and for a second, I had totally forgotten he had thrown a chained knife in my back. I could only think of his lips on mine, his dark eyes searching my face, his mouth that could do so much more then kiss me.

"Isa. Sweetheart," I heard.

"Huh, what?" I answered and looked at Averey who was now a hell lot closer than first. His warmth had started radiating into me.

"I asked, 'why did you let him escape?'"

I looked up at him. "I don't know," I told him honestly, okay, almost honestly.

"Can you tell me more about him, so we can keep an eye out?" Averey asked, his voice was low and seductive when he said that.

"Yeah. Short black hair, dark eyes, and he wore all black." I started, I was still looking into Averey's eyes. Those stormy silver-grey eyes that sucked you in and kept you there. I almost forgot one important thing.

"The chain he used." I closed my eyes for a short time, the closeness and the heat of Averey made my head spin a little, the memory of the man's lips on mine helped, too.

"It turned into ink on his arm, when he pulled it back." I used my own finger to indicate what I meant on my arm, swirling it from my hand up to my shoulder. Averey's eyes followed the movement, turning even darker. His hand moved towards my arm, trailing the same path I had just made, making the hairs on my arm rise and my body shiver.

"It sank into his skin?" he murmured, while his eyes followed his own fingers. They reached up to my shoulder, to stop there and move back down again. He kept doing it for a few times, until I stepped back. His hand dropped next to his body, and it seemed it snapped him out of wherever he had been.

"I need to talk to the others about that."

"Okay, Go." I motioned with my hands towards the door, shooing him out of the room.

"No," he growled out again, and I rolled my eyes. That man changed his mood as fast as a woman could.

"Why not?" I asked him.

"Because you are still holding something back. And you need to tell it."

"No." I mimicked him.

"Isadora Seraphina Savill Royal." He moved even closer, his chest pressing against mine, his chest expanded with his breath, it pushed me back a little. His hands were clenched by his side, almost as if he had wanted to keep his hands away from me. It made me a little sad, I had loved the way his finger had moved over my arm, the tingling sensation it left. Even when I stepped away, I wished I hadn't.

"Using my full name doesn't make me want to tell you." I narrowed my eyes at him.

"Ha, there is something more."

"Duckface and pancakes," I swore at him. "Yes, and no, I'm not telling you. It will not help you with anything. Just fuck off, okay? Let me get my shower. I smell," I growled out at him, angry we were still talking about it. I made a move to turn around, instead he grabbed hold of my arm.

I froze.

"Averey Thorne–" I started, except for him to chuckle.

"Using my full name doesn't work, either." I looked at him, there was a ghost of a smile on his lips.

"Your Highness. Please, let go of me?" I asked as sweetly as I could, and for a moment, his face fell, all the play leaving it.

"Isa, sweetheart," he started, still holding my arm.

I yanked it out of his grip and placed my hands on my sides, narrowed my eyes, and told him what I thought. "Don't start 'sweethearting' me. I'm not your sweetheart, I'm not your bonded, I'm not your Protector or in your service. Meaning," I held up my hand, which stopped him from speaking, "that I don't have to explain anything to you, don't have to tell you anything, or do whatever the fish sticks you asked. So no, I will not tell you everything that happened on that roof. It is none of your freaking business, and like I said," I waited for a second before continuing, letting it all sink in, "it. Will. Not. Help. You. With. Anything." I growled the last part and turned around again. I moved to the bathroom, but before I could open the door, he bellowed.

"You will tell me, even if I need to make you!" I could feel the air moving around him, the magic told me how angry he was. I turned around slowly, arched my eyebrow at him, and looked him over. His breath came fast, and his hands were fisted next to him.

"Make me," was the only thing I said, the challenge clear in it. He stood there, not moving at all.

Suddenly, he moved, his magic making him blur until he stood in front of me with a smile on his lips and his eyes focused on mine.

"Are you sure?" he breathed out, and all I could do was nod. His mouth slammed into mine, hard and demanding. I stood there, his lips against mine, and a sigh escaped me, opening my lips a little to him. He pushed his tongue in, deepening the kiss. This had me reacting to him. I pressed myself against him, moving my hands up his arms, towards his neck and face. Holding my hands on either side of him, I pulled us apart. Looking up into his eyes, I saw they were full of passion. It had darkened them, made them beautiful. I sighed again and slammed my mouth back onto his, pressing my body against him.

His hands moved towards my hips, pulling me against his hardness. It made me gasp, and he took advantage, nibbling on my bottom lip. I groaned at the sensation it gave me. I moved back, taking in a breath. My voice was husky when I spoke, "How is this going to make me tell you?"

"Oh, you will. I plan on making you scream, cum, and tell all your secrets to me. And then, I'll make you mine." His eyes moved over my face, and my heartbeat picked up, faster and faster until I thought it would have beat out of my chest.

"Oh," I answered back. What in crab's name do you say to something like that?

"Yes," he said, almost as if he had read my mind.

His hands started kneading my hips, slowly moving one up towards my back and the other down towards my ass. As he stroked and kneaded, I gave in and relaxed against him. He chuckled. His hands moved around again, towards my shoulders, my back, and then my ass again.

In one motion, he lifted me up, and I wrapped my legs around him. He growled a little at that and pressed me hard against the wall. His lips found mine again, this time softer and slower when moving over mine. I nibbled at his bottom lip and then bit hard. He growled again, pushing his cock against my center, making me gasp. He moved towards my jaw kissing down it, towards my earlobe and nibbling on it. I writhed against him. He slowly moved lower, kissing the side of my neck, sucking at it, and kissing it over and over. I leaned my head back against the wall, closed my eyes and sighed, it felt so amazing.

His hands were still on my ass, holding me up. He moved towards my mouth again, parting my lips with his, our tongues meeting each other. My hands moved up his body, I took hold of one of his braids and pulled him back a little. It made him growl, low and so freaking hot.

Only, I needed to say something first; so, I placed my finger on his lips, letting him know to stop. My other hand still held his braid. Before I could say anything, his tongue darted out and licked my finger, it made me shiver, and for a moment, I forgot what I had wanted to say.

When I found my voice again, I said one word to him. "Virgin."

This made him still. My finger was still on his lips, and

he moved them a little, sucking my finger into his mouth. It was so hot, and my core turned even wetter than it already was. I moaned, and that was all he needed to hear because he pressed his hardness into me and claimed my lips again.

26

He started moving; his cock rubbed against me. It made my pants rub against my clit, and a moan escaped me. He pressed me harder against the wall, pinning me between him and it. His hands were free to move over my body. He trailed one over my legs and back up, towards my sides and then to my sports bra, over my breasts. My nipples turned hard from the friction, pressing through the fabric. He looked at them, hunger in his eyes.

I let go of his braid and moved my hands towards his back, his muscles moved under them. His hands started exploring me again; moving over my stomach, my hips, and back to my ass. He pressed against me with his whole body. I sucked in a sharp breath when my wound pressed harder against the wall, a shooting pain made me squeeze my eyes shut, and a whimper escaped me.

"Are you okay?" he asked me, while pulling back a little, making me sag against him, my breathing hard.

"Yes, shoulder," I said to him.

"Sorry," he said, concern now in his eyes.

"Don't worry. But, no wall?" I asked him, while I gave him a lopsided smile. He chuckled, his hands grabbed my hips and pulled me harder against him. I folded my arms around his neck and held onto him. He kissed my cheek, my nose, and then my eyes before he moved back to my mouth. We kissed for a time, my breathing picking up again, and I started moving my hips in his hands, rubbing myself against him.

"Isa," he growled out.

"What?" I asked against his mouth.

"Stop doing that."

"Why?" I giggled at him and pulled back. He sighed and squeezed my ass, pressing me against him, and I wiggled with it. He moaned when I felt his hard cock press against me again, and a soft sigh escaped me.

"Bed?" I asked him, I wanted more of his skin against mine, I wanted to know what his tongue could do.

"Are you sure?" he asked me, sweet but not what I wanted to hear. I wiggled myself out of his grip, letting myself slide along his body, his hardness pressed against my lower stomach. I looked at him, licked my lips, and moved away from him. He let me, his eyes followed every movement I made.

When I stood before my bed, I shimmied out of my sweatpants, moving my hips from side to side. His eyes stayed glued on my black panties. I tsked at him. "Eyes up here, honey," I told him and pointed at my own eyes. He did what I suggested, but slowly. His eyes roamed my body, setting it on fire just by looking at it. When his eyes landed on mine, it took me a moment to remember what I was doing. His silver-grey eyes, lit up; they sucked me in and kept me there.

I moved my hands towards my sports bra, his eyes caught the movement, and it made me swallow as they turned even darker. I placed my hands under the rim of it and pulled it slowly up, setting my breasts, which now heavy from arousal, free. My nipples hardened again, and his eyes focused on them, a hunger filling them—something I hadn't seen in Averey's eyes. Before I could start pulling off my panties, he moved. Steps slow and deliberate, his chest rising slowly, and his eyes roamed over my half naked body, the hunger intensifying.

He stood before me then, his hands still at his sides. Slowly, he moved them up, and I held my breath, he moved them to the hem of his shirt. Pulling it over his head, he showed me that perfect body I had kept dreaming about. I moved my hands to his chest, the warmth seeping into them the moment I laid them on his skin. I could feel his heartbeat, beating fast under them. I moved my hands towards his shoulders and down his arms–those strong arms that would keep me safe, hold me no matter what would happen. I moved lower, towards his hands. His fingers held onto mine for a moment, entwining them in a lover's embrace. I pulled them loose and moved back up, using my fingernails to trail over his arms. He shivered a little, which made me grin; I already loved the effect I had on him.

My hands moved towards his chest, slowly towards his nipples. I moved over them, softly at first, and as he leaned into me a little soft moan escaped him. I moved back; circled around them and played with them. When I pinched one, he growled at me. I loved that sound from him, manly and natural.

I moved my hands lower, skimming his skin and enjoying the feel of it. I moved my hands over his abs, hard and chiseled. He was hairless except for the small streak of hair from his abdomen towards the edge of his pants. They hung low, the 'V' shape perfect, disappearing into his pants, too. It made me disappointed and angry at the same time, and I narrowed my eyes at his pants, my hands moved towards them. I wanted to touch more, see more, and explore more. I needed more. I licked my lips at the idea of tasting more. But his hands stopped me, their grip firm, and he pulled them away. I looked up at him, he shook his head no at the question that was written on my face.

He pushed me back a little, and I felt the edge of my bed against my knees before he pushed further, and I fell back.

He stood in front of me, staring down, his hands still holding onto mine.

He looked me over, his eyes stopping on my panties. He moved towards me, placing my hands above my head. "Leave them there," he said. His hands slid down my arms, over my breasts and towards my hips. It made me squirm under them. He hooked his thumbs under my panties and pulled them down. He threw them on the ground and looked at me, his eyes drinking me in. Wherever they touched, my skin heated up, and my breathing became even more ragged.

He slowly moved his hands towards the bulge in his pants and stroked himself a few times. It had me heating up even more, I pressed my knees together and wiggled, trying to release the pressure between my legs, to give me some friction against myself.

"Stop that," he growled out, and I made a small noise of disappointment. "Or don't you want my help?" He was still slowly stroking himself, my eyes followed the movement. "Sweetheart?" he growled out at me when I didn't say anything.

"Yes?" I breathed, and I looked at him. He smiled at me, which made me heat up even more. The room had to be on fire right then.

"You are perfect," he said while his eyes kept moving over my naked body. He stopped stroking himself and moved towards me, slowly lowering over me, my arms still above my head. It made my breasts stand out more, catching his attention. He looked at my pebbled nipples and slowly blew on one. I writhed at the sensation, then his tongue darted out, and he licked it. That had me closing my eyes, they opened wide when he sucked my nipple into his mouth. I opened my mouth, but no sound come out of it.

His hand moved over my skin, trailing towards my other breast. His fingers, slowly moved over my nipple making it even harder than it already was. I arched into his hand when he placed it over my breast, squeezing it softly. He kept sucking at my other nipple, used his tongue to play with it. Before he let it go, he bit into it, and I moaned.

I could feel him chuckle against me, the vibration going straight to my core. I wanted to rub myself against something, I needed friction. Averey moved then, placing his leg between mine, pushing against me. I moved my hips, using the friction of his pants to release the sensation between my legs. Only, I needed more, so much more.

His mouth moved towards my throat, towards my ear, and he sucked at it before going back towards my mouth. He kissed me, deeply and full of passion and hunger. I sucked in a breath when he moved again, kissing and biting down towards my other breast, teasing it before he moved lower. I moved my hands towards his hair, wanting to touch him so badly.

"No," he said and pulled away from my skin. He placed my hands back above my head.

"Leave them there," he said to me, his voice low and coarse. I merely nodded at him, I was lost for words. My breathing was fast and shallow.

"Good," he said and started to kiss my right arm, slowly moving back towards where he had stopped. He moved his leg away, and before I could say something about it, his hand filled up the spot his leg had left.

He started circling around my clit, not really touching it, solely staying around it. He was teasing me, and I rocked against him, wanting more. I grabbed the sheets with my hands while I writhed under him.

Then he flicked his thumb over my clit, and I screamed at the sensation. He chuckled. Slowly he started rubbing it, putting more pressure to it and releasing it when I started to buck against his thumb.

"Off," I breathed, I couldn't even make full sentences anymore by then. He wasn't even in me, and he had already had me writhing around him, moving and panting.

"What?" he asked, his hand stilled on my core, his fingers laying over it.

"Pants, off," I said and looked at them, trying to get them to vanish. I wanted to feel more of him, see more of him. I wanted him.

"Okay," he said and pulled his hand away, I whimpered at the loss of heat there. His hands moved towards his pants, opening the buttons slowly. My eyes took it all in, but I wanted to help, make him go faster. But I remembered his threat and kept my arms above my head.

He let his pants drop, and his cock bulged even more in his boxers. I licked my lips. His hands moved towards his boxers, and he slowly pulled them down. His cock sprung free, it was big and amazing. My breathing hitched at the full sight of him, and I greedily drunk it in. His silver eyes were full of lust, his chest rising, his powerful muscles all on display for me, and his cock was tempting me to taste him.

I moved before he could do anything; I moved my hand around his shaft and stroked it. Fuck the threat. His cock was soft and hard at the same time. He moaned, and I smiled at him, my eyes focused on his cock in front of me. I licked my lips again, and then darted my tongue out, tasting the pre-cum on the tip. He bucked, and I gripped a little harder.

"No," I said, the roles were changed now. He chuckled, he knew.

I licked again, slowly, tasting him. My tongue moved over the tip of him, he was so big. I trailed my fingers over his shaft, slowly up and then down, stroking him gently as his cock became harder and his breathing picked up. I reached his balls and stroked them, too, kneaded them softly, letting them roll in my hand before trailing my fingers back towards the tip.

I had never done this, but I loved it. And I had let myself go, reacting to his moans and small movements. When I wrapped my hand all around him, I slowly moved towards his balls, and my mouth followed, swallowing him up. He groaned at that, and I could feel him move against me. His movement pressed him deeper into my mouth. I took it all, swirled my tongue around it and sucked. His hands moved to my head, his fingers entwined into my hair. The strong grip made me suck even harder, moving back a little. I used my teeth to scrape slowly and softly over his shaft, making him shiver. I sucked him back in and repeated myself, playing with his balls and using my tongue to lap up all the pre-cum of his. His hands became more pressing against the back of my head, and I sucked harder, moved faster. He growled out something and pulled himself out of my mouth. I whimpered for real that time, the sound actually came out of my mouth. His breathing was shallow and fast.

"Sweetheart, don't worry," he said, and he pushed me back on the bed, his body moving over mine. He slowly kissed his way back down again, it had me moving under him. Tasting him had been so amazing, and it had my core throbbing. When he reached my clit, he blew on it, the soft air tickled, and I moaned. His tongue darted out, and I was lost. He played with my clit as if it was the most precious thing in the world. He sucked, licked, and then pushed a finger into me.

"You're so wet, sweetheart. So wet for me," he said against my folds. His finger slowly moved in and out of me. I pressed myself against his finger, riding it. He added another, stroking the inside of my core. He pumped into me fast and then even faster. My core tingled, and I moaned, writhed, and rode his hand. The sensation brought me higher and higher, it soared through me, setting my nerves on fire. I closed my eyes and moaned, but it turned into a scream when everything released. Averey kept on licking me, his tongue slowly stroking my slit, licking up all the juices the dripped out of my core. I panted when the wave slowed down, still he kept licking me, his tongue slowly moved up and down my folds.

"I . . ." I started and took a breath. "I want you," I said and looked at the man between my legs. I wanted him, deep and buried in me, I wanted to feel him explode inside me, feel him shudder when he emptied himself. He pulled out his fingers, gave me a kiss down there and moved above me, his lips trailing over my skin, leaving heat in its wake.

He kissed me, and I tasted myself on his lips. It made me heat up all over again, I could feel his cock against my entrance. He looked into my eyes, and softly pressed. He entered me slowly, all the while he looked at me, his eyes focused on my face.

I arched my back, pressed my hips against him and fully took him. I sighed when he was fully in. The pain had been there, the one everyone always talked about. It was just for a moment, then it changed when he started to move. Slowly. He still looked at me. His cock moved into me and back out. The rhythm even and steady, all about me getting used to his cock. It filled me completely.

I moaned, and he started moving faster. My breasts bounced at the movement, and he lowered his mouth to one. Sucking the nipple into his mouth made me arch my back, and he pumped harder and harder. My hands roamed over his back, feeling the muscles move under them. I moved a hand towards his ass and squeezed it, pushing him deeper into me. His mouth moved towards mine to swallow my moans. And we kissed, his tongue moving around mine as he pumped harder and harder. I pressed against him more, wanting to take everything he gave me. I wrapped my legs around him, and he started a harder rhythm. When I thought I couldn't take anymore, he pressed even deeper, faster. My core was throbbing, and my nerves were back on fire again. The sensation moved through me, my breathing hitched, and I came again. Riding out the wave, he kept pumping into me, pulling out everything of my orgasm. Then he growled and shuddered. I could feel him pulsing inside me when he came. I pressed him closer against me, pulled him on top of me when his arms couldn't hold him up. He relaxed in my arms, and I breathed in his scent, mixed with my own scent and sweat.

"Hmm," I said to him.

"A good hmm?" he asked.

"Yeah," I answered and kissed his brow.

"Good. Can we do it again?" he softly asked me when he looked into my eyes.

"Now?" My eyes went wide.

"No," he chuckled, "another time." I relaxed in his arms. "Many times," he added, and I nodded. He moved off of me, pulling out of me, and I missed him immediately. He pulled me up the bed and laid down next to me.

"Did I hurt you?" he asked me, while his hand slowly trailed over my stomach.

"No." It was true, it did hurt a little, just not enough to mention. He had made it perfect.

"It was perfect," I said my last thought out loud. This earned me the biggest smile I had ever seen on his face.

"Are you going to tell me everything now?" he asked. For a second, I was taken back with that. Then I laughed.

"No." And I snuggled against him, my back against his chest and my head on his arm. I closed my eyes. "Like I said, you could try."

I felt the rumble of his laugh, and I smiled.

"Maybe I should try harder next time."

"Yeah, maybe," I said and yawned.

"Go to sleep, sweetheart. Rest." He pulled me even closer and pulled the sheets over us. I fell asleep in moments, content and happy.

27

Averey

Her breathing was soft against my skin, her face serene, and her hair splayed out over the cushion. I trailed my fingers over her arm, slowly moving towards her shoulders and her back. She hadn't stirred yet, only the goosebumps showed me that she was starting to wake. I moved to her back, slowly moving down. I had been hard the moment I had felt her soft breath against my chest, her warm body pressed against mine, and her heartbeat softly thumping against my chest.

It was heavenly, waking up like this. She was my bonded, my Natural Bonded. She belonged to me, to us, and it was the best feeling ever. That strong, stubborn woman belonged to us. And the sex, my cock twitched with the memory of it. How she had sucked me, moaned, and teased me, she had tasted amazing; she was heaven.

"Stop poking me," she murmured against my chest, her voice soft from sleep.

I chuckled at that. "Sorry, sweetheart. Can't help it when a goddess lays naked next to me." I kissed the top of her head, breathing her in. She smelled like me, sweat, and sex, and her own soft smell of summers on a beach. She pushed away a little, and I had to stop myself from pulling her back. She looked into my eyes, and I was lost in hers, the brown was surrounded by this honey-gold circle and was full of emotions. She had never really showed emotions on her face, except in her eyes. Those were the windows into her soul. She was looking at me then, as if she could look right into mine.

"About last night," she started. It totally surprised me, and I had to stop myself from pulling away. She regretted it, it wasn't something easy, losing your virginity.

"It was amazing." She breathed out, her cheeks turning red. She looked even better that way, her eyes downcast a little and her mouth a little open. I let go of the breath I was holding.

"But I will not tell you more of what happened on the roof." Her eyes were hard and defiant.

I nodded at her. "That is fine." She would tell me when she was ready, still, I said after it, "I like making you." And I kissed her on the lips. They parted for me, and a soft sigh escaped them. We kissed for some time, our limbs entangled, and our breathing started to pick up. Her hands stroked my back, and her breasts were pressed against my chest. I hated what I would be doing next.

I pulled back a little. "I need to go." I could feel her freeze before she asked.

"Why?"

"Sweetheart, I have a ball to organize."

She relaxed in my arms. I kissed her again and moved out of bed.

"Averey," she said before I was fully dressed and out of the door.

"Yes?" I turned and looked at her; that goddess, half-covered in the sheets, her nipples hard and her breasts teasing me, one leg from under the covers pulled up and her arms under her head she lay there, looking at me. I felt myself harden again, the inner battle to crawl back into bed was hard, and I would have lost it, if not for what she had said next.

Isadora

"Thank you," I said to him, he stood there with his shirt in his hands. His eyes moved over my body, I knew what I must have looked like. And I felt feminine in that moment, how his eyes heated up more and more, they heated me up. I really meant it.

"Don't leave me," I said softly, I kept my hands from wringing under my head.

I saw him deflate. "Sweetheart, I never would. You are my heart." Before he moved closer, the door opened in the other room, and Flynn stepped into my bedroom. His eyes landed on me, and if I thought I had known how lust looked, I was wrong. The lust that filled Flynn's eyes had my breath stopping and my heart skipping a beat. I wanted to be ashamed, for him finding me there, with Averey still half naked, but I couldn't, not with the heat that filled his eyes.

Averey made a low sound in his throat that snapped me and Flynn out of it.

"The council called," Flynn said to Averey, still his eyes were on me, his hands were fisted next to his body. I could see the bulge in his pants, it made me lick my lips.

"They want a meeting." His voice rumbled over me, and I wanted to moan just at the sound of his voice.

"Sorry, sweetheart. We have to go. Another time?" Averey said, which pulled my eyes to him, he winked and placed a hand on Flynn's chest to push him back. "Come on, Flynn, next time, we'll share," he told the other King, and I sucked in a breath, my nipples hardened even more at the idea of having them both.

Flynn kept looking at me when he said, "Soon." He then turned around and walked away with Averey.

I was left alone in the room, which had turned colder

instantly. I sighed and pulled up the sheets, then laid there, watching the ceiling. A tingle interrupted my thoughts, and I looked around, finding Mara standing next to my bed.

"Hi, Hunny bear," I said to her and smiled. I pulled the sheets higher and sat up.

"I found something," she blurted out.

"Tell me." I moved towards her, holding the sheets close to my body.

"My uncle, he is collecting magical beings. Not only Witches, also Elementals," she started, her hands holding on to the fabric of her pants.

"Do you know what for?"

She nodded her head, "He drains them."

I kept looking at her, waiting for more. "To do what?" I asked her when nothing came.

She looked over her shoulder, and when she looked back at me her eyes were wide.

"I don't know, something big." She looked again over her shoulder. I followed her line of sight, except seeing nothing.

"I have to go, something is hunting me. I need to go, I need to hide." Her wide brown eyes looked at me, and a chill ran up my spine with the fear I saw in her eyes. "Go," I mouthed to her, and she vanished.

I kept staring at the spot where Mara had been, wondering what Nox must have been planning. All kinds of scenarios ran through my head. It was quickly giving me a headache, and I pressed my palms into my eyes.

"Shower first," I said to myself and got up, the sheet falling down my body as I made my way towards the shower. When the hot water trailed over my skin, I closed my eyes, and a plan started to form in my head. I needed Banu and the others for it. It would be the first thing I'd do before anything else. I moved out of the shower, dried myself, and put on my clothing. I strapped my swords and other weapons onto my body and moved towards the hallway.

That time, there were no other Witches there, and I breathed out a sigh of relief.

"They are in the ballroom," someone next to me said. I looked over finding Liv standing at the door of the Kings' Quarters.

"Who?" I asked her.

"The other Witches. They are practicing dancing. One of them found out the Kings like to dance, so the Witches are trying to win their hearts with that. Or their cocks, not sure which one they wanted first." Liv chuckled at that.

I smiled at her.

"I'm looking for the three Protectors who came to the Castle yesterday."

"You mean the blonde happy girl, the short-haired serious lady, and the silent one?"

I chuckled at that. "Yeah, those three."

"The blonde one and the silent one, they are training with the Chief, and the other, not sure." Liv looked around. Almost as if Banu was hiding behind a curtain and would jump out and yell 'surprise'.

"It's okay, I will find her." I told Liv and moved towards the main entrance. There were people walking in and out of the big doors, carrying flowers and other things into the ballroom. I hadn't seen any of the Kings there, which made me a little relieved. I was still a little sour after Averey, and I don't know how I would react if the other two saw me then. It was hot and bad enough to have Flynn walking in on us, and we weren't even doing something then.

I looked down from the balcony, my mind wandering to the evening before. How his hands had felt against my skin, his tongue teasing me, and his cock that had slowly entered me. I sighed a little and opened my eyes to look down again.

I moved down the stairs and walked towards the ballroom. The other Witches were dancing in a corner of the room. Swirling around, their dresses moving around their legs. I hoped I wouldn't have to dance, I was not made for that. I moved away before they noticed me. I didn't want a repeat of last night. Okay, not of them and me. Averey and me, hell yes, and Flynn, yes him, too. Oh, and Cian and Rayan. My mind was too occupied to keep track of my surroundings. I almost walked into someone, holding a vase of flowers.

"Sorry," I mumbled and moved on. Something made me turn around to look, seeing a glimpse of short black hair. I moved after it, merely to lose the person in the group of other servants. I kept looking around me, trying to find the person. There was something about that person that had triggered me. It had me on high alert, and I needed to find him. Figure out why I was reacting like that.

"What are you doing here?" I heard and looked at the voice, totally forgetting the black hair, I rolled my eyes and flipped them off when I walked out of the ballroom. I didn't have time for those Witches, I needed to find Banu. Even more so then.

I walked towards the throne room, hoping she would be there. It was filled with other Protectors, just not Banu. Moving towards the servant's side of the castle, I walked into the Kitchen, there was a chance she would be there. Banu liked food as much as I did.

"Hello, girl," the cook greeted me.

"Hi. Did you see Banu?" I asked him, while I looked around.

"Who do you mean?" he asked me while he kept stirring in a big, amazingly good-smelling, pot.

"This other protector, my height, short hair and always serious-looking."

He chuckled at that. "I think I know who you meant, she was in here earlier. Took some food with her and left."

"Do you know where to?" I asked him, he shook his head.

"Thanks," I said.

"Girl, take some bread with you." The cook motioned towards the table, filled with bread and other foods. I looked at it, my stomach agreed with the cook.

"Maybe I'll just eat first," I said, while I rubbed my stomach. Averey and I had slept in late, missing breakfast and almost lunch. He laughed and his belly shook. "You do that, girl, eat as much as you want."

I sat down and started to eat. The kitchen was busy, people came in and out, some carrying empty plates, others supplies. I thanked the cook when I was done and made my way out of the kitchen. When I was in the hall-way, I looked to the left and right, contemplating where to go next.

I needed to find Banu, we needed to discuss what to do about the ball and the plan Icas Nox was forming. I needed her and the girls to keep Astra safe, he had taken her once. Maybe he would try again.

There was one thing that kept bugging me. He wanted to have powerful witches and take their magic, draining them dry. Why go for Astra and not me? He must have known that I was more than I looked?

I shook my head, I needed to find Banu. With what had happened on the roof, that guy had snuck into the Castle without a problem. Who was to say he wouldn't do it again? The glimpse of black hair behind flowers came into my mind again.

"Purple pancakes," I grumbled out, I looked at the door that would lead towards the main hall. I knew who that guy was, the one who had attacked me. And I knew I would never find him again, he would have recognized me. I moved towards the wall next to the kitchen door, I needed to focus, I needed to find Banu. I closed my eyes and set my magic out, searching for her. I had lived with her for years in the same school, I knew how she felt. I skimmed the people around me, touching the cook and the servants. I moved further throughout the castle, finding the Kings in their office. I lingered on them, loving the feel of their magic. It entwined with mine, and it took me a moment to push further. Finding the Witches in the ballroom, I didn't linger on them. I moved through the whole castle, only to end up at the swimming pool where Rayan had taken me and Astra. I could feel them both there. I pushed myself off of the wall and moved towards the training rooms where I had felt the other two.

Walking in, I immediately found DeeDee and Lena, I approached them.

"Girls, meet me in thirty minutes, my room." They nodded and went on with their training. There were a few other Protectors training. I guessed that the rest were on duty. I moved towards the doors, heading outside, the sun was high then. Which made me aware of the time, and I grumbled at Averey for letting us sleep this long.

I walked over the terrain and moved towards the pool house that stood near the wall. There was one Protector at the door that time. He mumbled chief when he saw me coming, and I nodded at him and moved to open the door. There was nobody in the pool, so they should have been in the dressing rooms. I moved towards them. A soft noise reached me, my hand on the door. Before I could push it open the noise came again. It hadn't sounded like someone was in distress.

I pushed the door open. My mouth hung open at what I had found.

Banu, with her hands in Astra's hair and their mouths locked into a passionate kiss. They hadn't noticed me, and I was not sure what to do right then. Astra's hands moved down Banu's body, and I noticed they both were in swimming clothing, leaving a lot of skin to be touched.

"Um." I cleared my throat when I saw Banu's hands moving towards Astra's swimming top. I loved Astra, had seen her boobs more times then I could count, but I didn't really want to see them like that. They both jumped back, panting, and they looked at me. When Astra had registered it was me, her face had turned a deep shade of red.

"Don't worry, girl," I said to her and gave her a wink. "I'm happy for you both." I looked over at Banu who just looked at the ground, not meeting my eyes.

"Banu," I said softly and moved towards her. "It is okay, I'm really happy for you both." I held her shoulder and shook her a little.

"You aren't mad?" she asked me.

"Why would I be?" I was genuinely shocked to hear her asking me that.

"I know how people look at me, how they reacted when they knew I liked women." She looked at me, her eyes filled with tears.

"Banu, I will never look at you differently, I never have and will not start now. I'm happy that Astra finally came out to me, and found you." I gave her a cheeky smile and squeezed her shoulder. "Only, we need to talk." I looked at them both. "Meet me in thirty minutes in my room. There are some things you girls need to know." I moved away, and before I went out of the door I shouted, "I am truly happy for you both!" I closed the door behind me and walked towards my room.

28

DeeDee and Lena were already in my room when I walked in. They lounged on the sofas.

"Hi, girls," I said and sat down next to them.

"You found Banu?" DeeDee asked me. I nodded at her, and they started talking about the training they were doing with the Chiefs of the castle, while we waited for the rest.

"We learned a lot of new stuff, and the other Protectors are really helping us out," DeeDee started.

"We never thought they would be this nice," Lena added to it.

"What do you mean?" I asked them. Normally, Protectors were nice towards each other.

"We heard stories about working in the castle. That it was this hard place, where you needed to prove yourself constantly. And if you wanted to become chief it would be impossible," DeeDee said.

"That's why we never really wanted to go here," Lena added.

"We don't like the whole hierarchy thing, that you need to be better to receive a better position. Only, it isn't like that. They all work hard, and they help each other out."

I looked at them both. "Where did you get that information? That working here sucked?" I asked them, worried about it.

"There are rumours going around the school, I thought you would have heard of it, too," Lena said, she pulled out her ponytail holder, her long brown hair falling down, before she shook it all loose.

"No. Haven't heard of it. I wasn't really planning on ending up here, you know?" I winked at her. We ended up talking about some of the male Protectors before Banu and Astra came walking in. I looked at them and gave them a wink, teasing them a little. Astra just stuck out her tongue, and Banu looked at the floor, I saw her cheeks turn a soft pink.

"Good, you both are here." I waved them towards the sofa. They sat next to each other, keeping space between them.

"First." I looked at DeeDee and Lena, they both looked at me, questions in their eyes at my grin on my face. "Banu and Astra are dating, this will be something between us," I started. I heard Astra gasp, and Banu growled. "Ah, hush, ladies. It is a good thing, and if we want to keep this a secret they should know."

"You can't keep this a secret from the Kings," Banu started.

"No not them, those other Witches out here. The Kings know," I explained.

"Wait, they know? Did you tell them?" Astra asked, she leaned towards me, her eyes narrowed.

"Yes and no. They'd already figured it out. And they promised me that you could stay here, in the Selection." I told her, and she relaxed, Astra looked at Banu and then the others before she moved closer to Banu, leaning against her. I saw Banu freeze for a second before she relaxed and pulled Astra more against her. It made me smile, seeing them so comfortable.

"The reason why I asked you girls here is this." I looked at them all, made eye contact before I started speaking.

They needed to know that it was serious. "There are some things that I need to tell you. You know who I am and what I am. What you didn't know, and me neither, until recently; I can talk to dead people." I tried to smile at that. It didn't reach my eyes. Nobody said anything, so I kept on talking. "When I rescued Astra, I talked to this little girl, Mara. She is the little sister of Flynn. Only, she died when she was twelve. She stayed here, in this world. She saw everything that Icas Nox did in that house." I looked at Astra, who sat up straight, her hand now in Banu's holding it. "I asked her to keep looking around, and she found out that he was draining Magical creatures, not only Witches and Elementals. Everything that holds some magic." I held up my hand towards Lena, who had opened her mouth to speak, telling her I wasn't done. "She doesn't know for what, or what his plan is. There was something hunting her, something that knew she was there. I told her to hide."

"Okay, what do you need from us?" DeeDee asked. I loved those girls, they never backed down from anything, and without much question, they did everything for each other.

"I think he is planning something at the ball. I don't know what, and I want you girls to keep an eye on Astra." I looked at my sister. "He wanted her before, and I'm afraid he wants her again." I could see her blue eyes go cold with the idea.

"We will keep you safe." Banu whispered to her, and I was even more grateful that they had found each other then.

"What about you?" Lena asked, and I looked at her.

"What about me?" I didn't know what she meant. I could keep myself safe.

"Why doesn't he want you? No offence, As," Astra shrugged with that, and Lena continued, "but you are more powerful than Astra is. If he is draining magical things, If I was him, I would want you." She looked at me, an eyebrow arched. It was the same thing I had thought.

"I don't know. Then there is something else."

"What happened?" Astra asked, she was now leaning towards me, her eyes focused on my face. She knew me too well.

"I was on this date, with Rayan. On the roof, and I was attacked," I started.

"Yeah?" she asked.

"The servant who helped us with the food, came in after Rayan had left. I offered to help the girl, I moved to pick up things and walked behind her towards the door. Before we reached the door, something hit me. And the servant changed after that, she became this walking dead person." I pulled my eyebrows together at the memory. "The person who attacked me sat on the railing of the roof. He had a chain in his hands that led towards me and a blade between my shoulder blades. When I made the servant immobile, he got angry and told me how he needed to find someone else. He used magic to kill her." I shuddered at that. "It was weird. Except it wasn't the strangest thing. I started attacking him, and he just laughed when I hit his face. Told me it tickled. I needed to find another way to hurt him." I looked at Astra, her blue eyes now filled with anger. "I moved closer and kissed him." The girls gasped. "It meant that I could grab the knife on the table behind him, and I stabbed him."

"You go, girl," DeeDee said, while she gave me two thumbs up and a crazy smile. I chuckled a little. "I could pull the knife out of my back while he was distracted. However, the weird part was. I liked the kiss. Oh, and I slept with Averey."

I kept still, my face had turned red a little as they all looked at me. I could see a smile starting on Astra's face, and Banu pressed her lips together to stop smiling, too. Lena's mouth hung open, and DeeDee gave me another thumbs up, which made me roll my eyes.

"So, you kissed this guy who wanted to kill you, and then you slept with Averey?" Astra asked, chuckling.

I shook my head. "No, the sleeping with Averey was last night, the guy trying to hurt me was two nights ago." And this had them squealing like little girls. They totally forgot the attack, I did, too.

"How was it?" Lena asked.

I shrugged. "Amazing," I said and blushed.

"Did it hurt?" was the next question.

"A little. Only, wow. He was so amazingly soft, sweet, and powerful." I felt my cheeks heat up at the memory, it made me heat up in other places, too. I kept myself from rubbing my legs against each other.

"Why didn't you start with this?" Astra asked.

"I didn't really want to tell you girls at first. And we need to find something against Nox, and we still need to plan on how to keep you safe." I pulled up my feet and hugged my knees.

"Only, after I saw you two sitting there, I really wanted to share it. I needed to share it. It was amazing, and I need my girls to talk about it."

"Okay, but what are we going to do about that man who attacked you?" Banu asked, she was and would always be the level-headed one.

"Not sure. I thought I saw him today again, when I was looking for you. But I don't know for sure. I walked into someone. That man was carrying a vase with flowers, and when he walked further, I saw this short black hair. It was the same as the man who attacked me. I'm not even sure it was him." I got up from the sofa and started pacing the room. "It was only a glimpse, and I walked after him, but couldn't find him again." I looked at the girls.

"Maybe it was just a servant who looked like him, or his hair. You just got attacked by him, you're just jumpy," DeeDee said. I nodded at her, that must be it.

"Okay, still. Tomorrow is the ball. I want you girls on high alert. And I want all three of you close to Astra. If Nox wants her, he will try to take her. We aren't letting that happen."

"I can fight, too," Astra said. I moved towards her and lowered to my knees in front of her.

"I know, As, you are strong and can handle whatever comes at you. I just need to know you are protected and safe. It sounded like he was planning something big, and I can't worry about you and look out for myself. And I have the Kings," I told her and squeezed her hands. She nodded at me, understanding dawning on her face.

"What are you going to do now?" DeeDee asked.

"Not sure. Cian gave me my Great-Grandmother's journal, I think I will be reading that some more, and trying to find out how the Gate was opened. And then sleep. There isn't much I can do. Icas should be at his own house, and I can't go there again. And I don't want to tell the Kings anything yet, we don't have solid proof."

"Okay, we will protect Astra, keep an eye out for trouble, and go searching for more information tonight," Banu said while she got up, her hand wrapped around Astra's.

"DeeDee, Lena," she said to them, her voice strong. "I want you both to go and search the ballroom, I want to know what hiding places there are, if there are spots where you have a full view of the room, and spots that could lead to blind spots. I need to know where the food comes from, the musicians, and how many servants there will be. A full report in two hours, please." I looked at her, impressed.

"Yes, sir," Lena and DeeDee said together and moved out of the room. I looked at Banu again, that amazing woman who had made sure I would feel at ease at that ball the next day. Her short black hair reached her ears, and her grey eyes shone with so much brightness it made me wonder what she saw when she looked at me.

"Give me an update in two hours, too. And if there are changes, let me know." She nodded and moved with Astra towards the door.

"Banu," I called after her. "Thank you, and stay with Astra no matter what," I told her. She nodded and looked over at Astra, as love filled her eyes. It made me breathe a little better, knowing that she would be safe. They left together, leaving me alone in my room.

It wasn't late yet, so I moved towards the bedroom and grabbed the journal. I sat back on the sofa and started reading.

"We had this amazing ball. Everyone was invited, and my men were there. I got to introduce them to the world; the men who would help me rule this world. It was the happiest day of my life."

Seraphina had kept on talking about the ball for a few more pages, nothing really came up. Until I read the word bonded.

"They are my Natural Bonded, and these four men will be mine tonight. It will be amazing, the first time we will share each other. The first time they will share me. Everyone thinks that the Bonding ceremony is about the words you speak. It is so much more; the real bonding begins when you choose to be with each other. And the night, staying together it isn't all about the sex, it is about the love we feel for each other. The love that makes us one, that makes us stronger."

I closed the journal for a moment, looked up and stared at the ceiling. Not really seeing anything, just letting my mind wander. If the bonding wasn't all about the ceremonies, why did they hold them? A thought popped into my mind, making me sit up straight. Seraphina said it wasn't about the sex, it just sounded like it was a part of the whole bonding thing. *Does this mean I'm bonded with Averey?*

I shook my head at the thought, no I can't be. I liked him, I had feelings for him. For all of them. Only, to say I love them? No, that was something that wasn't there. It could have been, but for now, it was like, not love.

I opened the journal again and read more. She had mostly talked about being Queen, her males, and how amazing they were. It had given me a good idea of what kind of person my Great-Grandmother had been. Kind, harsh, and forgiving. She had wanted to do her best for the people around her even, if it meant sacrificing her own life and that of the men she had loved deeply. That was for sure, she would have gone through fire to save them. Would I? I didn't want to answer my own question, because I knew I would have. Before my thoughts could go further towards that, somebody knocked at the door.

"Yes?" I asked, looking towards the door. Banu walked in. She had a tray with food with her. She placed it in front of me on the coffee table. "Oh, girl, thank you," I said and got up.

"I thought you could use some food," she said and stepped back. She then took the standard Protector position in front of me, legs a spread a little and her hands behind her back.

"Isa, we couldn't find anything strange with the ballroom, and we checked all the servants. I sent DeeDee to keep an eye on the servants more closely, see if she would find something wrong with them."

"Mmh, okay. And any strategic points in the ballroom that we need to cover?" I asked her.

"Yes, there are two blind spots, one is the corner behind the musicians, there is a door. But it is half covered by a curtain. And second are the doors that lead to the garden. There are too many blind spots in the garden."

I nodded at that. "Go tell the chief that we need more Protectors overlooking the garden, and that we want that door covered as well." Banu nodded at that.

"What do I tell them?" she asked me. I understood what she meant. She was a nobody here, and nobody would really listen to her.

"Tell them I said so. Use my name if need be, and if nobody listens, send them here. Or ask Liv to help you. She knows who I am," I told her and picked up the journal.

"Isa?" Banu asked softly. I looked up at her.

"Yes."

"Are you truly okay, with me and Astra?" She had moved to a more relaxed posture, her hands now in front of her, and her fingers were fidgeting.

"Banu, I will always be okay with what makes you and Astra happy. If that's each other, then it is that. If it is with someone else, also, fine, as long as you both are happy." I smiled at her.

"Thanks, I always liked her, a lot," Banu said, a smile on her face. It took one second before my smile widened, I had never seen her smile like that. In that moment, she had looked younger than she ever looked.

"Be good to her," I said before Banu walked out of the door.

I heard her answer me. "I will protect her with my life, Isa, don't worry." And with that, she closed the door, leaving me alone again.

I sighed and looked outside, the sun was already down, and the night would consume the world in seconds. That next day would be long, I picked up the plate with food and ate some. After I had finished my plate, I moved to the bedroom, changed, jumped into bed, and fell asleep right away, only to dream about black hair, tattoos, and lips that softly caressed my body.

29

My eyes flew open when I felt something heavy move next to me. I kept still, pushing out my magic, I just didn't expect to feel Averey next to me. I breathed out and let myself relax.

"What in the purple kitten's name are you doing here?" I asked him when I turned around to look at the male that was lying next to me, his bare chest right in my face. I needed to keep myself in check, so I didn't start licking it. Oh, his chest, every man should have one like his.

I looked up at his face, a smirk on his lips. "I couldn't sleep," he said casually.

"And that gave you the right to move into my bed?" I asked him while I narrowed my eyes at him, trying to be angry at him and failing miserably.

"Yes." His face turned even more smug. "You didn't complain last night." That had me sitting upright, and I looked at him.

"Last night?" I asked. He laughed aloud. If he was more in tune with the earth, the castle would have shook with his laughter.

"Yes. I came in and got in the bed, you turned towards me, mumbled something, and carried on sleeping."

My eyebrows must have flown off my face by then. "I

did not!" I threw my hands up, trying to cover the fact that I maybe had. Only, I thought I had dreamt it. He chuckled.

"Sweetheart, you totally did. You even said. What was it?" He tapped his chin, his eyes twinkling. "Oh yeah, that you already missed something long and hard." He winked at me, and my face flushed.

"I never said that, I said I missed you, not your dick. Don't get them confused!" I squealed at him. He laughed at that again, and I crossed my arms, fuming that he had gotten me to repeat what I had said the night before, acknowledging that I knew he had been there. I eyed the pillow in front of me, grabbed it, and smashed him hard.

He oomphed, and I hit him again, the next moment I was hit back by a pillow, too. I hadn't seen him grabbing his. We started fighting with the pillows. When he knocked me over with a hard smash against my head, I laughed. He jumped on top of me and started kissing my face.

"Stop, Averey. Stop." I laughed even harder. He stopped and looked at me, his grey eyes soft, and I needed to swallow the lump that existed in my throat. He lowered towards me, his eyes focused on my mouth, and I licked my lips. His eyes heated up, and I could feel something grow harder against my stomach.

His lips touched mine, softly. And I moaned a little at the feel of his lips against mine. He pushed his cock against my core, and I groaned. He moved his hands towards mine, holding them above my head, he kissed me deeper, his tongue moving around. I moved my legs around his hips, pulling him closer towards me, pressing him against my center. I moved against him, which made him groan into my mouth. I could feel the rumble of it in his chest pressed against mine.

"Are you two done playing?" I heard someone ask. I knew it was Rayan, I could feel his magic. I didn't react at all towards him. I slowly kept moving against Averey. It made his breathing come faster. I could hear Rayan move towards us. I broke away from Averey to look at him. His eyes were filled with lust, making my own body react to him. My magic reached out to him, wrapping around him. He moved towards us, his eyes lowered to my mouth and stayed there. I watched him as he bent down and kissed me softly. A sweet kiss from my sweet King. He pulled back and smiled at me.

"Come on, you have to get ready for the ball tonight. And Averey needs to rule a world." Rayan gave me another quick kiss, before he moved towards the door. I growled at him, for reminding me of the ball that night. Rayan moved out of the bedroom, but before he left the room, he yelled back, "Your dress was finished, it is in the living room!" And then the door closed.

I turned my head back, towards Averey who was still on top of me. I searched his eyes for a second before I said, "You aren't going to introduce me as a Protector, right?" He softly shook his head.

"Purple balls," I swore at him, and he cracked a grin.

"You really love swearing with purple," he said.

I rolled my eyes and answered. "Yeah, love the colour, and if you don't move it will be the colour of your balls," I growled out.

Hurt flickered through his silver-grey eyes, they dimmed. And it made me freeze.

"I didn't mean it like that. Sorry," I started. "I like you, the ball not so much, and being Queen, it isn't for me. You guys need to know that. I'm not Queen material." I gave him a quick kiss on the lips, his smile returning to his face.

He nuzzled closer, kissing up my neck before he whispered into it, "It's okay, sweetheart. We will be there for you." He kissed my earlobe and moved away. I wanted to hold on to him and stay there for the rest of my life. Averey walked over towards his pants. He hadn't slept naked next to me, which I found kind of disappointing.

"Averey." I waited for him to turn around and look at me.

"I'm not a Queen. You need to know that." I hugged my knees closer and looked at him.

"Isa, you are a Queen, by power and blood. You are the strongest here. You are our only choice as Queen," he added.

My eyes widened at that. "No, no. I don't want to be. I'm not a Queen, I'm not a broodmare. I just want to be free," I murmured. I lay my head down on my knees, and tears started flowing, followed by sobs. Averey's hand softly touched my back, slowly moving up and down, the bed dipped where he sat down.

"Isa." I pulled away a little, which made him growl out at me. "Isa," he said again, his voice low with a warning in it.

"What?" I asked and looked at him, he was blurred by the tears still in my eyes.

"You will never be a Broodmare. You will be magnificent and free. You will always be free," he said. "Only, we need you, not for the world, not for closing the Gate. *We* need you. All four of us, we can't live without you, anymore."

"Why do you want to make me Queen then?" I sobbed out.

"Because, Isadora. You are the rightful heir to the throne, you are the power that will keep this world in balance. If the High houses had never rebelled at the idea of your Queen Seraphina offering herself up, this all would have been prevented. We want to make it right. But most of all, we want you." He kept stroking my back, slowly, and I eased into his hand.

"That's merely because of the bond," I said. My biggest fear was that they wouldn't have liked me without the bond.

"No, Isadora, the bond is something that means we could be great together. It doesn't mean we instantly love you. That is something that needs to grow, we can resist the bond if we wanted to." I looked at him my mouth opening, and he shook his head.

"We always looked for our bonded, for the one that would complete us. We never wanted to settle with a Witch that would be *sort of* compatible. Only, we needed to start searching. The power it costs to keep the Gate almost closed is too much for us alone. They are winning power on the other side. That is why we started searching for Queens." He placed his hand under my chin and lifted it up.

"Then, we found you. Our Natural Bonded, our better half, the lost pieces of our hearts. That you are meant for all four of us, it makes it even better. It meant we chose to get to know you, we choose to love you. And we will be by your side, no matter what." He softly kissed my brow.

"You aren't going to make me into a broodmare?" I asked softly.

"No," was his answer.

"Also, not to make more Full-Bloods?" I asked him.

"No, we can make more," he answered.

"You have other Full-Bloods?" This had me sitting up right.

"No, we don't."

"What do you mean, then?"

"If we cross powerful Witches and Elementals with each other, there would be a chance that they will make new Full-Bloods." I started shaking my head with that. "What is it?" His brow pulled low.

"I don't know who told you that, only one of the parents need to be a Full-Blood. Why did you think my Gran made me promise to never come here?" I told him.

"No, it can happen, Icas . . ." He stopped there. His face turned into a mask of anger.

"I don't know what Icas told you, but it can't happen. Otherwise, there would be more Full-Bloods."

"I need to talk to the others." He started to move away from me, and I grabbed his hands.

"Don't make me a broodmare. Please?" I begged, my eyes wide, new tears filling them.

He lowered himself back on the bed, pulled me close and said, "You will never be something you don't want, sweetheart. We will never let that happen, and I know for sure that you would fight against it every moment you get." He held me closer against him, my head against his chest where I heard his heartbeat. It made me relax.

"And you losing your freedom? That will never happen. None of us wanted to become Kings. We didn't want to lose our freedom, either. What we didn't realize at the time was that we would gain a new sort of freedom. One that would help this world and us." He kissed the top of my head and moved away. I let him.

"Go take a shower, prepare for the ball tonight. It will be alright, don't worry," he said while he pulled on his shirt. Then he moved towards the door and left. I stayed there for a while, sitting in the bed not wanting to move. My face had puffed up from the tears, and my heart still raced with the idea of losing my freedom.

After a moment, I got up and walked towards the bathroom. A shower would help me calm my mind. I turned it on and waited for it to heat up, before I moved in. The hot water ran down my body, and I felt myself relax.

They sort of loved me, all four of them wanted to be with me, for me. I rubbed my eyes, it was all so much. I wanted them, too, wanted them to be mine. Would it have been a terrible thing for me to be Queen? It meant I would keep them. Them with me, standing next to me as equals. Because that is what they would be, my other half.

Still, how would the world react to me being a Full-Blood, being a Royal? That ball would be making one of my nightmares come true. People would know who I was, and I wasn't sure about how they would react. I had really hoped it would be nice. I turned off the shower and pulled on something easy. When I entered the room, there were three strange ladies waiting.

"What are you doing here?" I asked, my magic ready under my skin. I had never been a big fan of strange people, and after the roof encounter it had dropped even lower. All three of them bowed, their black clothing indicated they were maids. "We were sent to help you to get dressed."

"Oh, no need for that," I said and waved them towards the door.

"But, Miss, you need help with your hair and," one of them started and had looked me over. My hair was still wet, hanging down my back. I arched an eyebrow, challenging her to say more.

"No, it will be fine. I'll help her," I heard from my right.

"Astra, hi," I said as a greeting, not even looking at her. My eyes were still focused on the ladies in front of me, expecting one of them to become a half-dead thing at any moment. Only, they bowed again and walked out of the room. When the door closed behind them, I breathed out and turned towards Astra.

She looked at me. "Why is your magic so close?" she asked me, indicating the shimmer that ran over my arms.

"The servant girl," I told her, and she nodded in understanding.

"I'm here to help you, thought you might want to have some girl talk." She smiled at that.

"Yeah, love to." She moved towards the dress that hung over the backrest of the sofa. She opened the cover and whistled low.

"That looks amazing. And it will look even better when you have it on." Astra pulled out the dress and held it up for me. The navy blue fell down to the ground, I saw some glimpses of the silver fabric Stella had picked. It looked beautiful, and I had to admit, I was curious about how it would have looked on me.

"Come on, girl, let's move to the bedroom and fix your hair then add some make up." Astra looked me over. I could see her mind whirling around, she was always the one who knew how to look good. And I would be in safe hands with her. I walked after her when she walked into the bedroom, laid down the dress, and placed me on the chair before a mirror.

I looked at myself, my wet black hair hung down. It came below my shoulders. My brown eyes looked back at me, I had always liked them. When I got angry, they seemed to turn black. Gran always said that they would become as dark as the night and that she knew I was really angry then. I wished that I knew what my mom had looked like, or my Great-Grandmother. Gran had said I looked like them, almost identical. It had made me feel empty, not knowing my mom. I shook my head and focused back on Astra, not wanting to go down that road. She had started talking to me, and I hadn't been listening.

"What do you think, hair up or loose?" she asked. She was holding up my hair and then let it fall.

"I don't know. You are better at this, go and do your thing," I told her.

She once more pulled my hair up and shook her head. "No loose, maybe if we made two braids at the side of your head, the rest loose and falling down at the back, it will keep your hair out of your face. Which I know you like." She mumbled the last part and moved to grab a brush, she combed my hair out and started braiding one side. "Thank you," Astra said.

I pulled my eyebrow up in question. "For what?"

"For being my best friend."

I turned around at that and looked at her. "Girl, you will never get rid of me. I'm here, and I will always be there for you." I squeezed her hands. A tear rolled down her cheek, and I wiped it away. "You may know this or not. But, you are my sister, not in blood but by choice." I squeezed her cheek, and she laughed.

"Good, because you are mine, and I will be the best sister you could ever imagine." She squeezed my hand in return and made me turn around again. She finished up the other braid in my hair and let the rest of it fall in waves. Then she applied some make up. Black around my eyes, making them stand out more. And red on my lips, it wasn't that much makeup, still it had made me look like somebody else.

I kept looking at myself. "Come on, let's get you into the dress," Astra said while she held up the dress.

"Yes, but first," I said to her as I turned around, so my back was now facing the mirror. I needed to get rid of this bandage. I pulled it off and looked at the soft-pink scar that sat between my shoulder blades. It wasn't long, and people wouldn't notice it because of my hair falling over it. Still, it would always be there; a reminder of that night.

"Okay, now we can put on the dress," I said to Astra and turned around again. She nodded at me and moved towards me with the dress.

30

Astra held up the dress while I pulled off my clothing, leaving my underwear on. She handed me the dress, and I pulled it on. It fell down my body, softly. Almost as a lover who kissed my skin. It had made me shiver.

The dress had a high neckline that left my shoulders and back open. Trailing down my body, it reached the floor, and when I moved towards the mirror, I found the dress had a slit, which gave me room to move. I grinned at that. Stella had really thought about my need to keep my legs free. When I looked into the mirror, I saw I looked really good in that dress. The silver underneath the blue made it look like the night sky even more. When I moved, the fabrics moved separately from each other, giving glimpses of the silver. The back was even more beautiful, with the silver fabric falling over the top of my ass, and the blue one a little lower, cascading down towards the floor in a waterfall of fabric. Everything hung loosely on my body, but it still showed off my hips, breasts, and my ass in the most perfect way. I looked stunning.

"You look amazing," Astra said when she gave me a pair of heels that would match perfectly with the dress. I pulled them on and stood up. The dark-blue straps reached up towards my ankles. It took me a second to adjust and then move around. I walked back towards my bag and pulled out two small knives, placing them in their holsters on my upper legs. When I looked back at Astra, she had crossed her arms in front of her.

"You really thought I would leave without any weapons?" That made her laugh, and she shook her head.

"No. And luckily for you, you can't see them." She pointed at the spot where I had placed them. The dress fell loosely over the holsters covering them up. I grinned at her. "Stella is the best," I said and moved towards the living room. When I looked outside, the sun was already setting.

"They brought some food," I said to Astra when I saw the table filled with plates of food.

"I know, I let them in. You were putting on the dress," she said when she moved towards the table, too. It looked great, so I filled a plate and started eating. I had totally forgotten breakfast when I woke up with Averey, finding the maids in my room, and having Astra dress me. I hadn't known time could go so fast. Maybe I had woken up late? I shrugged at myself and stuffed my face.

"Isa, careful. Don't smear your lipstick around." Astra grumbled at me when she picked up her own plate and started eating, too.

"Are you excited about it?" Astra asked me.

"The ball?" I asked around a mouthful of food.

"Yes, what else?"

"No, not really." I told her the truth. Why lie?

"Why not? We can dance together. You get to dance with the Kings." She wiggled her eyebrows at me.

"Yes and no, the dancing sounds fun. Not in these heels, though. I'm not really excited about the part where they will tell everyone who I am."

"It will be fine, Isa, you will be great." We both ate in silence after that. Both lost in our own thoughts. When we were done, Astra fixed my red lips and went to her own room to change.

A knock sounded on my door a little while later, and I

opened it. It was to find the four Kings standing there. Their eyes moved up and down my body.

"Hi," I said and waved a little. "What are you guys doing here?" I asked.

"We couldn't decide who would take you to the ball. We thought you could decide," Cian said.

"Maybe it is for the best if I go alone," I said, I didn't want to make a scene before I even entered the ballroom. I already knew people would be shocked when they found out who I was.

"No," All four of them said at the same time.

"Oh, yes. We aren't going to play like this. I'm not going with any of you. I'm going by myself." I crossed my arms in front of my chest. It drew their eyes towards it, and I felt my nipples harden. "Please?" I added.

"Okay," Cian said, and he started moving away.

"Thank you," I said to him. The others walked behind him and moved towards the main hall.

When I moved out of my own room, the door next to mine opened. Astra walked out of it in a red dress, her blonde hair in a neat bun on her head, red lips finished the whole look. She winked at me when Banu walked out of her room, too, all dressed in black, her weapons strapped on.

"Can you take my swords, too?" I asked Banu.

"Yes." She looked a little confused at that question.

"I want them close if something happens," I told her. She nodded and walked into my room. When she came out, the swords were strapped at her back. "Thanks, girl," I said to her and moved towards Astra.

"Where are the other Witches?" I asked her.

"They are already at the ball. It started thirty minutes ago."

This had me stopping. "What do you mean thirty minutes? I thought it would start in fifteen?"

"No, didn't they tell you that?" Astra asked me, I could see her looking back at Banu.

"No. They didn't. Those purple bastards," I growled out at them, wiggling my fingers to keep them relaxed. No time to start punching someone. I focused on other things, like asking Banu if the other girls were ready.

"They are ready and in position. Liv, the Protector you told me about, helped us set things up. They increased the overall protection of the room and the garden, too." I nodded at her and moved towards the main hall again.

"Keep her safe," I whispered to Banu when I walked next to her.

"Always," she answered and moved towards Astra. I walked a little slower, not really wanting to go to the ball. Everything would change from the moment I walked into that room. I wasn't sure how or if it would be good or bad. Things would change and that would be the biggest thing. I braced myself when I reached the main hall. Music filtered through the double doors, laughter and voices followed. I walked down the stairs, proud of myself when I reached the bottom, and I hadn't fallen down in the heels.

The light of the room fell into the hallway, the people who were dancing and the talking people hadn't noticed me standing there. Except for the Protectors who stood on guard. "Chief," one mumbled, while another nodded at me. I squared my shoulders and moved into the room.

The room was decorated beautifully, lanterns hung from the ceiling, the lights were dimmed, and the musicians in the corner played soft dancing music. Everything was covered in golds and blues, even the curtains had been changed from red to blue. It almost gave the room a feeling of the night sky and stars. I looked around, seeing so many people. I didn't recognize any of them.

I moved further into the room, seeing DeeDee near the musicians and Lena standing near the garden. I nodded at them, and they nodded back at me. I kept looking around the room, trying to find something wrong with it. My instincts had been screaming at me, telling me to run. I just couldn't, not with my Kings there, not with Astra still under threat. I ignored my screaming instincts and moved towards the raised dais, wanting to be closer to the Kings.

They were looking out into the room, Cian smiled at me when he saw me moving towards them. The others found me quickly, too. Flynn gave me a wink, which had me stopping, and a smile spread across my face.

When I was almost at the dais, Averey stepped forward. The whole room slowly quieted down, and the music stopped. I made it to the front, finding the other Witches standing there, too. They glared at me, and I rolled my eyes. Just my luck. Before any of them could say anything to me, Averey's strong voice boomed through the room.

"Good evening, Ladies and Gentleman. We are grateful for you coming here tonight. This night is a special night because we have an important announcement to make. However first, relax, eat, and dance." He clapped his hands, and the musicians started playing a simple tune. Some people had moved towards the centre of the room, starting to dance.

The Selection Witches were whispering to each other and ignoring me, which I was happy with. The Kings came down from the dais, as soon as they did, they were swarmed by the Selection Witches and some other people. I turned away from them and looked around the room, my instincts still screaming at me. I searched for the reason, only to find my least favourite person walking towards me.

"Hello, Isadora Seraphina Savill Royal," Icas Nox drawled, how he had said my name made my neck hairs rise.

"What?" I folded my arms in front of my chest, keeping them from reaching towards the knives that were strapped at my legs.

"That isn't the way you greet a Council member," he said. Darkness filled his eyes, and I felt his magic vibrate around him.

"You aren't my council member or someone I respect, or like. So, nope, not going to happen. What do you want?"

I asked, my fingers itching to grab my knives. Suddenly, I felt the air around me change, and his face turned from night to day. His face was serene, and all the darkness left his eyes.

I knew the Kings were standing behind me, I felt them. To be precise, I felt Averey the most. His air had wrapped around me, kissing the bare skin on my back, it made me shiver in the best way.

"Good evening, Your Highnesses," Icas said, his voice smooth. "We didn't know you would have an important announcement tonight." Icas arched an eyebrow, his eyes moved over all four of them, lingering on Flynn. I moved closer to the male, shielding him with my body. He placed his hand on my lower back.

"Not everything has to go through the council, Icas, this is one of those things," Averey answered.

"And as far as we know, you aren't part of that Council anymore," Cian added.

Icas's face turned white and then red in a moment's notice. I tsked at him before he could speak.

"I don't think you want to make a scene here, Icas. It wouldn't do you any good." I waved around the room, indicating that people had already started watching us.

"The Council will not be pleased with the news or with me being out of it. They will turn against you four," Icas hissed quietly at us. I rolled my eyes at him, and that felt so freaking good.

"Go suck it, Icas. We don't care." I waved at him with my hand, indicating for him to leave. If he could have made steam come out of his ears, it would have happened there and then. Icas turned on his heels and moved away from us. I couldn't see if he had left the ballroom, because we were swarmed by people. I pressed closer to the Kings, not used to that many people around us. Flynn's hand moved towards my shoulders slowly, it left fire in its wake, and I shivered.

Cian bowed in front of me, ignoring the people who stood around us.

"Care for a dance?" he asked and held his hand out.

I placed mine in it and bowed my head while I said, "Yes." He pulled me closer to him and moved us through the people towards the dancefloor.

When we were in the centre of the room, Cian bowed again, and I did, too, remembering the dancing lessons, we'd had in school; not my best class. When I looked up, I could see the other Kings looking at us, ignoring the group of people around them. Their eyes focused on me, I gave them a soft smile and a wink before I took Cian's hand. The musicians changed their song, a slower one starting up.

"Cian," I growled out at him, playfully slapping his chest. He cocked his head and grinned. He pulled me closer, his hand low on my back. We started moving through the room.

"Why are we the only ones on the floor?" I whispered to him.

"Because we are doing a first dance," he whispered back, now smiling from ear to ear. It had me mesmerized, and I forgot what he had said.

"Wait, what?" He winked at me, and I rolled my eyes, smug bastard. "Why dance with me?" I asked him, when it had fully sunk in. The first dances were special, normally it was with their Queens. And when they didn't have a Queen, they used the first dance to show favour to a woman they liked. I knew they liked me, but that they were willing to show it on a night like that, made my heart stutter and my stomach flutter. Cheesy shit happened in my head when I was in the clouds.

My thoughts were interrupted when I glimpsed short black hair in a corner. Before I could look closer at the person, Cian had swirled me around. I turned my head towards the spot except to find two servants standing there. No one with black hair. I let Cian lead and kept looking around the room, my mind searching for the thing that I was missing, just for Cian to stroke softly up and down my back, pulling my focus back to him. I got lost in his green eyes. It was only him and me on this floor, the music played around us, cocooning us in a bubble. I smiled at him, letting him see how much it meant to me. Forgetting about the threat, forgetting about my nerves, I let myself relax for a moment.

His eyes filled with an emotion I didn't want to name, an emotion I wasn't ready for. Before I could look away and focus back on my surroundings, the music stopped, and Cian stopped, too. He bowed low and kissed my hand. Before he led me away from the centre of the room, he stepped close. I heard shocked gasps around us. He lowered his head, and for a second, I thought he would kiss me. Except his mouth stroked softly over my cheek, and when he was at my ear, he whispered, "It may be that Averey is the only one of us who has had you, yet. But you are ours, and soon, we will have you in more ways than one." He softly kissed my earlobe and pulled back. He smiled and said a little louder, "You look amazing in this dress, the whole court needed to see how amazing you look in it." He winked, and I blushed, suppressing the giggle that wanted to escape. He softly stroked his thumb over my hand and brought me back to the others. When we were almost at the others, he moved closer with his head to whisper something one more time, "And you will look even better without that dress, my hands on your skin, and my head buried between your legs." I almost faltered in my steps. He pulled me closer, steadying me with a hand on my back. It made my core wet. When we reached the others, I let go of his hand and bowed at him.

"Thank you, my King," I said.

"You never bowed to us, don't start now," Rayan chuckled, and I winked at him. Another hand landed on my back; Flynn.

"Now it is my turn," he whispered in my ear, his thumb

stroking my lower back. I nodded at him. He moved me towards the centre of the room, there were more people then, and I really hoped that they would stay there.

I didn't protest against him dancing with me, even when I heard the whispers starting. I liked how his hand felt on my back and how he held my other hand in his. As well as how he guided me around the room. We didn't speak, just looked at each other while I got lost in his dark eyes. His magic surrounded us, mine mingling with his as we danced. I knew I was smiling when I saw a small one reflected on Flynn's face. When the music came to an end, and I could hear the people around us again, Flynn lowered his head towards me. I almost froze, scared that he would kiss me in front of everyone, only, for him to say, "I'll be the one taking off that dress tonight, slowly." He trailed his hand up and down my back, making my body react to him. I wanted to moan right there, but the sound of the people around was what kept me from doing it.

We parted before I could bow, though he bowed to me. This had the people around us murmuring, not whispering anymore. A King never bowed to anybody, let alone to somebody they didn't know. A blush had crept onto my face, I quickly bowed back. He took my hand in his and guided us back towards the others. Rayan held out a glass of wine for me, and I took it gratefully, slowly sipping on it while I looked around the room. Searching for Astra, I spotted her near a table, Banu still with her. I sighed in relief. I kept looking around the room, searching for that specific black hair and the man that came with it. I wasn't sure if I had been looking for him to keep the rest safe or for other reasons.

"What is it?" Rayan asked.

"Nothing," I said and focused back on them. Enjoying their closeness, I looked around, only to notice that Averey wasn't with us.

"Where is Averey?" I asked them.

"He is on the dais, we have to go there, too. It is time for our announcement."

I looked at Rayan. "What announcement?" I asked him.

"You will find that out with the rest of them." He pointed towards the other Selection Witches who were still glaring at me. He took my hand and kissed the back of it. He moved towards Averey. Cian stepped in front of me.

He kissed the back of my hand, too, and winked when he said, "Don't worry, love." and walked off to the other two. Flynn took my hand, too, and kissed the top as well. His thumb stroked my palm before he let go of it. He moved towards the rest, and the whole room turned from me to them. I breathed out the breath I had been holding and looked at my Kings.

"Ladies and Gentleman, members of the Council." Averey nodded towards a group of people close by. "We are here to announce something that will change the world for the better," he started. My hands had turned sweaty, and I had to hold them together to keep from wiping them on my dress.

"We aren't here to announce the Selection Witches."

The girls he had talked about all squealed, a high-pitched noise. It made me chuckle, I mentally sent them a 'suck it, bitches,' and kept looking at the Kings on the stage. There were now murmurs going around the room.

"We," he moved his arms to indicate the other three, "are here tonight to resign our duties as Kings." That had me freezing, and the whole crowd exploded in noise. All four of them moved and looked at me, my heart stopped.

"We are here to pledge our loyalty to the last Savill and the rightful Queen of this world."

My heart exploded, and anger rushed through me. Those sons of a sheep had promised me they wouldn't do that. I had been sort of okay with them telling the world who I was, but they were making me Queen, they were giving up their throne, to hand it over to me.

Their eyes were focused on me. I looked at Averey, his

silver-grey eyes filled with hope and understanding. He lowered them, as if to say 'I'm sorry.' I looked at Flynn, his dark eyes showing me nothing but love. Rayan's blue eyes bore into mine, pleading with me to do what I had to. Finally, Cian and his forest-green eyes, the ones I loved to disappear into. They calmed me down, and I took the breath I needed to focus back on the world around me.

Averey cleared his throat, but still his voice wavered. Everything flashed through my head, from, turning around, running away, and never looking back, to having my freedom, my own future. But, what kind of future would that have been? Me, alone in the forest, without those men, who had slowly made their way into my heart. And I wasn't sure I wanted to push them out of it then, they were my Natural Bonded. My other part, the ones who would always be there for me. My rocks. If I placed my hand in theirs, I would be agreeing to them making me Queen. It would mean that I would have to sacrifice something of myself. Would that be so terrible if it meant I would have a family back for it? To have love?

I gave him a small nod, letting him know I was okay with it. For a little while, anyway.

"We want to introduce you all to Isadora Seraphina Savill Royal." He held out his hand, the crowd in front of me parted, and they looked at me. I pulled my shoulders back, breathed out, and moved to the stage. I was done hiding, it was time then for me to claim what I had wanted. And not what the world or Gran wanted me to do. Averey pulled me on to the raised platform. When I stood in front of them, they all lowered themselves, placing one knee on the floor, their heads bent.

"We, Averey Thorne," Averey said.

"Cian Reeve." Cian's voice flowed through the room.

"Flynn Nox." I followed them with my eyes.

"And Rayan Leighlin."

"Pledge our lives and magic to the rightful Queen of this world. We swear to never leave her side and protect her from anything that would want to harm her. We would love her forever and beyond, we swear on the magic that flows through us." I could feel a pull in my magic when they spoke those last words. I let it flow where it filled the room, and I could hear people moving behind me. But my eyes were focused on the four Kings on the floor, and my magic, which made them glow.

31

I was stunned for a moment, the feeling of being almost complete filled me, my eyes watered, and I opened my mouth. "I accept," I whispered, accepting more than the role of Queen. Before I could say more, the room exploded in screams.

An explosion had sounded next to me, and all four of the Kings jumped up. They moved around me, protecting me. I pushed past them, searching for Astra. The Kings let their magic go, and I was filled with power, it swirled around me. It took some time for me to adjust. They were truly powerful.

"What is going on?" Rayan asked. His head moved over the screaming people, some were hunched low. I was still looking for Astra, I couldn't find her, and I hoped that the girls were with her. My focus moved towards something else, magic. Another explosion sounded. The castle vibrated with that one.

"We need to get these people to safety, send them to the strongest place in the palace," I directed a Protector close to us. He nodded and moved towards the doors behind the musicians. Another Protector ran up towards us.

"King, chief," he said, taking in a big breath. "We are

under attack. Dark-world monsters." That had me looking at the others.

"Where and how?" I asked. Before he could answer, more people screamed even louder. In the doorway, were creatures, creatures we hadn't wanted to see in this world again. Some of them were on four long legs, others on two. None of them even looked close to human. With another rush of magic, the glass doors from the garden blew in, scattering the whole room in glass. I cast magic, trying to shield as many people from the flying glass as I could.

More creatures ran into the room.

"Get these people out!" I screamed at the Protectors around me. "Leave the creatures to us, get them out first, then help!" I pulled out my knives and cut the dress above my knees. I pulled off my heels and started running towards the creatures, my knives in my hand.

"ISA!" I heard a bellow behind me. Ignoring him, I kept running. I pushed out a wall of air, pushing the creatures back towards the garden. I needed to focus on the ones that still stood in the door. Their mouths were already covered in blood, and bodies littered the floor in front of them.

I pushed faster, and when I reached the first creature, I slid underneath it, cutting through its belly. It screamed and dropped to the floor. I jumped up and moved towards the next. They were focused on me then, their hound-like mouths opened up, full of teeth. They moved their spidery legs towards me. The other two creatures stayed standing, not moving at all. I kept my focus on the three that had come towards me. I jumped and pushed myself into the air, landing on top of one with my knife right in its head. It bucked and then fell to the floor. Two down, two to go. I moved off of the creature, my knife making a sickening sound when I pulled it out of its head.

When I turned around, I saw the man who had attacked me on the roof. It made me hesitate. He was looking at me, his arms crossed in front of his chest and a smirk on his face. Before I could throw magic at him, I was knocked to the ground. I groaned and turned around, just in time to pull up stone around me, using it as a shield against the snapping mouth of the spider-dog. I needed to get out from under it. Before I could do anything, the creature flew off of me. I looked up, seeing Averey standing in front of me, his hand held out towards me. I grabbed it, and he pulled me up. The creature lay on the floor, its legs twitching. Before it could get up, Flynn threw a fireball at it. It incinerated right there on the spot. I wished it had smelled like bacon or popcorn, but it didn't, the smell made me gag, and I turned my head away.

"We have saved as many as we could," Averey started.

"Good, let's clean them up then," I said and moved towards the last spider-dog. "Good doggy," I said to it and threw my knife at it only for it to dodge. "Sprinkles," I cursed and moved towards it, I pulled at the earth, using the stone to throw it at the creature. Hitting it with disc after disc of stone, it crumpled down to the ground.

"Good, stay there," I heard, and I moved on, knowing that Flynn was right behind me. I heard the creature scream when it was burned to nothing but ash. The other two creatures were still standing in the door, doing nothing. They reminded me of the servant girl that man had controlled. I looked around for him, he was there, and I knew it.

"What are you looking for?" Flynn asked me.

"That man," I started, and a growl escaped Flynn. "Kill those two, they are his puppets," I told him, and we both moved towards them. "Averey, our backs," I said to him. I didn't wait for his reply, I moved towards the creatures. They looked like the Ilunias, but these two didn't move or breathe at all. They just stood there, giving me the chills.

Flynn and I moved closer, slowly, keeping our eyes on them, trusting Averey for having our backs. Before we could slice our knives through them, they moved. Faster than the wind, they shimmered in front of us, and then they were at the other end of the room. I blinked and moved into the room. There was fighting all around us, Protectors holding the creatures out of the room. I ignored them and moved towards the two creatures.

"Help!" I heard someone yell.

"Go," I told Averey. Not checking if he had gone, I kept walking towards the creatures, my feet slow. My magic tingled under my skin, warning me of the danger in front of me. When we were close, I motioned for Flynn to slow. "Do what I do," I told him, and crouched lower, making me look less like a threat. I summoned air, slowly letting it fall around them. "Now," I growled at Flynn, hoping he would understand what I was doing. He threw fire at them, at the same time, I opened the air cages enough to let it pass through. I added some more fire of my own and watched them burn. But they shimmered away again. I cursed and whirled around, trying to find them.

"Why haven't they attacked us?" Flynn asked. I pulled up my shoulders, not having an answer. As if they heard what he had said, they reappeared a few feet in front of us and opened their mouths. A scream came out of them. It made me grab my head, covering my ears. I could see the others doing the same. Protectors fell down to the ground. I needed to do something. I was a Full-Blood, and I could use the elements, but it didn't mean I had to use them like every other Witch.

I filled my lungs with air, and screamed, throwing out magic against the two creatures, their own hands flew at their heads. My scream didn't have any sound, just magic. I made it vibrate through the air, used the heat of my fire to make the air boil. They were boiled from the inside out. They slumped to the ground. It was silent for a heartbeat. The fight picked up when the Protectors got up from the ground. I saw Flynn moving towards my side, and Averey was still fighting more creatures with the Protectors.

"Where are Rayan and Cian?" I asked Flynn.

"Over there." He pointed towards the garden, I could see glimpses of them.

"Okay." I moved towards them. "We need to push them back," I told Flynn, my head spinning with ideas.

"How?" he asked me.

"Protectors, fall back!" I yelled at them. They all reacted in an instant, moving back towards us. I saw Averey following them as well.

"Form a line," I told them. "Keep the creatures off of our backs, and we will start killing them." I threw out a fireball towards a smaller dog animal. It turned into ash. Flynn and Averey stood next to me, and we started picking off the creatures. Moving forward trying to keep as many of the creatures away from the Protectors as we could. We only let the smaller ones through and took out the tougher ones. Slowly, we moved forward, towards the garden.

I used my water to throw one of the creatures against the wall, a Protector stabbed it through its eye. I let go, and it slumped down to the ground. I trapped a few with earth, letting the Protectors cut off their heads.

Steadily, we walked into the garden. There were so many different creatures, some the size of wolves, others the size of bears. Their glowing red eyes would haunt me in my dreams for many nights. Some creatures flew with wings made out of leather. There were human-looking creatures, which walked on two legs, some with claws as arms, some of them with claws as feet. Others were almost human, wielding magic. I focused on them, they were a bigger threat than the smaller creatures.

"Cian, Rayan!" I yelled at them. I pulled up a wall of earth, running towards them.

"Thanks," Rayan said when he caught his breath. But then the earth started to crumble, and I pushed another wave of magic into it.

"We need to make sure the Protectors are safe from the magic-wielding creatures. Make sure they stay behind us and pick off the ones without elemental magic." They both nodded, and I let the wall of earth drop, only, to come face to face with a woman. A dark Witch.

She wasn't like our Witches, she lived from the magic she took from the world around her. I wouldn't say she lived truly, she just chose to use black magic and lived from that. It made her the strongest creature there and totally mine.

I grinned at her. From the corner of my eye, I saw a wolf creature running at me, I threw him away towards the Protectors. I could feel the others next to me, fighting as well. I kept my eyes focused on the dark Witch. She needed to die.

"There is the little Witch," the dark Witch sneered when she saw me running towards her. "She is mine!" she screeched and ran at me. I pulled up air and pushed it towards her, she waved her hand, and it disappeared. I threw fire, and she waved her hand again, making the fire sizzle out.

"Fuck a duck," I growled and moved closer.

"Isa!" I heard someone scream, which made me look over my shoulder, seeing Banu and Astra.

"Here!" she yelled and threw both of my swords my way. I caught them with air and pulled them towards me. Relieved to see them both alive and to have my swords back, I unsheathed them and relaxed in a fighting stance. I may have been powerful with magic, but I was deadly with my swords.

The dark Witch's eyes flickered towards my swords, and she smiled at them, her black and brown-stained teeth showing. "You are a pretty thing aren't you?" I said to her. Her mouth closed, and anger burned through her eyes. I moved towards her, swinging with my right arm towards her, she ducked, and I swung my left sword lower, cutting her on her face. She screamed and then laughed. The dark Witch punched, hitting me in the ribs. I sucked in a breath and moved out of her reach.

"Come then, little thing," she taunted. And I moved,

pulling the ground away from her, instead she just hovered in the air. "Magic, little thing, is what I know best." She laughed at that.

"Do you know steel, too?" I asked, I gave myself a boost and flung myself at her, my swords pointed at her throat and stomach. I almost hit home, but was pushed away by her air. I landed on the ground with a thud, jumping up as I braced myself for the next attack. She moved, faster than I ever had seen anything move before. She hit me in the back, then kicked me in the knee. I screamed at the feel of something popping. Still I kept standing, swinging my swords around me, trying to hit her.

She stopped in front of me, just out of my reach.

"I thought you were stronger, they told me you were stronger," she taunted and kept on talking, "They lied." She tsked at me.

My mind moved around, I needed to think of something, I needed to end this fast. I grabbed hold of my magic and pushed it out. A white shimmering wall pushed out of me, through her, and she screamed for a moment. And then, it was behind her. She cocked her head at me.

"We are playing together now?"

"Yes," I growled out, the pain in my ribcage making it harder to breathe.

She moved, and I did, too. I needed it to end, quickly. I pushed all my magic into my body, making me move faster than I ever had. I sliced at her and heard her scream. I moved behind her, quickly cutting on her back before she could turn around. I could feel my magic draining, that fight had cost me so much. Still, I pushed.

"Mmh, this is more the fight than I thought I would have." She giggled at that, actually giggled.

"Go swim," I said and moved towards her again, I aimed high, then let myself drop down and cut through her legs. She screamed again, blood poured over me, and I swirled around and got on my feet. I threw more magic at her, using air, fire, and water to drown her. I even threw raw magic at her, not bothering to form it into anything.

She laughed at me. "Little thing. You are giving me everything I need," she said, that had me stopping. I looked at her, watching her cuts heal and a shit-eating grin form on her face.

"How?" I asked not expecting her to answer. Except she did.

"I'm magic, little thing, I absorb it. It becomes what I want. Magic can't harm magic," she said. And for a moment, I wavered. She reacted and threw fire at me. The heat engulfed me, burning me, and I screamed. My lungs were sucked dry, and no air filled them again, I could feel my body boiling. Until it stopped, my instincts kicked in and, my magic took it all in.

"What how?" the witch started, and I looked at her and grinned.

"That trick, yeah. I know that one, too." I told her, not telling her that I couldn't do it on command and had only done it one other time. She was stunned, and I moved.

"You are done!" I yelled at her and ran towards her. Her eyes widened in shock when I pushed my sword through her heart. "How?" she gurgled around the blood that welled up in her throat. "Only Darmors can . . ." she gurgled again, and then she fell silent. I let my magic drop, the shimmering wall disappeared, and the world came into focus again. It was just silent; no fighting. Just my panting breaking the quiet.

"Isa, Babe?" I heard from my side. I looked up to find all four of the Kings standing at the side. There were no more creatures, the silence stretched around us. I looked at them, looked them over. Finding no terrible injuries, I moved towards them. I was pulled into the arms of Rayan, I breathed in his summer rain smell and whooshed out a relieved breath. I pulled back a little and looked at the others.

"How many did we lose?" I asked them. I had seen the bodies littered around the room.

"We saved most of them. We aren't sure how many we lost," Averey said, his voice soft, and I heard the hurt. I let go of Rayan and moved towards him, my hand on his cheek. "It isn't your fault," I said to him. "If it is anyone's fault, it is mine. I knew something would happen tonight," I said.

"What do you mean?" Flynn asked before Averey could.

"Your sister, she told me Nox was planning something big, and I think she meant this."

"Where is Icas Nox?" Cian growled out, I could see Protectors moving around us.

"Sirs," someone said to us. I looked over my shoulder to find Lars.

"I'm sorry to say, we lost seven Protectors, and three of the Selection Witches didn't make it out in time. We also lost one council member and four others," he said, his eyes on the ground. We started moving back towards the ballroom, I saw Liv running towards us.

"Queen." She nodded her head at me. I looked at her waiting of her to speak.

"We can't find Icas Nox or Astra," she said. My head spun, and I grabbed hold of someone, almost falling down.

"What do you mean?" I asked, fully knowing what she had meant.

"We couldn't find her," she said again.

"Where are Banu, DeeDee, and Lena?" I asked her. "I just saw them." I turned around to looked at the spot where Banu had been when she had thrown me my swords.

"Isa," I heard from my other side and whirled around, I knew that voice.

"Banu," I said. Her face was covered in blood and bruises. "Where is As?" I grabbed hold of her hands.

"They took her," she sobbed out. I had never seen her cry. "I, we, I wanted her to be safe, so we moved towards the garden the moment we could. I wanted her to get to your room. She would be safe there. She said you had spelled it. Lena and Deedee," her voice broke, and she swallowed, "they found us and moved with us. I saw you fighting with that monster." Her hands were now shaking, and I pulled her against me, not caring about the blood. She sobbed even harder; in between her sobs, she spoke.

"I threw you your swords, knowing you needed them. I took my eyes away from Astra for a second. When I turned around, she was gone. I looked around and found her being dragged through the garden to the other side. I ran after her. Lena, and DeeDee . . ." Another sob racked her body. "They followed. When we entered the small door they left through, they ambushed us. It was stupid for us to go after them like that." She pushed away from me, shaking her head.

"They killed DeeDee." She balled her fists and then looked at me. Tears streamed down my face from seeing the sorrow in her eyes. "She was the first to run into the hallway. They killed her Slit her throat. We-we had to fight them off." Banu shook her head, almost if she could make it all go away.

"They took Astra." She sobbed again, my heart beat against my chest.

"Do you know where?" I asked her.

"I think the dark world." Banu shuddered at that.

"Why?" Averey asked.

"The creatures who took her, they were more human than monster. They said to hurry, that the master wanted her, that they needed to cross before the magic ran out." She looked at Averey.

"It sounded as if they were talking about the Gate, that it was opened?"

I could hear one of the men behind me swear and move away.

"Where is Lena?" I asked her, I needed to focus on the things here and now. We weren't sure if Astra would be taken to the Dark-world.

"She is in the sickbay, she was hurt badly."

"You did good, Banu. Go to her and stay with her. I'll let you know when we know more about Astra," Cian said, he placed a hand on her shoulder and squeezed. I was grateful for him stepping in because I was losing it, I didn't know what to do then. DeeDee wasn't there anymore and Lena lay in the sickbay, and Astra, I couldn't even think about that.

"I'll walk with you. I want them to take a look at you, too," Rayan said, and I mouthed a thank you at him.

Cian moved towards me. "Are you alright Love?"

I shook my head. "No," I croaked out, and my eyes closed as darkness caught me.

32

I woke up, disoriented for a second and surrounded by warm bodies, a heavy arm over my stomach, and my leg between someone else's. I tried to move, instead I heard a grunt next to me. I wanted to smile, waking up like this would be amazing. But not then.

"How long was I out?" I asked the room.

"A few hours, it is morning," I heard Flynn's soft voice next to me. I turned my head to look at him, his dark eyes searched mine and then settled on my lips. I moved towards him and kissed him softly, giving myself and him the reassurance that we were still there.

"You are safe," he whispered to me.

"I know," I said to him. I moved the arm off of my stomach and pushed myself upright. I looked around, finding myself in a room I didn't recognize.

"Where are we?" I asked the room again.

This time, Rayan answered. "Your room, my Queen."

I groaned at him using the title Queen. Still, I looked around. The room had soft blue colours and some purple accents. There were high arched windows where the blue curtains were pulled closed. A big desk stood in the left corner, it was mostly empty except for a small picture frame. I couldn't see who was in it. The rest was white, and the floor was a dark brown, there were small doors and a double door that probably led to another room. The bed was huge, the soft sheets sliding against my body. When I looked up, I found dark-purple fabric covering the top of the bed. It draped down all four of the bed posts, giving the bed even more of a grand feel. I looked around the room again, a feeling of belonging had settled deep inside me. It was my Great-Grandmother's room, she had lived here, and I could live here, too, I could live here with my men. And that bed, it would be perfect for the things I wanted to do with them. Not the time for that. I shook my head and looked towards my men.

"Where is Astra?" I asked Flynn, when my gaze focused on him again. He was the one who had left last night, the one who went to check what had happened at the Gate. He would be the one who knew where Astra would be,

"I'm sorry," he started, and for that moment, my world stopped spinning.

"What do you mean?" I croaked out, my throat closing. Tears filled my eyes, and I prepared for the worst. That they had found her body, that Banu had heard it wrong, and that she had been killed.

"Banu was right, the Gate was opened further, and they probably took her back through it," he said, his eyes downcast. I sagged at that, relieved and terrified at what would happen to her. I made up my mind.

"Okay, we need to go after her." I started moving out of the bed.

"Isa," Averey growled out. "You can't go now," he said. I looked at him and arched an eyebrow.

"Watch me," I said and moved further, this time it was for Cian to stop me.

"Love, we need you here now. You can't go after her," he started.

"That you are wrong about. I will go after her, and you

can't stop me. She is my sister. And I can't leave her in the hands of whatever this *master* is." I pulled his hand off of my stomach and moved out of the bed.

Averey sat upright in the bed, his naked chest distracting me for a second.

"Okay," he said, and that me blown away.

"What?" I answered.

"Okay, you can go. But we are coming with you, and you will be crowned Queen before you go," he said.

"No, not that. What if I'm killed?" I asked. This had them all growling.

"You will not be killed." The room filled with magic, and I took it all in. Now that I had done it twice, it became easier. Still, it made my skin crawl to think about what the Witch had tried to say.

"We bond," Cian said. My head whipped around to look at him.

"I'm sorry what?" My mouth hung open.

"We bond. You are our Natural Bonded. We will make this bond official. It will give you, and us, more power. It will make us one."

I looked at him, seeing the logic behind it all. Bonding, for real, with them, it would be better than being Queen. And they would be mine for sure. Something inside me screamed 'Yes!'

"If we bond, I can go?" I asked them.

"Now you make it sound like you have to but don't want to," Rayan said, his blue eyes focused on me, his fingers playing with the sheet in his lap. I was reminded of what he had said about the Witch who made him believe she was his bonded. It made me shake my head.

"No, hunni. I didn't mean it like that. I would love to bond with you guys, I want you guys to be mine and solely mine. But I need to go after Astra, she is my family. And I need to know for sure that if we bond, if I become a part of you and you of me, that you guys will still give me the freedom to make my own choices." Cian nodded at that, and I could see Flynn and Averey looking at each other. After what seemed forever, they looked at me and nodded, too. I looked back at Rayan, his blue eyes waiting, he slowly nodded. I gave him a soft smile.

"Still, I need to know that you guys aren't going to lock me up when we are bonded. I don't want to become a broodmare," I said to them, my own fears rising with that.

"We would never," they all said.

"We love you," Rayan said, and my head whipped up at that.

"We really do," Flynn added.

"Why?" I asked them.

"You are amazing, Isa, you fight with your whole heart for what you want. You protect what is yours fiercely, and you love more than you receive back," Averey said.

"You guys are my Natural Bonded, the pull," I started.

"Like I said earlier. We still would have fallen in love with you. The bond doesn't decide for you if you love us or not. It only makes us stronger, we are a part of you and you of us. And with that bond, you make it real. It isn't about the pull, it is about the choice that you make with it. If you accept the bond, if you accept us, and we accept you. That is the power behind it, that is what you share, you will share the choice to love each other, you choose to give freely," Averey said, while he moved towards me. His hand was on my hip and I looked down at him.

"And we choose to love you also. We choose to share everything we have and are with you. We want to be yours and yours only," he said and kissed my ribs softly.

"You are our other half, you are the missing part in our life," Cian said, and he kissed my hand that lay on Averey's shoulder. Flynn moved out of the bed and walked behind me.

"You are the light in our darkness, you are the darkness that helps us hide from the light. You are our strength and weakness," he said and kissed my neck. I looked over

Averey's head, my eyes filling up with tears. Rayan's blue eyes sparkled when I looked in them.

"You are the one we choose to be with, you are the one we give our lives for. We choose this," he said and held his hand over his heart. That broke me then, and I sobbed.

They were silent, and I swallowed my tears away and spoke up.

"And I choose you, to be my other half, to be my power and my life, to be my love and my hate, to be my strength and my weakness. I choose to give myself freely to each of you." My voice was soft, I looked at all of them as I leaned back against Flynn, and we stayed like that for a while. Nobody said anything, nothing needed to be said anymore.

I stood there between my four men, between the parts that would be my life and my love. I had accepted them freely into my heart, and I would make it real, I would bond with them. We would do that, and we would save Astra, because I needed her. I knew that thought to be self-ish, but she was my sister, not by blood but by choice. And I knew that it would be stronger than anything. Because you choose to be something, you choose to do something or to become something. Maybe life had a way of putting you into tough spots, and it would make it harder for you to choose, but it was a choice you made, you decided what was the best in that moment.

And I knew that choosing those four men, placing them into my heart wouldn't be the easy way or the hard way. It would be the right way. Because from the moment I had seen them, I had known that they were mine. I whispered the words, echoing my own thoughts.

"You are mine."

"You are ours," they said in sync, and I smiled at them. All four of them were touching me then, Averey still held both of my hips, Flynn stood against my back, and both Cian and Rayan were holding my hands. The tears in my eyes were dried up, and I looked at them and nodded.

"So, let's do this," I said to them. This made Averey

chuckle. He pulled me against him, making the others drop their hands.

"Sweetheart, there are other things we have to do first." He pulled me onto his lap. If that was that other thing, then it was starting to be a really good other thing.

I rolled my eyes at him and asked, "What?"

THE END . . . ALMOST

TIRAN

"Can I get more wine?" someone asked, and I scowled at them. It sucked, I hadn't planned on being a servant there. If it wasn't for that woman, I would have had eyes inside the room without being there. I hadn't had enough time to get another puppet, and they had increased their wards, they would have noticed too much if I had used my magic more. "Go away," I growled out and looked back towards the room. It was filled with people who were laughing and dancing. I hated it there. If they had known what was happening on the other side of that Gate, they wouldn't have been laughing at all. I scowled at the next person who walked up to me.

It wasn't working, I needed to keep a low profile. I had already alerted her of my presence there. Only, I couldn't resist when I had seen her the day before. I had needed to be closer to her, touch her again. She had recognized me, which had made my heart beat faster. But I couldn't let her find me. I needed that mission, it would help me free myself.

Something pulled at my attention, and I looked up. She had walked into the room, her hair cascading down her exposed back, the dress she wore flowed around her. The colours made her look like a goddess. I wanted to move closer, trail my fingers over her back, going lower and lower until I would slip into her dress. I would move my fingers over her core, feeling her wet and ready for me.

She was looking around the room, and I knew she was looking for me. But then, her eyes landed on someone else. I followed her eyes, she was looking at my target for the night. The blonde Witch, she was what they wanted. Then she moved further, towards the four Kings who stood on the dais. They saw her, and they smiled, I knew she was smiling back at them. Her whole body had changed when they looked at her like that, her head was held higher, and her steps were sure.

I hadn't wanted to see more, couldn't see more.

I searched the room for that obnoxious little prick Nox, finding him in a corner, scowling at that woman. He was such a suck up. How those four Kings tolerated him, I had never understood. Master could barely tolerate him, and that was just because the man served a bigger goal than he had been aware of.

I smirked at that, that foolish man would meet his end soon.

The music started, the crowd parted, and I moved more into the shades of the room. I followed their eyes and whispers until I saw her. She was dancing with one of the Kings. Her eyes focused on him, she turned out of my view, and I moved with her.

Her eyes had focused on me, widened, and then the King turned her again, and I moved away. I saw her searching for me, she kept looking around the room. But I wouldn't be found again. Nice trick the Ilunias had, even better that I had learned it, too.

"Who is she?" someone whispered next to me, they didn't know I was there.

"Some Witch or Protector," another answered. I stayed still next to them, hoping I would find out more.

"Isadora something." the first one whispered again. I looked at the woman on the dance floor, the goddess that moved there. I wanted to say her name out loud, wanted to know how it sounded on my tongue. But, I couldn't, they would have heard me. Instead, I moved again.

I needed to focus on my mission. I moved closer to the blonde girl and waited. Waited for Icas Nox to open the Gates further, so my army could get inside the castle. I waited.

———

I stood at the back of the room, watching the Kings on the dais. Isadora walked to it. I hadn't heard what was said, except that it was a big deal. The whole crowd had gasped at what they said. Then the Kings lowered to the floor, kneeling before her.

She let go of her magic, and it surged through the room; through everyone who was there. It lit up the four Kings in front of her. Someone gasped, and I looked at them, they had seen me.

"Fuck!" I growled out and moved away only to notice that my hands were glowing. It stopped me in my tracks, I looked at them. The soft glow was coming from my skin, the same as the four Kings had. What had she done? I looked back at her, the woman who made my heart beat faster and my cock harden in seconds. What was happening? I needed to move; things needed to be set in motion. Nox needed to do his part, we had waited for long enough.

A smile crept on my face when the earth vibrated, and the first screams entered the room. It was time. I looked at the dais again. They were surrounding her then, the woman. Isadora.

Before I moved away, I could see her rip her dress and jump off the dais. Her heels were off, and she had ran towards me. I moved away, slipped past the creatures that stood in the doorway and waited for her.

She swirled inside, cutting down the first Dangla and moved on to the second. She looked amazing, her hair spinning behind her when she turned, her knives glittering in her hands. She jumped up and danced around the creatures.

How I had wanted her right then; to take her there and then. Then she saw me and froze. It had cost her, and my stomach turned when I saw that Dangla on her. Before I could do anything, the Dangla was thrown off. I disappeared, so the King couldn't see me. Besides, I had a mission to complete. I adjusted my cock in my pants, it was harder than hard. I moved away from her then, leaving her, and I could swear I felt something try to tug me back.

THE REAL END

Dear reader,

Thank you for reading the book, for being part of this adventure. If you liked it, give me a review, it will mean so much to me and also book two will be more reality if you did. I'm working on it and going as fast as I can, and all the while being this crazy girl with a Super-girl day job. And sadly, for me I'm not a night person. Or made from magic, can't snap my fingers and the book appears finished in front of me. Still that would be by the way so freaking cool.

Again thank you for reading, keep me around for the second book, for the next adventure of Isadora and her men. And for more steamy parts that hopefully makes you buy a hell lot of new panties because I just melted yours off.

ABOUT THE AUTHOR

Check out my facebook page's here for more information about book two.

And for more contact points you can find my books on Amazon and me on goodreads.

Printed in Great Britain
by Amazon